A Reluctant Bride

Books by Jody Hedlund

The Preacher's Bride

The Doctor's Lady

Unending Devotion

A Noble Groom

Rebellious Heart

Captured by Love

BEACONS OF HOPE

Out of the Storm: A BEACONS OF HOPE *Novella*

Love Unexpected

Hearts Made Whole

Undaunted Hope

ORPHAN TRAIN

An Awakened Heart: An ORPHAN TRAIN *Novella*

With You Always

Together Forever

Searching for You

THE BRIDE SHIPS

A Reluctant Bride

THE BRIDE SHIPS ⚓ BOOK ONE

A RELUCTANT BRIDE

JODY HEDLUND

BETHANYHOUSE
a division of Baker Publishing Group
Minneapolis, Minnesota

Published by Bethany House Publishers
11400 Hampshire Avenue South
Bloomington, Minnesota 55438
www.bethanyhouse.com

Bethany House Publishers is a division of
Baker Publishing Group, Grand Rapids, Michigan

Printed in the United States of America

Library of Congress Cataloging-in-Publication Data
Names: Hedlund, Jody, author.
Title: A reluctant bride / Jody Hedlund.
Description: Bloomington, Minnesota : Bethany House, a division of Baker Publishing Group, [2019] | Series: The bride ships ; 1
Identifiers: LCCN 2018048926 | ISBN 9780764232954 (trade paper) | ISBN 9780764234149 (cloth) | ISBN 9781493418688 (ebook)
Subjects: | GSAFD: Love stories.
Classification: LCC PS3608.E333 R44 2019 | DDC 813/.6—dc23
LC record available at https://lccn.loc.gov/2018048926

Scripture quotations are from the King James Version of the Bible.

Cover design by Jennifer Parker
Cover photography by Mike Habermann Photography, LLC

Author is represented by Natasha Kern Literary Agency, Inc.

19 20 21 22 23 24 25 7 6 5 4 3 2 1

But we have this treasure
in earthen vessels, that the
excellency of the power may be of
God, and not of us. We are troubled
on every side, yet not distressed; we
are perplexed, but not in despair;
persecuted, but not forsaken;
cast down, but not
destroyed.

2 Corinthians 4:7–9

One

London, England
May 1862

"Hang on a little longer, my lamb." Mercy Wilkins shifted the listless infant in her arms without slowing her pace.

Clara had stopped responding on Chilton Street, but the slightly warm breath coming from between the little girl's colorless lips told Mercy she wasn't too late . . . so long as the Shoreditch Dispensary wasn't crowded and so long as Dr. Bates was available. He'd treat the infant even though Mercy had no way to pay for his services.

"Don't you fret," she murmured. "If Dr. Bates isn't there, I'll sell my shoes to pay the fee."

Mercy ignored the cold dampness between her toes, the puckered skin on feet that hadn't been dry since spring had chased away the chill of winter and invited a familiar tormentor in its place—rain.

The frequent showers not only soaked her half boots but also turned the streets into swamps of mud and horse manure. The mixture oozed through the holes where her toes had worn through the leather and threatened to suck the shoes off her feet.

She'd tied the frayed laces tight, causing them to break and forcing her to knot them yet again. Though the strings didn't reach the tops of her boots anymore, she was lucky to have them, lucky to have boots at all when so many wore nothing on their feet but rags.

"I'll gladly trade my boots for you to be seen to by a doctor, my sweet one." She brushed a kiss against Clara's cheek. The infant's face was as pale as the fog that hung over the rooftops, and as thin and hollow as the terraced houses that lined either side of the street.

Several boys bumped against Mercy, jostling her. Fingers darted in and out of her skirt pocket with the nimbleness of an expert thief. She had nothing for the boys to steal. The looks of her should have told them that. Except that with the sick infant, maybe they supposed she had a halfpenny tucked away to pay the doctor.

She caught sight of the face of one of the boys, recognizing him in spite of the layer of soot and filth. "Mr. Martins is looking for another boy to clean the streets. Go talk to him and earn your bread the honest way. D'ye hear me?"

The boy didn't acknowledge her comment except to hunch further into his man-sized greatcoat and tip his round cap down to shield his face.

Mercy shook her head but plodded forward. If Mr. Martins would only offer her the street-cleaner job, she'd take it in a snap. But no amount of her pleading had changed his mind about giving the work to a young woman.

"Heaven save us all," he'd exclaimed. "What's the world coming to with women thinking they can do a fellow's job?"

Mercy had wanted to retort that dodging betwixt horses and carriages to shovel up steaming piles of dung didn't take any special talent. Surely a woman could do the job just as well as a man. But Mr. Martins made it clear enough he wouldn't hire her, just like the dozen other people she'd approached that day.

"No matter," she whispered. "I'll find something. Just you wait and see."

Clara's head lolled, and Mercy shifted the infant again. Not quite two years old, the child didn't weigh much more than Twiggy's newborn babe. Even so, after carrying the girl for blocks, Mercy's arms burned from the burden.

Through the foggy mist hovering in the narrow street, she glimpsed the Shoreditch Dispensary. Like the surrounding businesses, it leaned outward and was propped up by beams to the building across the street. The beams were almost like canes, meant to keep the aged, tottering structures from collapsing into the filth below.

Between high windows hung strings of soggy garments, so threadbare and gray they resembled the rags Twiggy sorted at the factory. Their soaking from the recent rain would wash away the grime for a moment, but never for long. In this part of London, the filth was as constant a companion as the rats.

"Almost there, dear heart." If only she'd known how sick the girl was, she would have brought her earlier. At least in the late afternoon, the streets weren't as crowded. And at least the rain had decided to show some compassion.

Upon reaching the dispensary door, Mercy fumbled at the handle, kicking her boots against the brick step, attempting to dislodge the muck. As she entered, the dark gloom of the hallway greeted her.

An old man crouched in the corridor cradling his arm. A mother sat opposite him, holding a bundle of blankets with a tiny bare foot poking through the fabric. The babe's stillness, as well as the mother's vacant gaze, told a story Mercy had heard too many times.

"Doctor!" Mercy strode down the hallway, her footsteps squeaking and squishing with each step. "I'm in desperate need of help."

"Wait your turn, you young cur," growled the old man. "There be others needing the doctor first." He nodded to the mother and babe. The woman stared at the faded green wallpaper, the remnants of a time when the home had been fancy and belonged to a family of means. Such families had long since moved away and built larger homes in parts of London Mercy had only heard about but never seen.

Mercy regarded the babe's unmoving outline, then faced the older man. "The doctor may be able to save a life. Do you want two children dead instead of one?"

She held his angry gaze until finally he dropped his sights to the muddy footprints that caked the wood floor.

"Doctor," Mercy called again as she made her way to the room Dr. Bates used as his office. "Please, I need your help. Straightaway."

Seeing the door was ajar, she bumped it open with her hip. The massive desk positioned near a boarded window was cluttered with books and papers and inkpots. A lantern was lit and illuminated its dusty globe painted with delicate flowers. But Dr. Bates wasn't there.

The door of the adjacent room swung open, and a young man exited, his hand swathed in bandages. He didn't spare her or the others a glance, as if they didn't exist.

Mercy supposed it was easier for some people to pretend the problems weren't there. The heartache, the burdens, the needs . . . it was all so overwhelming at times.

Clara's weight dragged at Mercy. For an instant, she was tempted to slide down next to the mother with the dead babe and stare at the wallpaper too. But at a clank from the open doorway, Mercy forced herself to move, gathering the strength to fight for one more life.

"Doctor?" She entered the room unbidden. "Can you give a look at my little lamb?"

At the room's lone table, a young man stood in front of a basin of water where he was washing his hands. Beside the basin lay a scattering of instruments and supplies—a scalpel, small scissors, ligature thread, and needles. He'd discarded his coat over the back of a nearby chair to reveal a striped waistcoat and a finely tailored shirt, its sleeves rolled up to his elbows. His dark brown hair was tousled, likely the result of a long day of rushing from one urgent need to the next.

His face was unfamiliar, not one of the usual doctors who gave of their time at the dispensary. Since Clara needed immediate attention, this man would have to do.

He glanced up and paused in his scrubbing. Exhaustion crinkled the corners of his eyes and forehead. "I shall be with you in a moment." He didn't speak unkindly, just wearily.

"I don't have a moment, sir." Mercy crossed the room toward the cot. "This sweet child is failing fast, that she is."

Gently Mercy lowered the girl, whose limbs flopped about, her strength and life all but gone. Mercy dropped to her knees beside the cot and caressed Clara's cheek and forehead, brushing back strands of matted hair. The girl's dirty face was shriveled, her eyes shrunken, her lips cracked.

"Don't you leave me, dear heart. The kind doctor will fix you up. I promise."

Thankfully, the doctor didn't delay and instead crossed to them quickly. He knelt on the opposite side of the cot and checked the infant's pulse, an air of urgency emanating from every brisk movement he made. "What are your daughter's symptoms?" he asked as he lifted first one eyelid and then the other.

"She's not . . ." Clara wasn't Mercy's daughter. Yes, they shared the same blond hair. But couldn't the doctor see Mercy wasn't wearing a wedding band?

As soon as she asked the silent question, she chastised herself. A wedding band wasn't necessary to have children, especially not where she came from. This doctor apparently knew it too.

He placed an instrument against Clara's chest. "Her symptoms?"

"She can't keep anything down, sir. No liquids or solids. It all comes out one way or the other."

The doctor rose so suddenly that Mercy started. "How long has she had the vomiting and diarrhea?"

"It began last night—"

"And you are just now bringing her in?" Irritation edged his voice.

"I'd have brought her earlier if I'd known, sir," Mercy replied. If only Clara's mother had thought to call for her sooner.

"Fever?"

"Come and gone."

The doctor muttered something under his breath as he rummaged through supplies in a chest. He returned with a teaspoon and a small brown vial. "I would normally suggest having the child drink a mild solution of salt and warm water until the poison is eliminated and vomit runs clear."

"Poison, sir?"

"Her symptoms point to cholera infantum."

A chill crept up Mercy's spine. Most people called it summer diarrhea because it occurred in the summer months when the heat made the foulness of streets and ditches almost unbearable. She'd watched helplessly last August as a dozen little ones in her neighborhood had wasted away, including her own baby brother.

"That cannot be it, sir," Mercy said. "It's not summer yet."

"Cholera infantum can strike at any time of the year." The doctor unscrewed the lid on the brown bottle and poured a scant amount into the spoon. "The condition is related to tainted food, possibly spoiled milk."

Mercy used her fingers to comb back Clara's hair. Milk was rare in the slums. Had Clara's mother found some? If so, she'd have given the treat to the girl expecting it to nourish, not poison, her.

"Raise her head," he instructed.

Mercy lifted Clara's body.

He brought the spoon to the girl's mouth. "She's too dehydrated and won't rouse to drink. Our best hope is to administer the acetozone every ten to fifteen minutes."

With surprising tenderness, he tipped the contents between her lips. He watched the pale, unresponsive face for a long moment before holding out the spoon and brown bottle to Mercy.

She took the items hesitantly. "Sir?"

"You may administer the next dose when I tell you it is time. Meanwhile, I shall prepare an enema for her."

Mercy nodded.

He crossed the room and searched in the chest again. Then he laid out a syringe and catheter and began mixing a solution from a number of bottles. From the fine cut of his garments to the way he held himself, she could see he was a gentleman. But strangely his face and arms were as sun-bronzed as a dockhand's.

Perhaps he'd recently returned from India or Africa or one of the other tropical colonies. She'd heard such places were blissfully warm all the year long. Those were the kinds of places that occupied her dreams during the winter, when they had only enough coal to keep from freezing to death but never enough to be warm.

"You're new to the dispensary, sir?" she asked, letting her curiosity get the better of her as usual.

"No." His stir stick clanked against the glass container as he swirled the cloudy liquid. "I'm only helping Dr. Bates for a few days now and then while I'm in town."

"Oh, Dr. Bates. Now, he's a right fine gent." Not only didn't he charge her for his treatments, but he was always kind and offering her helpful advice.

She swished the contents of the brown bottle. How much would this new doctor charge her today? Would the offer of her shoes be enough? They were the last thing she owned of any value. She'd long since pawned the rest of her possessions. Would she, like some of the women she knew, have to start trading favors for what she needed?

The very idea repulsed her. But as she ran a finger along Clara's delicate nose and traced the outline of her face to her chin, she could begin to understand what drove some women to such desperate measures.

Mercy glanced at the doctor and caught him staring at her. She half expected he'd read her thoughts, that she'd see lewd calculation in his eyes the same that she'd seen in Tom Kilkenny's eyes when he'd told her she could be a serving wench in his pub. She knew as well as everybody else that Tom's wenches did more than hand out mugs of beer.

She'd told Tom she'd rather go to the workhouse.

He'd only laughed and warned her the workhouse would ruin her pretty features and turn her into a hag so that no one would ever want her.

Mercy had only to think about how much Patience had changed in the few months she'd lived at St. Matthew's Bethanl Green Workhouse. Before going in, Patience had been like a rare blade of green grass poking through the piles of garbage in a dark alley. But she'd withered so that whenever Mercy visited the workhouse, she hardly recognized her sister anymore.

All the more reason why Mercy needed to find a job, so Patience could live at home again.

The doctor shifted his attention to Clara, but not before Mercy glimpsed the compassion in his expression. He felt sorry for her because he thought Clara was her daughter. She ought to correct him, but what if his assumption motivated him to work harder to save the child?

"It's time for another spoonful of the acetozone," he said as he readied the catheter.

Mercy poured the medicine into the spoon, cradled Clara in her free arm, then slowly tipped the liquid into the girl's mouth the way the doctor had. "There you are, sweet one."

She envisioned Clara's adorable smile, the one she'd given Mercy yesterday morning when Mercy had delivered half rolls to the children who lived in her building. Occasionally Mr. Hughes, the old baker over on High Street, gave Mercy the rolls that had gone stale. It was a kind gesture. She supposed he did it because she'd once stopped a boy from thieving a basket of fresh bread from his shop.

Even if the rolls were harder than a pewter pot, they were nourishment all the same. And Clara was just one of the children Mercy made a point of helping whenever she could.

She bent and pressed a kiss against Clara's sunken cheek, waiting to feel the faint warmth of the little one's breath. Instead, there was stillness. Mercy sat up only to find the gray liquid dribbling from the corner of Clara's mouth.

Her stomach twisted with a deep knowing, one she wanted to ignore. She dragged the spoon under the leaking medicine and brought it back to the girl's lips. "Come now, lamb. You have to take this."

She attempted to pour it in, but it trickled back out. She tried again and again, murmuring, "Please sweet one, please . . ."

Finally she became aware of gentle fingers tugging at the spoon, attempting to pull it from her. She tore her gaze from Clara to find the doctor across from her. His brows slanted above eyes brimming with pity.

How dare he give up so easily? She wanted to shove his hand away, to scream her protest and cling to the spoon, as if by doing so she could cling to hope. But having seen death too many times in her eighteen years, she knew the fight would be futile.

She released her hold and let her hands fall to her lap. The pain in her chest was not as easy to release. It gripped so tightly she struggled to suck in a breath. Then she fought to push away the ache just as she always did. She'd learned long ago to stuff it out of sight or she might just go mad from the sorrow.

"I'm sorry." The doctor sat back on his heels, haggardness grooving more lines into his face.

Mercy bent low and kissed the little girl's forehead, praying her kiss would anoint the child as she journeyed to a better place.

Surely anyplace in heaven or earth would be better than London.

two

"You'll be back again tomorrow, will you not?" Bates placed the last of the medical supplies into the chest and closed the lid.

Joseph Colville finished rolling down his sleeves and fumbled at his cuff links, grasping for any excuse he could find to avoid another day at the Shoreditch Dispensary. "I'm afraid I already have plans for the morrow." His game of cricket at Marylebone Cricket Club was as valid a reason as any.

"What about the day after?" Bates persisted.

"You know I'll be leaving soon for Wiltshire. I must visit the estate and my aunt before too much time passes."

Bates stood to his full height, which fell well below Joseph's chin. At six-feet-two, Joseph didn't consider himself overly tall, but he towered above Bates. Even though his old friend was diminutive in stature, he had a boundless energy that Joseph envied. And boundless compassion.

The simple truth was that Dr. Bates was a saint. How else could the man devote so much time to London's poorest of the poor?

"Then upon your return from the country, you must consider joining me," Bates said. "I would put a good word in for you at the college, and you could teach a few classes."

"They won't want an inexperienced and young doctor like myself."

"Nonsense. They'll want you, and we both know it."

Joseph shrugged. He'd been a stellar scholar. More than that, however, the college would want him for the prestige his titles and wealth would bring.

Bates cleared his throat. "If you taught, then you could spend the rest of your time here at the dispensary. It turns out my partner is retiring this summer, and I'll need someone to take his place."

Turning his back on Bates, Joseph slipped his arms into his coat. Although the man had become like a father, replacing the one Joseph had lost, he couldn't reconcile himself to Bates's life.

They'd known each other since Joseph had attended Harrow School, where Dr. Bates had served as the parochial surgeon. Bates had been there when Joseph received the news his family had taken ill with cholera during an epidemic that had ravaged London. And Bates had been there when Joseph learned his mother, father, and brother had all succumbed.

After Joseph finished his studies at Oxford, Bates had been the one to support him when he'd sought to attend the Royal College of Physicians. None of the members of the peerage had understood how the titled Lord Colville, Baron of Wiltshire, could cast aside his duty to Parliament and to the other privileges of his station to pursue a commoner's work of becoming a physician.

His fellow gentry hadn't concerned themselves over the fact that a title and his family's estate were never meant to be his as second-born son. They hadn't cared that he'd sensed God's call to do something more with his life than smoke cigars and drink brandy at The London Tavern and eat turtle cutlets in the Surrey Oak dining room. They certainly hadn't understood his decision to become a doctor and then later to become a ship's surgeon for a yearlong voyage to India. He'd caused more gossip when, shortly after his return, he left again as the ship's surgeon on a tea clipper to Shanghai.

Joseph couldn't explain the choices he'd made, couldn't explain what was driving him. All he knew was that he'd needed to go. And all he knew now was that he'd have to leave again. Soon.

Since the *Kate Carnie* had docked last month, the unsettled urge had been pacing back and forth inside him, like one of the caged tigers he'd seen in India, always restless, always anxious to prowl, as if that could somehow dispel the darkness hovering deep in his soul.

Silence settled about the office, heightening the sharp patter of raindrops against the boarded window. The May evening had grown in length, but the shadows of night had crept in with the return of rain. The lantern at the center of the desk failed to drive away the gloom.

Joseph rolled his shoulders in an attempt to release the tension that had built in his chest as he'd tended one poor soul after another all day. But the tension only tightened, like violin strings being tuned under a maestro's adept fingers. He forced himself to pivot and face Bates. His friend deserved the truth from him.

Bates leaned against the desk, his feet crossed at the ankles and his arms folded comfortably. Although his wispy white hair stood in disarray and his suit was rumpled, he maintained a distinguished air. Joseph was always amazed that this man, who worked so tirelessly, never appeared weary or ruffled.

His eyes were round behind his tortoiseshell spectacles and brimmed with a fatherly concern that brought an unwelcome ache to Joseph's heart.

"I'm not ready to settle down just yet." Joseph offered Bates the only explanation he'd been able to come up with, the same one he'd given the doctor the last time he was home.

The older man now taught at the King's Royal College of Physicians, where he took every opportunity to encourage his medical students to consider the plight of the poor.

It was no secret the first city had become a national disgrace. Over the past decade, the influx of laborers into London had far outmatched the availability of jobs and housing.

Conditions within the city had reached a crisis level of a magnitude heretofore unknown. Shortages of work and housing were leading to severe hunger, poverty, and disease in the overflowing slum areas.

The problems threatened to choke the life from the world's most magnificent city, just as the stench and thick sewage in the River Thames threatened to choke the air from anyone who breathed it in.

Bates wanted to make a difference with the Shoreditch Dispensary, was reaching out and showing compassion to hurting people day after day. But his efforts hadn't made any difference in the Shoreditch community as far as Joseph could tell. The building, the street, the neighborhood had only grown more dilapidated since the last time Joseph had been there. And the people had only grown more haggard and hollow-cheeked.

The troubles seemed insurmountable, as enormous as the mountain ranges he'd seen in Indonesia. Who could scale such a divide between the rich and poor? The contrast between the two separate worlds seemed completely irreconcilable.

"How can you bear it, Bates?" The question slipped out before Joseph could stop it.

"Bear what?"

"The desperation in each face, the heartache, the ability to do so little for them . . ."

Bates regarded Joseph, his wise eyes narrowing in thought. Joseph appreciated that his friend never gave glib answers. He could count on Bates for the truth, even when it wasn't easy to hear.

"I may not be able to help everyone," Bates said slowly, "but I help those God places in my path each day. One life at a time, one small difference at a time. My methods are not revolutionary. But I'm doing the small part God's called me to, and when I obey Him, He gives me the strength I need to accomplish the task at hand."

"What about those you cannot help?" Joseph persisted. "Like

the child with the cholera infantum? Her mother brought her in too late. The infant was practically dead when she arrived."

"Do you mean the child Mercy brought to us?"

"She's too young to be a mother." Joseph couldn't contain his exasperation. "At her age, she ought not to have any children, since she clearly has no idea how to take care of them."

Joseph didn't agree with every philosophy his friends espoused regarding the poor, particularly blunt statements such as "If they cannot feed, they should not breed." Perhaps he didn't go quite so far as to think the poor should stop having babies, but after the neglect he'd witnessed time and again during his work at the dispensary, he was beginning to think that at the very least, poor women needed to be educated on how to take care of their young.

"Mercy wasn't the child's mother." Bates took off his spectacles and wiped them with the edge of his waistcoat. "My guess is the mother was at work or perhaps sick herself so that she was unable to bring the child. And Mercy, seeing the child in need, rushed her here hoping to save her."

Joseph envisioned the young woman bending over the dead child, her delicate features taut with agony, her eyes swelling with grief. Pretty eyes, he remembered thinking, especially their blue-green color. "You must be mistaken. She was the infant's mother—"

"Mercy comes in all the time with one child or another. She's an angel of mercy in that community, though she doesn't know it." Bates chuckled softly. "Her name certainly befits her."

Again, Joseph pictured the woman as she'd finally stood. She'd surprised Joseph by bending over and unlacing her boot. *"Thank ye for trying, sir,"* she said in a broken voice. *"I'm very much obliged to you."* She then tugged her sockless foot out of the boot and held it out to him. *"Will you take my boots as payment, sir? It's all I've got."*

Joseph had tried not to recoil at the prospect of touching the filthy excuse for a shoe, much less the idea of allowing the woman to walk the London streets barefoot. Of course, he'd insisted she keep her boots, that he required no payment. He figured she would need every penny she could find to pay the undertaker for a coffin and a proper burial.

"Mercy is doing her part to make a difference," Bates continued. "Now, imagine if everyone did that—took a small part in reaching out. Then imagine if all those small parts were added together. We'd be able to accomplish a great deal of good."

Joseph nodded. He knew the changes had to begin somewhere. Starting small was better than sitting around and simply complaining about the problems, as many of his peers were wont to do. He'd heard of organizations forming charities, of other concerned members of the upper class who genuinely desired to provide relief to the poor as his father had wanted to do. But was it too little, too late?

"The question I have for you, son, is this." Bates replaced his spectacles and peered through the lenses in his direct manner. "What's the small part God's calling you to? Are you seeking His leading or are you running away from it?"

Joseph tugged at the large gold buttons on his coat. He'd defied convention by becoming a physcian. He was helping sailors and passengers during their voyages. Moreover, he didn't demand the courtesy and rights of his station and title. What else did God expect of him? Wasn't he already doing enough?

Though the questions choked him like the sooty fog that permeated the city, he swallowed the bitter taste. "You always know how to make me think deeper."

Bates pushed away from the desk and crossed the room toward Joseph. The older man grabbed him into an embrace, squeezed him hard, then thumped his back. When Bates stepped away, he wore a tender smile. "You can count on me, Joseph, for anything. Always. I hope you know that, son."

"Of course," Joseph said. "Thank you. And likewise."

"Does that mean you'll consider the partnership?" The seriousness in Bates's expression told Joseph more than his words. Bates needed him if he had any hope of keeping the dispensary open long term.

"Your students," Joseph said, "are not any of them willing?"

Bates's shoulders slumped in the first sign of discouragement he'd shown today. "I need someone with both time and money, Joseph. Most of them have only the time, and even that's limited."

Joseph held back a sigh. He wasn't the solution to Bates's problem. Surely his friend could see he wasn't the right man to enter into a partnership at the dispensary. Yes, he cared about the people of this community, and yes, he always went away knowing his services were necessary and appreciated.

But the mission here was Bates's passion, not his own. At least it couldn't be his passion at this point in his life.

"I am sorry." Joseph chose his words with care. "I cannot make a commitment I fear I would only break."

The older man smiled ruefully, then patted Joseph's cheek before turning to go. Bates stepped into the hallway and spoke a few words to the driver of their hackney coach, who had arrived a short while ago to transport them and the medical supplies back to their homes.

When he returned to the room, the distress in his face was gone and he tossed Joseph a grin. "Since I cannot convince you to stay, can I count on you for another sizable donation to the operating expenses of the dispensary?"

"Consider it done." The knot inside Joseph's gut eased a bit. Maybe he couldn't serve the poor the way Bates was doing, but he could give his money toward the cause. Surely that counted for something.

three

Joseph threw aside his white bowler hat and wiped his brow with a hand towel one of the attendants offered him. He'd discarded his white flannel cricket coat during the game, unbuttoned his high collar, and loosened his bow tie. Even so, his starched shirt stuck to his back with perspiration.

"Excellent game today, Lord Colville."

Joseph accepted the compliments from the other men as he lounged in an armchair in the elegant Long Room of Marylebone Cricket Club's pavilion. The high ornate ceiling and tall windows provided ample light despite an overcast afternoon as the men came inside off the field.

Even though Joseph had played cricket here for as long as he could remember, his brother, Anthony, had always been the star and darling of the club. Anthony had set the record for the most wickets and runs. Even after a decade since his passing, he was still a legend.

"You've gotten faster," said another friend, sitting nearby. "Maybe those sea legs of yours are giving you the advantage."

Joseph had endured the good-natured teasing of his peers often over the past years. He didn't care that many thought he was a tad touched in the head. The truth was, he liked being his own man, breaking free of the constraints of his class and doing whatever he pleased.

His aunt took every occasion she could to remind him of his place, the social graces he lacked, and the family name he must honor. He loved his aunt and was grateful for her managing Wiltshire in his absence. Nevertheless, he'd learned to keep his visits short and thus curtail her lectures regarding his "wild behavior" and his need to find a proper wife.

He had enough pressure without hers. Every time he was home from a voyage, he received invitations from wealthy and titled families hoping to introduce him to their daughters and initiate a match. He tried to resist, but his friends cajoled him and dragged him along to various outings, dinner parties, and dances.

Over the past few weeks, he'd enjoyed spending time with the fairer sex, especially since such company was rare during his travels. Yet he'd been careful not to form attachments or mislead any young ladies into thinking he wanted more from them than friendship.

He was no more ready to take a wife than he was to settle down. Of course, one day he'd get married and have a large family—a family to take the place of the one he'd lost. Just not yet . . .

"Excuse me, my lord." One of the attendants offered Joseph a glass of brandy. "This is compliments of the gentleman, Captain Hellyer."

Joseph accepted the thick glass and followed the attendant's nod to a man sitting stiffly among a cluster of chairs a short distance away. In a sharp navy coat, military trousers, and an old-fashioned silk cravat tied at his neck, he emanated an aura of authority. With slight threads of gray in a trim mustache and beard, the man appeared about the age Joseph's father would have been.

Captain Hellyer raised his glass, filled only a quarter with the amber liquid, and silently greeted Joseph.

Joseph returned the gesture, took a sip, and let the brandy burn a hot trail down his throat.

Something in the captain's eyes beckoned him, an intensity that informed Joseph the drink was but a bridge to a conversation he wished to have.

Who exactly was Captain Hellyer? And what could he possibly have to say? Joseph searched his mind for some knowledge of the man, any connection. But he could think of nothing of consequence. He'd been gone too often in recent years to keep abreast of the local news and gossip.

"Excuse me, gentlemen." Joseph pushed himself up from his chair, handed his bat to the attendant hovering nearby, and crossed toward the captain.

"Captain Hellyer." Joseph gave a slight bow. "Joseph Colville at your service, sir."

The captain nodded at Joseph and waved to the empty chair next to him. "Lord Colville. Please. Sit."

Joseph lowered himself into the chair, which was positioned so that the entire playing field spread out before him. A new game of cricket was under way, this one by younger fellows.

He and Anthony had been a part of a group like that, so full of zeal and excitement and industry. They'd had good times together, and if anyone should have had his life cut short, it should have been him, not Anthony.

"We haven't had the pleasure of meeting before, Captain," Joseph began, diverting his thoughts away from his brother.

"I knew your father."

Joseph wanted to shrug but didn't. Many had known the late Lord Colville. He'd been prominent in the House of Lords for many years.

As if sensing Joseph's indifference, Captain Hellyer continued, "He was a good man. And if you're even half the man he was, then I suspect you're a good chap too."

Joseph didn't respond except to take another sip of brandy. He stared out the window, attempting to keep at bay the memories of his father. He had no wish to think on his father any more than he did his brother.

"I hear you're a ship's surgeon," Captain Hellyer said.

"I've given it a go, yes."

"Did it suit you?"

"Well enough."

"Enough to do it again?"

Something in the captain's tone drew Joseph's attention away from the field. At the hopeful glimmer in the captain's eyes, Joseph's blood began to pump a little faster. "What do you have in mind, Captain?"

"Lindsay and Stringer hired me to command the *Tynemouth*. She's an A1, 1,500 tons, 600 horsepower."

"Sounds as though she's a decent size."

The captain nodded. "She was a troopship in the Crimea. Survived a savage winter in the Black Sea when most of the other ships didn't."

"Then she's a sturdy ship as well."

"That she is. With the steam engines and her sails, she's ready for the voyage to Vancouver Island and British Columbia."

"Vancouver Island and British Columbia?" Joseph set his glass down on the low table near his chair and leaned forward. Gold had recently been discovered in the British colonies on the western edge of North America and was apparently drawing immigrants from nearby California and Oregon. England was scrambling to keep the colonies populated with her own people, so the gold wouldn't trickle down into the United States but would instead profit the motherland.

Joseph didn't need the gold, but he'd heard tales of the beauty and grandeur of British colonies in the Pacific Northwest and couldn't deny he longed to voyage to the Western Hemisphere. With the unrest and war dividing the United States, British ships were steering clear of the conflict. As a result, Joseph hadn't dared to hope he'd get an opportunity anytime soon to sail to North America.

Was this his chance?

The captain was watching him keenly, observing his every reaction. "First, we'll cross the Atlantic to South America, stopping in the Falkland Islands for coal, fresh provisions, and water. Next we'll head up the Pacific coast and dock again in San Francisco before sailing to Vancouver Island and eventually the Hawaiian Islands."

"I've heard the Falkland Islands are incredible, unlike anything else."

"Then you'll want to see the place for yourself," the captain said.

Joseph hadn't realized he'd shifted to the edge of his chair and perched there as if he were ready to jump up and leave today if possible. He forced himself to scoot back, pick up his glass of brandy, and relax his shoulders. "When do you leave?"

"I'll be loading the *Tynemouth* next week at the London Docks, and I'll be embarking passengers at Dartmouth a few days after that."

A week. He could wrap up his business here in London, travel to Wiltshire, and make it to Dartmouth in a week. That was more than enough time.

What of Bates? The conversation with his mentor yesterday had replayed in his head a dozen times since he'd ridden away from Shoreditch. Bates was in dire need of a new partner in order to keep the dispensary open. The work and the logistics of the mission were too great for one man to shoulder alone. That had been clear enough yesterday with both of them needed to treat all the patients.

But surely his old friend would understand he wasn't meant for the job, at least not now. Bates had to know Joseph wasn't ready to live in London permanently.

The very thought of returning home every night to the empty hallways and silent rooms of Arlington House draped a dismal veil across Joseph's heart every bit as ghastly as the coverings that shrouded the mansion's furnishings. Upon his return to London, the few servants who remained at Arlington House had begun the process of opening up rooms and removing the coverings. But he'd stopped them and instructed them to leave things as they were.

He hadn't told them he had no desire to use any of the rooms in the house, that he'd rather be anywhere but in his childhood home. Now, confronted with the possibility of leaving again, he couldn't deny his wish to get away. Far away.

"I'd be honored and obliged to have you as part of my crew." Captain Hellyer finally said the words he'd been leading up to.

Joseph met the captain's gaze and realized the conversation was more than simply crossing a bridge. It was an invitation to another journey, a journey he couldn't wait to begin.

four

Mercy stood in the long line of tenants waiting for a turn at the water spigot at the back of the building. The house agent switched on the water only once every other day and only for thirty minutes, hardly enough time for everyone to fill their buckets and pots. Still, Mercy made a point of getting her family's share every opportunity she could.

With the blackened pot in one hand, Mercy adjusted the tiny squirming bundle in her other arm, sweet baby Paul, her newest sibling. At two weeks old, he was plump and rosy-cheeked and could squall louder than a hungry tomcat. All good signs he was thriving, all the more reason not to complain about the extra work, and all reminders to be grateful and pray he'd survive longer than the last babe.

"Hold tight to my skirt, Charity," Mercy admonished her youngest sister. "And stop splashing in the dirty water, d'ye hear me?"

At four years old, Charity was growing more independent—and more belligerent. When her hair was clean, it was the same shade of blond as Mercy's. But most of the time, the layer of dust and soot turned the autumn gold to winter gray. As with baby Paul, Charity's energy and attitude were preferable to the listlessness of some of the neighborhood children, who were either too hungry or too sick to make trouble.

Like Clara.

Mercy tried to shove aside her thoughts of the girl. She'd done what she could but had failed. After she'd carried the lifeless body home, Clara's mother hadn't been surprised and hadn't shed a tear.

Was death so common a visitor in these parts that people expected it, maybe even welcomed it as the only true savior from their pain? Or had they, like her, closed off their hearts to the pain in order to continue on?

Charity stomped her foot again in the nearest puddle, sending a spray of mud so high that some of it splattered Mercy's face.

Dirty was too mild a word in describing the puddles. After the recent downpours, the kennels had overflowed into the streets. Added to that, piles of trash remained from the winter months, along with the rotting privy that served the several hundred people who lived in the old houses surrounding the stone courtyard.

The sour reek of human waste and rotting garbage was ever present. And now that the days were becoming warmer, the stench was growing. By summer it would be an enormous, invisible beast that twisted and slithered through every corridor, suffocating them with its noxious fumes.

"Charity Wilkins, I daresay," Mercy said in her sternest voice as she wiped her sleeve across her cheek. "Twiggy will set you sniveling once she gets home from work after I tell her you've been naughty."

"Mum's already home." Charity pointed past the line behind them to the courtyard entrance.

Sure enough, their mum stood with several other women who worked with her at the rag factory. Somehow, in spite of the long hours, Twiggy always managed to look pretty. Maybe it was her long thick hair, or her smooth skin, or her curvy figure.

Mercy glanced at the patch of sky visible above the crowded

rooftops. She couldn't see the sun behind the clouds to tell what time of day it was, but certainly it was too early for Twiggy and the others to be home from work.

When Mercy had last heard St. Matthew's church bell toll, she figured she had plenty of time to make beef broth from the bones she'd found earlier in the trash behind the butcher shop. With the onion and the biscuit pieces she'd hoarded, she hoped to surprise Twiggy with the fine meal when she arrived home from the factory, tired as always.

As though sensing Mercy's questions, Twiggy looked their way. People told Mercy she was pretty like Twiggy, that she had her mum's blue-green eyes, yet Mercy couldn't remember the last time she'd looked into a mirror to see for herself.

Now a sadness in Twiggy's eyes dulled the beautiful blue-green, a sadness that clawed at Mercy's insides.

Charity broke away from Mercy and skipped through the muddy yard toward their mum. Mercy wanted to break out of line too and run over to Twiggy the same way, skipping along without a care in the world, trusting that the one who'd birthed her would always love and protect her.

But Mercy couldn't run to Twiggy with her problems any more than she could run to God. Both had abandoned her long ago.

Twiggy snatched Charity up into a hug, one that seemed tighter than normal, which scratched at Mercy's insides all the more. Something was amiss, and Mercy wasn't sure she wanted to find out what.

She finished waiting her turn in line, filled her pot from the trickling spigot, and slowly made her way across the courtyard, bouncing sweet Paul as his hungry grunts and squeaks grew louder.

At the courtyard entrance, Twiggy took the babe from Mercy, snuggling into Paul's neck and breathing in deeply of his downy hair that was as black as coal, unlike Twiggy's or Ash's.

Mercy never said anything about the landlord climbing up to the garret room with Twiggy whenever he came into the neighborhood in his fancy hackney. Mercy never said anything when

Twiggy shooed everyone out of their home while her boss from the rag factory came calling. And Mercy never said anything when Twiggy had new babes who didn't look like Ash. Mercy understood well enough how Twiggy came by the occasional extra food or the additional lumps of coal.

But that hadn't stopped Mercy from silently chastising Twiggy. Twiggy wasn't being fair to Ash, who worked long and hard for their family. She wasn't being fair to the children she already had by bringing more babes into the family. And she wasn't being fair to the babe, knowing the child would eventually go hungry and wear castoffs that weren't fit for the rag factory. They didn't have any more space in the garret room they rented. And besides, a new babe only gave the housing agent another reason to increase their rent.

"He's as smart as a sixpence, ain't he?" Twiggy whispered as she kissed Paul's perfect nose.

"He's a right dear lamb," Mercy agreed. It wasn't the babe's fault he'd been born. What was done was done, and there was no changing it now. They'd have to make the best of things, which was why Mercy hadn't let up on her job search even though she'd exhausted nearly every possibility.

It was all the more reason Mercy had made up her mind never to get married and have babies. This wasn't the kind of world to bring a child into. Besides, if she ever got a hankering for a child, she only had to walk a city block to find a homeless orphan living in an alley and needing a home.

"The mill let us go." Twiggy said the words so softly that Mercy almost missed them.

"You mean let you go early?" The question was a plea followed by a quaking deep inside.

Twiggy lifted her face away from Paul and met Mercy's gaze directly. "I mean let us go, go."

"But why?" Mercy couldn't keep the desperation from her question.

"Don't rightly know since there be plenty of rags piled high for sorting. But some are a-saying the need for paper ain't what it used to be."

The nearby paper mill employed women to do the dirty work of sorting through rags, pulling out the cloth that was too grimy and stained to be recycled, cutting away buttons, clips, and other small items, along with sorting out the garbage.

The women worked long shifts while standing on their feet all day, setting aside the usable rags, which were later taken to a different part of the factory where the fibers were broken down, bleached, and beaten. The pulp was eventually turned into the brown paper shopkeepers used to wrap everything from butter and tea to pins and sewing needles.

While being a rag girl was dirty work and rumored by some to spread disease, it was one of the few jobs women could get, one Twiggy had been lucky to have.

"You'll be able to go back again right soon," Mercy said. "You'll see."

Paul gave a disgruntled cry, this one louder than the previous. Twiggy bounced him. "Hush-a-bye now. Guess I can feed you myself this time."

Twiggy wouldn't need her to take care of Paul anymore. And she wouldn't need her to watch over the other little ones or make dinner or stand in line for water.

With her waterpot bumping against her leg and Charity in tow, Mercy followed along as Twiggy made her way through a dark alley to the front of the building. Like the terraced houses in Shoreditch, the Nichol's homes were just as aged, hardly able to hold themselves up under the weight of the masses who squeezed into every nook.

You're adding to the burden, Mercy Wilkins, said a nagging voice inside, the one that had started as soft as a newborn's breath but was growing into the clatter of a dozen coaches over cobblestone. *And now that Twiggy's out of work, she won't need you—if she ever did—and you'll be just another mouth to feed.*

Another mouth to feed. That was why her older sister, Patience, had left over the winter and why two of her younger brothers had long since moved out and now lived on the docks. At fourteen and twelve, the boys could fend for themselves. That still left five children at home, including Mercy, with never enough food to go around.

Mercy quickened her pace until she was practically stepping on Twiggy's heels. "Maybe Ash can find more night-soil work until the factory hires you back."

"The poor man hardly sleeps now." Twiggy opened the main door. "You don't expect me to ask him to do more, do you?"

Mercy didn't answer as she trudged up the sagging staircase behind Twiggy. All she had to do was picture Ash's exhausted face when he arrived home in the wee hours of the morning, threw his reeking body onto the floor, and fell asleep in an instant.

While the rest of the city slept, Ash spent hours crawling through privy seats into underground cesspools that were built into basements or back gardens away from homes. He shoveled the solid waste into baskets that were later carted off to the countryside.

The stench from cleaning the cesspools was too disturbing for the daytime, and so men like Ash made a little extra money doing the foul work at night on the side.

Whenever he cleaned cesspools, he managed to sleep for an hour or two before rising and heading off to his day job collecting coal ash from houses and businesses around the city. He and a partner hauled load after load to the yard along the River Thames where the ashes were then sold to brickmakers.

Ash was one of the lucky ones who hadn't been let go after the market had collapsed several years ago. He and Twiggy had celebrated their good fortune the way they did on most occasions, by lots of hugging and kissing beneath the blankets.

Those were the times when Mercy felt the sorriest for Ash and most ashamed of Twiggy. Surely he questioned where Twiggy got the extra food and coal. And yet if he did, he never let on. He just kept on loving Twiggy and every babe she bore.

"Maybe it's time for you to think about getting yourself a husband," Twiggy said breathlessly as they reached the top landing. "When I was your age, Ash and me were already married."

Mercy froze in the hallway, letting the heavy pot of water dangle at her side. Twiggy would never ask her to leave, would never demand it of her. But Mercy knew that was what her mum was implying. The truth was, Twiggy adored her babes but outgrew her older kids, especially when they were no longer useful.

Twiggy ducked into the tiny room with the slanted ceiling and soot-blackened walls. She lowered herself into the room's only chair and set to nursing Paul, kissing the babe's head and humming as she did so.

Charity, who'd lagged behind, finally stomped up the last few steps and bumped Mercy from behind, causing water to slosh from the pot.

The nagging voice spilled over too. *See, Twiggy doesn't need you anymore. And she doesn't want you either. Maybe long ago, when you were a pretty little babe, she loved you. But now all you are to her is a burden. A big burden.*

Mercy folded her hands around her sister's. Not only were Patience's hands little more than skin and bones, but her fingers were blackened and full of sores that came from picking oakum all day.

The tedious work was required of all who lived at the workhouse, mostly old men and women who could no longer survive on their own. The large facility also housed widows and their children along with other young women like Patience who'd decided they'd rather die in the workhouse than sell their souls on the streets.

They spent their days unraveling, unpicking, and uncoiling old pieces of rope until all that remained were thin fibers called oakum. The oakum was then mixed with tar to create a caulking that was applied to ships to make them watertight.

"There's a dear," Mercy said as Patience bit off another piece of roll. "If you don't eat every little last crumb, I'll throttle you, that I will."

"Bless you, Mercy." Patience chewed slowly, her once-delicate features now gaunt, her thick hair now stringy, her womanly form now emaciated. "I'm just trying to savor each bite."

Although her sister never complained about her food rationing at the workhouse, Mercy heard tales about the gruel, that the gray liquid was so thin and distasteful that even ravenous dogs turned their noses up at it. Even so, the workhouse residents were given two servings of the gruel morning and night and licked their bowls so clean they hardly needed washing.

"You're as thin as a chimney sweeper," Mercy teased, hoping for a smile.

Patience gave her the ghost of one, which was soon chased away by a fit of coughing that wracked the young woman's body. Even though people told Mercy she was as pretty as Twiggy, Mercy always thought Patience was more beautiful. Even now in her sickly condition, she radiated a beauty that contained all the loveliness of her sweet spirit.

She lived up to her name, having the patience of a saint. Twiggy had claimed she'd named her boys after the apostles and her girls with divine traits in the hopes that God might bless her children as a result. As far as Mercy could see, her mum's strategy hadn't worked.

In the waning dusk, only a few other residents with visitors sat in the fenced-in courtyard. The evening had taken on a chill, and Mercy watched Patience struggle to regain her breath and suppress the cough that seemed to be getting worse with every visit.

"We should go in." Mercy started to rise. "It's too damp out here for you."

"Come out with it." Patience laid a hand on Mercy's arm and held her in place. "I know you have something to say. I can see it in your eyes right so."

Mercy shifted on the wooden bench. She didn't want to burden

Patience with her problems. Heaven knew her sister had enough of her own. But that was why she'd stopped by the workhouse, wasn't it? Not only to give Patience the roll but to seek her sister's advice.

"Twiggy lost her ragpicker job."

Patience lowered the remainder of the roll to her lap and then swallowed hard, clearly having to work to get her last bite down.

"She told me to get myself a husband." Mercy blurted the words as if they were a curse. Twiggy had told Patience the same thing several months ago during the bitter days of winter when both food and fuel had been scarce.

"No, no, no," Patience said, dots of color flaring in her pale cheeks. "She can't push you out now. Not when I came here so you'd be able to stay at home and be safe."

At the rushed and passionate declaration, Mercy stared at her older sister. With only two years' difference in their ages, and even when they'd both been hardly more than infants, Patience had taken care of her during the endless hours when Twiggy had been away at work.

With each new babe that had come along and stolen Twiggy's time and affection, Patience had never wavered. She'd stepped in and loved Mercy with unending devotion. In some ways, Patience had been more of a mother than Twiggy had ever been.

But this? Coming to the workhouse for her? It was too much.

"Don't be cross with me." Patience grabbed Mercy's hands. "I did what I had to—"

"We could have made it work." Even as Mercy said the words, she knew there was no other way. Twiggy's efforts to get Patience a job as a rag girl had failed, as had Ash's efforts to find Patience work sorting through the piles at the ash yard. There were simply too many laborers needing employment and not enough jobs.

"You have to stay at home." Patience's tone was firm.

"And watch the little ones go hungry?" They were already hungry enough. And now, without Twiggy's meager income, there wouldn't be near enough to go around.

As if coming to the same conclusion, Patience's expression crumpled and tears began to slide down her hollow cheeks.

"I'll come here with you—"

"No!" The word came out shrill. "I won't let you!"

"At least then we can take care of each other."

Another fit of coughing wracked Patience. She shook her head adamantly, the tears streaking through the grime, providing the only cleansing Patience's face had seen in weeks. "You have to get a real job, Mercy," she said when she could breathe again. "You can find something. I know you can."

"I've tried."

Patience's bony fingers dug into Mercy's hands, as if she could grasp Mercy's soul through her skin and somehow save her.

"Don't fret," Mercy said softly, wishing she could ease her sister's anxiety.

"The Columbia Mission Society." Patience sat up taller, a light flaring in her eyes. "You have to go to the Columbia Mission Society."

She had no idea what Patience was talking about but had the feeling it wasn't a good idea.

"Several ladies from the Columbia Mission Society came to the workhouse last week looking for women interested in immigrating to Vancouver Island and British Columbia—"

"Stuff and nonsense!" Mercy extricated her hand and jumped up from the bench, drawing the attention of several older residents across the yard. Mercy lowered her voice into a growl. "I'm not leaving you. Don't even think about it."

"They want healthy young women of good repute," Patience continued as though she hadn't heard Mercy. "But most of the women here are too aged or sickly to qualify."

"Patience, please stop—"

"But you're perfect." Patience pushed herself up and reached for Mercy's face, holding her cheeks captive. "You're young and beautiful, healthy and strong."

The rare words of praise so startled Mercy that her stormy thoughts stopped raging and fell into an eerie calm.

Patience's eyes glowed with such love and pride that a lump formed in Mercy's throat. "The ladies from the mission society promised there'd be plenty of jobs waiting for each and every woman."

Plenty of jobs waiting? For women? Did such a place really exist?

"You need to do this, Mercy." Patience pressed her hands harder against Mercy's cheeks. "You have to go to the Columbia Mission Society building at once and ask them to sign you up. Tonight. Now."

At the anticipation in Patience's face, Mercy held back her ready protest. Could she make herself consider something so outlandish as getting a job in another country?

"I don't know where Columbia is—"

"British Columbia," Patience corrected. "It's near Australia, right where it's warm and sunny all the time."

She'd heard stories of prisoners being loaded onto ships and sent off to Australia, never to be seen or heard from again. "No, I'm not a-going. It's too far away, and then I'd never see you or anyone else again."

Patience dropped her hold and took a step back, her expression turning severe. "You listen to me, Mercy Wilkins. You're going and that's all there is to it. You're going, and then when you've been working for a mite, you can send me enough of your earnings to pay for my fare."

The determined set to Patience's chin told Mercy her sister wouldn't be swayed. "Why can't we both go now? You come with me to the society building, and we'll sign up for the trip together, that we will."

"I have to get over this cough first. And get strong again."

"You're strong enough." But even as Mercy spoke, she felt Patience letting go and setting her adrift. Murky water opened up betwixt them, and even though Mercy grasped after her sister, the chasm grew wider.

Patience smiled tenderly. "If you won't do this for yourself, then do it for me. Please."

"But I can't leave you here." Mercy waved at the barren courtyard and the imposing building behind them.

"Do you want to make me happy?"

"Of course I do."

"Then vow you'll go to British Columbia. I'll be happy if I know you're someplace where you can start a new life for yourself. A good life."

Before Mercy could respond, Patience started coughing again. The force of the hacks bent her over. Finally, breathing heavily, she straightened. The spots of color in her cheeks had deepened. She pushed against Mercy. "Go. Now."

Mercy took a step away but hesitated.

"Please, Mercy, go." The repeated pleas were like an ancient battering ram against Mercy's remaining defenses, hitting hard and crumbling her resistance. "Vow it."

"Fine, I'll go. But you best be ready to follow soon after. D'ye hear me?"

Patience nodded wearily.

There was so much more Mercy wanted to say, but her throat constricted, cutting off her words. Instead, she hugged her sister tightly and left her standing in the courtyard.

five

"What did you say your name was?" asked the woman from the opposite side of the desk.

"Mercy Wilkins, ma'am." Mercy perched on the edge of her chair, folding the material of her skirt to hide the worst of the stains.

The woman ran her smooth, clean fingernail down a long list of what appeared to be names. "I don't see that name on our list."

"No, ma'am." Mercy tucked her hands out of sight so the woman wouldn't see the black encrusted into her fingernails. Everything about the room spoke of a standard of cleanliness that was foreign to Mercy, from the shining glass windows to the richly polished desk, with every inkpot, ledger, and paper neatly organized.

The woman finally looked up. "If you're not on our list, why then are you here?" The words weren't spoken unkindly, but Mercy couldn't keep from cowering on the inside regardless.

"I was hoping to get on the list, ma'am. The fine gent I spoke to last night told me to come back this morning first thing. So here I am." After leaving Patience and the workhouse, Mercy had walked several miles to reach the Columbia Mission Society building only to discover it was dark and deserted. A man exiting the business next door informed Mercy that everyone had gone home for the night.

Darkness had long past fallen, along with a foggy mist. She'd had to make her way carefully through the maze of streets so she didn't call any attention to herself, especially as she ventured into Old Nichol.

Some claimed the name of the slum was taken after the devil himself, Old Nick. Whatever the case, the Prince of Darkness had made Old Nichol his home, for surely no other place so resembled hell on earth.

As she passed through the bowels of the slum, a deep weariness had cloaked her. She decided she wouldn't return to the Columbia Mission Society in the morning, that she couldn't leave Patience or her family. For in spite of everything, they still needed her.

But when she'd climbed to the garret room and found her younger siblings huddled together on the dark landing and heard Ash shouting and Twiggy crying behind the closed door of the apartment, it hadn't taken her long to realize they were fighting over which of the children had to leave.

At their mention of sending ten-year-old Matthew to the docks to make his way with the homeless boys who lived there, including her other brothers, Mercy finally understood why Patience had so willingly gone to the workhouse. She'd interrupted her parent's argument and told them that as long as they kept Matthew, she'd be the one to go and make her own way.

Now here she was again, hunger raging around her insides looking for something to devour, except there was nothing. Before leaving home that morning, she'd given her share to the little ones and determined that from now on, she'd find her own grub or else go hungry.

The woman on the other side of the desk shuffled her papers together. "I'm sorry you had to make the trip over here again so needlessly. But I'm afraid all sixty of our spots have already been filled."

Mercy stood, unsure whether to feel discouraged or elated. She hadn't wanted to let Patience down by ignoring this opportunity. On the other hand, she hadn't wanted to leave everything familiar and everyone she loved, even if they no longer wanted her.

At least now she could go back to the workhouse and tell Patience she'd tried but that it hadn't worked out, that together they'd find a way to survive.

The woman rose from her chair, revealing the full length of an elegant gown. Smiling apologetically, she said, "I'm sorry . . ."

"Mercy Wilkins."

"Mercy," she finished. "I do hope you'll find what you're seeking elsewhere."

What exactly was she *seeking*? Before Mercy could figure out a polite response, the front door opened. A petite lady bustled inside with rustling skirts and a swishing cloak, along with a pleasant scent Mercy didn't recognize but guessed resembled a bouquet of fresh flowers—though she'd never smelled flowers before.

"Miss Rye." The woman behind the desk dropped a curtsy. "You're here early this morning."

The newcomer untied a large ribbon under her chin and removed her hat to reveal sharply angled features made more severe by the tight pull of her plain brown hair into a coil at the back of her head.

"Good morning, Mrs. Dotta. It is early, but there's a great deal to be done and such a short time in which to accomplish it all." She hung her hat on a coat tree next to the door and slid out of her cloak, which was thick and velvety and begged Mercy for one touch of its fabric.

"The women need to be ready to go in less than a week, Mrs. Dotta. Less than a week." The petite lady spoke just as quickly as she moved, as if she couldn't bear to lose a single second of her day to idleness. "We must make certain every last detail is in order if we hope to send them successfully on their way."

Miss Rye draped her cloak next to her hat and then spun. Only then did she see Mercy. "And who, pray, is this?" Her sharp eyes scanned Mercy from her head to her toes.

"This is . . ." Mrs. Dotta stumbled over her introduction, clearly having forgotten Mercy's name again.

"Mercy Wilkins, ma'am." Mercy bobbed a curtsy, doing her best to imitate Mrs. Dotta's.

"She heard about our endeavors," Mrs. Dotta rushed to explain, "and wanted a place among the women chosen to emigrate. As we are limited with how many spots we've been given on the ship, I'm afraid she'll have to wait for the next group—"

"We have one spot left," Miss Rye interrupted.

"We do?" Mrs. Dotta reached for the list on the desk and scanned it.

With short, rapid footsteps, Miss Rye approached Mercy. "It became available last night when one of our women was arrested for immoral behavior."

Mrs. Dotta pressed a hand against her lips as though capturing a gasp. "Oh, for shame."

"Very much a shame, especially when she had such a good life ahead of her. Why she should throw away such a blessed opportunity is beyond my comprehension." All the while Miss Rye spoke, she circled Mercy and studied her.

Mercy dug her fingers deeper into her skirt and tried tucking her muddy boots out of sight.

"Are you single?" Miss Rye asked, finally standing back and crossing her arms.

"Aye."

"Any children?"

Mercy heated at the question but shook her head. "No, ma'am."

"What are your skills?"

"Skills, ma'am?"

"Well-to-do families on Vancouver Island and in British Columbia are looking for domestics. Do you know how to sew or cook or clean? What type of work have you engaged in?"

"I'm not skilled at much of anything," Mercy said. "Never been trained, nor have I had a job."

Miss Rye's severe expression didn't change. "And how, pray, do you spend your days?"

The insinuation in the woman's tone pricked Mercy. "I'm not immoral, ma'am. Not in the least."

"Then you fill your days with idleness?"

Again Mercy bristled, insulted by the common perception that poor people like her were lazy and would rather spend their days drinking and gambling and thieving than working an honest job. "I've been tending my wee siblings while my mum works."

Mercy couldn't even begin to explain to these women all the work she did on a daily basis to help her siblings and the other children in her neighborhood. They wouldn't understand how difficult her life was and how much energy it cost her. If people like her were idle, it wasn't by choice. They'd gladly take a job if any were to be found.

"So you know a little bit about childcare?" Miss Rye asked.

"Aye, more than a little. If I don't have one of my mum's own babes on my hip, I've got one of the neighbor babes, that I do."

Miss Rye nodded brusquely and strode toward a door on the opposite end of the room. "At such short notice, you'll have to do."

"Ma'am?" Mercy asked.

"Add her to the list, Mrs. Dotta."

"But shouldn't we interview her first?" Mrs. Dotta's worried expression trailed after her superior. "We also need to confirm references, ensure she has no criminal record, and have the physician check her for illness and disease."

"Have her provide a reference," Miss Rye remarked as she opened the door of what appeared to be another office. "As for the rest, we simply do not have time."

"But, Miss Rye . . ."

The petite lady paused and leveled a sharp look at Mercy. "Have you ever committed any crimes?"

"No, ma'am."

"Are you sick or diseased?"

"No, ma'am."

"You've been given a great opportunity to start a new life. Don't squander it."

"No, ma'am," Mercy replied quickly as she bobbed another curtsy. "I won't."

"There you are, Mrs. Dotta. She's had her interview." Miss Rye disappeared into the adjoining room and closed the door.

For long seconds, Mercy could only stare at the door. What had she gotten herself into? Was it too late to back out? All she had to do was leave the office and never return. She could simply pretend this interaction had never happened.

After all, these two women didn't seem thrilled to have her join the list. They likely wouldn't notice if she disappeared.

But by disappearing would she throw away her last chance at the *great opportunity to start a new life*? If she built a new life, then she could eventually rescue Patience from her miserable existence. However, if she stayed, she wouldn't be able to do much good for Patience except join in her misery.

"Sit down," Mrs. Dotta said as she lowered herself to her chair. "We have a good deal to accomplish if you're to be ready in three days' time."

"Three days?"

"Yes. Your train departs in three days."

"I thought I'd be a-going on a ship, ma'am."

Mrs. Dotta released an exasperated sigh. "Of course you're sailing by ship."

The full weight of her ignorance and inferiority slapped Mercy in the face. She lowered her head. What was she doing here? She was just a poor girl from the poorest part of London.

"As you'll be representing the Columbia Mission Society, we'll require you to wear clean apparel. You do have a clean skirt and blouse, do you not?"

Mercy was tempted to hang her head in further shame, but she forced her chin back up so she could meet Mrs. Dotta's gaze directly. "If I'm not good enough, ma'am, then just say so now and we can stop wasting each other's time."

Mrs. Dotta's brows rose, and something akin to remorse flitted through her eyes before she dropped her attention back to the list. "Before you leave, we'll provide you with an outfit. We've had donations from those wishing to support our program, and I'm certain we can find something your size."

Mercy wanted to tell the woman she didn't need the charity. She wished she didn't have to depend upon anyone else for her survival, that she could make it without help, that she had the means to protect everyone she loved. Yet in some ways she was as vulnerable as sweet baby Paul. She'd had to rely upon the charity of the baker, the doctor, Twiggy and Ash, and others for her survival. And if she stayed, she'd have to transfer her reliance either to a husband or the workhouse—neither of which she wanted.

She longed for the chance to finally stand on her own. This trip, this voyage, might be the only possibility she'd ever get to do that. If only she could find a way for Patience to go too.

"You said something about another group?" Mercy asked tentatively.

"Yes, the *Robert Lowe* is scheduled to leave by summer's end." Mrs. Dotta wrote something on a sheet in front of her. "But as we have a place for you now, Miss Rye wants you to be ready to leave in three days."

"Could my sister go on the next ship?"

"The *Robert Lowe*?"

"Aye."

"Is she single?"

"Aye, and she doesn't have any children either."

Mrs. Dotta didn't look up from her paper. "Tell her to come to the office at the beginning of July, and we shall conduct an interview to see if she qualifies."

"Her name is Patience Wilkins, ma'am."

"Very well."

Mercy suspected Mrs. Dotta wouldn't remember the name in five minutes, much less in five weeks. Even so, Mercy wanted Patience to be on the next Columbia Mission Society ship. She had to be.

If Mercy didn't find a way to get her sister out of the workhouse and onto the *Robert Lowe*, she suspected Patience wouldn't last until she saved up enough money to send for her.

Mercy pressed the cool cloth to the babe's feverish forehead. "Keep dipping it in the cold water and reapplying," she said to the young mother.

The woman did as Mercy instructed without question.

Mercy crossed the room to the medical-supply chest and dug through it until she found the syringe she'd seen Dr. Bates use to inject fluids into the mouths of infants too young or too weak to drink for themselves.

After entering the Shoreditch Dispensary a short while ago to find a line of sick people stretching down the hallway and out the door, she walked directly to one of the vacant rooms and began helping as many as she could. With her limited knowledge, she couldn't do much. But she figured she could at least pass out cool cloths and cups of fresh water.

Her stomach growled long and low, and she pressed her fist against it to keep the hunger from getting the best of her.

She'd come straight to the dispensary from the Columbia Mission Society building. Mrs. Dotta had explained she needed a reference—a short note that said Mercy was all she claimed to be—and had told Mercy to get the letter and return it to her by the end of the day.

Of all the people Mercy knew, Dr. Bates was the only gentleman. His reference letter would hold the most weight. And she aimed to beg him to include a reference for Patience too. With a man like Dr. Bates vouching for them both, how could the Columbia Mission Society turn them away?

"Mercy," said Dr. Bates as he entered the room. "I thought I saw you." His white hair was sticking on end as usual, and his suit was wrinkled as though he'd been moving nonstop for hours—which likely he had been.

"'Tis me just so." She pulled the syringe apart and began to fill the tube with water.

In spite of his busyness, Dr. Bates offered her a smile. Behind his thick glasses, his eyes filled with the compassion she'd come to expect from him. "And who did you bring today?" he asked, starting toward the woman and child.

"Only myself, Doctor."

He halted and turned to study her, lines creasing his brow. "Are you ill, my child?"

"Not at all. I'm just hoping you'll write me a letter stating my character is right well enough to sail with the Columbia Mission Society group."

"You're emigrating?" He spoke the question as if it were the last thing he'd ever expected her to do.

Once again, Mercy couldn't keep from wondering, as she already had a dozen times since leaving Mrs. Dotta, if she was doing the right thing.

In the silence that filled the room, her stomach released another ravenous growl. She again balled her fist and pressed her abdomen to subdue the noises. From the rise of Dr. Bates's eyebrows, she had the feeling he wasn't having any trouble figuring out her predicament.

"I got no other choice, Doctor," she explained, trying not to let her desperation show. "I'm real lucky the Mission Society had a spot open up for me."

Dr. Bates watched her for a moment longer, the sadness in his eyes telling her more than his words could.

She ducked her head and focused on putting the syringe back together. For once she hadn't come to him needing help with someone else. She'd come because she needed it. She was hungry, homeless, and had no one else to turn to. At the realization, her hands shook.

Thankfully, Dr. Bates didn't question her further but set to work helping the young mother with her sick babe. All the while he tended the infant, he gave Mercy directives in assisting him. And when they finished with the mother and babe, Dr. Bates asked her to start on the next patient.

Mercy was grateful for something to keep her mind off her hunger. By midafternoon, Dr. Bates called Mercy into the room he used as his office. He took a seat at his cluttered desk and began to unwrap a brown paper package, revealing thick slices of bread, cheese, and ham.

"Thank you for your assistance today." He spread out his meal.

Mercy glanced away from the food to the boarded window. "I'm much obliged to you for letting me stay and help, as I can't go home now and got nowhere else to go until I leave for Dartmouth."

He was silent as he arranged the food on the desktop. Finally he said, "Since I cannot pay you properly for your assistance today, will you at least allow me to give you part of this meal? My kitchen maid always sends too much along."

Mercy swallowed hard. "Thank ye, sir, but I'll be right well."

"Come now, Mercy. Sit down and have some of this. It's the least I can do for you."

She couldn't keep from glancing down at the desk. He'd pushed half of the food toward her. As he took a bite of his own portion, he picked up a blank piece of paper. "Now eat while I write this letter for you."

Her stomach gave an angry utterance as though demanding that she obey Dr. Bates. She couldn't tear her attention from the thick slices of bread slathered in butter. Maybe just a few bites . . . that wouldn't hurt any. Maybe it would be enough to tide her over until she left London.

She sidled over to the desk and lowered herself into the chair he'd positioned opposite him. As she picked up the bread, she was embarrassed that her fingers trembled with eagerness. But when she chanced a look at Dr. Bates, he was busy dipping his pen into the inkpot.

For several moments she ate in silence, relishing every bite. She couldn't remember ever eating such fine bread or cheese or ham. It was a feast, and she soon found she'd consumed every morsel.

"I was hoping you might also put in a good word for my sister, Patience," Mercy said, dabbing at the crumbs left on the brown paper. "I'd be right happy to have her come on the *Robert Lowe*, the next ship the Columbia Mission Society is planning to send out to Vancouver Island and British Columbia."

Dr. Bates paused in his writing and peered at her through his spectacles. His eyes were wide and full of questions. "Why can she not travel with you now?"

"She's sick. But she'll get well soon enough to join the next ship, that she will."

"Why don't you bring her into the dispensary? I'll have a look at her and see if I can help."

"She's at St. Matthew's Bethanl Green Workhouse. If she leaves her work, the master will kick her out and she'd have nowhere to go."

Dr. Bates turned back to his letter, his hand poised above it as though deciding whether to write any more.

"She's a right nice girl," Mercy said. "You'd like her, Doctor, if you met her."

"If she's anything like you, I have no doubt I would."

Mercy warmed at the praise. But she trained her attention upon her hands in her lap.

"However, I think you know as well as I do that most sick people at the workhouses don't get better."

"Patience will get better," Mercy insisted. "You'll see."

Dr. Bates put his pen to the paper. "I'll do what I can, Mercy. You know I will."

"Thank ye, sir. I'm in debt to you, that I am."

"Now, Mercy, the only one you owe anything to is God. He's already using you, and I know He still has much more for you to do."

Mercy nodded but didn't say anything. Whenever Dr. Bates talked about God, she didn't know how to respond. He spoke as if God truly cared about her. Yet if God cared, she hadn't felt it, hadn't felt His nearness, hadn't felt His directing her. If anything, she'd always felt as though her life hadn't mattered.

Maybe it never would amount to much. But she had to try. It was the least she could do for Patience.

six

Joseph kissed his aunt's cheek. "Good-bye, Aunt Pen."

"Oh, Joseph." Penelope Colville dabbed at the corner of first one eye, then the other with her lace handkerchief. "Must you really go? You've only just arrived."

The coachman had already loaded the trunks and now stood by the door, ready to open it upon Joseph's approach. Beyond the waiting coach and team spread Wiltshire's lush yard with its manicured hedges interspersed with small ponds and gravel walkways.

In May, with the warmth of sunshine pouring over the estate, the scent of damp grass and soil hung heavily in the air, and the songs of warblers and sparrows rose throughout the garden. Joseph took a deep breath and could almost find beauty in his boyhood home.

Almost. But not enough to make him want to stay.

"I must be on my way to Dartmouth," Joseph said. "I'd like to board the ship and make sure I have all my supplies at the ready before the passengers arrive."

"Oh, my dear, dear boy," Aunt Pen lamented again, her eyes glassy and her lips quivering. Joseph had seen enough dramatics from women to know when their tears were genuine and when they were manipulative. And he could tell that his aunt was truly sorry to see him go.

"I shall write often." He squeezed her plump hand. His father's only sister had never married. In her younger years, she'd devoted her life to caring for her father—Joseph's grandfather—after he'd been injured in a hunting accident. At the time of his death, Aunt Pen had been considered a spinster, too old to find a suitable husband. Years later, after the death of her brother, she'd found a new cause in caring for Joseph.

In front of the wide veranda with its towering portico and the sprawling stone spreading out like an ancient palace, Aunt Pen appeared somewhat small, even dainty, although she was a stout woman.

"I thought for sure this time you'd be home for good," Aunt Pen said again as she already had multiple times since he'd told her he'd accepted another ship's surgeon position.

Joseph hadn't known how to explain to the dear woman why he couldn't stay. He couldn't explain it to her any more than he'd been able to do so to Bates. At hearing the news, his friend's eyes had been sad but not surprised.

Thankfully, Bates hadn't asked him any more questions about what God wanted from him. And he hadn't pressured Joseph any further about joining him as a partner at the dispensary. Instead, he'd clamped his shoulder and wished him the best.

If only his exchange with Aunt Pen had been as easy. She'd already reminded him that his father would have wanted him to stay, find a wife, and produce a Colville heir. She then went on to lecture him on the dangers of travel and the pernicious temptations awaiting him in foreign lands.

Now as he bent to kiss her cheek one last time, she gave a half sob. "I was hoping to spare you the rumors, but it cannot be helped."

Joseph had half a mind to bound down the last few steps and jump into the coach before his aunt could say anything more. It was his training as a gentleman that held him firmly in place.

"At church yesterday, Lady Carlyle informed me that your ship, the *Tynemouth*, is being called a 'bride ship.'" Aunt Pen dabbed at her eyes again.

A bride ship? Like the ships carrying young women that had been sent to Australia to help populate the colony? He'd heard tales about such women, that many had come from overcrowded prisons. Surely the *Tynemouth* was more civilized. "That's nonsense," Joseph said.

"Lady Carlyle heard it directly from one of her friends, who is on the board of the Columbia Mission Society. Apparently, the committee received a letter from Reverend Lundin Brown, a missionary in British Columbia, asking the society to send good Christian women to marry the men there. With the influx of miners and other settlers, there simply aren't enough women in the colony for the men to marry."

Joseph shook his head. "You cannot believe everything you hear, Aunt Pen."

"But I have it on good word, Joseph, that the *Tynemouth* is taking aboard sixty single women. Why else would they be going, if not to become brides?"

Sixty single women? If his aunt's gossip was true, why hadn't Captain Hellyer mentioned it?

"If no other reason will persuade you to abandon your plans to set sail, you must let this one change your course." His aunt laid a steadying hand upon his arm, her expression grave. "The situation is positively scandalous, and you cannot involve yourself in it."

By scandalous, his aunt was referring to the nature of the women involved, likely those drawn from the lowest strata of society and of the basest nature. Surely Captain Hellyer wouldn't agree to command a ship containing thieves and prostitutes?

All the more reason to arrive in Dartmouth ahead of the passengers, so that he could clarify with the captain the precise makeup of their transport.

"You see," Aunt Pen went on, taking his silence as confirmation that he was as appalled as she, "you're meant to stop running away and stay home."

"Not you too." Joseph tried to lighten the conversation with a smile.

"So I'm not the first to accuse you of running away from all that happened to you?" she said softly, reaching up to cup his cheek.

Her motherly touch opened a painful abyss inside him. He stood at the precipice and tottered, longing to give in, to let himself fall into the darkness.

"I have to go." He moved down a step, breaking free of his aunt's gentle hold. He didn't want to consider her accusation of running away any more than he had Bates's.

Once again, tears welled in her eyes.

"You have no need to fret," Joseph assured. "I've been informed that the *Tynemouth* will carry close to three hundred passengers. If sixty of them are single women, they'll be of no more consequence to me than any of the other two hundred passengers and crew."

"I pray you are right," she replied.

Whether the ship was full of single women or not, he wouldn't be swayed. Whether he was running away or not, he didn't care. Nothing would keep him from being aboard the *Tynemouth* when she set sail next week.

Mercy waited for Patience to tuck the blanket about the old widow's frail body. The workhouse infirmary in the gable was icy cold even though warmth lingered in the evening air after the exceptionally warm May day.

"I'll come back to check on you later," Patience said as she stroked the woman's sunken cheek.

"I'm so cold," the woman replied in a plaintive whisper.

Patience looked longingly at the coal stove in the corner, which stood empty and unlit. The overseers of the workhouse doled out coal as sparingly as they did gruel.

All the beds in the infirmary were full, with many patients lying in the aisle on the floor upon straw with naught but ragged blankets to cover them. The sour acridness of urine permeated the room, and Mercy guessed some of the invalids were so ill that they had no choice but to lie in their own filth.

As Patience straightened, she was overcome by a fit of coughing that hunched her back and shook her thin body.

Dr. Bates's words from two days ago crept into Mercy's thoughts and taunted her. *"Sick people at the workhouses don't get better."*

Not Patience. Patience wouldn't die.

Her once-vibrant sister straightened to reveal the ghost she'd become, her face skeletal, pasty, and lifeless. All except her eyes, which now met Mercy's and were filled with peace.

Whenever she'd asked Patience about how she could be at such peace amidst the hardships threatening to drown them, Patience said that whenever she started to feel sorry for herself, she'd think about all those who were worse off. Then her problems would shrink in comparison.

"I must be a-going, Patience." Mercy looked to the small, circular window, the only source of ventilation in the squalor. The darkness of night was creeping in, and she had yet to say farewell to Twiggy and Ash and her other brothers and sisters before she headed to the train station.

She'd already spent most of the day saying good-bye to all the children and neighbors who had come to rely upon her for assistance. She'd given them food and advice and as much love in a day as she could. She hated leaving them on their own, but she'd made arrangements with Mr. Hughes, the baker, and several other shop owners, hoping they would continue their kindness to the children in her neighborhood.

Patience reached for Mercy's hand, and together they wound through the infirmary until Patience closed the door behind them and they stood in the equally cold hallway with only the tiny flicker of the flame from the candle Patience held. It illuminated the dark stairwell and the trails of mold growing on the wall.

"Now remember," Mercy said as she already had at least a dozen times, "you have to be at the Columbia Mission Society building the first week of July for your interview."

"How will I know when it's July?" Patience asked.

"You must mark off the days somehow."

"I'll try."

"Mrs. Dotta and Miss Rye will be expecting you, that they will. They have Dr. Bates's letter and know right well who you are and where you're at. They'll be saving a spot for you on the *Robert Lowe*."

Patience started down the steps, leading the way with the stub of candle shoved into the top of a bottle. Mercy wanted to say a hundred more things but couldn't formulate the words. Instead the slap of their footsteps echoed too loudly in the corridors until they reached the front of the workhouse.

As Mercy stepped outside onto the front stoop, she had the sudden urge to drag Patience along with her. Surely she could sneak Patience aboard the ship. What was one more frail woman among so many passengers?

But even as Mercy contemplated how to force Patience to come with, her sister started to cough again, this time so violently she would have dropped the candle and set herself afire if Mercy hadn't rescued it and placed it on the brick wall bordering the stoop.

When Patience finally stopped coughing, Mercy's heart thudded with the awful premonition that this was it, that she'd never see her sister again. An ache formed in Mercy's chest and swelled until it felt nigh unto bursting.

For a long moment she could only stare at her sister, the young woman who'd raised her, who'd tended so lovingly to her every need, who'd ultimately sacrificed everything for her. Mercy's eyes suddenly stung with the need to cry and scream her protest at how unfair life was.

"I want you to remember that when we're troubled on every side," Patience said, her voice wavering, "we can't get caught up in seeing the problems from our view. God's so much bigger and has things worked out in His ways—ways we can't begin to understand."

Mercy nodded, unable to speak past the tightness in her throat. She wouldn't—couldn't—cry. She had to stay strong.

Patience lifted her blackened and blistered fingers and caressed Mercy's face. Her eyes filled with tears. "You're gonna be just fine and have a good new life."

"And you'll join me right soon."

Patience touched Mercy's face again, tracing it as though memorizing every line.

"Promise me you'll come," Mercy insisted. "Vow it."

"I told you I'd try and I will." Patience offered a trembling smile.

Mercy attempted to swallow but couldn't.

"You best go on now." Patience swiped at her cheeks. "I don't like you wandering about in the dark."

"I'll be fine."

"Yes, you will be." And with that, Patience grabbed Mercy into a fierce hug. "You know I'll always love you."

Mercy squeezed her sister in return, letting Patience's love bathe her for a final time. Patience released her and spun but not before Mercy saw the tears streaming down her sister's cheeks.

"I love you too." Mercy's voice broke and sobs pressed for release.

Then Patience stepped inside, closed the door, and was gone, leaving Mercy to pray this parting wouldn't be their last.

seven

Joseph held on to the small open drawer and steadied himself against the familiar sway of the ship. The bottles inside rattled, and he shifted them closer to make room for the remainder of the medicines he'd brought along for the ailments sailors or passengers might encounter during the voyage.

He'd boarded the *Tynemouth* too late the previous evening to unpack. Now by the light of day, he was able to explore his accommodations. To be sure, the room allotted for the sick bay wasn't big, but it was more sizable than what he'd been given on other voyages.

Fortunately he had a porthole, although it was small and surrounded by rust. Still, it allowed for some natural lighting, enough to aid him during surgeries and suturing. A bunk bed had been affixed to one wall, providing a place in which to tend the sick. Against the opposite wall stood a counter containing the drawers where he was storing his medicine. A set of shelves above the counter gave him space for additional supplies and linens.

A writing table and chair had been squeezed into another nook. The screws holding the table in place appeared new. The captain had likely arranged for the furniture to be put into this cabin as a special courtesy. He would have to thank Captain Hellyer for so fine a room. With limited space on board the ship, he was grateful for the generosity. He'd yet to speak with the captain but guessed he would have plenty of time over the next few days before they embarked on their voyage.

He'd already learned from acquaintances in London that Captain Hellyer had been trained in the Royal Navy as an officer, that during the past years without any wars to fight he'd been in the Royal Navy Reserves. Though the *Tynemouth* was his first merchant command, Joseph expected the captain would have no trouble making the adjustment.

Hearing a knock, Joseph quickly smoothed back his hair, straightened his cuffs, and moved to open the door. He half expected to see the captain and instead discovered a short man peering up at him, a mixture of awe and trepidation in his severe expression.

He wore a black suit with a high starched white collar that almost seemed to strangle him. He swallowed, struggling to get his Adam's apple past the collar, then bowed at the waist.

"Lord Colville" came the man's muffled voice from his bent position. "I am most delighted to make your esteemed acquaintance."

The man held his bow for so long, Joseph began to wonder if he should pry him up. Finally he cleared his throat. "I'm pleased to meet you as well . . ."

"Reverend William Richard Scott." The man popped up so quickly, Joseph was taken aback. "Mr. Scott of St. Mary Magdalene Church in Harlow?" The reverend watched Joseph expectantly. "One of my patrons is the esteemed Lady Carlyle." Again the reverend waited.

Joseph had known Lady Carlyle his whole life, but that didn't mean he knew everyone she decided to help.

"She has likely spoken of me or at the very least of my sermons, as I'm told my eloquence is unmatched."

"I'm sorry to say she has not mentioned you, Mr. Scott." Joseph glanced past the man to the second- and third-class staterooms that were being readied by the ship's officers going in and out of the rooms with luggage and linens. While the large majority of passengers, particularly poor immigrants, would reside in steerage, there were a good number of cabins reserved for passengers who could pay a higher fee.

Some of the third-class cabins stretched out beyond the sick bay, just behind the ship's funnel. Farther aft, behind the mizzenmast, ran another row of slightly larger second-class rooms.

"I do hope you'll be able to attend services, Lord Colville, and hear for yourself my soliloquies. I have no doubt you will find yourself quite pleased with them, the same as Lady Carlyle, especially since I often read and expound upon Bishop Law's *A Serious Call to a Devout and Holy Life*, as well as Bishop Butler's *Sermons*. I'm sure you will find my lectures enlightening."

"I'm sure," Joseph said politely, even as his attention strayed to the ship's railing and to Dart Harbor, where a hundred or more ships, fishing boats, coaling hulks, and even naval training vessels were moored along with the *Tynemouth*.

The port town of Dartmouth and Bayards Cove spread out along the harbor. Rows of tightly packed homes looked as if they were stacked on top of one another like stair steps up the cliff, with the ancient stone Bearscore Castle standing at the base as a stout sentinel.

The harbor was a murky brown-gray due to the recent spring rains clouding the water. Thankfully the waves were gentle, and the sunshine of the May afternoon held a hint of summer.

"I and my family will be occupying one of the second-class cabins on the other end of the deck." The reverend's expression remained grave, his voice almost monotone. "I do hope to have the pleasure of introducing you to my wife and two daughters, Lord Colville. I'm told my daughters are quite fetching, intelligent, and accomplished at sewing, embroidery, drawing, painting, and the like."

"I will look forward to meeting them," Joseph said. "However, as the ship's only surgeon and without an assistant, I'm afraid I won't have much time for leisure."

"I understand completely, my lord." Mr. Scott ducked his head in deference. "I too will likely find myself taxed beyond endurance in shepherding the flock the Lord has given me for this voyage."

Joseph nodded and stepped back into his room, intending to bid the reverend farewell, but the man shuffled forward until he stood stiffly in the doorway, blocking Joseph's retreat.

"I had hoped to sail to Sandwich Islands with the illustrious Reverend Thomas Nettleship Staley, the newly consecrated Bishop of Honolulu. Perhaps you've heard of him?"

Joseph shook his head.

"I was honored to be asked to serve with him in an effort to convert the natives and spread the gospel among the heathen aboriginals. However, Miss Angela Georgina Burdett Coutts—have you met the delightful Miss Coutts?"

As heiress to the Coutts Bank's millions, every member of London's aristocracy knew of Angela Coutts. "Indeed, I have a time or two—"

"She's quite the devoted philanthropist and social reformer, is she not? Her good deeds and Christian charity along with Charles Dickens inspire us all. I was honored when she singled me out as the champion of her cause."

"Which cause is that, Mr. Scott?" Joseph asked, even as he scrambled to find a way to excuse himself from the reverend's company.

"I am to chaperone and guide the young single women being sponsored by the Columbia Mission Society. I've been tasked with the important job of keeping them away from the temptations of evil, so that when they arrive to Vancouver Island and unite with the men anxiously awaiting their appearance, the women can enter the sacrament of holy matrimony as pure brides."

"So the rumors about the *Tynemouth* being a bride ship are true?" Joseph wasn't surprised by the news, thanks to Aunt

Pen's warning, and yet irritation niggled him nonetheless. Captain Hellyer should have told him more about the nature of the *Tynemouth*'s mission.

Mr. Scott pulled himself up and lifted his chin above his stiff collar as though preparing to launch into a sermon. "I know what you are thinking, Lord Colville—of past such endeavors made by our great country. But let me put your anxieties to rest. Maria Rye, the founder of the London Middle-Class Emigration Society, has screened and chosen the women herself."

"The women are not from the prisons, then?"

"Oh no, my lord. I'm told the group is comprised mostly of distressed middle-class gentlewomen seeking governess positions until suitable husbands are found for them."

"I see."

"Of course, the Columbia Mission Society, under the influence of our dear Miss Angela Burdett Coutts, insisted that Miss Rye also make an effort to rescue young women from the workhouses and orphanages. And she was quite right to insist such a thing, if I may say so. Quite right as usual. Such souls deserve saving, don't you agree?"

Joseph started to respond, but Mr. Scott was like a ship with full sail and couldn't be stopped.

"Needless to say, Miss Rye made her selections of such lost souls very rigorously, so that only the most deserving among the lower class were chosen. After all, there is a need for domestics in Victoria. The poor, friendless girls will be glad to have the work—that is, until they're able to enter into matrimony, which I'm assured will be soon after landing, as the laborers in the colony are most eagerly awaiting the arrival of this first ship."

"So there are to be other bride ships?"

"If we have any hope of keeping the colony civilized, then we must send more women." Mr. Scott glanced over his shoulder as if gauging who might be listening to their conversation. He then leaned in closer to Joseph and lowered his voice. "My fellow missionaries who reside on Vancouver Island and in British Columbia report that the miners are positively heathen and that it is the fault of the native women who entice them into cohabitation. They need rescuing from their vices, and the influence of virtuous, servile, and good Christian women will be just what the men need to save them for God and country alike."

Joseph had seen enough in his voyages to dispute Mr. Scott's assumption that the native women were at fault for their *enticing*. From what Joseph had seen in other British colonies, the immigrant men were largely to blame for seeking out and often taking advantage of foreign women. Joseph had always been appalled at the arrogant view so many took regarding the natives and the abuses they piled upon them—as if they were inferior, somehow less human.

As Joseph had long ago thrown away convention, he'd since allowed himself the freedom to speak his mind, even when his ideas and opinions were less than popular.

"If the miners are full of vice," Joseph said, "then perhaps *they* are the ones enticing the natives and not the other way around."

For the first time since making his introduction, the reverend opened his mouth and nothing came out.

"Now, please excuse me, Mr. Scott." Joseph began closing the door, leaving Mr. Scott no choice but to stumble backward out of the way. "I really must resume my unpacking. I bid you good day."

eight

On the bench in the tender, Mercy wrapped her arm around Sarah, one of the orphans she'd befriended during the train ride from London to Dartmouth. With each dip of the oars, the waves slapped hard as though to keep the small boat from reaching her destination, the steamship anchored ahead.

Sarah shuddered. "I'm gonna be sick real soon."

"We're almost there, sweet lamb," Mercy murmured. "Take a deep breath of air. That'll help, to be sure."

Several of the others attempted to do as Mercy instructed, breathing in gulps of salty air to stave off the rush of seasickness. Their faces were as chalky as the limestone cliffs they'd left behind on the shore. And the pallor only highlighted the gauntness in each face.

The Columbia Mission Society had attempted to help the young women clean up and wash away all traces of grime before the voyage, giving them each a twopence to take baths and wash their hair at a public bathhouse near the Society's building.

Although the dirt had been washed from their bodies, they hadn't been able to wash away the sickly hollowness that came from living and breathing in the filth of their slum neighborhoods.

Mercy had only been to a bathhouse once before in her life, and the experience of immersing her entire body in a tub of water—even if it had been lukewarm and murky after several women had gone before her—had been a luxury.

She still marveled as well at the fine garments Mrs. Dotta had provided for her, the finest she'd ever owned or worn. The dark blue cotton skirt was serviceable and somewhat tattered along the hem but was thick, sturdy, and best of all it had no stains. The blouse was the same color of blue as the skirt and buttoned up the front.

Mercy ran a hand over one of the long sleeves, relishing the soft, almost silky texture. She even marveled at the freshness of her chemise, as well as the drawers. While a bit more frayed than her outerwear, they were whiter and cleaner than anything she'd ever worn.

"Are we almost there yet?" Sarah asked, burying her face into Mercy's arm.

"Just a mite longer." Mercy peered ahead at the ship that didn't seem to be drawing any closer. An elegant figurehead graced the long bowsprit, and a funnel rose from the top deck into the air alongside several masts.

One of the men rowing the tender had explained that the ship had a large screw propeller fueled by steam, which came from coal engines deep in the belly of the ship. He'd said there were times when the ship needed the propeller and steam engine to move her along, and other times when the ship used her sails for power.

Whatever the case, Mercy stared at the vessel that was to be their home for the next three or four months. The train car they'd ridden in yesterday had been strange enough, the speed unsettling, the noise and commotion and excitement overwhelming. But it hadn't prepared her for the magnitude of the ship or the reality that came with seeing it—namely that she was leaving England's shores, perhaps never to return, and she was sailing halfway around the world to a strange place where she wouldn't know anyone or anything.

Her sights strayed past the dozen or more women in the tender to the land she was leaving behind. She drank in the vibrant green of the grass and woods decorating the hills overlooking the town, the riot of white, yellow, and purple flowers growing in clusters, and the vast blue sky that went on forever and ever.

The scenery was so unlike anything she'd ever witnessed. She could go on staring at it without ever tiring of the view, much like yesterday when she'd gazed out the window the entire train ride without losing interest. The passing countryside, small towns, sprawling farms, and lush vegetation had awakened a longing within her—a longing to dig her bare toes into the grass, to breathe in the clear air, to stroll among the tall trees.

With so much land spreading out as far as the eye could see, why were the masses of poor people crammed into such small rooms in narrow houses, built so close together that a person could hardly glimpse the sky above them? With the rich resources she'd witnessed, why were hordes of people hungry and jobless and without hope?

During her visits to the dispensary, Dr. Bates had talked about how much God loved her, about the joy and peace and hope He offered. But why would a loving God allow so much suffering? Why would He turn His back on the pain and trouble that afflicted Twiggy and Ash, Patience, and so many others? With all the beauty in the world, why couldn't God spread it out and make it available to everyone rather than just a few privileged folks?

Mercy's questions had swelled to hurting the farther she'd traveled from London. It was as if she'd been stuck her entire life in a tiny overcrowded corner that had defined her existence, ignorant of the spacious world that existed beyond her. If only she'd thought to turn around sooner and see what she was missing.

But even as she wished she'd ventured beyond London sooner, she knew the turning around wasn't easy, not for poor women like her. If not for the help of the Columbia Mission Society, she wouldn't have been able to afford a train ticket out of the city. Even if she'd decided to walk to the countryside, parishes were swift to punish beggars, vagrants, trespassers, and anyone who didn't belong.

"How am I gonna last months at sea," Sarah asked miserably, "when I can hardly make it an hour?"

"You'll get used to it," Mercy assured, praying she was right.

Sarah started to speak again, but then hung her head over the side of the tender and released the contents of the morning meal they'd eaten at the public house, a meal they'd ravenously devoured: hot fresh bread, cooked eggs, thick slices of bacon and sausage, and coffee—real coffee. Mercy'd never had anything so filling or tasty before in her life and guessed the others hadn't either.

And now Sarah was losing the sustenance she so badly needed.

For the remainder of the row to the steamer, Mercy gently rubbed Sarah's back, held her hair out of the way when she vomited again, and caressed the girl's cheek.

Barely older than fifteen, Sarah and some of the other youngest women in their group had been gathered out of St. Margaret's Home, which Mercy learned was an orphanage. The girls had informed her they were getting too old to stay at the orphanage and would have soon been cast out to make room for younger children who needed the help more. This voyage had spared them from having to live on the streets.

When the tender pulled alongside the ship, Mercy noticed a haggardness about the steam vessel, as if she'd been pushed too hard for too long in her young life. The fresh coat of paint couldn't disguise the dents and scratches, and coal soot had blackened much of the ship's hull.

As the gangplank was lowered and they boarded the main deck, Mercy kept a tight hold on Sarah, gathering the other orphans around her as well.

"Ladies, your attention, please." A tall woman, who was as thin and flat as an iron bedstead, stood several feet away. She wasn't old, but the downturned lines at the corners of her mouth and prominent veins in her temples indicated that she hadn't necessarily had an easy life.

"My name is Mrs. Robb," she said firmly. "I'm to be one of your chaperones during your voyage on the *Tynemouth*."

Mercy should have known the Columbia Mission Society wouldn't allow sixty women to travel unsupervised. With already half their number having boarded, she supposed someone would need to provide instruction and guidance if Mrs. Dotta and Miss Rye were staying behind to organize the next shipment of women.

"Gather your belongings and follow me." Mrs. Robb started moving toward a passageway.

"Belongings?" scoffed Ann, another of the orphan girls. "'Xactly who does she think we are? Her Royal Majesties?"

Some of the others tittered. Yet all of them followed along the same as Mercy, empty-handed, with only the clothes they wore to accompany them into their new lives.

Mercy was surprised when they passed by a cow in a makeshift stall on the deck, as well as several pigs and chickens in crates. Barefoot sailors mending sails and scrubbing the deck paused in their work to gawk at the women. But Mrs. Robb hurried them along, giving them no time to explore or interact.

"Here you are." Mrs. Robb finally stopped next to the ship's funnel and motioned to a row of cabins directly behind it. "Count yourselves very blessed that you will have separate living quarters for the duration of this trip, meaning you won't have to reside in steerage along with the other poor passengers. The Columbia Mission Society has raised enough money to pay for you to stay in cabins of your own."

Mercy could only guess what the conditions of steerage were like—probably dark, cramped, and dismal, similar to what they were already accustomed to back in the slums. Although the ache in her heart hadn't gone away since saying good-bye to Patience and everyone else, she was beginning to understand more and more the enormity of the opportunity she'd been given.

"There will be six of you bunking together," Mrs. Robb added. "Once you choose your stateroom, I'll expect you to remain there for the duration of the voyage."

The women began to disperse. Mercy had led Sarah and the other orphans to the closest cabin when Mrs. Robb called out sharply, "Ladies, you will wait to pick your rooms until after I'm finished with my instructions."

She stood silently until all the women had gathered again in front of her. "It is important for you to follow the rules set down by the Columbia Mission Society for the length of our trip. We must have orderliness on such a voyage and be above reproach if we hope to continue the good work of the Society in the future."

Mercy stood straighter. Was the voyage of the *Robert Lowe* dependent upon how well her shipload of women behaved? If so, Mercy would be the model passenger, that she would.

"The most important rule for this voyage," Mrs. Robb continued, "is that you are forbidden to fraternize with the other passengers, especially the men."

At the general murmurings of discontent, Mrs. Robb pursed her lips and waited.

Mercy didn't mind the rule. She had no desire to talk to any men now or in the future. She didn't figure there was a reason to form relationships or friendships with any men, not when she had no intention of getting married. As far as she'd ever been able to tell, marriage brought a whole lot of trouble, including unfaithfulness and more babies.

There were too many desperate women who married the first man who showed them any attention, thinking marriage would rescue them and perhaps finally give them a mite of stability and happiness.

Many of Mercy's friends had fallen prey to such thinking. One by one they'd paired off and married men in the neighborhood. But instead of being happier, her friends had ended up with more heartache, especially when the babes came along only to die of hunger or disease.

The truth was, Mercy hadn't witnessed many successful or happy marriages in her tiny dark corner of the world. As a result, marriage didn't appeal to her any more than the thought of having children.

But not everyone was committed to singleness the way she was. She guessed most of the women who'd boarded the *Tynemouth* hoped to find good husbands someday.

Mrs. Robb swept her gaze over the women. "Once we reach the colonies, I'm told there are at least a thousand young men earnestly awaiting your arrival. The minute you step off the ship, you will each have a host of admirers making you offers of marriage."

The comment brought a round of giggles and laughter from the women, save Mercy, who recoiled at the prospect and prayed that Mrs. Robb was exaggerating.

The tall woman's face, however, was as solemn as a gravedigger's. "I hope you can see the serious nature of maintaining your reputations and virtue during our long weeks of traveling. You wouldn't want any hint of impropriety to prevent you from making a good match upon your arrival. Thus you must take very seriously the rule not to fraternize with other passengers. Do you understand?"

The women chattered among themselves with a barely restrained excitement Mercy didn't share.

"I asked, do you understand?" Mrs. Robb spoke sharply above the commotion.

Mercy was quick to join the others in voicing her affirmation. Mrs. Robb would soon find she had nothing to worry about with Mercy Wilkins. Nothing at all.

nine

Sarah's sick again," Ann whispered when Mercy stepped into their cabin, which had only enough standing room to allow a few of them at a time to be out of their berths.

Ann peered at Mercy from the bed above Sarah's. Flo and Minnie shared the bunk on the far wall, while Kip had taken the top bed above Mercy.

The smell of vomit permeated the cabin. Even though Mercy had already emptied the floral china washbasin several times over the ship's railing, the stench still hung heavily in the air.

Mercy shook the rain from her skirt and hair before bending over Sarah, who was curled into a ball on her straw-filled mattress in the narrow bunk.

Sarah had seemed fine yesterday after they'd boarded the ship. She'd been as excited as the rest of the girls to pick their room. Despite its being plain and windowless, without any furnishings except for the wooden bunks, the washbasin and a matching pitcher, they'd each exclaimed over the room and had taken turns lounging on the different beds.

At some point during the night, rain began pelting the ship, and the wind howled as the storm became more intense. Soon large waves were buffeting the ship, tilting it to and fro like a drunkard stumbling out of a tavern. It wasn't long afterward that Sarah woke up moaning, dizzy with nausea.

Mercy had tended the girl through the rest of the night, until Sarah had finally fallen asleep at the first light of dawn. Mercy had used the opportunity to leave the cabin and explore the deck. At the early hour it had been deserted, and she relished a few moments of privacy, catching a breath of fresh air under an overhang while letting the pitcher from their cabin fill with rainwater. It seemed the worst of the storm was over.

"Bless your sweet face," Mercy said, brushing Sarah's cheek with the back of her hand. "A cool drink should help, that it will." She poured some of the rainwater into a tin cup, then held Sarah up and brought the cup to her lips. "Come now, dear heart."

Just as soon as Sarah swallowed the water, it came back up.

The other girls hung over the edges of their beds, watching. Ann slipped down and dropped to her knees next to Mercy. "What can I do to help?"

Mercy patted Ann's arm. In the short time with the girls, Mercy had come to see that Ann was their leader. Her features were dainty, and she wore her dark hair plaited into two long braids, giving her a childlike appearance. Like many of the waifs, she'd had to grow up much too soon and had an inner strength and hard edge that lent a maturity beyond her years.

"You want me to fetch the doctor?" Ann asked.

The light peeking in from under the door revealed Sarah's face. It was as sunken and shriveled as Clara's had been on the day she'd died at the Shoreditch Dispensary. Clara's mother had waited too long in seeking help for the child. Mercy wouldn't repeat the same mistake with Sarah. During her time spent walking the deck earlier, she'd passed a door marked with a medical symbol not far from her cabin and guessed it was the ship's surgeon's quarters.

Though the hour was early, surely the doctor would be awake and wouldn't mind helping Sarah.

"I can get anything you need," Ann added, a note of pride in her tone. "You just tell me what, and I'll find it. I've never once got caught."

Mercy was saddened to think how so many homeless children resorted to stealing to survive. Even more disturbing was that pilfering often became second nature to them. She shook her head. "We can't be starting this voyage by doing wrong. We gotta do the honest and right thing, even if it's hard."

"Have it your way," Ann said as she climbed back onto her bed.

Mercy wanted to say more but bit back a reply. She had weeks ahead to help these young women learn about doing right, the same way Patience had always helped her. There was no sense in forcing the matter now.

Instead, she assisted Sarah off the bunk, slipped an arm around the girl, and led her out of the stateroom and down the deck. The rain had tapered to a mist, but the wind was still swirling in gusts. With the ship's rocking and Sarah's weakness, Mercy had to half carry the girl.

"Doctor," she called after reaching the door marked with the medical symbol. She knocked lightly. "I've got a very sick girl here."

The wind ripped away her words and tossed them out to sea. She waited a moment longer, then pressed her ear to the door. Hearing nothing, she knocked again, louder this time.

When the door swung open suddenly, she didn't bother greeting the doctor, not sparing him even a glance. Instead, she stumbled into the room with Sarah, her arm wrapped tightly around the girl's waist. Spotting the bed—which from the tangle of covers appeared as if it'd been recently occupied—she led Sarah there and gently lowered her, helping to lift her feet until she was curled up once again.

Behind her, the doctor seemed to be fumbling at something. A moment later a lantern flickered to life and allowed Mercy to see Sarah's face clearly. The girl's eyes were glassy, her skin pale, her lips dry and cracked.

"Please, Doctor," Mercy said, turning around, "could you—?"

Her words stalled. Standing only a few paces away, a man was in the process of hanging the lantern on a metal wall hook. His back was facing her—his very naked back.

For an eternal second, Mercy couldn't look away. Thickly corded muscles flexed with every movement he made. Not wearing suspenders, his trousers sagged low enough to reveal a narrow but well-defined waist. From the messy locks of dark hair, broad shoulders, and tanned arms, she could see he was much younger than she'd anticipated. She wasn't sure exactly what she'd expected from a ship's doctor, but certainly not this.

After making quick work of adjusting the lantern's flame, brightening the room, he spun to face her.

Before he could catch her ogling, she dropped her sights to the floor, to his bare feet showing beneath the hem of his trousers. In her haste she'd given the doctor no time to make himself presentable before opening the door.

Not that she was naïve about the human body. In the close confines of her family's living quarters, she'd seen all manner of nakedness. Around her neighborhood and other parts of the slums, she'd happened upon people in varying states of undress and indecency.

She ought not to be surprised or embarrassed now. Even so, there was something about this man's sculpted physique that made her uncomfortable in a strange way.

"I beg your pardon, Doctor. I didn't know . . . didn't realize—"

"It is I who must apologize, madam," he interrupted. Out of the corner of her eye, she glimpsed him hastily reaching for a shirt from a peg on the back of the now-closed door.

"It's just that I was hoping you could help this sweet little lamb."

In the midst of shoving an arm into his shirtsleeve, he halted. Mercy could sense him studying her. She dared to peek at him again, this time forcing her attention away from his half-clad torso to his face.

Something about him seemed familiar. His hair was a rich dark brown, his eyes equally dark. The shadow of whiskers couldn't hide the handsome face beneath—the long cheekbones tapering into a strong jaw and well-defined chin.

One of his brows quirked. "Have I met you before?"

She started to shake her head, but then stopped abruptly at the memory of his tired face the day she'd brought Clara to the dispensary. He was the doctor who'd tried to help the girl.

And she'd tried to pay him by offering her boots. At the memory of his recoiling in pity, Mercy dropped her attention to the floor again. He'd probably thought she was pathetic, perhaps believed she was a prostitute. After all, he'd assumed Clara was her daughter.

Maybe if she didn't remind him of their meeting, he wouldn't recognize her, especially now that she was clean and wearing new garments.

"Ah, yes, now I remember," he said, tugging at his shirt and stuffing his arm into the other sleeve. "You brought the little girl with cholera infantum to the Shoreditch Dispensary."

Her heart sank. So much for remaining anonymous. "Aye, sir. 'Twas me."

"What is your name again?" He snapped his suspenders in place over his shirt.

"Mercy Wilkins, sir." She couldn't bring herself to meet his gaze. She didn't know why she should be so embarrassed, why it should matter what this doctor believed about her. He was nothing to her.

Except she'd likely see him often over the next few months of their voyage, and she didn't want him to think ill of her.

"I'm Dr. Colville," he said as he closed the distance between them. "Who have you brought to me this time, Miss Wilkins?"

The sound of her name spoken so formally and respectfully took her by surprise. Poor women like her were rarely given the courtesy of a title.

He brushed past her and lowered himself on one knee before Sarah.

"This is Sarah, sir." She knelt next to him. "She's been mighty sick all the night long. Would that she and the sea could become friends, but alas, they don't seem to be getting along right yet."

Dr. Colville glanced at Mercy. Although he didn't smile, humor crinkled the corners of his eyes.

Did he find her amusing? Maybe he thought she was a simpleton. Before Mercy could decide whether or not to be offended, Sarah moaned.

"Hello, Sarah." The doctor felt the young woman's forehead and then the pulse in her neck. "I hear you're not making friends with the sea. Well, not to worry. You aren't the first to find the sea a foe, nor will you be the last."

Sarah finally opened her eyes. Through her haze she seemed to be studying Dr. Colville's face.

"I'm afraid that those who find a foe in the sea can rarely mend the broken relationship." He offered Mercy the hint of a smile, his eyes warm and devoid of mockery. She could almost believe he was genuine and that he meant her no offense.

Even so, she couldn't find it within herself to smile back. "Are you saying poor Sarah will be sick for the whole long voyage?"

"It will likely come and go, depending upon the severity of the ship's movement. But yes, I'm afraid most of the voyage will be very unpleasant for her."

"Should she be taken back to land?"

"No," Sarah croaked, her ashen face creasing with anxiety. "Please don't make me leave the ship. I ain't got nowhere to go, no place to live, no job."

She tried to sit up, but Mercy eased her down, her chest swelling with compassion. She understood the girl's plight all too well. "Of course we won't be making you leave the ship. But you must promise you'll be strong and that you won't give up."

Sinking into the bed and closing her eyes, Sarah nodded weakly. "I promise."

"Good girl." Mercy brushed Sarah's loose hair away from her

face. "The voyage'll be right difficult, but we can't forget what awaits us on the other side."

Again Sarah nodded. "I won't forget."

Joseph rose and crossed the cabin to the drawers containing his medicines. He located what remained of the wormwood ointment he'd concocted during his last voyage. He opened the tin and breathed in the scent of mint that mingled with the ground wormwood, wine vinegar, and olive oil.

He'd been in a deep sleep when the knock awoke him. With a pounding heart, he'd jumped from the bed and was glad now he'd had the foresight to slide on his trousers before throwing open the door.

In previous voyages, he'd been disturbed only by sailors or the ships' officers needing his services. Without any women aboard, he hadn't needed to consider his own modesty or that of others.

But obviously he needed to be more careful now.

He glanced at Mercy, who was still kneeling next to Sarah. Her eyes had widened at the sight of his nearly bare body. He'd immediately recognized her blue-green eyes but hadn't been able to place her until she'd started speaking. The kindness in her tone took him immediately back to the Shoreditch Dispensary.

The lantern light highlighted her hair, showing it to be a soft gold. Apparently, in the urgency of caring for the sick girl, she'd neglected to pin up her hair, which hung in thick waves down her back nearly to her waist. He didn't recall such fairness from their previous meeting. Of course, he'd been overly tired at the time, and she herself had been harried. And the occasion had been clouded with grief over the death neither of them had been able to prevent.

He couldn't remember the name of the child she'd brought in, but he did recall thinking what an incompetent mother Mercy had been, only to discover later from Bates that she wasn't the child's mother after all.

As though sensing his perusal, she looked up at him. He quickly shifted his attention to the drawer and drew out another medicine—this one a tonic. "So, Miss Wilkins, I must admit that when I first met you, I assumed you were the mother of the infant you brought to me."

"I figured as much, sir."

"And you felt no need to correct me?"

"I was more concerned about Clara than my reputation."

He couldn't keep his eyes from drifting back to Mercy. Her expression was resigned, as though she was accustomed to being insulted on a regular basis.

She certainly was beautiful, especially the way her long lashes framed her eyes, making them appear bigger and more luminous. For one so pretty, he was rather surprised she hadn't already been claimed. Surely she had any number of men vying for her and could have her pick of a husband at the snap of her fingers. So why join a bride ship?

His question begged for an answer, but he was too polite to speak about so private a matter.

"You can rest assured," he said, closing the drawer, "this time I won't insult you by insinuating that Sarah is your daughter."

"Thank ye, sir." She ducked her head, taking him much too seriously since Sarah was too old to be her child.

"Dr. Bates informed me of your generosity in caring for many of the children in your neighborhood."

She only gave a slight nod to acknowledge his statement.

"And Sarah?" he asked. "Is she a youth from your neighborhood?"

"I just met her, sir. On the train ride here."

He stopped short and stared at Mercy with growing fascination.

"Is there anything, anything at all I can do to help her?" Mercy stroked the girl's cheek.

"She's an angel of mercy, though she doesn't know it." Bates's words rushed back to Joseph's mind.

"Doctor?" Her lashes swept up to reveal trusting and generous eyes. She clearly gave of herself with no thought of getting anything in return. He'd do well to follow her example.

"I have a couple of remedies." He started to swish the liquid in the bottle he was holding. "Hopefully they will lessen the discomfort and allow her to keep down some sustenance."

Since Sarah seemed to be resting more comfortably, Joseph used the lull to administer medicine. He lined her nostrils with the minty wormwood ointment and then gave her a spoonful of the tonic. Seeing that Sarah was tolerating the medicine, he allowed Mercy to feed her a few sips of water. Before Mercy could finish, Sarah fell asleep.

Mercy stood and stretched. "Do you think she'll endure the voyage, Doctor?"

"With you watching over her, I have a feeling she'll be just fine."

Her cheeks flushed at his words of praise, and she buried her fingers into the folds of her skirt, twisting the blue material. "I best be checking on the other girls and making sure they're getting their rations."

Before he could respond, several taps drew him to the door.

He opened it to reveal a tall, dour-faced woman. "Good morning, Doctor. I'm looking for two of my charges. I've been informed they are likely in your company."

Without waiting for permission to enter, the woman poked her head past him. At the sight of Mercy, the woman's lips pinched into tight disapproval. "Mercy Wilkins?"

Mercy curtsied. "Yes, Mrs. Robb."

"What is our number-one rule for this voyage?"

"I thought Sarah was dying, ma'am," Mercy rushed to explain. "That I did."

"Our number-one rule, Mercy?"

"I didn't think the doctor counted, ma'am."

"*The rule?*" the tall woman insisted.

Mercy's chin dipped. "No fraternizing with the other passengers."

"Especially no fraternizing with whom?"

"With the men, ma'am."

The exchange was happening so rapidly that Joseph scarcely had time to comprehend who this Mrs. Robb was and what she was insinuating.

"Mrs. Robb," he interrupted. "Please let me assure you that Miss Wilkins did the right thing by bringing Sarah here—"

"Doctor," she replied in a sharp but calm tone, "did anyone put you in charge of the women on this ship?"

Her condescending question prickled his scalp. "When someone on this ship becomes ill, madam, then *yes*, they do fall under my jurisdiction—regardless of their gender."

She narrowed her eyes at him. "Let us be clear about one thing, Doctor. The Columbia Mission Society has placed these women under my watchful care. I will decide when and if the women need medical attention. Not you."

"'Tis my fault entirely, Mrs. Robb," Mercy interjected, her worried eyes darting between Joseph and Mrs. Robb. "I brought Sarah here this morn 'cause I thought she was in danger of dying. Please don't blame the good doctor, ma'am."

Mrs. Robb gave Mercy a look that promised punishment. The young woman lowered her head, clearly knowing and accepting her place at the bottom of the social strata.

Joseph pulled himself to his full height. Apparently, Mrs. Robb had no idea who he was. From the simplicity of her gown, he guessed she was far from wealthy. He had half a mind to demean her and put her in her place.

But doing so would make him no different from her, using one's class to subjugate another. He had, after all, thrown off his title for the voyage, already having informed his fellow officers to call him doctor rather than lord.

He decided to adopt a civil tone and approach. "Mrs. Robb, let me also be clear about one thing. As the ship's surgeon, Captain Hellyer has put every passenger's well-being under my watchful care. Please understand, neither you nor anyone else can dictate how and when I practice medicine while we're aboard this ship."

The matron had the audacity to stare him in the eyes. He held her gaze until finally she shifted her attention to Mercy. "Gather Sarah and return to your cabin at once."

Mercy jumped to obey the order.

Joseph wanted to stop her and insist that Sarah be left where she was for the time being, undisturbed. Yet he sensed that doing so would only make matters worse for both Mercy and Sarah. Instead, he gathered the tonic and ointment he'd used to ease Sarah's discomfort.

As Mercy passed by, bearing the weight of the drowsy girl, he pressed the items into her free hand. "Reserve the medicine for when Sarah is especially sick. And if she gets worse, be sure to bring her to me again."

Mrs. Robb spun sharply at the blatant disregard for her instructions.

Mercy nodded briefly, not daring to look at him.

After Mrs. Robb exited and closed the stateroom door, Joseph could only shake his head at the strangeness of his morning. Although part of him wanted to rush after Mrs. Robb and insist that she treat Mercy and Sarah with leniency, another part of him hesitated.

In some ways, the matron was right. The bride-ship women weren't his concern. He hadn't taken on the ship's surgeon position to champion the cause of these poor women. But even as he attempted to shove aside all thoughts of the would-be brides, he couldn't dislodge the image of Mercy Wilkins's compassionate face.

She was clearly doing her part to make a difference.

What was he doing?

ten

"Oho! Those are some real fine ladies," Ann remarked, peeking out their cabin door.

Mercy scrubbed at the stains in Sarah's shift, attempting to remove the spots along with the smell. After lying abed most of yesterday, the sweet girl was sitting up today. Mercy had helped her shed her clothes, wrapped her in a clean blanket, and now was trying as best she could to wash the garments in the floral washbasin.

"Strike me blind!" Ann said. "Fancy clothes, fancy shoes, and fancy hats everywhere!"

Kip sprawled out on her bed while Flo and Minnie scrambled behind Ann in the doorway to get their first glimpses of the ladies who were joining their group.

While the other girls had been in and out of orphanages most of their lives, Sarah was the exception. She'd lived with her mum until only a year or two ago. From what Mercy had gleaned, Sarah's mum had been loving, the kind of mum that made them all envious.

Like Mercy, they'd all lived in London's slums their whole existence, never going beyond their neighborhoods much less beyond the city. Everything about their journey so far had been new and exciting—including seeing the wealthy passengers.

Mrs. Robb had instructed the women already aboard to remain in their cabins until all the newcomers settled in. Mrs. Robb didn't want them getting in the way of the other bride-ship women, as well as the additional second- and third-class passengers who'd paid for passage.

After the rain had confined them to their cabins yesterday, Mercy was as antsy as the others to stroll around the deck. Yet even when they'd been allowed out, Mrs. Robb had placed ropes at both ends of their row of cabins, leaving them only a small stretch of deck for their use.

The matron had looked directly at Mercy when she instructed the women not to go beyond the ropes. Mercy wasn't sure if the enclosure was punishment for taking Sarah to see the doctor yesterday, or if the chaperones would have confined them anyway. Whatever the case, she hadn't argued or protested. None of them had. She supposed they were all too afraid Mrs. Robb might send them back to London and the slums if they didn't obey.

"To be sure," Ann lamented, "them fancy ladies will grab up husbands quicker than we will."

"You're too young to *grab* a husband," Mercy said from her position on the edge of Sarah's bed.

The other girls giggled, and Ann just shrugged. "If a husband keeps me from a life of worry and hardship, then I don't care a jot how old I be."

Sarah twirled a loose strand of Mercy's hair around her finger. "You're so pretty, I daresay the instant you step foot off the ship, you'll have a dozen fellows all uncommon sweet on you."

Mercy smiled at the girl. "Stuff and nonsense. I didn't come on this trip to find a husband. I'm not planning to get married."

"You're not?" Sarah asked.

"No. Not ever."

The girls in the doorway grew silent, and Sarah's eyes rounded in her pale face.

"But ain't that why we're going to the colony?" Ann asked. "'Cause the men there sent for us to come and be their brides?"

Mercy let her hands fall idle in the washbasin. "We're a-going to get jobs."

The girls all exchanged glances.

"'Course we'll get jobs," Ann said. "But Miss Rye made it mighty clear that this is a bride ship, and we'll be expected to get married at some point."

Flo nodded, her face wreathed in seriousness. "We're going cause the fellows are asking for wives."

"That's right. They don't got enough women for all the men," Minnie added.

Mercy sat back and stared at the girls, the true nature and purpose of the voyage hitting her full in the face. How had she been so naïve as to miss the truth? She supposed since she'd joined the group late, Miss Rye and Mrs. Dotta had been too busy to outline all the expectations, but surely they could have mentioned the teeny-tiny fact that they meant for her to become a bride.

Suddenly Mrs. Robb's words after they'd boarded the ship made sense. "*There are at least a thousand young men earnestly awaiting your arrival. The minute you step off the ship, you will each have a host of admirers making you offers of marriage.*"

No wonder Mrs. Robb was so zealously guarding the women from interacting with the men on the ship. The Columbia Mission Society was counting on the chaperones to deliver the brides to the men in the colonies. That explained why the Society had appointed a second chaperone, a Mr. Scott, who would serve as their reverend during the trip as well.

With only sixty women compared to so many waiting men, the Society expected every woman to cooperate.

Nausea began to rise in Mercy's throat.

"Mercy?" Sarah asked softly. "What'll you do?"

Mercy cupped a hand over her mouth and swallowed the bile. She couldn't be sick. She had to stay clear-minded and figure out how to get herself out of the mess she was in.

"You're not gonna leave us, are you?" Sarah persisted, her eyes welling with tears.

Mercy glanced past the girls out the door to the deck. Dartmouth was only a boat ride away. It wasn't too late to jump ship. She could board one of the tenders delivering the other women, return to shore, and make her way back to London.

But what would she find there?

Of course, she'd get to be with Patience again. And yet she'd already come to accept that traveling to the colony was the best chance she had at saving her sister. If she didn't go, if she didn't prepare the way for Patience, what hope did either of them have?

"Mercy?" Sarah whispered.

"I'm just thinking, is all," Mercy replied. If Miss Rye and Mrs. Dotta wanted to send brides to the colony, Mercy had no business being on the ship since she had no intention of becoming any man's bride.

"You might not have a hankering to get married now," Ann said. "But you'll be got over once you see all those available men."

The idea of facing "a host of admirers making offers of marriage" turned Mercy's stomach all the more sour. Despite that, she nodded and forced her lips into a smile. "Maybe you're right." She knew Ann was absolutely wrong, but the lie spilled out anyway.

What other choice did she have but to go along with the plan? She'd have to pretend she felt just like everyone else. And once they arrived to Vancouver Island, she'd figure out a way to avoid getting coerced into a marriage she didn't want.

"Then you'll stay?" Sarah's expression was hopeful.

"I can't leave you now, can I?" She squeezed the girl's hand, already feeling responsible for this ragtag group of orphans.

"Good," Sarah said with a smile. "Ann is right, you know. You'll be 'got over' by some handsome fella soon enough."

Mercy didn't respond except to squeeze the girl's hand again.

Joseph exited Captain Hellyer's quarters and let the scent of salt and sea greet him like an old friend. He took a deep breath and basked in the early June sunshine. According to the captain, they would be boarding passengers for a couple more days before weighing anchor.

"Lord Colville." The diminutive Mr. Scott was walking briskly toward him, a retinue of women following behind, attempting to keep up. "You are just the person I am seeking."

Joseph considered retreating into the captain's stateroom on the quarterdeck. He had no wish to engage in small talk with Mr. Scott—which always seemed to devolve into lengthy one-sided discourses—but he could see no way to politely avoid the encounter.

"Mr. Scott," he said in greeting.

The man halted abruptly and bowed low, almost as if Joseph were a king. The women curtsied and held their bows too, watching Mr. Scott, clearly taking their cues from him.

Finally Mr. Scott straightened, his back looking as stiff as the mainmast. "My lord, permit me to introduce my family. They came aboard the *Tynemouth* earlier today. The moment they stepped foot upon the ship, I informed them all of your presence, and they are as eager to meet you as I am to make the introductions."

Joseph bowed slightly at the women, noting that there were three of them.

"My wife, Mrs. Scott, along with our daughter, Miss Charlotte Scott, and our other daughter, Miss Lavinia Scott."

Again the ladies curtsied. As they did so, Joseph caught sight of a woman in blue farther down the deck. Although she wore a bonnet, her pale golden hair couldn't be contained. Tendrils blew in abandon, apparently having come loose from her long plait.

Mercy Wilkins.

She stood at the railing, surrounded by several younger girls. With their faces raised to the sunshine, Joseph guessed they were enjoying the warmth of the afternoon after the past cloudy days. He hadn't seen her since Mrs. Robb had marched her out of his cabin yesterday morning. In the ensuing hours, he'd considered visiting her and checking on Sarah. But he'd pushed aside the strange urge. Sarah was suffering from a mild case of seasickness, not scarlet fever.

"My daughters and wife are delighted to make your acquaintance, Lord Colville," Mr. Scott said. Once more, his starched collar pushed his chin upward, almost as if it were strangling him. "We are all quite relieved to have such an esteemed man such as yourself serving in so lowly a position. I'm sure we shall rest much easier knowing you are accompanying us on so arduous a journey."

The women straightened, forcing Joseph's attention away from Mercy and back to Mr. Scott. "Thank you, Mr. Scott. I hope my services will not be needed by your family, but if they are, I pray I will be of aid."

"Very true, Lord Colville," Mr. Scott said. "We hope we shall not need your services either. But I must say that it is my greatest hope you will honor us with your company during the long voyage."

Once again, Joseph was distracted by the women beyond Mr. Scott and his family, particularly by Mercy. She was in the process of removing her bonnet, lifting it away to allow the sunshine to bathe her entire head. She closed her eyes and smiled—a smile that transformed her face from pretty to utterly alluring.

"As I've already mentioned, my daughters are quite accomplished at many things, Lord Colville," Mr. Scott continued in his even tone. "Not only that, but they've been tutored in geography, science, history, and even languages. I'm sure you'll find their companionship and conversation quite scintillating."

"Perhaps I shall." Joseph nodded at Mr. Scott's daughters, who beamed at him with wide smiles. Like their father, they were both short in stature. Whereas he was thin, they seemed to take after their stouter mother. And although they appeared graceful and poised, Joseph could find nothing remarkable about them to draw his attention.

Unlike Mercy. His eyes drifted to her once again. He had the suspicion that Mercy's smile was rare, that she had little occasion for it. It was beautiful nonetheless.

He wasn't surprised to discover she wanted to emigrate. He'd only needed to work in the Shoreditch neighborhood one day during his time in London to witness for himself the worsening conditions for the poor who lived there. Still, he couldn't help but wonder again why she felt she must join a bride ship. Surely she could find a husband elsewhere, rather than sailing halfway around the world with the purpose of marrying a stranger.

"My daughters are also quite well read, Lord Colville," Mr. Scott was saying with the utmost gravity. "They have persuaded me to bring along a chest of their favorite books. Perhaps you will join us in the evening for a time of reading aloud? I guarantee you'll find the time most entertaining."

At a sharp command, Mercy's eyes flew open and her smile faded. Joseph searched for the source of the interruption at the same time Mercy did, landing upon Mrs. Robb, who was exiting one of the staterooms farther down.

"Young ladies, you must put your hats back on this instant," Mrs. Robb called.

Mercy and the girls bobbed a curtsy at the matron and rushed to do her bidding, their fingers fumbling in their haste to don their hats.

Mr. Scott shook his head, having followed Joseph's gaze. "The poor lost souls are in need of much instruction, Lord Colville. But I am happy to report that Mrs. Robb is up to the task. She is indeed a wonderful role model for those in our midst who haven't had the proper training in what is acceptable."

"And what, Mr. Scott, is unacceptable about removing one's hat in order to enjoy a few moments of sunshine?" The question was out before Joseph could stop it.

The man's mouth hung open as he struggled to utter his next comment.

Mrs. Robb stepped in front of Mercy and peered down at her with undisguised irritation. "You are to be a good example to the younger ladies, Mercy. But thus far you are leading them astray."

Joseph couldn't hear Mercy's response, but from the dip of her head she'd obviously accepted the harsh words of condemnation.

"What shall I do with you?" Mrs. Robb went on.

Joseph strode toward the women. He had no idea what he planned to do, and that other part of him again warned that he had no business interfering with the brides. Nevertheless, his feet carried him down the deck, his soles echoing with the indignant thud of his heartbeat.

"Lord Colville." Mr. Scott's choppy steps rushed after him. "At the very least, may we have the honor of your company this eve for dinner in the passenger salon?"

At a cord cutting across the deck, Joseph stopped abruptly, causing Mr. Scott to bump into him. "My sincere apologies, my lord" came a quick response behind him.

"What is this?" Joseph took hold of the cord. His question carried so that it drew the attention of the women, who stood only a dozen paces away.

Seeing him there, Mrs. Robb sniffed. "It is rope, Doctor, as you can plainly see."

"I am quite aware what it is, madam. But *why* is it here?"

"I should think that would be quite obvious." Mrs. Robb glared at him as if he were a common ruffian coming to prey upon her charges.

Mr. Scott sidled next to him. "Mrs. Robb, have you met our highly esteemed ship's surgeon, Lord Colville, Baron of Wiltshire?"

At the mention of his title, Mrs. Robb curtsied, even if her expression didn't change. Mercy and the other young women turned wide eyes upon him.

He found himself looking directly at Mercy. Up close and with the bright afternoon sunshine upon her, he could distinguish a slight dusting of freckles upon her nose and a rosy pink in her cheeks.

"Miss Wilkins." He nodded. "How is Sarah today? As I do not see her on deck, am I to assume she is still feeling ill?"

Mercy gave Mrs. Robb a sideways glance as though asking for permission to speak to him. Now that the chaperone knew he belonged to the aristocracy and was titled, she wouldn't dare slight him, would she?

The matron pinched her lips together and hesitated before finally inclining her head toward Joseph.

Mercy curtsied. "She's faring better today, sir, that she is. Thank ye for asking."

"I would suggest she get as much sunshine and fresh air as possible while we are still moored, and perhaps an extra portion of water and food while her stomach is calm."

"Thank ye, sir. I'll see to it right away."

For a reason Joseph couldn't explain, he felt uncomfortable hearing Mercy's subservient response. He rather liked her better when she was free to be herself. He'd expected that taking on a physician's role would show people he had no wish to put on airs. And to a degree, it had. He'd gained the respect of the sailors and passengers on previous voyages—respect for himself alone and not simply because of his family name.

Perhaps he would have to constantly wage such a battle to earn respect for his deeds rather than his title.

Of course, he hadn't set off with such lofty goals. Rather, his desire to pursue physician training had been fueled by his grief. After he'd finished Oxford, he didn't want to return home and walk in his father's footsteps. The very idea of doing so had been paralyzing. Instead, he'd buried himself in his studies at the Royal College of Physicians.

It was then he discovered how distancing himself from his past not only eased the ache and emptiness but also had helped to expand his view of the greater world. Outside his grand homes and exclusive clubs, he came upon opportunities to meet ordinary people and discover what life was really like.

"We will be at sea together for many long days," Joseph said to all the women there, hoping Mercy would take particular note of his wish not to be treated deferentially. "I do pray you will see me as your servant and nothing more."

Without waiting for their reaction, Joseph excused himself and walked away.

eleven

The swaying of the ship tossed Mercy against the bunk. She grabbed on to the upper bed to hold herself steady. The seawater seeping in under the door wasn't helping her to keep her balance either. It made a steady nuisance of entering the cabin whenever the ship leaned leeward. And then the water would flow back out when the ship rocked the opposite way.

In the darkness of the windowless room, she had to feel her way around and pray she didn't trip over or bump into anything that had been dislodged during the ship's tossing.

She'd already made sure their food rations were picked up and tucked away for safekeeping: biscuits, butter, preserved beef and fish, potatoes, raisins and currants, soup and bouillon, oatmeal, coffee, and even lime juice to prevent scurvy. They'd been given more for one week than they would have eaten in a month at home.

Mrs. Robb allowed one woman per cabin to prepare the food and do the cooking. Of course, the girls had nominated Mercy. So twice a day she went to the galley in the forecastle. There, along with the other women, she used the ship's stove, pots, pans, and utensils to cook the meals under the watchful eye of the ship's quartermaster. Mrs. Robb was present too, of course. When finished, Mercy returned to her cabin, where she and the girls ate each morsel with gratefulness, knowing how fortunate they were compared to the ones they'd left behind in London's slums.

Even if they were more fortunate, Mercy wasn't about to take any chances with having their weekly rations ruined by the water flooding their cabin. Already her new boots and stockings were soaked through, her skin was shriveled, and her toes felt numb from the cold. She aimed to keep the others from suffering too.

But her task had grown more impossible as the rough night had turned into an equally rough day. After waiting in Dartmouth nigh onto a week for everyone to board, including the steerage passengers, they'd finally set sail on the morning tide two days ago.

They'd been out into the English Channel, entering what Mr. Scott had informed them was the Western Approaches, when a southeast gale struck.

And it hadn't let up since.

Gripping the bunk, Mercy slid along the wooden beam until she came to Ann, who was curled into a ball. In the darkness, Mercy brushed a hand over Ann's warm cheeks and down her back over her long braids. The girl groaned in reply.

"Bless you, little lamb," Mercy crooned. "Can you drink a sip of water?"

Ann shook her head.

Mercy applied some of the minty ointment to the girl's nostrils before making her rounds to Flo, Minnie, then Kip. One by one, the girls had given way to sickness until each had become violently ill. Even Mercy had battled the churning in her stomach, which seemed to rival the churning of the sea.

Finally, Mercy knelt in front of Sarah and touched the girl's forehead. It was hot and clammy. The girl was faring the worst. Still weak from her last bout of sickness, she'd grown nearly delirious.

"Sarah?" Mercy attempted to draw the girl back to reality. "Don't you give up."

She didn't respond, not even to moan, and her silence sent fresh anxiety skittering up Mercy's backbone.

As the ship began to sway again, a loud creaking accompanied it. The vessel acted like a huge rocking chair rolling back and forth, her old timbers protesting every move, her groan rising above the shouts of sailors and the constant crashing of the waves.

With the water receding again, Mercy allowed the ship's momentum to carry her to the door. She'd waited long enough. She needed to fetch the doctor to help Sarah.

"I do pray you will see me as your servant and nothing more." Dr. Colville's statement from several days ago had hovered in her mind. She didn't understand exactly what he'd meant by it, but his kindness was clear enough. She was confident he'd treat Sarah again if she but made him aware of the need.

As she struggled to close the door after stepping outside, the wind clutched at her, ripping at her hair and garments as if to tear them from her body. She fought against the invisible foe as she'd done before when going to check on the other women.

Most had taken to their beds. Yet there were a few like her whom God had spared from the misery of the sickness, and they were all doing their best to ease the discomfort of the others.

Mrs. Robb had been one such sturdy soul. The last time Mercy had ventured from her cabin, Mrs. Robb was emptying basins and pitchers, having spent the night tending to one sick woman after another.

Clutching the doorframes, Mercy made her way from one stateroom to the next. She wanted to rush to the doctor's cabin without delay, but after the fuss Mrs. Robb had made over the previous visit, Mercy didn't dare go beyond the rope without permission.

"Mrs. Robb!" she called as she knocked on the last door of the third-class cabins.

"She's bumped 'er head," someone replied from inside, "and she's bleedin' like a stuck pig."

Mercy pushed open the door to find Mrs. Robb hunched on

the edge of her bunk, her eyes closed, a towel pressed against her forehead. Streaks of blood ran down her thin face, dribbling off her chin.

"Mrs. Robb." Mercy crouched next to her. "Are you cut bad, ma'am?"

The woman's face was unusually pale. When she didn't respond, Mercy reached out and gently shook her arm.

"I think I should fetch the doctor for you, ma'am."

Either the movement or hearing the word *doctor* was enough to stir Mrs. Robb. Her eyes fluttered open. She glanced around as though dazed before settling her gaze upon Mercy.

"Yes, the doctor," Mrs. Robb said breathlessly. "The gash is deep and needs suturing."

Mercy patted the woman's hand to reassure her before rising. Then, without wasting further time, Mercy fought the wind and rain and spray of the waves as she made her way down the deck, under the rope, and to the ship's surgeon's cabin.

She pounded on the door and then waited, her chest seizing with the sudden anticipation of coming face-to-face again with the kind, handsome doctor. Mercy hadn't spoken with him since their meeting on the deck when he'd inquired after Sarah's well-being.

Of course, she'd glimpsed him on several occasions when she and the other women strolled along in the roped-off area. Not that she'd been looking for him. Not in the least. It was difficult, however, not to notice his appearance, especially when the other women—mainly the wealthy middle-class ladies—stopped to fix their eyes full upon him.

These women in their fancy gowns and hats and parasols made a right pretty sight. In their roomier second-class cabins, they had trunks of clothing and books and other amusements to help them pass the time while at sea. One woman was rumored to have brought along a piano, another a treadle sewing machine, with both items stored safely away belowdecks.

The middle-class ladies protested the ropes that hemmed them into their small section of the ship just as much as the poor women had. But no amount of complaining had swayed Mr. Scott or Mrs. Robb from taking the barrier down.

Mercy wiped a strand of wet hair out of her eyes and lifted her hand to knock again.

"The doctor ain't there!" shouted a sailor from farther along the deck. He was an older, burly man with a shaggy head of gray hair and an equally shaggy gray beard. His skin resembled cracked old leather, brittle and tough from the years spent at sea, and the few teeth he had left were of varying shades of gray.

During the few times she'd watched the barefoot sailors climbing the rigging far above the deck, she'd heard them shout out questions to the older man, referring to him as Gully. He wore an oilskin overcoat with a hood that appeared to be waterproof. Even so, seawater dripped from his face and beard.

"D'ye know where he be?" Mercy shouted above the crashing waves and roaring wind.

Gully nodded and motioned for her to follow him. She tried to imitate his even gait as she fought against the pitching of the ship and the waves that sprayed over the side and threatened to soak her. When they reached the quarterdeck, he crouched before a blackened hatch and lifted it.

A waft of foul air rose up to greet her. The stench was so overwhelming, she almost retched. She could sense Gully gauging her reaction, testing her. Did she have the stomach to enter?

She didn't need his test, not after living for so many years in Old Nichol, the devil's home. Without waiting for Gully's instruction, she lowered herself to the first rung of a ladder. It was slippery, and the air was damp. She gripped the ladder tightly, even as her slick soles fumbled for traction.

The rain followed her downward, until Gully lowered the hatch and plunged her into darkness. Without the noise of wind and waves, the moans and cries coming from below swirled up to taunt her, making her wonder if indeed she was descending into the pit of hell.

As her feet connected with a landing, she steeled herself. A chicken flew up, clucking in distress and flapping its wings in her face. The motion startled her, and she would have fallen if her hands hadn't found the ladder again.

Dull lantern light glowed through a square opening. She bent and ducked through the entrance and found another, shorter ladder that led down to crowded accommodations that she guessed to be steerage. Without any windows, the cramped quarters were especially dark. The only light came from a lone lantern that hung from a beam near the far end of the deck.

Thick wooden bunk beds, similar to the style in their cabins above in third class, lined the walls on both sides. It appeared some families and passengers had erected makeshift partitions with sheets in order to gain a semblance of privacy between them. But without separate rooms or separate areas for men and women, Mercy guessed that privacy was as absent here in steerage as it had been in the slums.

Dozens upon dozens of people were crammed into every spare spot, along with their cooking pots, bundles of clothing and blankets, ragged shoes, wooden crates, and the rest of their earthly possessions. Except for the chickens and a small group of children slapping hands in play, there was very little movement. Most people were huddled in their beds or lying on the floor.

From the stench of the place, Mercy realized the passengers here were as ill as those above, if not more so. The hard knocking of the waves against the lower deck pounded louder, and the swaying was more dizzying.

She forced herself to breathe evenly so she wouldn't be sick to her stomach. Turning toward the square opening from which she'd come, she felt a powerful need to scramble back up the ladder as fast as her feet could carry her. But as a woman sat up nearby and vomited into a basin, Mercy halted her retreat.

These were her people. This was where she belonged. In fact, if not for the Columbia Mission Society, she would have been living among these poor immigrants for the duration of the voyage. No, the truth was, she was lower than them. She wouldn't have been able to afford to pay for steerage, not even if she lived two lifetimes. The least she could do was offer them comfort, the same she was offering to the women above.

Mercy stepped over the legs of a prostrate man, ducking her head so as not to bump it against the beams. With a sudden lurching of the ship, she grabbed on to a post to keep from falling and hurting herself, or worse, hurting someone else. The lantern swayed and cast its faint light upon a bent head and familiar profile.

Dr. Colville.

Mercy carefully picked her way across the floor until she reached the doctor, who was kneeling next to a man sprawled out on a lower wooden bunk. It was devoid of its straw-filled mattress, which lay on the floor nearby. Children were curled up together on the mattress, one of them in the process of heaving and the others crying.

Next to Dr. Colville, a woman was attempting to help the doctor, but then she paused, bent over, and threw up into a basin. Mercy touched the woman's shoulder gently and drew her hair out of the way. When finished, the woman wiped her sleeve across her mouth. Fatigue lined her face.

"Rest with your children." Mercy nodded toward the wee ones. "I'll help the doctor."

Dr. Colville glanced her way. His dark eyes were solemn, his hair mussed, and his jaw covered with thick stubble. With his coat discarded and his shirtsleeves rolled up, she was reminded of how he'd looked the first day she met him at the dispensary—tired and harried.

He returned his attention to the patient in front of him. In the dim, swaying light, she glimpsed the man's arm, a mangle of flesh and bones, and understood why he lay there unconscious, and blessedly so. Nausea burned a path up her throat, and she looked again toward the ladder that would take her to the upper deck.

As tempting as it was to escape, she could no more walk away from the suffering around her than she could ignore it in the cabins above. Swallowing the sickness, she knelt next to the doctor. "How can I help you, Doctor?"

He nodded at the sheet next to the man. "Finish ripping that linen into strips. I'll need it to bind his arm to the splint."

Mercy quickly set to work. When Dr. Colville asked her to help hold the arm in place while he sutured and then wrapped it, her queasiness was soon replaced by her fascination and admiration of his deftness. His long fingers worked with a skill and precision that made her forget about everything else but assisting in whatever he needed.

When finally the arm was set, the flesh sewn together, and the wound wrapped, Dr. Colville wiped his bloody fingers on the remains of the sheet. "My deepest gratitude, Miss Wilkins. I wouldn't have been able to set the break as cleanly if not for your assistance."

"You deserve better help than me, sir." She added a curtsy. He was, after all, a lord, a member of the highest level of society, one far above hers and even above Mrs. Robb's. She'd never met a lord before, had only seen such fine gentlemen from a distance.

Even so, she suspected most weren't like Dr. Colville. Very few of his class would take the time to speak with her, much less thank her. Even fewer would subject themselves to the lowly conditions of a place like steerage.

"Your assistance is more than sufficient, Miss Wilkins," he said wearily. "Out here we are all subjects of the same taskmaster, the sea. He has a way of bringing us to our knees and making us equals, does he not?"

Mercy couldn't understand the doctor's poetic language. Instead, she nodded her acquiescence and kept her face hidden from him lest he see her admiration, which only seemed to grow with each encounter.

Joseph sagged into the armchair he'd dragged out of his cabin onto the deck. He leaned his head back and closed his eyes. Though the gray clouds were racing faster than the sun and hiding it from view, every now and then warm rays broke through and caressed his face.

They'd finally sailed out of the Channel, leaving the storms behind, and were now well on their way southward toward the Bay of Biscay and the Azores. The water was still choppy, but the wind was gentling, which meant the worst of the seasickness was over. Most of the passengers would be out of their beds by tonight, if not by the following morning.

"Doctor."

At Mercy's voice, he opened his eyes and sat forward.

She stood in front of him and held out a steaming mug of coffee. The aroma of the brew awakened his senses, and his stomach gurgled. He hadn't eaten since the storm had started over twenty-four hours ago.

"I thought you could use a strong cup, to be sure."

Rather than taking the tin mug, he stared up at her. Though her hair was damp and unkempt, face smudged and weary, her garments soggy and splattered with all manner of filth, for a reason he couldn't explain, she had grown more beautiful and not less.

He couldn't stop himself from studying her pale face, the cupid's bow in her upper lip, the high cheekbones, the thinly sculpted brows. And her eyes . . .

Her lashes dropped before he could drown in the blue-green sea of her eyes. The mug in her hand shook just slightly. "If you'd rather have a meal, sir, I can go back to the galley—"

"No, Miss Wilkins," he said rapidly and took the mug. "The coffee is perfect."

She took a step back as though to leave.

"But only," he continued, "if you'll sit with me a moment and have some too."

She'd worked tirelessly at his side since the early hours of the morning when she'd come down into steerage to find him. Thankfully, the broken arm had been the worst of the injuries there. He'd sutured several lacerations, removed a nail from a foot, and treated a concussion.

After they finished, they'd gone above and first tended Sarah and Mrs. Robb before moving on to help the rest of the sick passengers. They then returned to steerage to check on the patients, and all the while Mercy had soothed and loved everyone she came across.

He'd never met anyone like her. And now all he could think about was how much he wanted to sit with her, drink a cup of coffee, and find out more about her.

"Sir?" She lifted her gaze, giving him a glimpse of her confusion.

Poor young women didn't sit and drink coffee and talk with wealthy lords. Especially the poor women on this bride ship who'd been forbidden to interact with the other passengers.

"Wait just a moment." He stood and thrust the mug back into her hands. Then he strode two doors down to the passenger salon, retrieved another armchair, and dragged it outside.

Her eyes widened at the sight of the chair, particularly when he positioned it next to his. He took the coffee from her, lowered himself into his seat, and waved at the new chair. "Please, Miss Wilkins. You deserve a short rest."

She glanced with longing at the chair but then peered over her shoulder in the direction of the bride cabins. The worry crinkling the corners of her eyes revealed her concern that her vigilant chaperones might come out of their cabins and observe her sitting with him. Surely she knew she had nothing to worry about, at least for a few more hours. Mrs. Robb was still under the effects of the laudanum he'd administered to ease the pain of her head injury. And Mr. Scott and his family were miserably still abed.

"As the ship's surgeon, no one can argue with my orders—

expressly the order that you must take a moment to rest, otherwise you will find yourself just as ill as the others."

At the mention of *order*, she took a step closer to the chair, and he immediately regretted his word choice. He didn't want her to spend time with him because she felt coerced.

"I have no wish to force you to sit with me, Miss Wilkins," he rushed to explain, not sure why he should care what this woman did or didn't do. "If you have no desire for my company, I would not detain you."

She dragged the chair away from his, putting a respectable distance between them, and lowered herself into it. For a long moment, she didn't say anything and held herself stiffly, peering past the rail out at the endless expanse of whitecap waves.

Taking a sip of his coffee, he did likewise. At last, from the edge of his vision, he could see her shoulders relax and her body ease deeper into the chair.

He waited a few more moments, then extended the tin mug to her. He attempted nonchalance, keeping his sights half on the sea. She hesitated, but when he didn't withdraw his offer, she accepted the coffee and took a drink. She closed her eyes, her expression radiating pleasure.

Warmth plumed in his chest like a breath of sweet tobacco smoke. "Tell me about yourself, Miss Wilkins." He tried to keep his voice casual so he wouldn't frighten her away. "What made you decide to join the bride ship and voyage to Vancouver Island?"

She turned and handed him the mug.

He shook his head and indicated she should have more.

She lifted the cup and sipped again. He couldn't tear his sights from the touch of her mouth to the rim, the long curve of her throat as she swallowed, and the drop of coffee lingering on her bottom lip.

He'd almost given up hope she'd talk to him when she shifted slightly and spoke. "I wasn't planning on leaving, didn't really want to."

"Then why did you?"

"When Twiggy lost her job picking rags, it was either me or Matthew who had to leave home." She expelled a sigh. "I wouldn't hear of Matthew a-going to the docks and scrapping for himself. So I offered to leave."

"Who's Twiggy?"

"My mother."

"And Matthew's your brother?"

She nodded. "He's not a mite older than ten years."

Joseph attempted to digest all the things she hadn't revealed but implied: the inability to find new employment, the loss of income, the shortage of food for everyone, the direness of her situation. Mercy very well could have ended up on the streets.

His stomach roiled at the thought. A beautiful young woman like Mercy wouldn't have lasted long, not before being snatched up and sorely used.

"Certainly you had a dozen offers of marriage?"

"A dozen?" Her lips curled into a wisp of a smile. "You flatter me, sir."

"Not at all. You're a fair young maiden. I have no doubt you could have had any number of fine men, rather than sailing to a new land and marrying a stranger."

The trace of smile disappeared. She pressed her lips together and stared out at the sea again. Her fingers tightened around the mug.

He was being forward. "I have spoken too freely. I do apologize—"

"Shouldn't you be married by now too, Doctor?" She turned her full gaze upon him. Her eyes churned with something he couldn't quite identify. . . . Was it guilt?

Before he could probe, she spoke again. "A rich gent and fine-looking fellow like yourself could have any woman he wanted."

He reclined further in his chair. "Fine-looking fellow, am I?"

She dropped her attention to the mug, stared at it a moment, and then lifted it and took a drink as though to hide behind it. "I'm only repeating what I heard them fancy ladies saying."

"Then you don't agree?"

The spot of color that rose into her cheeks gave her answer. So she thought he was handsome? He crossed his arms, allowing himself a smile.

"You'll have to be right careful, sir," she said. "If the fancy ladies have their way, you'll end up wed to one of them before the voyage's end."

"You needn't worry yourself over my welfare." He'd rebuffed plenty of advances of well-meaning friends who'd attempted to negotiate marriage unions. He'd had enough practice in saying no to hold him in good stead. "If God so pleases, someday I shall have a wife and many children. But at the present, I am a free spirit and wish to travel the world."

"I've never stepped a foot outside London in all my life," she admitted.

He wasn't sure why such a fact should surprise him, even more that it should dismay him. He wasn't so oblivious to the plight of the poor not to know that most had no means to go beyond their neighborhoods. Even so, the thought that this angel of mercy had never experienced anything but the squalor of the London slums made his heart ache.

"The fancy ladies are sayin' our new home'll be real nice and pretty," she rushed to say as if to cover the embarrassment of her previous statement. "Being close to Australia, I suppose it'll be warm all the year long?"

He almost chuckled at her assumption. But when she turned her eyes upon him, the vulnerability, openness, and sweetness within them stopped him. He took for granted so much of his upbringing, education, the privileges of his status, the means and ability to go wherever he wanted. How could she be expected to know where Vancouver Island and British Columbia were when she'd likely never seen a map?

"Vancouver Island and British Columbia are an ocean away from Australia and quite a bit farther north."

She shifted in her chair and stared at the mug, the fresh pink in her cheeks indicating her mortification at her mistake.

He held out his hand and used his finger to sketch an island. "Here's Great Britain." He drew a line to the opposite side. "Here are the continents of North and South America."

Almost shyly, she shifted to watch his inkless drawing and followed as he traced their journey across the Atlantic, down the coast of South America, around the Falkland Islands at the tip, and then back up the other side until they reached the far reaches of the United States.

"Vancouver Island is just a short distance away from Washington Territory, so close, in fact, that you can see the Olympic Mountains. While Vancouver Island and British Columbia are separate English colonies, I've heard the two have much in common."

Joseph lost track of the time as he explained everything he'd read and learned about the Pacific Northwest, including the mild weather that was similar to England, the recent discovery of gold in the mountains along the Fraser River, the rich history of the fur trade and the Hudson's Bay Company's influence, the conflict with the natives, and the abundance of natural resources.

"I'm told the beauty is unparalleled," he said. "I hope to have time to explore the region before the *Tynemouth* sets sail again."

"What'll you see first?" She watched him eagerly, almost as if she were planning to explore alongside him.

Before he could respond, the gruff call of a sailor down the deck interrupted him. Gully was lumbering toward them, his weathered old face creased with worry. "Mr. Allen done hurt his arm again. And he's howlin' worse than a newborn babe."

Joseph stood slowly, reluctant to end his time with Mercy. To his surprise, she was already moving toward Gully, her firm steps every indication she planned to help him again.

A part of him knew he should resist, at the very least encourage her to rest a little longer. But he ignored the warning and the dangerous fact that he liked having her at his side.

twelve

Mercy leaned her head against her cabin door.

"Captain Hellyer has moved Miss Lawrence to special quarters amidships to lessen the motion." Dr. Colville's voice on the opposite side was confident yet compassionate.

Mercy's chest had begun a strange motion of rising and falling the moment she'd heard Dr. Colville on the deck. And the longer she listened to him, the more her insides dipped.

She hadn't spoken to him for several days, not since the morning after the gale in the Channel. Yet she couldn't stop thinking about the kindness he'd shown to the passengers in steerage. That he'd gone down there at all to aid their discomfort was out of the ordinary, to be sure. She suspected most doctors would've let the poor passengers tend to their own needs.

Aye, he'd been tender and efficient with the sick, but he'd done much more than care for their ailments. He'd allowed a mother with a sick babe an extra ration of milk, gave a handful of marbles to a group of children, and found a cane for a man who'd sprained his ankle. He never once spoke harshly but displayed great patience. In fact, he interacted almost as if he considered himself one of the steerage passengers, never putting on airs nor speaking with a condescending tone. As a result, she'd seen the respect and admiration on their faces. No doubt it mirrored her own.

As much as she was tempted to crack open her cabin door and peek at him, she let the weight of her body hold the door closed and prevent her from acting foolishly. He might have appreciated her help during the recent storm, and he might have taken a few moments on the deck to pull up a chair and talk with her when the others were too sick to keep him company, but that didn't mean he wanted to make a regular practice of mingling with her.

"Our captain is indeed most gracious" came Mr. Scott's voice. "We are beholden to him for his kindness. As we are to you too, Lord Colville."

The girls crowded at the door with Mercy, eager for any news that would break the monotony of their days confined to the cabin—except for the short periods their chaperones allowed them to walk outside on their small stretch of deck.

She ought to tell the girls to move away from the door and stop trying to listen to the conversation outside, but how could she rebuke her charges for eavesdropping when she was doing the same?

"As Miss Lawrence is still not eating or drinking," the doctor continued, "the captain and I are growing increasingly concerned."

"Such a shame, such a shame," Mr. Scott remarked.

"Can you save her, Lord Colville?" Mrs. Robb asked at the same time.

Mercy tried to picture Miss Lawrence's face from among the fancy ladies of their group, but they rarely mingled with or spoke to any of the poor women.

"I shall continue to do my best," Dr. Colville said. "But as I am unable to be with her at all times, I'm requesting that one of your other women nurse Miss Lawrence."

"The women aren't allowed beyond the ropes," Mrs. Robb stated.

Mercy trembled to think what Mrs. Robb would do if she discovered Mercy's visit down into steerage and the short while she'd sat on the deck with the doctor and sipped his coffee. Even if Mrs. Robb had given Mercy leave to fetch him, she certainly wouldn't approve of such familiarity. If Mrs. Robb found out, she'd put Mercy on the first ship back to London. Or perhaps even throw Mercy overboard.

"Surely you can understand the need to make an exception in the case of illness," Dr. Colville said. "As Miss Lawrence is confined in a different part of the ship, and you're busy with your duties here, she has need not only for a nurse but also a chaperone."

Silence stretched in which the creaking of the ship reminded them that their voyage was at the mercy of the ocean and its ever-changing temperament.

"Very well, Doctor," Mrs. Robb said reluctantly.

"Perhaps one of my daughters?" Mr. Scott offered. "They are almost recovered—"

Dr. Colville cut off the man. "I would like the assistance of Mercy Wilkins, if she is so agreeable."

At the mention of her name, Mercy sucked in a breath. In the same moment, the girls nudged Mercy.

"Mercy?" Mrs. Robb's voice rang with surprise.

"She has already proven to be a capable nurse," Dr. Colville added. "She has quickly learned to ride the ship and has a strong stomach."

Warmth radiated through Mercy at the words of praise. The girls elbowed her again, clearly as flustered by the unusual attention as she was.

"My lord," Mr. Scott said, his voice laced with concern, "our dearest Miss Lawrence will most certainly want to have another gentlewoman at her attendance, not a ruffian pulled from the streets."

The comment was like a splash of icy seawater against Mercy's skin. She froze as the warmth of the doctor's words was dashed away by the reality of who she was and her place in the world.

"Have a care, Mr. Scott." Dr. Colville's tone hardened. "If not for Miss Wilkins's untiring devotion during the gale, many more of your women would be in the same position as Miss Lawrence."

"Of course, of course, my lord," Mr. Scott rushed to reply. "You are indeed right as usual. The young girl of whom we speak is stalwart in nature. Nevertheless, are you certain you do not wish for a more genteel woman to be at your disposal? My daughters have oft spoken of their wish to serve you."

"Thank you, Mr. Scott. But I need an assistant, not a companion."

"Very well then, Doctor," Mrs. Robb interjected. "We shall send Mercy to nurse Miss Lawrence straightaway."

"My sincerest gratitude." The sound of Dr. Colville's footsteps faded, leaving only the rush of the wind and the never-ending crash of the waves against the hull.

As the girls returned to the bunks and flopped themselves onto their thin mattresses, Mercy pressed her forehead against the cool wood of the door, not sure whether to feel embarrassed about the conversation or excited.

"There, there, Mr. Scott." Mrs. Robb was still on the deck nearby, obviously waiting to speak again until the doctor was gone. "Don't fret. You have nothing to worry about. A man of Lord Colville's stature would never consider a woman of such low rank."

"Very true, Mrs. Robb. Very true. At least not as a marriageable option."

"You don't think Lord Colville would attempt a—" Mrs. Robb paused and cleared her throat—"a dalliance with the girl?"

A dalliance? Mercy lifted her head. Was Mrs. Robb insinuating the doctor had an ulterior motive for requesting Mercy's assistance?

"Lord Colville is a man of honor," Mr. Scott replied almost too quietly for Mercy to hear. "But he is also just a man, after all."

"Then we should reconsider our allowing any of the women near him. I made a vow to Miss Rye, to see that all the women in my charge remained chaste in body and soul."

"As did I" came Mr. Scott's solemn reply. "Still, we most certainly cannot refuse an esteemed and illustrious man such as Lord Colville."

"Heaven save us." Mrs. Robb's voice was filled with horror. "Whatever shall we do?"

"We shall do all we can to oversee the situation, Mrs. Robb. And perhaps if Lord Colville is presented oft with my lovely daughters, they will serve to distract him from temptation."

The voices grew distant as the two began walking down the deck. Even after their conversation wafted away altogether, Mercy couldn't move herself from the door.

In all her interactions with Dr. Colville, he'd been kind, compassionate, and considerate, never giving her the slightest impression his motives were anything less than honorable. But then he *had* invited her to sit with him and had shared his coffee. Why would he do so unless he had some kind of interest in her?

Mrs. Robb and Mr. Scott were right in saying an important, wealthy man like Dr. Colville would never consider a woman of her station to be his wife. And that was perfectly fine by her. Even if she and Dr. Colville had been equally matched, nothing would affect her decision against marriage.

Unless Dr. Colville was contemplating something else entirely . . .

"Oho." Ann whistled softly. "Do you think Lord Colville be wanting you as a mistress?"

"No!" Mercy spun and plunked her hands on her hips. Even if Ann had given voice to Mercy's fear, she had no intention of letting such a fear grow into a reality. "That's rot. All rot."

"If he wanted me, I'd snatch him up quicker than a fogle hunter snatching a gold coin from a pocket." The others laughed at Ann's bold statement.

"You'd do no such thing, d'ye hear me?" Mercy retorted, her glare taking in all the girls in the cabin. "That kind of thinking will only get you in a heap of trouble."

Wide eyes stared back at her from their beds.

Sarah, from her curled-up position on the bottom bunk, said quietly, "I never knew my dad. My mum didn't talk about him. But I 'spect he was a rich fellow somewhere 'cause she always warned me not to let myself dream about being together with someone who weren't like me. Told me he'd just use me and then leave me."

"That's right. We haven't come this far to start letting men use us." Mercy said the words fiercely, thinking of Twiggy and the men she'd let use her. Her mum could have resisted them and their gifts. Surely she could have found a different way to help the family. "We'll stay strong and build new lives for ourselves."

Mercy closed her eyes and willed herself to believe the words. She had to stay strong. She couldn't let herself be swayed by a man—no matter how handsome and kind he might be.

"Miss Lawrence?" Mercy knelt next to the prostrate woman.

"Be she dead?" Harry, the ship's boy, stood behind Mercy and peered over her shoulder.

Mercy tugged down Miss Lawrence's high collar and touched the vein in the woman's neck as she'd seen Dr. Bates and Dr. Colville do to their patients. She avoided a bruised spot that looked strangely like teeth marks—almost as if someone had taken a vicious bite out of the woman's neck. At the steady rhythm of a pulse, Mercy expelled her breath. "No, she's yet alive."

The lanky, freckle-faced boy shrugged his shoulders as if disappointed there wouldn't be any unfolding drama to entertain him.

"Then I guess I'll be on my way." Harry backed out of the stateroom. "Dr. Colville said to holler if you need me to fetch 'im."

"Thank ye," Mercy said, although she wasn't planning to be near Dr. Colville any more than she had to, not after the conversation she'd overheard between Mrs. Robb and Mr. Scott.

She'd do best to stay as far from him as possible.

After Harry closed the door, Mercy glanced around the private berth given to Miss Lawrence. It was tiny, with a single bed attached to the wall, a built-in writing table that could only hold one sheet of paper at a time, and a simple three-legged stool. There was hardly enough space to stand next to the bed, much less kneel. Regardless, Mercy could sense right away that the wave-tossed motion at the middle of the ship was calmer than in the cabins at the aft.

Mercy skimmed her fingers across the woman's forehead, feeling for fever. Though her skin was clammy, it wasn't hot, not even warm.

The stench of vomit permeated the cramped cabin. The lantern Harry had hung above the bed revealed that Miss Lawrence's lovely satin gown was coated with the filth.

Mercy set about fetching warm water and clean clothes for Miss Lawrence. When she returned, the woman was still in the same position as before. Mercy gently rolled her patient over, noting her delicate features, unblemished pale skin, and hair that was a beautiful copper color. Waves had come loose from an elegant coil and lay in tangled strands around her neck and down her back.

Miss Lawrence's long lashes resting against her skin made the contrast between her burnished hair and light skin more pronounced, as did the sprinkling of freckles over her face.

"I'll get you cleaned up right well," Mercy said softly, not sure if the woman could hear her. "Then you'll set to feeling better in no time."

As Mercy began to unbutton the woman's shirt, her lashes flittered up, revealing green eyes. The hue was lovely, one Mercy hadn't seen before. She didn't have anything to compare the color to, except perhaps the sun-warmed fields they'd passed during their train journey from London to Dartmouth.

"Thank you . . . ?"

"Mercy Wilkins, miss."

"Thank you, Mercy," Miss Lawrence whispered in a raspy voice. "But I shall wait to change until I'm no longer sick."

"When's the last time you heaved?"

"I cannot recall."

Mercy searched Miss Lawrence's gown. "You're dry, which means you're most likely over the worst of it."

Miss Lawrence's lashes fell, and she held herself so still that Mercy began to wonder if she'd fallen asleep again. "Miss Lawrence?"

"If you leave the clean garments," the woman whispered, "I shall change momentarily."

"Dr. Colville thought you'd prefer to have a woman tending you, miss. I'm here to stay and help where I can."

It had been mighty generous of the captain and Dr. Colville to move Miss Lawrence amidships to make her more comfortable. If only Sarah could be moved as well. But Mercy knew well enough that a street orphan like Sarah wouldn't get the same fine treatment as a wealthy gentlewoman.

Miss Lawrence opened her eyes, and Mercy caught sight of shadows of pain in them. The beautiful woman's lips parted as if she might protest further, but then she seemed to school her face into resignation.

Mercy finished unbuttoning and slid the gown over Miss Lawrence's shoulders. She nearly gasped at the sight that met her. The chemise couldn't hide the vibrant red welts and bruises covering the woman's back. Miss Lawrence looked as if she'd been recently whipped with a cat-o'-nine-tails. Some of the lacerations had opened up and were scabbed over, while others were still raw.

The gentlewoman stiffened as Mercy gently peeled the layers of her garments away but didn't say anything.

What had happened to this poor lamb? Had she been attacked by an angry mob?

Mercy waited several heartbeats for Miss Lawrence to give an explanation. But when she offered nothing, Mercy knew she had to say something. "You must be a right strong woman to hold up against whatever happened to you."

"I took a tumble while out riding." Miss Lawrence spoke quickly—too quickly—almost as if she'd rehearsed her answer. "'Tis of no consequence and will mend soon enough."

Mercy didn't know much about horse riding. But whatever had happened to this woman hadn't been an accident. She'd clearly been attacked. But by whom, and for what reason?

She bathed Miss Lawrence as tenderly as she could and then helped her into a clean gown, taking care to leave the fastenings loose. When Miss Lawrence was finally attired, Mercy worked at untangling the woman's hair and washing the vomit out of it. She brushed and plaited it simply so that it hung down her back and out of the way of any further seasickness.

"Thank you," Miss Lawrence said as Mercy settled her back into the bed. "You have been very kind."

"Think nothing of it, miss." Mercy propped up the gentlewoman with pillows.

Miss Lawrence winced at the contact against her back. "I should not like anyone else to know about my accident. I pray you will be discreet?"

"'Course, miss. You've got nothing to worry about with me."

Miss Lawrence tugged the collar of her gown up over the mark on her neck. When she realized Mercy was watching her, she dropped her hands into her lap. "You seem to be a strong woman, Mercy. How is it you can withstand the ship's tossing and turning so well?"

"Not sure why some are stronger than others, miss. My sister always said if we're stronger in body, that just means we've got more responsibility from the good Lord to take care of any who are weaker."

Weariness settled over Miss Lawrence's pretty but gaunt features, and the same shadow of pain from earlier flickered in her eyes—a pain that went much deeper than just physical. Mercy had no doubt this woman was suffering in both body and soul.

Mercy had always believed life was easier for the wealthy, had assumed money and titles provided everything a person could ever want. Yet Miss Lawrence's battered body told a different story. Perhaps the devil could make his home in the wealthy parts of London every bit as much as in the slums.

"Is your sister along on the voyage?" Miss Lawrence asked weakly.

"No, I left her behind at the workhouse." Once the words were out, Mercy felt the weight of them, as if she'd locked Patience there herself. Had she done the right thing in leaving her sister behind? Could she have done more for Patience if she'd stayed with her?

"I shall most assuredly pray for her," Miss Lawrence said, reaching for Mercy's hand.

"She'll need the prayers, to be sure," Mercy replied. Then before she could fall into too much despair, she pushed the melancholy aside. She had to keep believing Patience would get better and come on the next ship to meet her. She couldn't give up hope. "And what about you, miss? You must be missing your family."

Miss Lawrence shrank back deeper into her pillows, her face growing paler, her lips trembling. "I think about them every day and wonder what has become of them."

"Become of them, miss?" Had they suffered the same abuse?

"I left them in a terrible predicament," Miss Lawrence said in a strained voice. "Very terrible."

Mercy wanted to press the gentlewoman further, but Miss Lawrence clamped her lips together as though she could say no more.

"A drink, miss?" Mercy lifted a tin cup and helped her take small sips before settling her back into the pillows.

"Thank you," Miss Lawrence whispered and closed her eyes.

Within seconds the gentlewoman's breathing was even with the peace of sleep.

Mercy watched the delicate face for a moment longer. She was sure she'd passed by Miss Lawrence many times during their excursions on the deck. But she wouldn't have guessed this woman was hiding painful secrets, that underneath the layers of frilly and fancy garments was a broken and bruised body.

Maybe Mercy was as guilty of making assumptions about the wealthy as they were of forming their views of the poor. She'd do well to stop rushing to judge and instead see beyond the surface to the real person.

thirteen

Joseph paused in the open doorway of the stateroom.

Mercy crooned words of encouragement as she spooned broth into Miss Lawrence's mouth.

When Arabella Lawrence had first come to his attention, she'd been so dehydrated, Joseph feared she would die. Thankfully, with Mercy's persistence, the sick woman was finally beginning to keep down some sustenance.

Of course, it helped that the ship was cutting her way into the calmer waters of the mid-Atlantic and that the wind had abated. The closer they navigated toward the equator and into the tropics, the smoother the sailing.

Nevertheless, Mercy's ministrations had coaxed life back into Miss Lawrence. Even now, as Mercy perched on the edge of the low bed, determination etched her profile. "One more sip, miss. Just one more," she murmured.

Miss Lawrence allowed Mercy to feed her another spoonful before sagging against the pillows. Mercy lowered the tin cup and then smoothed a loose strand of the woman's hair back under her nightcap.

"Thank you, Mercy," Miss Lawrence said drowsily.

Mercy kissed the woman's forehead with a tenderness that

made Joseph's chest pinch. How was she able to give so much to others when she had so little herself? She'd admitted to the direness of her living conditions and difficulty of her life. If such adversity had left its mark on her for the worse, he didn't see any sign of it.

She stood and began to stretch. At the sight of him, she stiffened and rapidly turned her back.

For the past few days while she'd been tending Miss Lawrence, he'd pushed aside her brusqueness, had told himself she was focused upon the sick woman and was simply too busy to acknowledge him.

He'd kept his distance as well, giving the women the privacy he thought they wanted. But now that Miss Lawrence was mending, Mercy had no reason to treat him as though he had the Black Plague, did she?

He leaned against the doorframe, unwilling to withdraw this time. "Have I offended you in some way, Miss Wilkins?"

She spun around, her eyes wide.

"I give you leave to speak freely."

"Sir?" Something flashed in her pretty eyes. Was it fear?

"Please do not mince the truth."

She glanced at Miss Lawrence. The gentlewoman's eyes were closed, and she was breathing restfully—likely asleep. Even so, Mercy slipped past him outside the room.

As he moved away from the stateroom, the sun blazed above the ship, drying the main deck from the drenching it had received during the previous week's gale. Only a few puddles remained, and soon he would be carefully rationing their water supply. As the ship's surgeon, his responsibilities included not only caring for the ill but also rationing food, checking for food poisoning, and overseeing the burial of the dead at sea.

The heat soaked into his dark coat, reminding him to wear his lighter colors from hence forward. He'd prefer to go about in his shirt and waistcoat, discarding his coat altogether as the sailors did, but he had already defied convention oft enough and so continued to wear his coat when outside his stateroom, even in the tropical sun.

Rather than finding a spot of shade, Mercy walked to the starboard rail into the sunlight. She peered over the side as the ship sliced through the water. Though the *Tynemouth* might have once been an elegant ship with her sails flying proudly in the wind, she was now patched in many areas, her throbbing engines belching black coal smoke that trailed in her wake.

Toward the stern, two sailors were hauling up buckets of seawater, likely at the request of passengers who wished to attempt to launder their vomit-splattered clothing and bedding and then hang the linens to dry. Little did they realize that without fresh water for rinsing, their garments would become caked with salt and would likely give them saltwater boils. Most would have to give up on washing soon enough.

Other than the sailors drawing water, the deck was deserted. Joseph leaned against the rail next to Mercy and watched as the sun turned the spray of water droplets into diamonds.

"The sea can be a beauty when she wants to be, can she not?" Joseph asked.

"Aye, she can." Mercy turned her attention to the horizon, an endless blue where the sky met the sea. "She's rather like an infant, isn't she? One day calm as can be, and the next throwing a tantrum."

"Sometimes she changes her mood by the hour."

The slight wind teased Mercy's hair, pulling fair tendrils across her flushed cheeks. "I like her best when she's quiet and content."

"As do I." His fingers twitched with the need to capture her flyaway strands, to test for himself their silkiness.

She inhaled deeply, as if the sea air contained the life-giving breath of God. Joseph supposed that compared to the thick air that choked London, the sunshine and the pure ocean air were exactly what her body needed. After all, she'd lost some of the pallor and gauntness from the first time he'd seen her at the dispensary. And now her face gave off a healthy glow.

"So, Miss Wilkins." He shifted his hands behind his back and clasped them together. "Will you put me out of my misery and inform me of my misdeed? Then I may beg your forgiveness and all shall be well."

She ducked her head.

He half expected her to peek at him coyly and tell him nothing was wrong, that there wasn't anything to forgive since he was the perfect gentleman as always. He was accustomed to such flattery. Even those who disagreed with his decision to become a physician followed the unspoken rule of his class—to dress criticism in elegant, flowery attire.

He was unprepared when Mercy turned to face him directly, her expression earnest and devoid of any guile. "I'll not be any man's mistress."

The words were so unexpected and blunt, he recoiled.

Though her eyes reflected the shame and embarrassment the words had cost her, she didn't back down. And though he was tempted to turn away at the indecency of her statement, he held her gaze. He saw then what he'd noticed the previous days. Accusation.

"Devil take all!" A burst of self-loathing exploded within his breast. He stalked away several long paces before stopping. Did she think he'd singled her out to be his assistant because he wanted to form an illicit liaison with her? What in the name of heaven above had he done to give her such an impression? He'd been nothing but kind and compassionate to her plight and those of the other poor women.

How dare she sling so unfair an allegation at him?

He spun around with every intention of berating her, but at the picture she made with the sunshine spinning her hair into gold, the sea reflecting in her eyes deep and blue, and her lovely features so pure and unspoiled, his anger blew away, leaving guilt in its place.

Even at that moment, when he didn't want to think about her loveliness, the breeze molded her gown to her body like a sculptor, leaving little to the imagination—pressing her skirt against long legs, as well as outlining her thin waist and curvy figure. There was no denying she was a beautiful woman in every sense of the word.

He hadn't wanted to desire her, hadn't wanted to admit to any attraction. But perhaps, against his best efforts, he'd desired her anyway. And perhaps against his best efforts to hide it, she'd noticed.

At his lengthening perusal, her chin rose a notch and the accusation in her eyes shouted louder.

"Miss Wilkins," he said, realizing he was only making matters worse, "I beg you to forgive me." Even if he found her attractive—as any man would—he surely hadn't meant to give her the impression he wanted her for his mistress. "Whatever I have done, whatever I have said, whatever my grievances, I assure you I have never given a single thought to—to ill-using you."

She cocked her head slightly, seeming to study his face.

"Rest assured I never have and never would consider having a mistress." Saying the word was enough to make him squirm. Although there were men of his station who indulged in such vices, his father had always been passionately devoted to his wife. He'd never hidden his deep love and adoration and had been openly affectionate with her. His father's example in marriage, as in other areas of his life, was one Joseph aspired to emulate someday.

At twenty-five, there were those within his class, including his aunt Pen, who believed men of his age ought to be marrying and starting families. But he'd convinced himself he still had time before he needed to get serious about looking for a wife and settling down. Meanwhile, he had no plans to indulge his flesh with fleeting encounters with women. Such relationships might temporarily fulfill a man's needs but almost always resulted in hurt and heartache.

"Again," he said, "I beg your sincere apology if I have in any way insinuated such a relationship. It was not my intention at all."

"What *is* your intention, sir?"

He couldn't say exactly why he'd singled Mercy out from the other women. Surely it wasn't simply because he found her physically appealing. Perhaps he'd been drawn to her because she was the only one with whom he had an acquaintance. And of course he liked her gentle and caring nature, along with her inner strength and independent spirit. Whatever the case, he had no plans—had never even considered—anything beyond a working relationship with her.

"I have no intentions toward you, Miss Wilkins," he said, reassuring himself. "I had hoped to engage your help. That is all. But if I make you uncomfortable, and if you'd rather not be near me—"

"Oh no, sir," she said, the accusation falling away. "I want to help. I don't have the training like a proper nurse, but I can learn fast."

"You do learn very quickly, Miss Wilkins. More important, you truly care about people, and trust me, they can sense it."

"You care greatly about people too, sir." She averted her eyes. "I could tell it the first time I met you. And I'm sorry for doubting you, sir. It's just that when I overheard the talk about becoming your mistress, I didn't know what to think."

He should have known other passengers might gossip and twist his intentions into something lewd.

"I tried to put the suggestion out of my mind, sir, that I did. But it stayed there. . . ."

Slowly he made his way toward her, stopping several feet away. "I hope I can prove to you I am honorable in every way." He wasn't sure how he'd be able to do that, but the desire to do so was powerful.

She nodded, her focus still on the deck.

He wanted to look into her eyes where he was beginning to learn to read her thoughts and emotions. Did she still doubt him? He was tempted to reach out and tip up her chin so she would have to meet his gaze. Instead, he clasped his hands behind his back again.

"Please know this, Miss Wilkins. I am most reservedly saving my affection for one woman only, the woman I plan to marry. When God brings that woman into my life, I pray I shall be found worthy of her love. That for having refrained from giving my love away to others, I might have an overflowing abundance to bestow upon her alone."

Her long lashes lifted to reveal eyes full of wonder. "'Tis beautiful, sir. She'll be lucky to have you."

"I pray you are right." Though he'd never put his marriage aspirations into such eloquent words before now, and had most certainly never spoken them so openly, he felt no shame in sharing with Mercy, rather only satisfaction.

"Thank ye for your kindness, sir. And now I must be asking for your pardon, for wrongly assuming things that weren't to be. I should have known better—"

"Mercy," he said, interrupting her, "there is no need for you to apologize."

Her lips curved into one of her rare smiles. He wanted to commission a portrait of her at that moment, wished he'd gone with his inclination to purchase one of those new machines that took a likeness—the daguerreotype camera.

"You ought to smile more oft."

She turned and peered out to sea, the smile turning wistful and nearly fading. "I suppose I'm sorely out of practice."

He leaned both arms on the rail next to her. "Forgive me. You have likely not had much to smile about in recent weeks."

"I haven't had much to smile about in all my life, sir."

His thoughts returned to Shoreditch, to the wretchedness of the place. He'd served at the dispensary with Dr. Bates enough to grasp the difficult life there for the poor. But the truth was, he'd never taken the time to get to know the people the way Bates had. He'd never bothered to see beyond their afflictions, hadn't wanted to. Rather, he always looked ahead to leaving so that he wasn't able or willing to truly look around him.

Even when Bates had needed him for the partnership, he'd refused to acknowledge just how desperate the situation there was. It had taken courage for his friend to humble himself and ask for help. And Joseph had probably done exactly what Bates had feared—he'd rejected him without even the slightest hesitation. The realization of his callous response to his older mentor brought a measure of shame.

And yet now, with this beautiful woman standing next to him, maybe he could begin to make up for what he'd missed. Maybe he could try to understand what life had been like for so many in London's slums. What kind of abuse and pain had she known? What were her scars? And what had shaped her into this amazing woman?

"Would you tell me what your life was like?" he asked. "I'd like to understand."

fourteen

Mercy could sense Dr. Colville's eyes upon her. In fact, he'd watched her the entire time she told him about her siblings and parents, also her grandparents who'd long since died.

Like so many others, the promise of steady work in London had lured her family to moving there. They arrived not knowing just how dire living in the city would be, how much they'd struggle to survive from week to week, hoping each rent day they'd have enough to pay the landlord's collector. The low wages left little for food, which they bought from the slum shops when and if they could afford it.

For a while, they'd been lucky enough to do piece work, getting supplies from a nearby match factory to make matchboxes. The small cardboard box pieces had to be glued together in a difficult and painstaking process. Eventually her mum and grandmother got fast enough that they could make over one thousand boxes in a day, which earned them enough to buy a loaf of bread.

Sometimes they had to work up to sixteen hours a day to reach their daily quota. When Patience and Mercy were old enough, they too helped with making the matchboxes. But then the match factory closed, hard times hit, and Twiggy and their grandmother weren't able to find any more piece work.

With Granddad hurting his back and unable to do manual labor, her grandparents had been the first to move to the workhouse. They'd both died there within a year. Thankfully, Twiggy had found a position at the rag factory. Even with both her parents working, they still had trouble paying rent and having enough to buy food, especially with each new babe Twiggy birthed.

"It sounds as though you have loving parents," Dr. Colville said.

Mercy hesitated. "Twiggy loves her babies. But beyond that, she never had enough energy to go around."

"Not even for you?"

"Patience raised me and loved me more than Twiggy ever could." Mercy's chest ached at the thought of her sister. It had been nigh onto three weeks since she'd seen Patience, and every passing day made their parting all the harder.

"Then she's to thank for your tender and compassionate heart?"

Mercy peeked sideways at him only to find herself mesmerized by his eyes. She'd only ever seen velvet before on the coats of the wealthier ladies among their group. Right now, Dr. Colville's eyes were like dark brown velvet—soft, rich, and thick. And sincere . . .

"Aye, anything good in me is all because of Patience, that it is. She taught me to live aright. Whenever I felt sad, she helped me to see there's always someone a mite worse off. She said that when we serve someone else, we're too busy to think much on our own problems. Leastways, our problems don't seem so big in comparison."

"She sounds wise."

"An old nun, Sister Agnes from St. Matthew's, befriended Patience when she was just a wee girl. I don't remember much about the nun save that she'd come visiting now and then, bringing bread or apples and teaching Patience stories from the Bible."

"Then this nun is the one we should thank."

"Aye," Mercy said quietly, her thoughts traveling back to those many visits from the nun. In some ways, Sister Agnes had been like a grandmother to Patience, offering guidance and wisdom and love, which Patience had in turn given to Mercy.

Patience had always believed God never let their troubles go to waste, that He was always using them to bring about good, often in ways they couldn't see. Mercy had tried to be like her sister, to have the same strong faith, to believe that God was with them in their afflictions. But she'd never been quite as strong as Patience.

Even so, she'd learned a great deal from both Sister Agnes and Patience about giving away love to others. "When we show kindness to someone, we never can know exactly how many lives that kindness may affect. And Lord knows how much kindness is needed where I come from."

Dr. Colville shifted his attention to the ocean, his brow furrowing. The breeze from the moving ship lifted a stray lock of his hair.

Dashing. That was the word she'd overheard some of the fancy ladies use to describe the doctor. He was indeed dashing, but more than that, Mercy admired his strength of character. In the face of her accusation, he'd handled himself with grace and dignity, as kind to her as always.

Her cheeks warmed just thinking about the brazenness of her words. She shouldn't have brought up the matter, should have realized Dr. Colville would never consider having a mistress. While she hadn't known him long, he'd never given her cause to believe he was anything but genuine and honorable.

"Do you hear that?" Dr. Colville straightened and looked toward the foredeck, his body stiff and unmoving.

Mercy tried to listen above the splash of the waves. "I don't hear anything, sir."

"Exactly." He moved to the middle of the deck. "The ship's engines are no longer running."

Mercy nodded. She too sensed a quietness to the ship that hadn't been there previously.

Dr. Colville glanced to the sea. "And we've stopped moving."

Mercy followed his line of vision, noting that the ship was no longer breaking through the water. The waves bumping against the hull were small, rocking the ship like a mother her babe.

The sailors at the bow were calling to one another, and Gully thundered down the deck in a hurry.

"Can you tell me what has happened?" Dr. Colville called.

"'T'aint good, my lord," the old sailor replied gruffly. "The coal haulers and stokers be mutinying."

Mutinying? Did that mean the workers were refusing to do their jobs?

"Guess they be thinking they're better than the lot of us," Gully grumbled as he lumbered past. "They been complaining 'bout too much work and not enough grub."

"Of course, they picked the opportune time to stop working now that we're in the doldrums," Dr. Colville responded.

"Got that right." Gully swung onto the forestay and started climbing the mast. "Without the engines and no wind to power the sails, we be stuck."

Mercy didn't quite know how to respond to the crisis. But thankfully Dr. Colville didn't seem to expect her to say anything. Instead, he excused himself and strode away.

Even as she pictured the ship drifting aimlessly on the ocean and everyone aboard dying of thirst and hunger, she returned to Miss Lawrence's stateroom with the same resignation that had held her in good stead in the past—the resignation not to dwell on her worries or sorrows. She'd seen too many others wallow in their problems, eventually sinking under the weight of them. She wouldn't do the same.

Soon the commotion on the decks turned into a frenzy as other second- and third-class passengers began to congregate. The main deck overflowed with people from steerage, who demanded to know what was happening.

As the hours passed with no sight of Dr. Colville, something inside her twisted until she felt as taut as the ship's rigging. She wanted to believe he was with the other passengers on the deck awaiting the outcome. Yet a deeper part of her knew he'd descended to the boiler rooms, straight into the heart of the mutiny, that he wasn't the kind of man to sit back and do nothing in the face of peril. He'd be at the forefront of it, searching for a solution, which would put him in very real danger.

Finally, when she could no longer sit still with Miss Lawrence, Mercy wound her way to the aft cabins to check on her charges. Most of the sixty women were waiting anxiously in their cramped roped-off area of the deck, wilting under the hot sun.

At the sight of Mercy, they bombarded her with questions. She told them the small amount she'd gathered about the mutiny but added that she was as uninformed as they were. Mr. Scott was nowhere to be seen, and Mrs. Robb was frazzled by her attempts to keep the women from carrying out their own mutiny against her strict confinement to their little corner of the ship.

Mercy was afraid Mrs. Robb might force her to remain there too. Eventually, though, she gave Mercy permission to return to Miss Lawrence's stateroom, but not without a withering glare that made Mercy feel dirty down to the core. She was mortified all over again to realize that if Mrs. Robb assumed she was ruining herself with Dr. Colville, then others must think so as well.

With the excessive heat of the tropics, she was helping to cool Miss Lawrence's face when the door banged open and Dr. Colville filled the frame.

Mercy leaped to her feet, searching for any sign of harm. His shirt was disheveled, his waistcoat unbuttoned, and his hair flattened to his head.

"How do you fare?" he asked breathlessly as though he'd just been running.

The question took Mercy by surprise. "Never mind me, sir." She had to restrain herself from circling him and making sure he had no hidden injuries. "I've been having visions of you cut to pieces by the mutineers and thrown to the sharks as bait."

He grinned. "I'm glad to know you've been worried."

"What d'ye expect, sir?" She tried to keep her voice light, but her heart raced with a strange anxiety over his well-being. "Disappearing all these long hours and leaving me to wonder what became of you?"

Coal soot mingled with perspiration on his forehead and neck, making him appear more rugged than aristocratic. He didn't immediately reply but instead seemed to take his time studying her face, as though the sight of her might somehow soothe him.

She soothe him? She silently chided herself for so prideful a thought. "Can you tell me how it goes?" She pulled her thoughts from a place she didn't want them wandering. She had no business thinking of him in any capacity other than their roles as doctor and assistant.

Before she allowed herself the pleasure of staring at him any longer, she reached for the pitcher of water she'd left beside Miss Lawrence's bed.

She could feel his gaze following her every movement. "We rounded up the insurgents," he replied, "and threw them into a makeshift brig. Captain Hellyer has charged them with mutiny on the high seas, and they are to be kept manacled and confined until they can be tried for their crimes."

"Are there many of them?"

"Not the entire crew, but enough that we'll be shorthanded forthwith."

She poured from the pitcher into Miss Lawrence's tin cup, conscious he was still watching her. "Then we're stuck here on the sea?"

"We've come up with a plan, having asked that any man among the passengers who is willing shall volunteer to help until a replacement crew can be acquired in the Falklands."

The news so startled Mercy that some of the water sloshed over the side of the cup. "You're in earnest?"

He nodded.

"Did the men volunteer?"

"Straightaway." His shoulders seemed to relax, and his features softened. "All the men, Mercy. Gentlemen and commoners alike."

The earnestness of his tone, the use of her given name, the realization that he was sharing so personally with her, sent her insides diving into unfamiliar territory that was warm and pleasurable.

She handed him the cup of water. As he tipped his head back and drank, she was the one doing the staring now, taking in the strength of his jaw and neck as he swallowed, the confident way he held himself.

"If it's rich and poor alike, then it's because of you," she said with more passion than she intended. "The men respect you and like you all around, to be sure."

After drinking the last drop, his eyes sought hers. And stayed there, even as he lowered the mug.

She felt breathless and hot and drawn to him, as if the intensity of his gaze had a magical power over her.

A faint voice behind her broke the spell. "Then will everything be all right, Lord Colville?"

Mercy pivoted and knelt beside Miss Lawrence, her pulse careening even more rapidly. She didn't understand her reaction to Dr. Colville, and suddenly it frightened her.

"Rest assured," Dr. Colville said smoothly, clearly not as ruffled as she was. "With every man doing his part, we shall reach the Falklands right on schedule."

"Thanks be to God," Miss Lawrence replied, looking past Mercy to Dr. Colville. "I fear I have become a burden to everyone and would not wish to impose longer than is necessary."

"There, there, dear." Mercy retrieved the cloth she'd abandoned upon Dr. Colville's appearance. She placed it back on Miss Lawrence's forehead. "You'll be right well soon enough, that you will."

"I signed up to work the first shift," Dr. Colville said. "Stoking the boilers."

His statement pulled Mercy's attention back around. She wanted to chastise him, for he was already plenty busy tending sick passengers. But the determined set of his jaw told her he wouldn't be swayed.

Something sweet expanded in her chest. She was proud of him, she realized. Proud of how humble he was to do the work of a common laborer. And proud she had the opportunity to serve alongside him.

"Lord Colville is a wonderful man," Miss Lawrence said wistfully once the doctor had left. "If only there were more men of his integrity and kindness. I pray that once we arrive to Vancouver Island, we shall all find men as kind and honorable as he is."

Mercy nodded and hoped Miss Lawrence took that as her agreement, even though she was far from agreeable about finding a husband on Vancouver Island. "You're right pretty and will have men fighting over you, to be sure."

Miss Lawrence tugged at a strand of her red hair as if the color explained her singleness. "While I was destined to be a spinster, my sister is the pretty one in our family. Though there aren't many eligible gentlemen left in London, my father made a good match for her."

Over the past few days, Miss Lawrence had shared only the barest of details regarding her family, mentioning her servant, Hayward, who had been special to her, along with her sister and her babe. Mercy was still curious about the stripes and bruises that covered the woman's body so carefully confined to areas where no one would notice them when she was fully dressed. But whenever Mercy asked Miss Lawrence about her past, she always quickly changed the subject.

Mercy wanted to ask more now, yet she knew her place well enough. For as sweet as the gentlewoman was, Mercy was more like a servant to her than a friend.

"Lord Colville will make some lucky woman a fine husband someday," Miss Lawrence said, reclining against her pillows. "For as much as I or any of the other women may dream about him, Joseph Colville will have his eyes set much higher—on a woman of noble birth, someone with both title and wealth."

Joseph Colville.

Mercy hadn't known his given name, had never heard it spoken. Now she allowed the name to play in her mind like a single low melody. *Joseph, Joseph, Joseph . . .*

Even if it was entirely improper for her to think his name, much less speak it aloud, the sweet tune played regardless.

The candle holder on the heavy oaken table slid with the swaying of the ship. Joseph grabbed it and did likewise with his plate of food.

Around him in the salon, the passengers chatted amiably, although the two long tables were decidedly sparser for the evening meal. The ship had finally crossed the line, sailed out of the doldrums, and was now in the choppier waters of the South Atlantic, causing a new bout of seasickness among those with weaker stomachs.

Across from him, Mr. Scott carried on a conversation with another gentleman, a Mr. Whymper. "We would be most delighted to have the pleasure of your presence again this eve, Mr. Whymper. Miss Scott will be reading from *The Vision of Judgment* by Lord Byron. She reads with such emotion. I have no doubt you will be completely enamored by her rendition."

Joseph took another bite of the tough pork, which rivaled the biscuit in its staleness. The semblance of gravy was thick and pasty and floated with dried peas. Nevertheless, he ate every bite, having increased his appetite from the hard work and heavy lifting in the boiler room. The noise of the engines was deafening, the heat unbearable, and the soot a nightmare.

Most mornings, when he and the other men returned from the

ship's bowels as black as coal, the sailors, who were in the process of washing the deck, would turn their hoses upon the men, cooling and cleaning them in one sweep. The equatorial heat dried them out soon enough. Afterward, Joseph would fall onto his bed and sleep for a few hours—so long as there weren't any medical emergencies demanding his attention.

After taking his turn at keeping the ship running, he had greater empathy for the men who'd mutinied. Even so, they had no right to put everyone else at risk because of their grudges.

Mr. Scott spoke again while twisting at his high collar as though to loosen it so that he could swallow his food. "Perhaps the other Miss Scott might provide further entertainment this eve with her singing. She is quite accomplished at a number of hymns and can sing 'God Save the Queen' beautifully, can she not, my dear?" He turned to his wife, who sat on his other side.

"Quite right, Mr. Scott," she said demurely. "Very beautifully indeed."

Joseph had learned that the Scott women rarely spoke. He oft thought Mr. Scott had enough voice for them all. Even with the attention Mr. Scott attempted to draw to his women, his loquaciousness seemed only to push them further into his shadow.

At least the heavy labor afforded Joseph a reprieve from Mr. Scott's invitations. Since he'd started shoveling and stoking coal a fortnight ago, he'd been able to excuse himself from the evening entertainment. Now it appeared Mr. Scott had set his designs upon Mr. Whymper.

The young man was cordial toward the reverend. Without any other diversions on the ship other than strolling the deck, Mr. Whymper appeared eager enough for the Scotts' companionship. And that suited Joseph, as he had no desire for it himself.

With the increase in the wind, Captain Hellyer had put a stop to the steam engines and unfurled the sails, letting the wind drive the ship onward. The air power would conserve their coal supply, as well as allow the men a respite from the backbreaking work.

Though the steady rumble of the ship beneath Joseph's boots was silent again, the ship hadn't lost any progress. It was almost as if the mutiny had never occurred. Only by the grace of God . . .

The altercation could have turned bloody, especially if more sailors had joined in the insurrection. As it was, the ship's officers had taken quick and decisive action, using their belaying pins to beat the mutineers into submission before dragging them away.

With another tilt of the ship, the candles and dinnerware slid again, this time more forcefully. Several utensils clattered to the floor, along with a goblet of wine, sending a splatter of Burgundy across the planking in every direction. Joseph lurched forward and managed to create a barrier with his arm, preventing even more from falling. Gasps of dismay and murmurs of worry replaced the conversation as passengers gripped the tables to hold themselves in their chairs.

A glance out the salon window showed the sky to be the same dark gray as earlier. And although the rain had held off, Joseph suspected they would have their fair share before the night was over.

The door to the room slammed open, and a ship's boy entered, bringing with him a gust of wind—cooler and hinting at a coming storm. "Dr. Colville?" the lanky boy called.

Joseph released his hold on the dinner items and stood. "What is it, Harry?"

The boy, not much older than fourteen, was as filthy as the rest of the sailors but gentler in spirit, not yet hardened from life at sea. Early on, Joseph had enlisted Harry's help in relaying to him the medical needs of the steerage passengers.

"Mrs. Donovan be having her labor pains in a bad way, sir," Harry said, his greasy hair hanging about his face.

Joseph stood hastily, his chair scraping the floor and nearly tipping over. "How long has she been travailing?"

"Don't rightly know, sir. Her mister is mighty afeared, seeing as the midwife said there ain't no more can be done."

When Joseph had last been down in steerage, Mrs. Donovan

was overdue, but since she'd already birthed half a dozen children, Joseph didn't expect her to have any difficulties with another.

"I shall gather a few supplies and be on my way," Joseph said. "In the meantime, I would like you to fetch Miss Wilkins."

Harry nodded and backed out of the room, wrestling with the wind to close the door behind him.

"Please excuse me," Joseph said to the remaining passengers before leaving the table.

"Lord Colville." Mr. Scott rose rapidly and held up a hand as though to stop Joseph's departure. "Surely you don't need Miss Wilkins when one of my daughters would be most willing to help you."

Joseph halted. "Mr. Scott, I do thank you for your kind offer, but as I recall, on the last occasion Miss Scott assisted me, she ended up in a faint."

Several evenings ago, one of the sailors had needed a festering tooth pulled. When Joseph had asked for Mercy's assistance, Mr. Scott insisted he take his daughter instead.

Joseph couldn't remember the names of the two daughters and wasn't able to tell them apart. Nevertheless, the one who'd tried to assist him shifted in her seat and flushed. At her obvious embarrassment at his bold statement, Joseph silently chastised himself for not being more tactful with his criticism.

"Please make use of the other Miss Scott," Mr. Scott insisted. "She is much less squeamish and will most certainly be of great aid to you."

Joseph paused, his hand on the door handle. He'd seen little of Mercy since Miss Lawrence had recovered enough to return to her quarters. He'd tried not to engage the women milling about on their section of deck, yet he found his attention irresistibly drawn there when passing by on his way to his stateroom, especially whenever Mercy was out. He was tempted to approach and talk to her but had refrained, knowing nothing good could come of it. After having time to contemplate the rumor that he'd taken Mercy as his mistress, he'd decided he needed to guard her reputation by staying away.

Even if he was able to hold himself back, keeping his thoughts at bay was another matter entirely. The truth was, he found his mind wandering to her quite regularly.

"I assure you, Lord Colville," Mr. Scott continued, his tone taking on a pleading quality. "My daughter can be of great benefit to you. You must take her with you."

While Joseph's spine stiffened in protest, his conscience told him he should heed Mr. Scott's plea. It was a beckoning to stay clear of the trouble he might stir up again by involving himself with Mercy.

The last thing he wanted to do was hurt Mercy. And if the rumors resurfaced, if he tainted her reputation, then she'd likely lose any chance of finding a husband once she reached Vancouver Island.

With an inward sigh, he nodded at Mr. Scott. "Very well—"

His acquiescence was cut short by Miss Scott cupping her mouth. With a pale face and wide eyes, she shot up from her seat. Before she could take a step, she stooped over and vomited on the floor.

Mrs. Scott rose from her chair in an instant. She slipped her arm around her daughter and guided her rapidly from the dining room, the second daughter scurrying closely behind. Once the door shut behind them, Mr. Scott kept his attention riveted to the table and wordlessly lowered himself to his seat.

Joseph nodded at the other passengers, then took his leave. As he hurried to his cabin, the wind and the first drops of rain buffeted him as though to warn him not to disturb Mercy. If he was completely honest, he knew he could use the midwife as his assistant. His calling after Mercy hadn't been necessary, and he suspected Mr. Scott had known it.

He'd send her back, he told himself as he entered his cabin and stomped about gathering his supplies, growing angrier at himself by the second.

Hearing a knock on his door, he took a deep breath, braced himself for what he must do, and swung open the door.

The rain had begun in earnest now and was pelting Mercy, so that she hung her head to avoid the sting of it against her face. The waves were splashing higher, and a sudden spray over the rail threatened to soak her.

Without a word of greeting, he dragged her out of the deluge into his cabin and shut the door.

Her breath came in gasps, and she leaned against the door as if needing it to brace herself up.

The interior of his cabin was dismal and dark, but not so much that he couldn't see the swell of her chest rising and falling in rapid succession or the tautness of her bare throat or the raindrops on her lips.

Against his will, his body reacted to her nearness, his muscles tightening, making him chastise himself all over again for involving her in this medical emergency. He shouldn't have allowed himself to entertain the possibility of utilizing her help again but should have kept in place the barrier between them.

She gave a slight tremble, and only then did he realize she wore no cloak or shawl for protection against the rain or the chill.

"Where is your cloak?" His irritation at himself made his voice sharper than he'd intended.

When her lashes swept up to reveal her large eyes, he wasn't able to see the blue-green in them. What he saw instead was her confusion in the slant of her brows.

"Sir?"

"Your cloak?"

"I don't have one. Never did."

Never had a cloak? He spun away from her, suddenly livid. At himself, at the world, at the unfairness of her life. He was overwhelmed by the realization of everything she'd had to live without, things any human being ought to possess. Not only should she own a proper cloak, but she ought to have lovely gowns and sturdy shoes and warm stockings and pretty hats and silky gloves . . .

He strode to his trunk, threw open the lid, and dug through it until he found one of his oiled capes. He returned to her, thrust it into her arms, then stalked back to the bag he'd been packing before she arrived. "Put it on."

She hesitated before slowly donning it. "You're angry with me, sir?"

His hands froze in midair, and his shoulders slumped as the anger drained from his body, leaving defeat in its wake. "No. I'm not cross with you, Mercy. I'm cross with myself."

When she didn't question him further, he finished stuffing the rest of what he needed in the bag. Then, leading the way, he started toward the steerage hatch. In the offing, dark clouds seemed to have mounted one upon the other, and he couldn't distinguish where the sea ended and the storm began. The waves were striking the ship harder, tossing the vessel and making walking more difficult.

"Hold on to my coat," he called over his shoulder.

She grasped his coattail, and he plunged forward just as a wave came over the deck, sending seawater rolling under their feet. Above them, sailors climbed the rigging to secure the sails, their shouts muffled by the roar of the wind and waves.

Joseph steered Mercy clear of the dozens of heavy ropes ferociously whipping about. He'd been stung by flyaway rigging on his first voyage and had to suture his own head with a dozen stitches. In a storm, and without the experience of a sailor who knew how to handle the loose serpents, he'd learned the ropes could be dangerous if not deadly.

At the hatch, Gully was already in the process of securing it with a heavy tarpaulin.

Joseph shook his head, motioning for the old sailor to uncover it. "I need to try to save Mrs. Donovan and the babe," he shouted above the crashing waves.

Gully's hardened eyes darted from Joseph to Mercy before

softening just a tad. With a nod, he yanked the canvas off and opened the hatch for them.

Immediately the water began pouring inside. Gully swept Mercy up and lowered her with a tenderness that surprised Joseph. Once Mercy was secure, Joseph quickly climbed down, slipping on the ladder rungs even after Gully closed the hatch above.

As his boots connected with the landing, the ship swayed and threw him against Mercy. He braced his hands on the wall, attempting to protect her from the full weight of his body. Even so, he found himself pressed against her, every soft exquisite part.

She drew in a sharp breath.

His attention dropped to her mouth, which was close enough he could feel the warmth of her exhalations against his chin. Though this was neither the time nor place to ponder what it would be like to lean in and capture her lips with his, the desire to kiss her sparked inside him nonetheless.

He forced his sights away from her mouth and found himself looking into her beautiful eyes, wide with confusion, along with something else that sent his pulse to racing. Was it desire? Was she feeling a pull toward him the same way he now felt toward her?

Such a foolhardy and impudent thought. Where was his integrity?

He shoved away from the wall and from her, groping for the square opening that led into steerage. He must stay in control and act upon all he knew to be right. For he'd meant what he told Mercy that day he refuted the rumors about having her as his mistress. He wouldn't use a woman in such a way, now or ever.

Without waiting for her to trail after him, he wound his way through steerage and the huddling mass of passengers. The swaying motion below was worse than above, and he had to clutch one bunk after another to guide him as he moved forward. He only needed to follow the anguished screams to know where to find Mrs. Donovan.

Once he reached the bedside, he set to work lighting a lantern. And as he lifted it and saw the bloodstained mattress beneath the writhing woman, he prayed he wasn't too late.

sixteen

Mercy wiped blood from her hands and extended the towel to Joseph. He took it wordlessly without looking at her and began to clean the blood from his hands. In the violently swinging lantern light, his expression was severe, his muscles taut.

Over the past hour, he'd spoken to her only when giving instructions and hadn't set his eyes upon her, not even for an instant. Not since their encounter when they'd entered steerage and he'd fallen against her, when he'd slanted his head and looked at her mouth as though he had every intention of pressing into her even further and kissing her.

She hadn't been repulsed and hadn't wanted to pull away. In fact, she'd surprised herself with the need to feel his lips against hers. She'd never kissed a man before, never desired it, had never expected to desire it. Not with her resolve to abstain from relationships with men.

Then why now? And why with Joseph?

"Thank ye, Doctor," Mr. Donovan said again, clamping down on Joseph's shoulder. They both swayed and nearly went down with the tilt of the boat. Mercy grabbed on to the beam of the bed to keep from toppling.

All throughout the long delivery, as Joseph worked to turn the babe so it would be born safely, Mrs. Donovan's screams of agony had drowned out everything else. Mercy had hardly noticed the churning of the ship or the water seeping in from the walls or the creaking of the dripping beams overhead.

But with Mrs. Donovan happily cradling her newborn babe, Mercy was well aware of the deteriorating conditions and the raging of the storm as she struggled to stay on her feet.

"They've battened down the hatches, that they have," Mr. Donovan said. "You won't be climbin' above until the storm's over."

Joseph nodded and glanced around, seeming to assess everyone. "I was aware that might happen when I came down here."

"Then I thank ye even more, Doctor." Mr. Donovan stared down at his wife and babe, his eyes glassy with tears. "I wish there were a way I could repay you."

"There is one thing you can do," Joseph said.

Mercy clung tightly as the ship tossed again, this time so high that many of the passengers cried out in fright. Surely this storm didn't have the power to turn the ship upside down, did it?

"Anything, sir, anything 'tall," Mr. Donovan called above the noise. "You just say it."

"A bed for my assistant, Miss Wilkins, where she can ride out the storm."

While Joseph still wouldn't look at her, Mr. Donovan did and nodded eagerly. He shouted instructions to a group of children crowded onto a nearby bottom bunk. At his command they scattered, some climbing into different beds, others crawling underneath the bunk.

Mr. Donovan waved his hand at the now-vacant bed. "It'll be as safe and dry as you can get here in steerage."

Joseph nodded his thanks before reaching out and grabbing on to Mercy's elbow. Although he was having trouble staying afoot too, he was managing better than she was, so she allowed him to guide her to the bunk. He didn't release her until she was seated comfortably. Then he backed away, not lingering a moment longer than he had to.

"You best take cover too, Doctor," Mr. Donovan shouted over the ship's creaking and groaning as he hunkered down next to his wife and new babe.

Joseph said something in reply, yet the words were lost by another swell and crash of a wave against the hull. Among the screams and cries of the passengers, Joseph made his way through steerage, offering aid and encouragement where he could.

Seeing his concern for their comfort and safety, Mercy couldn't keep at bay her admiration, though her heart warned her that she needed to try harder to stave off such feelings.

Claps of thunder and the hammering of the sea became fiercer. When the ship's stern rose and seemed to point toward heaven, Mercy could hardly hold on to the bed. An agonizing moment later, the ship plunged, charging down the trough, throwing everyone the opposite direction.

Mercy wondered if the ship would keep diving downward through the ocean, all the way to the very bottom. But then with a horrible creaking that sounded as if the ship were breaking apart, they rose again and beat back the onslaught of another great wave.

More screams and cries rang out in the cramped quarters. The banging and pounding coming from the decks beneath them sounded as though a sea monster had attacked the ship and was attempting to tear it to shreds.

Still clinging to the bed beam, Mercy squeezed her eyes shut. There were no such things as sea monsters. Nevertheless, her body shook with terror. If the storm above didn't sink them, the forces below would. They were going to die, and she wasn't ready for her life to end.

"God . . ." she whispered. She tried praying the way Patience had taught her, but the words caught in her throat. If she was about to sink with the ship and drown, then she needed to plead with God to take her to heaven in spite of all her bitterness toward Him.

"Mercy" came Joseph's voice from above her. "How do you fare?"

Her eyes flew open to utter darkness. He'd extinguished the lantern. Or perhaps the water leaking in from the deck above had put out its flame. Whatever the case, darkness had descended with a finality as certain as the grave.

His hand connected with her arm. "You're trembling."

She felt him wrapping something around her, and it took her a moment to realize he'd shed his coat and covered her with it.

An instant later, she felt his presence on the bed beside her as he lay down next to her. She was shaking so forcefully that when he slipped an arm around her and pulled her close, she collapsed into him and wanted to weep with fear but held it in.

"Rest easy now," he murmured against her ear, even as he enfolded her deeper within his embrace.

Soon she could feel her trembling subside. And though the ship continued to lurch and heave as if it might come apart beam by beam, Joseph's presence and the security of his arms brought her a measure of comfort, even if these were their last moments on earth.

"Are you starting to regain warmth?" he asked.

She was tempted to lie and tell him she was freezing so that he wouldn't release her. But in the throes of death, her conscience forbade her from any further sin. "My fear troubles me more than the cold, sir."

He was silent, and she waited for him to leave her side. But with another steep tilt of the ship, his hold only tightened. As the vessel dipped with the swell of a wave that was likely submerging the stern, Mercy buried her face against his chest.

"Are you ready to die, Doctor?" she asked.

"I'd like to think so." His voice was low. "I want to be ready to stand before my Maker and give an account for my life, but I'm not so certain."

"What have you to confess, sir? Cannot be overmuch, not compared to my sins."

"Your sins? From what I've seen, you have nothing but goodness in your heart."

"My transgressions are plentiful enough." With the storm threatening to take their lives, she might as well confess. "For one, I doubt God too oft."

"That's only human. God surely invites us to wrestle with Him the same way our forefathers did time after time in the Holy Scriptures."

Before Joseph could probe further, she confessed a worse sin, one that plagued her every day. "I left my sister Patience behind at the workhouse."

"From what you've told me of her, she wanted you to leave London and have a better life."

"Aye, she's always sacrificed for me. And now I need to survive for her so that I can help her start over too."

"Then you're hoping she can emigrate one day and join you?"

"I made arrangements for her to sail on the *Robert Lowe*, the next ship the Columbia Mission Society is sending out. Even so, I can't keep from doubting myself in leaving her behind and wishing I'd found another way."

"I'm sure if there had been another way, you would have taken advantage of it."

The ship pitched again, causing her stomach to plummet with it. For long moments, they couldn't speak amidst the crashing waves and battering wind that drowned out even the cries and calls of despair that rose from the other passengers.

Joseph's steady breathing close by helped to calm her nerves once more, so that she allowed herself to breathe freely.

"It has been pointed out to me," he finally said, "that perhaps I am running from God."

"Running from God? You who are a kindness and savior to everyone you meet?"

"Well, perhaps I'm like Jonah, running from God and what He is calling me to do with my life."

Mercy had only a vague recollection of the story of Jonah, the prophet who'd been tossed into the sea and swallowed by a giant fish because he'd refused to go and preach to the heathens.

"Perhaps if you throw me overboard," he said, "this storm will cease."

"Stuff and nonsense. I'll do no such thing."

Against her head, she could feel his mouth curve up into a smile. He'd been teasing her, and the realization left her breathless. "If not doctoring," she said hurriedly to cover her strange feelings, "what do you suppose be His calling for your life, sir?"

"The doctoring isn't in question, just the location of where to do it. Dr. Bates wanted me to stay at the Shoreditch Dispensary and enter into a partnership with him. I turned him down."

After watching Joseph work so tirelessly to save Clara, she'd sensed a kindness and generosity in him that was much needed in the slums. Dr. Bates had surely sensed it as well. But maybe Joseph didn't want to make the sacrifices necessary to work at the dispensary. "Does God have only one place for you? Can't He use you anywhere?"

"That's what I've been telling myself since I started this voyage. But if that's the case, why then do I feel so restless, as though I somehow went my own direction and took the easy way?"

Serving in the slums would certainly be a difficult life for someone of Joseph's social standing. "Patience always said that we might be troubled on every side, but God's still there working things out in His way. And God's way is something we can't always see or make sense of."

Joseph didn't respond. As his silence lengthened, Mercy guessed she'd overstepped her bounds. After all, she was just a poor woman from the worst part of the city. What did she know of God and His plans for Joseph when she couldn't begin to understand His plans for herself?

As the ship rose and then sank again, it threatened to wrest her from Joseph's arms. She clutched his waistcoat but expected the turbulent motion might send her flying like a loose button popped from its thread.

"If we are to perish this night, you most assuredly do not have anything to fear in standing before your Maker," he said and reached out with one arm to grab the beam of the bunk above while continuing to hold her with the other. "You are the closest to an angel I think I shall ever meet on this side of heaven."

His words spread warmth to her limbs, and despite the storm raging around them, some of her fear dissipated. If they survived, she would always cherish his compliment and the knowledge he regarded her so highly. "Thank ye, Joseph."

Once his given name left her lips, she realized her mistake too late to take it back. She closed her eyes and cringed, hoping he hadn't heard her. That was what came of allowing her thoughts to run away with too much familiarity these past weeks.

"Does the use of my given name mean you consider me a friend?"

"I'm sorry, my lord. I shouldn't have—"

"Yes, you should have."

"I would never presume, sir." A friend with Joseph? Who'd ever heard of such a thing—an important nobleman becoming friends with a lowly insignificant woman?

"I would cherish your friendship, Mercy. And I do desire that you put aside titles when we speak together."

Exactly what kind of friendship did Joseph have in mind? Her thoughts strayed to the moment they'd climbed down into steerage and he'd fallen against her and looked as though he might kiss her.

She forced the memory away. Hadn't he assured her he had no intention of seducing her? Hadn't he been a gentleman thus far in every way? If he was offering friendship, she could accept it, couldn't she?

"You're a lord," she said at last, "while I'm a simple poor woman. Who's ever heard of a friendship betwixt two so different?"

"Are we so different really? Perhaps we are more alike than we know."

She mulled over his words, which were like spicy warm ale, heating a deep place in her stomach.

"Since we are to be friends," he went on, "we shall do what we can to divert each other's attention from the peril at hand."

"How's that, sir?" Before he could answer, she became keenly conscious of the way their bodies fused together. She told herself the intimacy was for the sake of safety. He was keeping her warm and protecting her from the storm and danger all around them. Even so, she pictured him shifting so that his lips touched hers for the tiniest of kisses. That was all.

Such a kiss would certainly help to divert their attention from the storm.

But just as vividly as she pictured the shared moment of affection, she pictured Twiggy in the stairwell, the rich landlord's arms wrapped around her, their bodies pressed together, and their lips intertwined.

"He's just a friend, Mercy," Twiggy had told her later. *"That's all. Just a friend."*

Mercy ducked her head away from Joseph. She didn't want a kiss. Didn't want intimacy. Didn't want to chance *any* affection. The last thing she wanted was to become like Twiggy, dependent upon a man, falling into his arms for comfort, and having babies every year. She would be different. She was stronger than that.

"If you tell me a secret about yourself, Mercy, then I shall do likewise."

"I've no secrets, sir."

"I implore you to call me Joseph."

She hesitated.

"Please." His lips brushed against the hollow of her ear as he whispered the word. His plea reverberated in her body to her bones, turning them to liquid. The curve of his mouth and his warm breath were enough to make her want to arch up into him, to bury her own lips into his neck.

She swallowed the desire and instead nodded.

"Then say it," he said.

"Say what?"

"My name."

"Joseph," she whispered.

His fingers at her back tightened, and his breathing turned ragged.

She wanted to speak his name again, knowing that it pleased him, that somehow she had power over this man—although she didn't understand how that could be.

Just as before, he was the first to break the connection. He let his hand fall away from her back and lifted his face so that his mouth was against her hair now. "Tell me secrets from your childhood, something no one else knows."

The cogs in her mind were stuck like wheels in the mud after a heavy rain. She tried to think of something that might interest Joseph, but no matter the memory that came to mind, it was too pitiful to share with him.

"Tell me why you call your mother Twiggy."

Mercy expelled a breath, allowing herself to relax, even as the ship continued its deathly rising and plunging. "Twiggy didn't want us calling her *Mother*. She didn't want the rent collector knowing she had so many children."

Mercy went on to tell him about rent day, known as Black Monday, the day the women lined up outside the pawnshops with anything they might be able to sell so they were ready for the rent collector. He'd evict tenants who couldn't pay up or charge more for those who'd added people to their already-crowded living spaces.

"Twiggy thought she could fool the rent collector about how many youngun's were hers, and yet he always knew."

Joseph was unnaturally silent as she finished answering his question.

Had she disgusted him with the tale? Part of her wanted to bury her face in her hands in shame, for her past was so different from his. How could he even begin to understand what her life had been like? And how could he still want her for a friend?

Before he could apologize or say something to try to make her feel better, she pushed aside her woeful past and changed the subject. "What about you? I'd be right pleased to hear about your family. They'll be a mite more interesting than mine, that's to be sure."

Again he was strangely quiet. The moans of the other passengers blended with the incessant creaking of the ship's timbers and the pounding against the hull. The dampness, the stench, and the filth of the mattress beneath her didn't give her pause. Instead, it reminded her of the hell she'd left behind, the hell that most of these immigrants hoped to leave behind.

Like her, these people had stepped out of the only existence they'd ever known. They'd shown great courage in taking such a risk, embarking on a long, difficult journey, crossing an ocean in an attempt to find a glimmer of hope—a new life for themselves upon foreign shores.

But had they traded one hard life only to be swallowed up by another that was just as hard, just as stormy and fathomless?

She began to think Joseph wouldn't speak any further when he blurted, "My mother, father, and brother perished of cholera when I was away at boarding school."

Mercy listened without speaking as he shared the devastating event, the guilt he still carried that he hadn't been with them in their last hours, that he'd been spared when they hadn't. In the span of one week, he'd lost everyone he loved and was left behind, alone in the world.

She didn't offer him an apology or say anything to try to ease his pain and loss. Instead, she hugged him tighter, suddenly understanding there were different kinds of desperation that drove men and women from their homes out into the deep unknown.

A strange quiet awoke Joseph. After hours of the storm waging battle against the ship, battering her and beating her nearly into flotsam, Joseph was afraid of what would be left of the vessel if she survived.

Truthfully, he hadn't expected they'd live through the night. With the storm having turned into hurricane intensity, and with the ship plunging from fifty-foot waves, he'd waited for the swell that would finally grip the *Tynemouth* and not let go.

There had been one point in the night when a wave had crashed against starboard and rolled the ship broadside so dangerously that he whispered what he thought to be his last prayer. Somehow the ship had slowly righted itself and had endured many more hours of abuse at the hands of the angry sea.

He'd contemplated more than once his jest to Mercy that maybe he was like Jonah. Maybe God was angry at him for walking away from the dispensary and leaving Dr. Bates to flounder and possibly even have to close its doors. Maybe the storm really was his fault, and if he gave himself up and allowed the crew to throw him overboard, God would then calm the sea.

Was he indeed running away as Bates and his aunt had insinuated? He'd thought he could ignore their questions, but last night had shown him he could sail far away, yet he couldn't escape the mighty hand of God reaching out and beckoning him.

Joseph shifted, his muscles stiff and sore from the thrashing they had suffered. At his movement, Mercy stretched, her body still curved into his. The motion made him all too aware of her presence . . . all through the night.

When he'd climbed in next to her, he'd told himself he was sheltering her to keep her safe and to comfort her. Mostly, he'd rationalized that if the ship was sinking, then it wouldn't matter if he lay next to her and held her in his arms for their last hours of life. So he'd given in to his desire to pull her close—closer than necessary—and had savored every luxurious inch of her nearness.

But now, in the strange stillness that told him they'd survived the storm, guilt rushed in like icy waves, lapping at him, telling him he'd overstepped the boundaries of propriety.

Through the blackness permeating steerage, his senses honed in on the whimpering of a child, the healthy suckles of the Donovans' newborn babe, heavy snoring, and the slap of waves still rocking the ship.

It was clear most of the passengers were asleep, likely having only recently fallen into an exhausted slumber after the harrowing night. Joseph couldn't go anywhere yet, not without disturbing and waking the others. Besides, it would still be some time before the sailors opened the hatches and allowed anyone on deck. Even so, he couldn't in good conscience continue to lie on the bed with Mercy.

Her hand slid from his shoulder down to his rib cage. The trail left fire on his skin. But her even breathing near his neck told him she was resting peacefully, that she wasn't aware she'd moved her hand and was touching him with such familiarity.

Throughout the long night, she hadn't done a single thing to encourage his ardor. The problem was, she didn't need to do anything for his desires to flare to life. His body reacted to her whether he wanted it to or not.

Thankfully, the severity of the storm and their hours of talking had helped keep his mind off her nearness. She'd told him stories of her childhood, her antics with Patience, her love for her other siblings, the care she'd given to so many children and families in her neighborhood.

He'd shared too. But after revealing the depth of his pain regarding his family, he'd stayed away from talking about them again and was grateful she hadn't pressed him. She'd seemed content to hear his descriptions of India, China, and other exotic places he'd visited.

The truth was, he liked Mercy, perhaps more than he'd liked any woman in a very long time. But if he hoped to guard not only his integrity but also her innocence, he had to put distance between them. She was clearly naïve in the ways of men and much too trusting. And he couldn't bear to think what might have happened if she'd ended up down in steerage by herself or with another man who might have sorely misused her.

He'd need to warn her to be more careful.

Gently he tried to ease his arm out from underneath her. But she shifted her hand again, this time slipping it around to his back. As before, her merest touch set his skin on fire like sparks from a flint.

He squeezed his eyes closed as if by doing so he could snuff out his body's reaction to her.

"Joseph?" she whispered drowsily.

The sound of his given name on her lips did nothing to ease the low burning inside him.

"Are we saved?" she asked.

"I believe so." His voice came out hoarse and pained. He needed to move away from her without delay.

As if sensing the same, Mercy blessedly jerked her hands from him and scrambled up. The spot she'd just occupied lay open and bare. Without her there, suddenly he felt empty and cold.

"My stars, sir," she whispered, the mortification raw in her voice. "I don't know what's a-come over me. I rightly don't."

He could feel her sitting and gathering the cloak about her with quick, stiff movements. Although he couldn't see her features, he could imagine her mussed hair, flushed cheeks, and wide eyes. He had no doubt she was more beautiful first thing in the morning after awakening than at any other time.

What would it be like to wake up next to her every morning? Certainly not as his mistress, but perhaps as something more permanent?

The thought was entirely unexpected. And was completely inappropriate. He shook his head. The wrestle with death during the night had addled him and made him overly sentimental.

He had no wish for a wife at present, had in fact become the expert at avoiding women during his furloughs home. Even if he'd been ready to get married, he wouldn't dare consider a woman plucked out of London's slums.

He'd defied convention by working as a doctor. He'd defied convention with his outspoken views on issues. But certainly he couldn't throw away social expectations entirely by marrying a woman whose station in life was so far beneath his.

Marriage to someone like Mercy would be highly unacceptable. He would be ostracized by his peers, cast out of clubs, snubbed in social circles. He'd lose the admiration that came with his father's good name and quite possibly forfeit any future chance at serving in the House of Lords.

It was one thing to maintain a free spirit in his youth, to roam the world and delay settling down. Most of his peers had accepted his traveling—at least for the time being. But there was coming a point in the not-so-distant future when he'd have to finally return home and take his place in society.

When that time came, he'd always believed he would find a lovely young woman who would be able to fit into his life. She'd become Lady Colville and would take over running Wiltshire and his London home. She'd mingle among the top echelons of aristocracy and bear him sons, who would inherit his title and fortune.

He couldn't throw all of that away based on one pleasurable night spent next to Mercy. Doing so would make him a fool. Rather, he needed to clear his head and think rationally.

"I never meant anything betwixt us, sir," Mercy whispered. "Nothing at all. I vow it."

Joseph pushed himself up so that he was sitting beside her. He had to hunch over to prevent his head from hitting the beam of the bunk above theirs. "Mercy," he said softly. "Please, say no more. You are not to blame for anything that transpired."

She was quiet and motionless.

The boat rocked them back and forth. His shoulder brushed

against hers, but rather than letting it linger, he forced himself to slide another inch away from her.

"We are forging a friendship, are we not?" he asked, attempting to make sense of their relationship.

"Aye. You're kind to befriend a woman like me. I do thank ye, sir."

A woman like me. She understood the disparity in their stations just as much as he did. She'd said it herself last night. *"You're a lord, while I'm a simple poor woman. Who's ever heard of a friendship betwixt two so different?"*

Mercy realized that even friendship was unusual for two people like them, let alone anything beyond that. And she'd never presume more, would never even dream of it.

His response from the previous night came back to taunt him. *"Are we so different, really? Perhaps we are more alike than we know."*

Who determined their stations? Why did the world need such stations anyway? Would not the world be a better place if a man simply lived in humility and loved his brother or sister as himself, regardless of one's birth?

The questions bumped around in Joseph's mind, like the cargo floating and colliding in the hull's bilge water following the storm. They were the kind of questions that were noisy during storms but then quieted when the waters grew calm.

He'd wait for the calm, and his troubled thoughts would find a way to right themselves eventually. For now, he'd do best to get up and put distance between himself and Mercy.

"Sleep for now," he said as he stood and stepped away from the bunk. "I'll wake you when the hatch is opened."

She didn't respond except to lie back onto the bed.

At her easy acquiescence, inwardly he sighed, wishing for a simpler life where relationships didn't have to be so complicated.

seventeen

"The Falklands," Mercy murmured, unable to take her sights off the meadows with patches of black peat moss and watery bogs, along with the rolling green hills beyond where a herd of cattle roamed freely.

"We be going ashore today too, ain't we?" Ann asked, squeezing next to Mercy at the side of the ship, where the women crowded together to watch the longboat of passengers being rowed to Port Stanley. Even Sarah had ventured out of the cabin. Though pale and weak from the voyage, she'd gained some tolerance for the sea.

"Aye, they'll come back for us, that they will," Mercy assured Ann and the other girls.

The *Tynemouth* had been anchored in the landlocked basin of Stanley Harbor for several days now. None of the passengers had been allowed ashore, however, because the midwinter winds were forceful when they first arrived, too much to attempt the crossing.

Finally today the winds had diminished and the water was less choppy, apparently safe enough for the crew to begin transporting passengers to the shore. The ship had lost one of its longboats during the hurricane-like storm, so the transportation in the one remaining boat had been ongoing most of the morning.

Mercy turned her face slightly, letting the breeze coming off the water cool her cheeks and neck. Joseph had drawn another map on his hand and explained that they'd sailed nearly to the bottom of the world, and the seasons were opposite here.

In London during early August, the streets would be unbearably hot. The sun would bake the garbage, the waste ditches, and even the River Thames so that the stench was insufferable in almost every part of the city. Flies would be out in endless swarms, as would the children trying to escape their sweltering homes.

But here in the Falkland Islands, winter was just beginning to lessen its hold. Though the wind was frigid and the spray of the water icy, the bright green of the meadows and hills filled Mercy with awe. So did the wildlife—the black-browed albatrosses flying overhead and the sea lions calling out noisy greetings from the rocky shore.

Early that morning, she and Joseph had seen penguins through his spyglass. "King penguins," he called them. She'd been delighted to watch them waddling along, tall and straight and proud, their beaks pointed in the air with a snooty attitude. She was hardly able to tear herself away when they heard the first stirrings of passengers beginning to awaken and emerge from their cabins.

Since the storm a fortnight past, she'd taken to meeting Joseph at first light next to the rope that kept the women confined to their portion of the deck. She stood on her side and he remained on his, and their time together was always brief, well before any of the other passengers were awake.

She hadn't exactly planned to meet him there every morning, but after they'd come up from steerage after the storm, he escorted her back to the rope. When she ducked under and tried to give him back his cloak, he'd told her to keep it for the day since it was still raining, and he'd offered to get it from her the following dawn.

When she met him the next morn, the air was damp and foggy, so he'd suggested she keep the cloak another day. One morning had led to another, and he always had a reason for why she ought to have his cloak a day longer.

And she always came up with excuses to make herself feel less guilty about breaking Mrs. Robb's rules by spending time with him. After all, she needed to find out how their patients in steerage were faring, whether he needed her assistance, or how she might help the women who were still weak and sick from the storm.

The past few mornings he'd brought his spyglass to their meetings. They'd taken turns spotting various animals, with Joseph identifying them for her, describing their habitats and giving other fascinating details he'd learned from a book he was reading in his spare time.

Mercy searched the shore for any sign of the penguins she'd witnessed earlier with Joseph. But now that the port city was alive with people coming and going from the several ships in the harbor, the proud little creatures were nowhere to be seen.

The town of Port Stanley was a cluster of bright buildings, smaller than Dartmouth but an inviting place nonetheless. After six weeks at sea, Mercy supposed even a barren, deserted island would have been inviting. She longed to plant both feet on solid ground and walk for as long and as far as her legs would carry her.

Even from a distance, she caught the earthy scent of peat, which Joseph said the people here used for fuel. It was a fine change from the sea air they'd been breathing for weeks.

"There's your Dr. Colville," Ann said with an elbow to Mercy's side.

"Hush now, d'ye hear me," Mercy scolded.

The other girls followed Ann's gaze down the deck to where Joseph was exiting his stateroom. He'd changed his attire and looked every bit the fine gentleman he was. With a tall black hat, blue coat, and white trousers, he had the appearance of someone important and prosperous.

"Oh my eye . . ." Ann whistled under her breath. "That man's sure a fine fella."

Mercy silently agreed but didn't dare focus on him for too long. Already the girls half believed she'd become his mistress, though she'd been adamant that nothing had happened the night she found herself trapped with him in steerage. Since then she'd wanted to prove—especially to herself—that Joseph was a friend and nothing more.

There were still times in the dark hours of the night when she couldn't stop herself from remembering the strength of his arms around her, the solid length of his body shielding her, and the warmth of his whispers against her ear. She'd loved listening to him talk of his travels. He'd painted pictures in her mind about faraway places she'd never known existed.

With the storm raging around them, his closeness and the conversation had helped her to endure the anxiety and fear pressing in on her. More than that, for a few hours she'd forgotten who they were. In the darkness, as the waves threatened to drown them, everything else fell away and they were ordinary people without any differences or problems weighing them down.

She hadn't wanted the time with him to end. She liked him . . . too much so, and she didn't want to like him more and more every day. But she did regardless, and that frightened her.

What if she reached a point where she couldn't say no to him? What if she ended up living immorally like her mum? What if she gave way to the pressure and found fulfillment in the man who made her feel beautiful and wanted?

That wouldn't happen to her, Mercy reminded herself fiercely. She was stronger than Twiggy. And she'd make better choices, be smarter, and have greater self-control.

Mercy stared out at the longboat that was now at the dock, unloading passengers. As much as she liked Joseph, she needn't worry. He'd vowed he had no aspirations for her, that he was saving his affections for the woman he'd one day marry.

She trusted him. After all, if he wanted to initiate more, he could have already done so in steerage when they'd spent the night together. Instead, he'd treated her with kind consideration.

Besides, why would Joseph want a woman like her when he

could choose anyone he wanted? He wasn't even interested in the wealthy middle-class women, not even pretty Miss Lawrence, one of his most frequent patients. Miss Lawrence's comment about him had stayed with Mercy. *"Joseph Colville will have his eyes set much higher—on a woman of noble birth, someone with both title and wealth."*

Laughter from one of Mr. Scott's daughters wafted down the deck. Mercy glanced in time to see both of the young ladies smiling up at Joseph, likely admiring something witty he'd said.

Charlotte and Lavinia were the quiet sort and hadn't mingled with the Columbia Mission Society women, not even with the fancy ladies. Even so, Mercy had seen the daughters on the deck and at the church services Mr. Scott led. They were charming enough, the type of women Joseph could admire. The way Mr. Scott was always jabbering on about his daughters, Mercy suspected that was exactly what Mr. Scott had been aiming for—that Joseph would take an interest in one of them.

"Lord Colville, we'd be most honored and grateful to have you accompany us during our outing today," Mr. Scott said. "My daughters and wife are the most delightful shoppers and will be able to guide us quite skillfully."

At that moment, Joseph shifted so that he was looking directly at Mercy. His brow quirked as if he hadn't expected to connect with her and was perhaps doing his best to keep their friendship as secretive as she was.

She quickly turned her attention to the longboat. The sailors had begun rowing it back toward the *Tynemouth*.

"Thank you for the invitation, Mr. Scott," Joseph replied, "but I regret I must decline. I'm predisposed to do more sightseeing than shopping."

Mr. Scott turned unusually silent. Out of the corner of her eye, Mercy saw that the reverend was studying her with furrowed brows.

"I hate to disappoint you, Lord Colville." Mr. Scott lifted his chin from side to side so as to stretch his neck, something he was wont to do on occasion. "If you are considering sightseeing with one or more of our brides, I must inform you that they will not be going ashore here in the Falklands."

Around Mercy, the women released cries of protest and dismay. Inwardly she objected just as furiously but managed to bite back her words at the realization that Mr. Scott was still watching her.

Was he preventing their going to shore because he assumed Joseph planned to spend the day sightseeing with her?

If so, he couldn't be more wrong. Joseph wouldn't associate with her publicly.

"Not going ashore, Mr. Scott?" Joseph was saying. "Why, is something amiss?"

"Mrs. Robb and I spoke at great length regarding the well-being of our charges," Mr. Scott responded above the growing clamor of the women. "And we have come to the conclusion they will be served best by remaining on the ship, away from the pernicious aspirations of any man who might try to lead them astray."

"That is rather severe, is it not?" Joseph pressed.

"I think not, Lord Colville. Some of the women have already proven to be wayward, and we cannot allow them to have any occasion for giving in to their baser instincts."

Mr. Scott's eyes darted to Mercy again. Did he believe she was to blame for Joseph's indifference toward his daughters? Did he think that by keeping her on board the ship, he'd further entice Joseph to accept his invitation for the outing with his family?

The thought made Mercy feel sick. Maybe he and Mrs. Robb had already made the decision long before this incident with Joseph. Nevertheless, Mr. Scott's message was clear. He didn't want her interfering with his daughters gaining Lord Colville's good favor and affection.

She wanted to shout that she had no intention of sightseeing with Joseph today, that she'd beg Joseph to spend the day with Charlotte and Lavinia so long as Mr. Scott allowed the rest of the women to go to shore. She'd even volunteer to stay behind on the ship if she had to. She couldn't bear the thought that everyone had to suffer and remain on the ship on account of her.

The women's protests grew louder still, so much so that Mr. Scott and Mrs. Robb ordered them back to their cabins. As the door closed behind her and the cold darkness of the tiny room encased her, Mercy stood there frozen in place.

Muffled sobs echoed in the room as the girls threw themselves onto their beds and cried out their misery. But Mercy felt only dread. If she wasn't more careful, she had a feeling Mr. Scott would find a way to ruin her completely, ruin her chance of getting a job on Vancouver Island, and maybe even ruin the opportunity for Patience to come on the next ship.

She couldn't spend any more time with Joseph. She couldn't look at him, couldn't speak to him, couldn't be near him—not even in the smallest way. If she could prove to Mr. Scott that he had nothing to fear regarding her stealing Joseph's attention away from his two daughters, maybe then he'd forget all about her.

Being an invisible, poor nobody was for the best, she decided. She would be wise never to forget that.

eighteen

Joseph waited at the rope, leaning against the ship's rail with what he hoped was a casual posture, one that didn't reflect his inner turmoil and angst.

Mercy wasn't coming.

He glanced again in the direction of her cabin. But the door remained as resolutely closed this morning as it had yesterday.

The sun was rising, sending its brilliant rays across the now-calm bay, turning the water into dazzling blue sapphires and the distant hills into vibrant emeralds. It was a sight he would have enjoyed sharing with Mercy, just as he had many times before during their early-morning encounters.

He didn't want to admit their meetings had become the highlight of his day, yet he couldn't deny the fact any longer. He looked forward to being alone with her at daybreak, when he could watch as her beautiful features filled with wonder and her eyes widened with delight, when he could share all he'd been learning with someone as eager to learn, when he could simply be himself without any pressure to perform as someone who was titled.

True, they'd had but a few minutes together most days, and it had never been quite enough time. But he didn't want those moments to come to an end.

And now clearly they had.

The oranges he'd brought back from shore weighed heavily in his coat pockets. He'd planned to give them to her this morning, had wanted to see her face when she took her first bite, guessing she'd probably never had a fresh orange before.

He ought to be on his way. He had a busy day ahead helping Captain Hellyer transport the mutineers ashore to the British government courthouse, where they would be put on trial for their insubordination.

The captain of the Royal Navy warship that was part of the Pacific Squadron and anchored in the bay had boarded the *Tynemouth* yesterday and addressed the prisoners, reminding them that since they were sailors in the merchant marine, they were allowed to live. If they'd been serving in the Royal Navy, they would have been hung or shot dead for their crimes. The naval captain's words seemed to have sobered the prisoners.

Rather than face execution, the mutineers would be held in the British garrison prison onshore and given a sentence of imprisonment including hard labor. Captain Hellyer had confided in Joseph that he planned to ask for leniency for the mutineers. He considered their confinement in the brig sufficient punishment for their misdeeds, and he would take them on board again if they promised to carry out their work for the remainder of the voyage without giving any more trouble.

The fact was, sailors were hard to come by, and Captain Hellyer needed skilled crew members for the rest of the trip. His mercy toward the mutineers would likely earn him their loyalty.

Joseph had continued to take his turn in the ship's engine room during the past couple of weeks as they charted a course southward, particularly on the fair-weather days when they'd needed the coal engines to power the ship. However, he'd gladly hand the task back over to the sailors for the duration of his time aboard the *Tynemouth*.

While the ship still had many months of voyage before returning to England, only a month remained until they reached Vancouver Island. A month . . .

He pressed a hand against his pocket and the oranges. One month until Mercy disembarked. One month until he said farewell and never saw her again.

With a quick glance to ensure no other passengers were yet on deck, he ducked under the rope and strode toward her cabin door. Even if he was spotted, no one would question his presence or find fault with his delivering the oranges. After all, the fruit was most beneficial to the women's health.

He knocked firmly, then stood back and waited, straightening his cravat and his hat.

A moment later, the door opened a crack, and Mercy peeked through. At the sight of him, she shoved the door closed again.

He jammed his boot into the gap before she could shut him out. "Mercy, have a care. I beg you, just a word."

"We cannot be talking, sir." She rose to her toes and peered beyond him. "Cannot at all."

"Please—"

"'Tisn't prudent, sir."

He glanced over his shoulder. Who was she looking for? She was clearly afraid someone was watching her. He lowered his voice. "Pray, did someone discover our meeting together?"

She shook her head. "No. Maybe. I don't know."

"Then why? Why won't you see me? Did I offend you?"

"It's not on that score, I assure you." In the shadows of the doorway, her features were pale and tight with anxiety.

"What happened, Mercy?"

"Nothing to speak of. But it's what may happen by and by."

Something had definitely occurred to frighten her from meeting with him anymore. Whatever it was, surely she knew she had nothing to fear from him. He pulled the oranges from his pockets. "These are for you and the others." He nodded behind her to the young women watching him with open curiosity.

"I can't—" The excited whispers from behind halted her refusal.

He thrust the oranges into her hands, giving her no choice but to take them. "I shall bring you and the girls more. Tell me what you want and I shall be your humble servant."

Mercy paused and looked at the others as they bombarded her with their instructions. Finally, shaking her head, she faced him. "We've got no way to repay you, sir."

"I'm not asking for payment, Mercy." His voice dipped even lower so that only she could hear it. "I only wish to see you happy."

She ducked her head but not before he caught sight of the pleasure his words brought her. "You've been kind enough. No more is needed."

"You cut me to the quick and shall make a wretched man out of me if you don't allow me to bring you something more." He'd adamantly opposed Mr. Scott and Mrs. Robb's decision to keep the brides aboard the ship. He'd even gone to Captain Hellyer with his protests.

The captain had warned Joseph not to get involved and revealed that Mr. Scott and Mrs. Robb were under a great deal of pressure from the Columbia Mission Society to make sure all the women arrived to Vancouver Island. Apparently, the *Seaman's Bride*, another bride ship from Australia, had shown up in the Vancouver Island capital city of Victoria without any brides, because the eligible women had all jumped ship in San Francisco and made off with Yankees.

As much as Joseph wanted to sneak Mercy off the ship and let her explore Port Stanley in spite of her chaperones' protectiveness, he knew there was very little chance of such a move going undetected and subsequently causing upheaval.

For now, it seemed the only way to help her was by sneaking some of the island to her.

At the sound of a nearby door unlatching, Mercy's eyes widened, and she backed hastily away. "I'm much obliged, sir." She pushed the door again to close it. And this time he didn't have the heart to force her to keep it open. He stepped back and allowed it to shut completely.

"Lord Colville?" Mr. Scott called from the second-class cabins down the deck. "May I be of aid to your lordship?"

"No need to trouble yourself, Mr. Scott." Joseph had no wish for a confrontation with the reverend so early in the morning. He strode back toward the rope, hoping to get away before the man could consume his time and attention. Although Mr. Scott was a decent fellow, there were times, like now, when Joseph would rather be horsewhipped than forced to carry on small talk with him.

"Have you need of an assistant at this early hour?" Mr. Scott persisted, apparently realizing whose cabin Joseph had been visiting. His short, choppy steps resounded on the deck behind Joseph. "As always, I offer you one of my daughters. They are most eager to learn nursing skills and would be heartily pleased to spend time under your esteemed tutelage."

"Thank you, Mr. Scott." Joseph slipped under the rope. "But I have no need for an assistant this morn. Good day." He tipped his hat and proceeded forward.

If by some chance he needed help, the first person he wanted was Mercy. In fact, she was the only one he wanted.

Sitting on the deck, leaning against the cabin wall, Mercy sniffed her fingers. The sweetness of the orange still lingered on her hands even hours after she'd eaten it. She needed to thank Joseph for the treat, but as hard as it was, she couldn't give in to the desire to meet with him. No, she couldn't risk being seen with him again.

"I ain't never had duck," Ann said as she plucked the feathers of one of the wildfowl the men had shot while hiking around Port Stanley. They'd brought so many of the game birds back to the ship that they were more than willing to share the bounty with everyone. Not for the first time did Mercy wish she could give some to Patience and the rest of her family at home.

"I haven't either," Mercy replied. She captured a handful of the soft feathers and stuffed them into one of the mattresses she'd dragged from their cabin. She'd emptied some of the straw that had become flat and rotten from the days of sweating and seasickness, hoping to freshen their beds with the feathers.

The other girls from the cabin, including Sarah, were sprawled out nearby, playing a game with cards the ship's boy had smuggled them. Since Mrs. Robb had left earlier in the longboat to Port Stanley, they could mostly do as they pleased, so long as they stayed within their confined area of the deck.

Some of the other poor women were plucking and cleaning birds too, as happy as Mercy to have something to do to pass the time while they were forced to remain on the ship.

"After the roasting, what about soup?" Ann blew at a feather that drifted near her face.

"Duck soup sounds right good." Mercy scooped more feathers into the mattress.

"Can't remember the last time I had soup." After the weeks at sea, the girl's face was grimy, her black hair stringy and hanging in limp braids. All the more reason the women should've been allowed to go ashore, so that they could have washed up with something besides salty seawater.

Once again, Mercy's chest stung with the indignation of their being left behind. And with the guilt that their plight was partly her fault.

A shadow fell across them. "Why, you little thief!"

Lifting a hand, Mercy shielded her eyes from the sun to find that one of the middle-class women was standing in front of Ann and glaring down at her. She was one of the women in Miss Lawrence's cabin, though Mercy couldn't recall her name. She was short and husky with a wide face, made wider by the looped braids she wore on either side of her head, which drooped like the ears of a basset hound.

"You're a thief," she said again to Ann.

Ann leaped to her feet, her fists balled, eyes flashing before Mercy could set aside the mattress. "Curses on your head!" Ann spat out the words.

"I do declare, you're wearing my necklace." The woman reached for the chain and pendant that had slipped out of Ann's collar.

Mercy stood and brushed her feather-coated hands against her skirt, catching only a glimpse of the necklace—an oval shape with a few pearls and other small jewels affixed to it—before Ann's fingers closed about it in a protective gesture.

"It's mine, that it is," Ann insisted. "And I won't let the likes of you try to take it away from me."

The women lounging on the crowded deck grew quiet, all eyes upon Ann and her accuser.

"The likes of me? You're the dirty imp!" the woman snapped. "Now give me back my necklace this instant, or I shall report you to the captain and demand that he have you whipped for your insolence and thievery."

Mercy's neck pricked with the realization that in all the weeks she'd known Ann, she'd never once seen her wearing a necklace. Where could Ann have gotten it, if not by stealing? Of course, Ann was as good a pickpocket as any on London's streets, at least according to all her boasting and the stories she told of her many misdeeds.

"I swear it," Ann said to Mercy as though sensing her thoughts. "I didn't steal the necklace. Not this one."

The problem was, Ann was about as good at lying as she was stealing.

"I found it when I was emptying one of the pots overboard," Ann explained. "Figured I couldn't throw a thing like this away."

From the horror and disbelief widening the eyes of the middle-class ladies, Mercy guessed they'd never before fished a halfpenny out of the waste in a kennel or gutter. 'Twould be nothing at all to take a piece of jewelry out of a dirty chamber pot. Mercy would have done it herself without a second thought.

But keep the jewel for herself? No. Not here aboard the ship.

"You stole it right out of my cabin," the woman said.

"I ain't shamming." Ann kept a tight grip on the necklace. "It were in the pot, hidden-like, until I started to tip it out."

"Ask any of these other ladies," said the accuser, gesturing to them, "and they will tell you the necklace is mine."

Several of the ladies nodded.

Miss Lawrence was among those nodding. Her copper-colored hair was covered with a fashionable hat, which shielded her face from the sun. But even with the hat, she'd gained a fair amount of color and a smattering of new freckles. With the calm weather of late, she'd had a reprieve from feeling sick. No doubt the passing of weeks had helped ease the wounds on her neck and back, for she seemed to move about less stiffly than she had when she'd first boarded.

She nodded politely at Mercy, acknowledging her presence, and Mercy dipped her head in response. "Miss Spencer," Miss Lawrence said, stepping around the other poor women who'd been plucking and cleaning the fowl, "may I have a word?"

"Not now, Miss Lawrence." The stout woman didn't take her eyes off Ann, as though she was afraid that Ann would disappear with the necklace before she could get it back.

Miss Lawrence pursed her lips and lifted her chin as she approached Miss Spencer. She glanced from her roommate to Ann and back again, uncertainty flittering in her pretty green eyes.

Mercy had noticed Miss Lawrence wasn't talkative with the other ladies and held mostly to herself. She guessed the woman would probably prefer not to get involved in the dispute at hand, that she was likely accustomed to deferring. And yet here she stood, apparently hoping to help resolve the matter.

"Miss Spencer . . ." She paused and lowered her voice. "I was in the cabin when you dropped the necklace into the chamber pot."

Miss Spencer finally had the grace to release Ann from her glare. Instead, she turned embarrassed eyes upon Miss Lawrence. "Since you were there, you can attest to the fact that it was an accident. It slipped from my hands."

"Truly, 'twas most unfortunate." Miss Spencer started to respond, but Miss Lawrence continued before she could say anything more. "And yet I do distinctly remember you saying it was rubbish and that you had no need of it."

"That was because it was . . . well, irretrievable."

"'Twould appear it was retrievable after all."

Ann still hung on to the necklace, her expression wary. Mercy nudged her, hoping she'd take the hint that she needed to do the right thing and give the necklace back. But the girl averted her eyes.

Miss Lawrence cleared her throat. "If this girl went to the trouble of finding and . . . cleaning the necklace, then perhaps she deserves to have it."

The anger had dissipated from Miss Spencer's expression, leaving indecision in its place.

Miss Lawrence leaned in and whispered, "Surely you have no desire to wear the item now that everyone knows where it has been."

The blanching of Miss Spencer's face was answer enough.

Mercy guessed that in the world they came from, jewelry was disposable. Once lost, they could easily buy another. At the very least, neither would consider the value the necklace could bring once it was pawned, an amount sure to feed and house a poor family for days if not weeks.

Without another word, Miss Spencer spun and stalked away, heedless of the piles of feathers she disturbed in her wake.

Miss Lawrence stayed a moment longer, studying Ann as if she wanted to say more. But at Ann's defiant expression, the gentlewoman took a step back. She offered Mercy a tentative smile before continuing on to her side of the deck.

As Mercy watched her go, new admiration settled inside her for the gentlewoman. She sensed this voyage was the start of a journey for Miss Lawrence too, and she prayed the woman's scars would one day fully heal.

nineteen

A cry awoke Mercy. She jolted up in bed and listened. Through the complete darkness of the night, only the faint rumble of the engines and the soft lapping of waves met her ears.

They'd left the Falkland Islands several days ago and had sailed around Cape Horn without any problems. Some of the middle-class women had spread stories about traveling around the Horn and had stirred up fear regarding the rough waters, the strong winds and currents, the large waves, and even the possibility of icebergs. They told tales of the many shipwrecks, along with the treacherous williwaw winds that blasted down from the mountains, coming out of nowhere and driving ships to their death on the rocks. "A sailor's graveyard," they called it.

Thankfully, God spared the *Tynemouth* another brush with death. He'd apparently decided the gales they'd already encountered had been sufficient.

Instead, the ocean waters and breezes, while cold and crisp, had been calm even after they'd rounded the Horn and entered the Pacific Ocean. Although the peaceful waters were a blessing while rounding the dangerous tip of South America, the *Tynemouth* had gone for days with no wind to fill her sails and was apparently using up the new supply of coal much too quickly to fuel her engines when she should have sailed northward under the force of the wind.

"Mercy" came a whisper belonging to Ann. "You awake?"

"Aye, that I am, dear heart."

"It's Sarah. She's burning up with fever and retching until she ain't got nothin' left." Ann's whisper was laced with fear, a fear that curdled in Mercy's stomach like sour milk.

Mercy cast aside her coverlet and crawled from her bunk. She bumped against Ann, who was kneeling on the floor next to Sarah's bed. "Have you been awake for long with her?"

"Awhile now," Ann admitted softly. "I was hoping to let you sleep."

The gesture had been a kind one, especially after Mercy had been up the past night tending to the women who'd suffered from food poisoning.

With the bountiful catch of wildfowl hanging out on the decks in the cold of the Southern Ocean breeze, they'd gorged themselves on duck soup and goose drumsticks. The gentlewomen had declared it was a feast just like Christmas, although for Mercy and the others from the city slums, it was their first real taste of such rich, roasted meat.

After several of the women had gotten sick last night, Mercy overheard Mrs. Robb speaking with Mr. Scott about the fowl, that even with the cold weather the meat was turning rancid and causing the sickness. The captain and Dr. Colville made the unpopular decision to throw the remaining carcasses overboard to prevent any further contamination.

Mercy laid a hand on Sarah's forehead. The girl's skin was burning up. At Mercy's touch, Sarah thrashed and cried out, the same hoarse cry that had awoken Mercy moments ago.

"Is she suffering from the tainted food too?" Ann asked.

"I don't think so." The others hadn't been afflicted with fever, nor had they been delirious. They'd been miserable to be sure, but by morn they were through the worst of the ordeal.

Sarah's symptoms were different. Mercy ran her hands down the girl's arms and across her back. The fever radiated from the girl like water boiling on the hob.

"She's in a bad way, Mercy," Ann whispered. "I ain't never seen her so ill."

"Bring me the water pitcher," Mercy instructed as she began to unlace Sarah's nightshift.

"I've already been cooling her with a rag." Ann pressed a cold cloth into Mercy's hand. "She needs the doctor, that's what."

Mercy nodded. *Joseph*. She'd seen little of him during the rest of their stay in the Falklands. He'd knocked on her cabin door a few more times in the early morning hours to deliver fresh eggs, a loaf of bread, more oranges, and even some soap.

The girls were delighted with each of his gifts, and she had been too. Though she'd wanted him to linger, she didn't encourage it. And he hadn't stayed, as if he'd finally resigned himself to abiding by the strict rules that kept them from socializing.

Joseph had checked on the sick women the previous night but was gone by the time Mercy went to care for the ailing ladies.

"I'll go fetch the doctor," Ann said. Before Mercy could protest, the girl was out the door.

Mercy knew Ann was right. They needed Joseph. Even so, Mercy's heartbeat began to thud at the prospect of being near him. She couldn't deny she longed for his presence, dreamed about him, and hungrily took him in each time she glimpsed him from a distance.

Sarah cried out again, and Mercy dipped the cloth in the cool water and bathed the girl's face. She'd cared for plenty of sick children and knew, at the very least, she had to bring the fever down.

"There, there, my lamb," she murmured as she sponged the girl's forehead.

Only minutes later, the door opened, and Joseph rushed in along with a gust of cool night air. His shirt was askew and only buttoned halfway. Her face heated at the memory of the first time she'd brought Sarah to his cabin and she'd caught him in a state of undress.

He knelt on the floor next to her. Even as she moved to give him space, his presence overwhelmed her. He was close enough that she could almost feel the strength in his arm as he pressed his fingers against Sarah's pulse.

"What are her symptoms?" he asked without preamble. When tending patients, she'd learned he was single-minded, almost brusque in his determination and devotion. And she liked that about him.

"Fever and vomiting," Mercy answered.

"Did she voice any other complaints?"

Ann had followed the doctor inside the cabin and now stood behind him. "She complained of being sore."

"Aching in her joints?" Joseph pressed a hand to Sarah's forehead.

"Guess so," Ann replied. "That and being tired."

Joseph slipped his arms underneath Sarah. "I'm taking her to my cabin so I can examine her more thoroughly and administer something to help bring her fever under control."

Mercy nodded.

As Joseph stood with the girl, she opened the door for him. And as he stepped out onto the deck and started striding away, she remained where she was in the doorway. She was torn between wanting to be with Sarah and needing to keep her distance from Joseph.

"You ought to accompany her, Mercy," he said over his shoulder without breaking his stride. "She'll want you by her side."

Mercy let out a sigh, turned and grabbed her cloak, and wrapped it around her nightgown. Joseph was right. No matter the rules, she had to stay with Sarah. Besides, she could be back in her cabin before Mr. Scott or Mrs. Robb became any wiser.

Not bothering with her shoes, Mercy raced after Joseph. The

deck beneath her bare feet was frigid, the night air blowing off the open sea freezing. Sometimes she forgot they were still near the bottom of the world, where the weather was winter-like.

Once inside Joseph's cabin, she helped him lay Sarah out on the bed. Then for some time she worked with him at trying to bring Sarah's fever down. Finally, the medicine he'd given Sarah began to calm her thrashing.

As the girl rested more peacefully, the light of dawn brightened the porthole and cabin. "I must go," Mercy whispered.

Joseph stood at his counter, the lantern illuminating his medicines as he worked to mix another concoction. At her quiet declaration, his movements stilled along with the clinking of glass.

"I'll take Sarah with me," she said, not wanting to burden Joseph any longer with the girl's care.

Joseph pivoted, a small glass bottle in one hand and a stirring stick in his other. "She cannot leave here, Mercy." His grave expression sent a shiver through Mercy.

"I have to get back to my cabin before Mr. Scott figures out I've been gone."

He shook his head. "I'm quarantining Sarah here until I'm certain she's not contagious."

"Contagious, sir?"

"It's quite possible she has smallpox."

Mercy pressed a hand to her mouth to stifle a gasp.

"Her symptoms point to the disease. But I shan't know for certain until I see if she develops a rash."

Outbreaks of smallpox happened regularly in London. The disease spread rapidly, leaving both children and adults dead or disfigured with blister scars. The afflicted were always shunned, fear rising up to take the place of common decency.

"Have you experienced smallpox," Joseph asked, "or perhaps been inoculated?"

She shook her head.

"Precisely what I expected."

Her mind set off to scampering like a cornered kitten. "The other girls in my cabin?"

"I shall quarantine them as well, until I'm certain none of them has been exposed."

"Then we'll stay with them, sir. It'll be for the best thataway—"

"If the others haven't been infected yet, then Sarah surely will infect them."

The rest of Mercy's protest faded.

"If you leave Sarah here, there's yet the chance for you to return to the others and avoid further exposure."

"No, Doctor. I won't skulk away to safety and leave her alone."

"I shall be here with her."

"But she needs me."

Joseph nodded as though he'd expected her to say as much.

Even with her mind made up, the doubts lingered. "It's just that my chaperones won't take kindly to—"

"Lord Colville" came a voice from outside, followed by rapping against the door.

Mercy stiffened. It was Mr. Scott. He'd certainly wasted no time in coming after her.

Before Joseph could reach the door, the reverend continued, "When I was retrieving Mercy this morning to attend to the sick women, her cabin mates informed me that she has interrupted your sleep and burdened you with the care of one of the orphans who has taken ill with the tainted food. My lord, I—"

Before he was finished with his sentence, Joseph pulled open the door to reveal the short gentleman, already attired in his black suit and stiff white collar. He bowed at the waist and held himself in the position.

"How may I be of service to you, Mr. Scott?"

The reverend straightened, allowing himself a sweeping look inside the doctor's stateroom, taking in Sarah on the bed and halting on Mercy, who knelt on the floor next to the sick girl. His eyes widened, and he swiftly looked away.

Only then did Mercy realize she was still attired in her nightgown and the cloak. Her bare feet poked out shamefully, revealing her ankles. Mercy yanked at the thin material and attempted to cover herself.

Mr. Scott's expression turned grave, almost ashen. He bowed again before straightening and tugging down his coat hard as if that could somehow cover Mercy's feet. "I beg you to forgive me, my lord. It is I who must try to make amends on behalf of my wayward charges for disturbing you so indecently."

"They have not disturbed me, Mr. Scott. On the contrary, I prevailed upon them when I learned of Sarah's fever."

"You are indeed generous, Lord Colville. In fact, you are more generous than most men of your esteemed station. And I do thank you for understanding." The reverend gestured at Mercy and hissed, "Come now, girl. You must return to your cabin at once before you shame us all with any further misconduct."

Mercy stood, ducked her head, and rushed to obey, feeling his wrath upon her back as though he'd struck her there.

"Mr. Scott, do not be so hasty." Joseph's tone became stern.

"Have no fear, my lord. I shall not leave you without assistance. I shall send one of my daughters to your aid just as soon as they have partaken of the morning meal."

"Perhaps. But only if you wish to expose your family to a potential case of smallpox."

Mr. Scott stiffened, and his eyes filled with horror. He backed out of the doorway until he was standing well onto the deck. "I did not realize the illness was quite so serious, my lord. I regret this intrusion."

"I thank you for your concern, Mr. Scott," Joseph said. "Now, would you be so kind as to inform the young women in Mercy's cabin that they too are under quarantine until further notice? I shall be along soon to examine each of them."

"Quarantine? Very well." Mr. Scott swallowed hard, a visible lump sticking in his throat at his collar. "What about your own well-being, Lord Colville? You must take yourself out of the danger immediately."

"I have been inoculated. But even if I had not, I could not *skulk* away to safety."

At his emphasis on the word Mercy had spoken only moments ago, her gaze shifted to him, only to find that he'd glanced at her too. Something in the warm brown of his eyes told her that he was for her, that he wouldn't leave her to fend for herself against Mr. Scott or against the threat of disease.

The realization loosened the fastening that had locked her heart tight, the one that kept her outside the wicket garden gate peering at something she could never have and never be a part of. He'd offered his friendship and was certainly proving it to her now. She couldn't reject him any longer.

Mr. Scott continued to retreat from the cabin. From the panic evident in the reverend's expression, he seemed not to have taken offense at Joseph's comment but was too consumed with getting himself safely away from any danger.

Joseph closed the door and shut out the reverend completely. "Good riddance," he mumbled under his breath.

Mercy stood still, hesitant, unsure if he'd meant for her to overhear him.

He crossed his hands behind his back and faced her again. "Forgive me. I shouldn't have spoken my thought aloud."

"No matter, sir—"

"Mercy," he said softly. "You are no *girl*. And I certainly have no wish to be thought of as *sir*."

Was he referring to Mr. Scott's order to her? "Upon my word, I think nothing of it."

"His attitude shows a complete lack of regard for you as a person."

She didn't know what Joseph expected her to say in response. She was born into her station, and he born into his. There wasn't anything that could be done to change the way of things. "Maybe we're all like ships," she finally offered. "When we're born we're put out to sea and can't always control our fate or destination. We have only to ride out the journey as best we can."

As soon as the words left her mouth, she hurried to Sarah's bedside, the heat of embarrassment creeping up her neck and into her cheeks.

"Perhaps," he responded. "But having a friend along for the journey helps greatly in easing the burden. Would you not agree?"

"Aye, that I would." When she chanced a look at him, his brow slanted up. He didn't have to say any more for her to know he was asking about their friendship and what had become of it.

What *had* become of it? Had she let fear and shame stand in the way? Maybe theirs was an unusual friendship. But surely there were no rules that would prevent their being friends, especially for the short time they had left aboard the *Tynemouth*.

She offered him a smile.

When he smiled in return, she felt as if she'd been given a treasure, one she'd cherish long after their ships parted ways.

At the soft tap against the door, Mercy sat up. For a moment, she stared at the walls, unable to figure out where she was. As her focus moved to Sarah lying on the bed in front of her, Mercy released a breath.

She'd fallen asleep in the chair she'd pulled up next to Sarah. Apparently she was more tired than she'd realized. She reached out her hand to Sarah's forehead, only to feel hot skin. The poor girl was still burning up.

Silently, Mercy berated herself for slumbering. She needed to get more water and continue to cool Sarah's flesh. But even as she stood, she fought back a yawn.

Another knock came then, echoing loud in the stateroom.

Mercy froze.

What if Mrs. Robb had come this time to order her back to

her cabin? Mrs. Robb was not quite as awed by Joseph as Mr. Scott and wouldn't hesitate to force her to return if that's what she wanted. With Joseph gone to see to his other patients, who would defend her?

Actually, she wasn't breaking any rules by helping to take care of Sarah, and surely Joseph had explained by now that with the threat of smallpox, Mercy needed to stay with the sick girl. Yet as she mulled over the excuses in her mind, her heart quavered.

If only she had a little of Ann's belligerence or a tiny amount of her strength in standing up for herself. Ann had taken to proudly wearing the necklace she'd plucked from the dirty chamber pot. It was a badge of sorts, almost as if she wanted to prove her worth. She'd said society might consider her and the rest of the poor women to be nothing more than throwaway trash, but underneath they were really treasures.

"Mercy?" came a soft voice, nothing like Mrs. Robb's, from the other side of the door.

"Aye, 'tis me." Mercy tried to place the voice. "Miss Lawrence?"

"I've come to offer my assistance."

Mercy crossed to the door and opened it a crack to find the young woman pale but intact, a far cry from the moaning and wretched condition she'd been in only the night before. "You're still weak, miss, and ought to be abed."

"I am feeling a hundredfold better today." Miss Lawrence smiled. "I wanted to thank you once again for coming to my aid. I know the other ladies are just as grateful."

"No need for any thanks, miss. I'm happy to do it."

She nodded, then hesitated. "When I heard Sarah may have the smallpox, I knew I had to offer my help."

"Thank ye, miss. But the best thing you can do is stay away, that it is. Otherwise you'll be catching the illness too."

"Not to worry. I've already been vaccinated."

Mercy opened the door wider.

"My stepmother required it of both me and my sister," she

continued. "Her first husband died of the disease. And when she saw the way the smallpox ravaged the body, she was terrified of anyone else contracting it."

Mercy supposed she could use the assistance, as she was so tired still. But part of her protested allowing any other woman into Joseph's cabin. It was foolish, she knew. He'd offered her friendship, and she wanted to have that friendship all to herself. She didn't want to share it—not even with someone as considerate as Miss Lawrence.

"Dr. Colville is still waiting to learn what the disease is," she finally responded. "If it's not smallpox and is something else, we sure don't want to be exposing you or any of the other women, now, do we?"

"No, I suppose not," Miss Lawrence said reluctantly.

"I'll be right well," Mercy added. "You just go on and take good care of yourself, d'ye hear?"

Miss Lawrence smiled again, this time wearily. "Very well. But please do not hesitate to call for me if you need assistance. I shall be only too glad to help you."

As she walked away, Mercy quietly closed the door and leaned against it. Her heart thudded a hard tempo. Why had she sent Miss Lawrence away? Surely she wasn't jealous or concerned that Joseph would show interest in other women.

She shook her head adamantly but couldn't shake the realization that the only woman she wanted Joseph to be with was herself.

twenty

"How is Sarah this morning?" Joseph asked as he entered the sick bay. He shook the rain from his coat and had to brace himself against the sway of the ship as she battled the choppier waters north of the equator.

Mercy sat on the edge of Sarah's bed, holding a cloth against the girl's wan face. At the early hour, Mercy was already dressed in the blue gown she always wore. He'd ashamedly realized it was her only gown when he went to fetch her belongings from her cabin the first morning she was quarantined.

The girls in her quarters had handed him one set of clothing and her shoes. When he'd inquired after the rest, they shrugged and told him that was all. He was surprised by his anger over her meager wardrobe and was tempted to ask the captain to drop anchor at the next port city, so he could take Mercy into town and buy her a dozen gowns.

But such a demand would have mortified Mercy, causing her to retreat back into herself. And he didn't want to risk that again, not after they'd formed a solid friendship while she was quarantined with Sarah.

"I think she took a turn for the worse during the night, the poor lamb," Mercy answered without breaking from her ministrations.

"I suppose that means you didn't sleep much." He'd given Mercy leave of his stateroom and moved to another one amidships. Most of the passengers knew by now that Sarah was deathly ill with a possible case of smallpox. Yet with no sign of blisters, he'd begun to think they had escaped an outbreak.

None of the other girls from Mercy's cabin had developed any symptoms, so after several days he'd lifted their quarantine. Even so, he hadn't lifted the quarantine on Sarah or Mercy.

It wasn't safe yet, he'd told himself. There was still the chance that what Sarah suffered was contagious, typhus perhaps. Her fever lasting almost two weeks was symptomatic. But without the telltale red rash upon her abdomen and back, he couldn't be certain.

Sooner or later he'd have to allow Mercy to leave. But for now, she made no mention of it, and he hadn't suggested it either. Maybe he was being selfish. He could admit he thoroughly enjoyed her companionship. He'd been teaching her about the medicines and herbs he'd brought along. He'd shown her his medical instruments and explained what they were used for. Some evenings he'd taken to reading aloud to her from his books.

She always listened attentively and was a quick learner. More than that, she shared interesting perspectives he hadn't considered and was above all kind and thoughtful in everything she did.

Joseph crossed the cramped cabin and assessed Mercy first, taking in the dark circles under her eyes, the tired lines in her forehead, and the wilt of her chin. "I shall take over Sarah's care while you rest."

"I'm not tired." Even as she said the words, she yawned.

He smiled at the contradiction. "You're correct. You're not tired. You're exhausted."

"And you worry too much."

"If I didn't worry about you, you'd soon find yourself committed to the deep." He liked worrying about her. And a part of him had begun to panic at the realization the *Tynemouth* would reach San Francisco within a week's time. They would spend a few days in the American city refueling before sailing to Vancouver Island directly afterward.

If the rumors were true, the men in the colonies would be anxiously awaiting the bride ship's arrival. Mr. Scott had indicated that hundreds of men wanted wives. Hundreds. The mere idea of swarms of men coming down from the mining camps and mountains to greet the *Tynemouth* and the brides filled Joseph with foreboding.

The more he thought about other men staring at Mercy, lusting over her, and plotting how to have her, the more his gut twisted. She was too sweet, too lovely, too unspoiled and shouldn't have to be auctioned off like a prize horse to the highest bidder. She deserved better than that.

He didn't actually know how the brides would be distributed. Still, he had no doubt Mercy would be one of the first chosen. Her beauty was unrivaled. Even tired, she was exquisitely lovely.

"How was your meeting last night?" she asked. "Will we have enough fuel?"

Joseph had gathered late last night with Captain Hellyer and the other ship's officers. With the continued calm weather, they'd used up most of their coal reserves as they resorted to the steam engines instead of wind power to propel the ship forward. Now without coal, they were attempting to come up with solutions for how to reach San Francisco.

"Starting today we're collecting all available wood—crates, chairs, writing tables, anything we can do without."

Her eyes widened. "We'll be burning the furniture to fuel the engines?"

"Hopefully we'll continue to have wind in the sails. But if we don't, then yes, we'll have to burn what we can to keep moving."

She stifled another yawn.

"Come now." He motioned toward the spare bunk. "You really must rest." Though he was tempted to help her up into the bed, he'd maintained extraordinary self-control during her confinement and had refrained from any physical contact.

There were moments his mind reverted to his time holding her while they were in steerage together, to the memory of how soft and womanly she'd been. He could ill afford another incident like that. Rather, he needed to honor her and their friendship in every way—no matter how many temptations might come his way. He was a strong man. Surely this time with her had proven it.

"Mercy?" came Sarah's weak voice.

Mercy bent and pressed a kiss upon Sarah's brow. "Hush now, dear heart."

"Take this." Sarah slipped a ring off her thumb and held it out to Mercy with a shaking hand. The narrow gold band was devoid of any engraving or jewels.

"Stuff and nonsense." Mercy knelt, took the ring, and attempted to put it back on Sarah's thumb. The girl's hands were skeletal after the poor nourishment of the long voyage, especially the past two weeks with her eating next to nothing.

"'Tis the only thing I've got that was my mum's," she rasped out through labored breaths.

"You're keeping it, d'ye hear me?" Mercy said sternly.

Joseph dropped to his knees next to Mercy. Sarah was dying. Deep down he'd known it. He just hadn't wanted to say it, to give up hope for Mercy's sake. She was so desperate to save Sarah, and he didn't want to see her disappointed.

Even now, he sensed Mercy would fight for the girl's life until the very end.

"I want you to have it." Sarah's eyes were glassy with the fever that still ravaged her body.

"No," Mercy whispered almost harshly. "You're gonna get better, Sarah. Just you wait and see. And then you'll wear it again right proud, that you will."

Joseph wished there was something more he could do for the orphan. His mind scrambled for a solution, another concoction or tincture, anything to save the girl. But even as he searched for an answer, his experience told him he'd done all he could.

"Mercy?" Sarah said, this time more faintly.

Mercy placed another kiss upon the girl's cheek. "Don't say any more, my lamb. You must save your strength."

Sarah struggled to turn herself so she was facing Mercy directly. Then she thrust the ring into Mercy's hand again. "You're like her. My mum."

Mercy gently smoothed the girl's forehead, brushing away lusterless hair.

"I'd be right happy knowing you'll be wearing her ring."

"Then I'll wear it, that I will," Mercy whispered. She slid it on her finger and held it up for Sarah to see. "But just until you're better."

Sarah nodded, then closed her eyes as though she had no more strength to keep them open. With the task completed, she expelled a breath and fell silent.

Joseph could almost see the girl's spirit depart from her body. She was gone. He didn't need to check her pulse or breathing to know.

Mercy sat quietly, unmoving, and stared at the ring. The acquiescence in her expression told him that for all her brave words, she knew the truth as well—Sarah wouldn't be getting better. The sweet girl had left them.

Joseph waited for Mercy to say something, to unburden her sorrow, to express her disappointment. Surely her heart was overflowing with sadness. How could it not be? After pouring so much of herself into Sarah.

A moment later, Mercy stood.

Joseph rose too, still watching her face closely. He wanted to offer her comfort. In fact, his heart ached knowing how hard this was for her.

"I'll help you with her body." Mercy's voice was soft but didn't waver. "Tell me what to do."

For a while they worked together getting the body ready. Once Sarah was bathed, dressed, and her hair combed and neatly plaited,

Joseph carried her to the cabin where he was staying, called for the captain, and made the arrangements for a committal service.

Finally, having followed the proper procedures, he returned to the sick bay. Mercy was kneeling on the floor. She'd taken the sheet off the bed and was scrubbing at a stain from Sarah's vomit. She rubbed the bar of soap across the same spot over and over, her knuckles white, the veins in her wrist beating through her skin.

Closing the door quietly, he crossed to her. "Don't trouble yourself with the sheet."

She found another stain, dipped the soap into the basin, and attacked it.

Helplessness seeped through him. He wanted to say or do something to show her he understood the loss. But he had no words, and there was no way to soothe such grief. He knew that all too well.

He waited for tears to begin sliding down Mercy's cheeks, but she focused on the linen with dry eyes.

Finally, he knelt and took the sheet and the soap out of her hands.

Only then did she turn to look at him. Her sea blue eyes raged with stormy waves. But she waited with the same resignation he'd seen when the little girl she'd brought to the dispensary had died, the same resignation that filled her face when Mrs. Robb had come after her the first time she'd brought him Sarah, the same resignation when Mr. Scott had demeaned her and called her *girl*.

Was it possible Mercy had experienced so much death and despair in her life that she accepted it without question? Was it such a normal part of her existence that she could so easily move on?

He held her gaze, needing to understand her in a way he couldn't explain. As though sensing his questions, her eyes flashed, revealing depths of churning pain. Then just as quickly, the flash was gone.

"What else can I do?" she asked. "Maybe I should sterilize the washbasin and pitcher."

He didn't move, didn't say anything.

She dropped her attention to Sarah's ring and began twisting it on her finger.

"She said you're like her mum," Joseph whispered.

Mercy nodded.

"That's because you loved her so unconditionally and so thoroughly."

She slipped the ring off and held it out toward him. "I don't want it."

"You should have it, even if you don't wear it. It will keep her memory alive."

"Take it." She thrust it into his hand, but he pushed it back. With a jerk, she grabbed it and threw it with such force it bounced against the far wall above his desk. It landed on the floor, and the sway of the ship sent it rolling underneath the bed.

For a moment, she stared under the bed. She then looked at him and cupped a hand over her mouth, her eyes wide and radiating disbelief and embarrassment at her outburst.

Had she ever allowed herself to feel the pain of her losses? Or had she repressed everything for so long, she didn't know how to grieve?

"I'm sorry, Joseph. I shouldn't have thrown it." She began to feel around under the bed.

"There's no need to apologize," he replied.

She groped under the bed farther. "I don't know what came over me. I right promise I won't do that again."

He started to reach for her, wanting to make her understand that she needn't fear him, that she had every right to be angry, but then he hesitated, his fingers hovering over her shoulder. Did he dare touch her? He shouldn't do anything that might undermine his integrity, and yet it seemed the situation with Sarah's death permitted him some leeway.

She released a small cry of frustration. Far within that cry, he heard the echoes of her heartbreak.

"Mercy," he said softly, touching her shoulder and gently squeezing.

Her frantic movements ceased, but she didn't lift herself. Instead, her body slumped as if she'd given up her will to fight.

He ought to remove his hand and put space between them. But even as he willed himself to be noble and honorable, his desire to comfort her was stronger. He let his fingers linger, then slide slowly down her back before returning again to her shoulder.

She shuddered.

He closed his eyes and fought the battle against his flesh for an agonizing moment. He needed to hold and console her as much as he needed to breathe. Without hesitating any longer, he brought his hands to her waist, lifted her into his arms, and wrapped her close just as he'd done that night in steerage.

She came willingly, pressing her face into his chest. Her arms slid around him, and her fingers clung to his back, digging in as if she were drowning and he was her only hope.

"What's wrong with me, Joseph?" Her voice was ragged. "I don't want the ring. I don't want to remember Sarah. I don't want to keep her memory alive."

He stroked the length of her braid. "Maybe it's easier to forget." Was that what he'd been doing? Trying to forget about his family? He'd shoved and kicked his pain aside for years too. How could he offer advice to Mercy when he'd been running from his grief for so long that he'd nearly lost himself in the process?

"If you ignore your pain, you can go on," he whispered. "But it's still there, buried deep."

"I don't want to think on it. I can't." She sucked in a trembling breath.

He wanted to soothe her, to tell her she didn't have to remember, that it was all right to forget. Yet he sensed what the forgetting had already cost her, for she too had lost some of herself.

"Maybe unearthing the sorrow allows it to finally surface and then dissipate." He didn't know. Perhaps the sorrow would always be keen. Even so, if they never brought it up, he suspected the grief would only fester and hurt them all the more.

"I don't want to unearth my own grief," he admitted, "but maybe we can help each other to do so."

She pulled back and studied his face. "Will you tell me of your grief, Joseph? The pain you feel deep down?"

He hesitated. Could he really do it? Could he dig up the past and lay it bare? To Mercy?

She lifted a hand to his face and gently cupped his cheek as he'd seen her do oft to Sarah. "I'd bear your pain if I could."

His chest swelled with need—the need to know her, body and soul, the need to have and to hold her. "You already bear the sorrows of too many," he said quietly. "I would take yours instead."

While comforting her, she'd ended up almost sitting in his lap, her face mere inches from his, her lips so near, beckoning him.

A warning clanged within him like the ship's bell.

He knew he should put a healthy distance between them, but as he shifted his hands to her hips to move her away, her eyes widened as if she'd suddenly realized their predicament as well and didn't know what to think of the closeness. She dropped her sights to his mouth. As she did, desire darkened her pupils.

That was his undoing. His fingers tightened and drew her forward and not away, giving her little choice but to lean into him. As she pressed herself against his chest, he nearly groaned. Before the sound could escape, he caught her mouth and let his lips fuse with hers.

The meshing was warm—soft and pliant and passionate. She was timid but moved in a way that gave him all the permission he needed to deepen the kiss. Thirsty for her beyond anything he'd ever known, he gave way to the longing that had built within him for days, perhaps weeks.

twenty-one

Mercy was adrift in a sea of pleasure that swelled with greater intensity with each passing moment. Joseph's mouth moved like an unending current against hers. One hand claimed her waist, the other slid up her back to her neck.

This was where she could forget about her pain, forget about Sarah's death, and about everything else that was wrong in the world. This was where she wanted to be, the place she never wanted to leave.

What she couldn't understand was why she hadn't come to this place before? Why had she resisted the pleasure? Why had she resisted *him*?

His mouth broke from hers, and a small cry of protest slipped from her swollen lips. Before she could think of a way to draw him back, the warmth of his lips connected with her neck.

Another involuntary gasp slid out, her breathless ecstasy. Her escape. Losing herself to reality. No matter the cost.

Her mind spun back to the garret room, to the time she'd accidentally opened the door to find Twiggy gasping out her pleasure in the arms of her boss from the rag factory.

Mercy froze.

Had it been the same for Twiggy? What if the affairs and the resulting gifts had been more than just a way to help her family survive? Had her mum given herself over to carnal pleasures, perhaps to dull the pain and brokenness of her life? Or was it the one place in her life that Twiggy felt wanted and needed and in control?

At her stillness, Joseph broke his kiss again. His breathing was hot against her neck, his chest rising and falling against hers.

Mercy had believed she was so much stronger than Twiggy, that she was better, that she'd be different. But maybe she was more like her mother than she realized.

She closed her eyes tightly to ward off the unwelcome thoughts. She didn't want to think about Twiggy right now. She wanted to think about Joseph. Their relationship was special, wasn't it? It was different from her mother's illicit relationships. Joseph cared about her, desired her, treated her with such tenderness. They'd even become friends.

Yet the more she tried to justify the passion of the kisses she'd shared with Joseph, the more the reality of their stations—their very different stations—rose like a thick fortress wall that couldn't be scaled.

All she'd ever be to Joseph was a shipboard diversion. Perhaps he hadn't set out to kiss her any more than she had him. She wanted to believe he'd meant what he said about saving himself for his future wife. But she supposed their close proximity, their shared sorrow, their budding friendship had all led to this moment.

"Mercy." His whisper was strained. "You have my highest regard and affection—"

She stopped his declaration by pressing her fingers against his lips. "Don't say it."

His eyes were the rich velvety brown she loved, made darker with a flood of his desire. It would be so easy to lose herself in them, to lose herself to him.

He started to speak again, but she cut him off by pushing away and scrambling to her feet. "We've got no future together beyond this voyage. We both know it."

He stood and braced his feet apart to keep his balance against the swaying ship. She grabbed on to the top bunk beam to prevent herself from toppling against him. Next time she ended up in his arms, she wasn't sure she'd be able to make herself break away.

"Tell me you don't feel something too," he demanded hoarsely.

She wanted to deny him, deny her feelings, but his eyes begged for honesty. "Aye, you're right easy to like. Too easy. But we can't—I can't—that is, I won't be giving you favors."

"Devil be cursed." He thrust his fingers into his hair. "I meant what I told you. I don't want favors. I'd sooner be hung from a gibbet."

"Then what do you want from me, Joseph?" The question was a daring one for a woman like her. But she couldn't hold it back. She needed to know what he really wanted. Why did he bother with her at all?

He gripped the back of his neck, kneading his muscles.

She found herself holding her breath.

"I don't know," he finally said and dropped his arms in a posture of defeat.

Her breath slowly eased from her, along with a low burn of disappointment. She shouldn't be feeling let down, not in the least. She ought to be satisfied with friendship, which was more than anything she deserved from a gentleman like Joseph.

Besides, she'd made her decision long ago not to get involved with *any* man. There had been plenty who'd made offers. Plenty who'd wanted her. But she'd never paid them any heed. And she couldn't start now.

Against her will, her attention drifted to Joseph's mouth. And her thoughts shifted to the taste of his lips upon hers, the dizzying sensation of the connection. An exhilaration and a passion she never knew existed, one she craved again. With him. Only him.

Mercy wrestled to free herself from the pull of desire, dragging her sights up to his eyes only to find herself drowning in them, drowning in whatever this was between them.

She released her hold on the bunk. "I'm a-going back to my cabin now." She took several unsteady steps in the direction of the door.

He didn't say anything, didn't try to stop her.

The lurching of the ship propelled her in long stilted steps, giving her no choice but to grab on to the door handle. She knew she should be grateful the ship had pushed her away from Joseph instead of directly into his arms. She sensed he was as weak in this moment as she was, that he would have swept her close again, and he'd be as powerless to let go of her as she would him.

Her fingers tightened around the handle. She took a deep breath and forced the door open.

A cold sea wind threatened to shove her back inside the room. She fought against it, stepped onto the deck, and wrestled the door closed behind her.

The rushing of the ship as it cut through the sea, the spraying of the waves, and the splattering of rain pushed her against the outer wall of Joseph's cabin. She clutched the paneling as though she could somehow hang on to him.

Then the ship tilted and urged her away, and she let the motion carry her stumbling down the deck. Her ship and journey were different from Twiggy's. She was different. She had to be.

No matter how difficult it might be, she would prove to herself that she could chart a new way forward. That was all she'd ever wanted. And now that she was so close, she wouldn't let herself be thrown off course because of one stolen moment of pleasure.

She'd forget it ever happened. She'd forget about Joseph. And she'd forge ahead.

twenty-two

Joseph stared out into the thick fog and tried to focus on Captain Hellyer's prayers.

"'Man, that is born of a woman, hath but a short time to live, and is full of misery. He cometh up, and is cut down, like a flower; he fleeth as it were a shadow, and never continueth in one stay.'" The captain's voice rang out over the assembly.

Overhead, the ropes creaked and the sails whined as though mourning with them. The sailors stood at the railing, Sarah's body wrapped in canvas on a plank held between them.

"'Thou knowest, Lord, the secrets of our hearts,'" the captain went on, reading aloud in his strong baritone from the *Book of Common Prayer*. "'Shut not thy merciful ears to our prayer; but spare us, Lord most holy, thou most worthy Judge eternal. Suffer us not, at our last hour, for any pains of death, to fall from thee.'"

The Lord knew the secrets of their hearts.

Joseph shifted, his suit coat and cravat constricting him. He had half a mind to unbutton his coat, but what good would that do? He'd be just as uncomfortable. His secrets would still strangle him, the secrets that were bare before the Judge eternal.

Joseph had certainly done his best to conceal his indiscretion with Mercy from two days ago when he'd kissed her so shamelessly in his cabin. Hiding the deed from the other passengers had been easy enough. Even now, Mercy, standing on the main deck below with her arms around the girls from her cabin, hadn't looked up at him as he stood next to the captain on the quarterdeck. They could be strangers to each other for all the interaction they'd had since she'd walked away from his cabin—since he'd let her walk away.

He could conceal the kiss and their shared passion from the rest of the ship, but he couldn't hide it from himself. No matter how hard he tried not to think about kissing her, the moment of holding her and tasting her and wanting her refused to fade from his mind. If anything, his remembrance only fueled his need for her, the need to be with her again and kiss her without ceasing.

Even as he longed for her, he loathed his weak will, loathed the heat that speared him and the way his body betrayed him. He'd prided himself on being strong, a man of virtue and integrity, on possessing more self-control than other men.

And yet in the end he'd proven he wasn't any stronger. He'd allowed his passion to overrule his good judgment. He'd given of his affection and his ardor when he should have saved it.

"'Forasmuch as it hath pleased Almighty God,'" said the captain, "'in His wise providence to take out of this world the soul of our deceased sister, we therefore commit her body to the deep.'"

Joseph fingered the silver band in his coat pocket. He'd retrieved Sarah's ring from under the bed and was determined to give it back to Mercy. But he needed to find a way to speak with her privately, not only to give her the ring but also to beg for her forgiveness. He didn't deserve it, but he was cut to the quick to think that she now regarded him poorly for ill-using her when he'd vowed he wouldn't.

He'd rehearsed his apology on a dozen occasions. Guilt had a way of making a man into a poet.

The sailors began to tilt the plank. Sarah's body, weighted with a lead beam, slid quietly away and, an instant later, splashed into the sea. The waves then rose up to swallow her, and she sank out of sight.

Somberly the passengers watched, some crossing themselves, others dabbing at their eyes.

The captain spoke the last words of the service. "'Through our Lord Jesus Christ, at whose second coming in glorious majesty to judge the world, the sea shall give up her dead. The corruptible bodies of those who sleep in Him shall be changed and made like unto His glorious body.'"

"Amen," Joseph whispered along with the others gathered there.

As the crowd began to disperse, Joseph watched Mercy and the remaining girls from her cabin amble away.

"I know you tried valiantly to save her, Lord Colville," Captain Hellyer said. "I hate to lose anyone, but we can be grateful that whatever ailed her wasn't contagious."

In his navy coat, military trousers, and sharp black hat, the captain remained dignified and impeccable even after weeks at sea. His graying beard and mustache were neatly trimmed and his keen eyes kind.

"Yes, Captain," Joseph replied. "We most certainly can be grateful we lost no one else."

Mercy had been spared, and yet somehow he felt as though he'd lost her anyway.

Joseph couldn't stop from seeking her out again, surrounded by the other brides, as she returned to her portion of the ship. He considered going directly to her cabin and asking to have a word with her. But he suspected she wouldn't leave her room, and he certainly didn't want the young women in her charge to hear what he had to say.

"A word, Lord Colville?" the captain said.

Something in the man's tone brought Joseph's head around.

"I may speak to you freely, may I not?" Captain Hellyer asked. At their spot on the quarterdeck, they were alone except for the helmsman at the wheel.

"Of course."

"The woman. Do you love her?"

The captain's question took Joseph aback so that he nearly stumbled. "The woman?"

"The one you can't take your eyes from." The captain nodded in Mercy's direction. "Do you love her?"

"Come now, Captain. That's rather personal."

"It's clear she has turned your head."

Joseph peered off into the thick fog, struggling to maintain his composure. He assumed he'd hidden his attraction toward Mercy. But if the captain had noticed, how many others had as well?

"May I give you a piece of advice?" Captain Hellyer asked.

Already he knew what the captain would tell him, that a man of his station might love a woman like Mercy, but that nothing could come of it, that he must eventually let her go.

Joseph attempted a smile. "Will you allow me to refuse?"

"Your father was a good man."

Immediately Joseph stiffened.

"I asked you to be my ship's surgeon because I was convinced you were like him."

The need to escape the captain's discourse about his father pressed against him like a westerly. He especially had no wish to have his own shortcomings held up against his father's stellar character.

Joseph slipped his hands into his coat pockets and started to bow, needing to make his escape. His fingers brushed against Sarah's silver band and halted him.

He'd wanted Mercy to allow herself to weep over Sarah's death, knowing the open expression of grief would be healthy for her. Why then couldn't he do the same? When would he stop fleeing from every mention of his family and start facing his loss?

"I was correct," the captain said. "You are like him in many ways."

The unexpected statement eased the tightness in Joseph's chest just a little.

Captain Hellyer peered toward the horizon and spoke quietly.

"My older brother fell in love with a woman who was a commoner, a poor domestic who laundered our family's clothing."

Joseph shifted to study the captain's face. As usual, the man's expression was stoic.

"There were many among his circle who encouraged him to marry a woman of his station and to keep his laundress as his lover, if he must keep her at all." The captain paused, then added, "Your father was one of only a few who looked beyond the barriers of class to see Mary as the lovely and dignified woman she truly was."

His father had looked beyond the barriers of class? The revelation shouldn't have surprised Joseph, but it did nonetheless.

"Against all adversity and criticism, including my own, my brother married her. On the day of their wedding, my father disowned him."

Joseph could hardly breathe.

"Of course, after the scandal, I married the woman expected of me," the captain continued. "I so proudly believed I was doing what was right where my brother had sinned. I believed I would succeed where he had failed. And I would be happy while he was miserable."

"And were you?" Joseph asked.

"My brother learned early on what I would not understand until much later. When God gives us someone or something, we must not spurn the gift. We must cherish it until our dying breath."

Joseph sensed the captain's story went much deeper than he was sharing, but already he'd bared his soul and Joseph decided not to press him for more.

"I'm ashamed to admit I loathed your father for a long time for the stance he took with my brother."

"But you said you respected him—"

"I do now, but it's too late to tell him so, is it not?" The captain looked overhead to the sails and then to every part of the ship, his experienced eyes not missing a single detail. "He aided my brother. Gave him shelter and employment. Eventually he loaned him money so he could immigrate to Canada and start over there."

Joseph's throat closed up with a swell of unexpected emotion.

"As I said, your father was a good man. I was saddened to hear of his passing."

Joseph tried to swallow but couldn't get past the tightness.

Captain Hellyer fell silent then as if to allow the steady rhythm of the waves to soothe all regrets.

"My piece of advice, Lord Colville?" he finally said.

Their conversation had come full circle, only this time Joseph was ready to receive the advice. "You have convinced me not to refuse it, Captain."

"Good." The captain's mustache turned up with the hint of a smile. "As a physician, you do not let the barriers of class stand in your way. You have cared equally for every soul aboard this ship regardless of who they are and where they come from. . . ."

Captain Hellyer's words of affirmation reached deep into Joseph's heart. He knew his father would have said something similar. His father, who had championed the cause of the downtrodden, labored hard at changing the views of his peers in the House of Lords, who supported many causes he'd hoped would bring about positive change in London's poorer communities. Yes, his father would have approved of Joseph's willingness to serve rich and poor alike. A stinging pricked the back of Joseph's eyes.

"My advice," said the captain, his voice turning gentle, "do not let the barriers of class interfere with *anything*. Not work. Not life. And certainly not love."

With a nod, Captain Hellyer patted him on the shoulder, then strode away, leaving Joseph to stare after him, his thoughts tossing and turning in the captain's wake.

Love.

Did he love Mercy? He was attracted to her. Of that he had no doubt.

Joseph pictured her when she'd knelt in front of him and cupped his cheek. *"I would bear your pain if I could."* He pictured the earnestness in her eyes, her beautiful face. The sincerity, the selflessness, the depth of her kindness . . .

Not only was he drawn to her sweet spirit, but he'd been shaken to the core by the strength of his physical reaction to her. One touch was enough to upend his world and everything he'd believed about himself.

But love?

He wasn't so sure he could claim such life-enduring affection. Nor could he claim he was prepared to make that step into declaring his love, even if he did sense it. He was still restless, not ready to marry and settle down. Eventually when he was ready, he'd have to return to England and live there.

As for Mercy, she was aboard a bride ship on her way to finding a husband in a new land with new opportunities. After the difficult life she'd experienced, she was determined to leave behind London and the world she'd come from.

Joseph blew out a breath. The kindest thing he could do now was to proceed with his apology and then let her go.

twenty-three

With Sarah's death dampening everyone's spirits, the last days of the voyage seemed to drag on forever, especially as Mr. Scott and Mrs. Robb once again denied the women the opportunity to go ashore in San Francisco. At the news, the girls in Mercy's cabin became despondent, even more so than when they'd been left behind on the ship while in the Falklands.

Thankfully, they hadn't anchored in the American port for long, experiencing only a few days of misery while the others took in the town and all the pleasures it afforded. Hardest of all for Mercy was watching Joseph row away with Mr. Scott's daughters on either side of him, knowing they were the kind of women Joseph deserved and needed.

As the ship finally trudged up the Washington coast and they got their first glimpse of Vancouver Island, the excitement of being so near their destination began to push away the gloom. When they entered the Strait of Juan de Fuca on the evening of the seventeenth of September, a flaming sunset on the Pacific horizon seemed to give a final salute and guide them into the sheltered waterway.

Although the fast-falling night made sightseeing difficult, the beams of a lighthouse ushered the ship through a narrow passage into Esquimalt Lagoon, where they glimpsed the outline of the rugged rocky shore with its thick vegetation, as well as the naval base headquartered along the harbor.

At the first light of day, Mercy gathered with the other women unable to get enough of the Vancouver Island coastline spreading out before them, an endless array of thick evergreens blanketing the land. In the distance, cloud-capped mountains covered in snow towered to the heavens.

They'd had an early-morning visit from natives in their canoes paddling alongside the ship and attempting to barter fish. Most of the women had been frightened at the sight of brown-skinned people, but Mercy had been fascinated. The natives hadn't stayed long, especially with the angry shouts of marines on a patrol boat demanding that they leave.

Around the Esquimalt Lagoon flocks of birds perched on boulders or high in the trees, floated in the calm water, and graced the sky overhead. One of the other women had informed them that Vancouver Island was known for its migrating birds, that in the autumn they'd see ducks, geese, swans, loons, herons, and many others. The only one Mercy could name with certainty was the sea gull, which seemed to be the same in this new world as it was back in England.

At midmorning, Mercy still couldn't tear herself away from the rail. She let the gentle breeze wash over her with the scents of pine and soil. And she relished the music of the bird calls that had serenaded them since their arrival.

If only she could spend a few moments with Joseph, he'd share everything he knew about the area. He'd likely read all about the birds and would pull out his spyglass just as he'd done in the Falkland Islands and help her learn how to identify them. He'd tell her about the trees and the names of the mountain ranges. And he'd explain the history of the area, including why the naval base was necessary here in Esquimalt, so close to Victoria.

She glanced across the deck to where he stood with some of the welcoming committee members who had boarded the *Tynemouth* a short while ago. He was attired in a suit she'd never seen him wear before and looked more dashing than usual. She had to admit, she was relieved he hadn't left the ship yet.

Their vessel was too large to sail directly into the shallow waters surrounding Victoria. So earlier in the morning, the ship's passengers had been ferried to Victoria, including those from steerage. While watching groups leaving in smaller steamboats, the women had grumbled and talked about jumping ship. After all, they'd been on the *Tynemouth* for over a hundred days and hadn't been allowed off once.

But Mrs. Robb had quieted the complaints with news that a welcoming party would be arriving on board today, and that the Victoria Female Immigration Committee was making arrangements for their group to come ashore tomorrow.

The women had cheered. Although Mercy was excited about the prospect of soon being on land, a quiet misery had settled over her at the realization she would never see Joseph again.

She had no reason to wallow in their parting. She hadn't spoken to him and had hardly seen him since she'd left his cabin over two weeks ago after Sarah's death. And he hadn't sought her out. Not that she'd expected him to. Most certainly not. Such a notion was just as outlandish as the idea that he might want to be with her.

"*You have my highest regard and affection.*"

His declaration whispered through her mind as it often did. And every time the words brought back the sensations of their intimacy, the burning of his lips against hers, the passionate pleasure of his kisses . . .

"Come now, Mercy." Ann tugged her sleeve and drew her out of the forbidden memory. "Let's take a walk along the deck like them other women. They're gettin' all the attention wearing such pretty togs."

"Let them have it." Mercy squeezed Ann's arm and patted first Minnie's, then Flo's, then Kip's cheeks. The morning light showed the grime that rimmed their faces and hair and clothing, the result of three months without proper bathing.

The wealthier women had opened their trunks for clean garments. Later, Mercy noticed several of them dumping their soiled shipboard clothing into the sea. Mercy was half tempted to jump in and save the items. The dirty garments were better than anything she or the other poor girls wore. But she hadn't wanted to make a fuss and have one of the wealthy women accuse her of stealing the garments the same way Miss Spencer had accused Ann of taking her necklace.

Now in their pretty dresses, the middle-class women were drawing the introductions of the gentlemen of the welcoming committee. Even Miss Lawrence was talking with several important-looking men, who were attired in naval uniforms of white trousers and blue coats decorated with gold trim. Though the gentlewoman's expression remained pleasant and mild, Mercy could see cold fear in her eyes and couldn't keep from wondering again what had happened to Miss Lawrence.

The gentlewoman had been kind enough to offer to help with Sarah's care during the quarantine, but Joseph had been there when she visited for the second time and had insisted that Miss Lawrence stay well away until he could determine the cause of Sarah's illness. Mercy hadn't had the opportunity to interact with Miss Lawrence again, except for brief greetings in passing.

The pretty lady was having no shortage of admirers today even though she'd assumed she was too much of a spinster to draw attention.

After such a strict policy against interacting with men, Mercy was surprised Mrs. Robb and Mr. Scott were allowing the mingling. She supposed now that they'd arrived, the two chaperones would have no choice but to give them more freedom. At least Mercy prayed it was so. Then she could find a job without having to worry about finding a husband.

"You'll have plenty of notice right soon enough," Mercy

reminded the girls. "What with all the gentlemen have told us, the fellas on shore are getting ready—shining their shoes and buying new collars."

"Oho," Ann said. "I bet a crown you'll be the first one fetched right up."

"You know I'm not planning on letting any man fetch me," Mercy said quietly but firmly.

"That's a'cause you already got a rich fella uncommon sweet on you." Ann made kissing motions in the air, which drew the giggles of the other girls.

"I've got no such thing." Mercy refused to follow their glances in Joseph's direction. While she hadn't admitted to anyone how much she liked him, she supposed her attraction hadn't been hard to figure out.

"Then why's he keep looking at you like he's about to drink you for his morning dram?" Flo asked, her voice much too seductive for one so young.

"My stars," Mercy chided. "You sure know how to go on all the livelong day about him." Another reason why she was ready to get ashore—so the girls would stop talking about Joseph whenever they saw him. "Be on with you now. Take a walk over by them gents. But behave yourselves, d'ye hear me?"

As they moved along and left her alone, she felt strangely exposed. She hadn't wanted to come out of the cabin when the welcoming party boarded, not when she'd learned the party was comprised of Victoria's most prominent citizens and that they were all men. But Mrs. Robb had insisted the women clean up as best they could and then lectured them on appropriate conduct before ushering them out to the main deck.

Mercy turned her attention to the sky, to a broad-winged bird effortlessly soaring over the calm lagoon waters. Maybe she could make her escape back to the cabin and hide there until the ordeal was over.

With a final glance at the beauty of her new homeland, she

slipped away, promising herself she'd have plenty of time to take in the view in the days and weeks to come. And eventually, in a few months when the *Robert Lowe* arrived, she'd be able to share the beauty with Patience. Her sister would like Vancouver Island right well and would be healthy with all the fresh air and open space.

In the meantime, she had to figure out how to avoid becoming a bride.

Joseph's attention strayed again to Mercy. His pulse crested and then crashed at the realization she was moving away and seemed to be trying to leave the gathering unnoticed.

"I have to say I'm highly pleased with the quality of the women," said Lieutenant Commander Verney. "They overall appear to have been well raised and generally seem a superior lot to the women usually met with on immigrant vessels."

"Very true," said another as he sipped from the fine brandy the committee brought aboard to share among the men.

Joseph had hoped for an opportunity to speak to Mercy again, but his duties had kept him busy over the past week as the passengers began to reach their limits of endurance, their afflictions increasing with each passing day—scurvy, saltwater boils, rotting teeth, indigestion, and the like.

Even when he wasn't tending passengers, Mercy was nowhere to be seen.

With this being the last day the women would be aboard the ship, he'd decided he must seek her out, even if that meant going to her cabin and pleading with her to give him one last opportunity to see her.

Perhaps now, while the passengers and crew were occupied with other matters, he could finally speak with her and offer his overdue apology.

"Excuse me a moment, gentlemen," Joseph said with a slight bow. "I shall be back momentarily."

He wound through the clusters of people while maintaining an air of nonchalance. As he started in the direction she'd gone, he guessed she was heading back to her cabin. He veered down a different passageway, hoping he could catch up with her before she reached the cabin.

His footsteps thudded against the damp wood of the deck. As he neared the corner that would lead him to the starboard side near the bride rooms, he halted and listened. The steps drawing nigh were soft but quick.

Before she could pass him, he moved from the passageway.

At the sight of him, she halted abruptly and gasped. "Joseph. You scared me worse than a creeping tomcat."

"Forgive me. I didn't intend to frighten you." Up close, he feasted upon her lovely features—her high cheekbones, elegant brows, and the long lashes framing her blue eyes.

She dropped her attention to the deck, breaking the connection so that everything he'd tried to ignore and escape came rushing back. She was leaving the ship. She would soon find a husband. And she would belong to someone else.

He'd lose her forever.

He was well aware she wasn't his and therefore he couldn't truly lose her. Nevertheless, an ache swelled in his chest that he couldn't explain, which made him feel suddenly desperate.

Drawing in a breath, he forced himself to complete the task he'd come here to do. "I've longed for the occasion to speak with you again so that I might apologize for my behavior the last time we were together."

Her lashes flew up, revealing confusion in her eyes.

"For when we—when I—" he stammered, embarrassed now to speak of their encounter.

"You're sorry for kissing me?" Her question contained a note of hurt.

"No. I'm not sorry for . . ." He glanced around, making sure they were alone. Then he lowered his voice and finished, "Of course I'm not sorry for kissing you, Mercy. I'd kiss you again in a second if I could."

A flush flared in her cheeks. Did her question and that look mean she'd enjoyed kissing him as much as he had her?

The realization made him take a step closer. "I apologize for ill-using you, for taking advantage of the sadness and grief of the moment. You were not in your right frame of mind. And I am the lowest form of ocean scum and the foulest of creatures to have given you my affection in such a moment when I ought to have saved it."

Saved it for whom? The question smacked him in the chest.

He'd vowed he would save his wholehearted devotion and affection for the woman he planned to marry. But what if that woman was Mercy? What if he threw aside caution and took her as his wife? Then he'd no longer have to feel guilty about liking her so much. In fact, perhaps marrying Mercy was the noble way out of his predicament.

"You're being too hard on yourself, Joseph," she chided lightly. "You meant well, and I did too. But we let the situation get the right best of us, that's all."

"I'm not too hard on myself. Rather, I'm not severe enough, and wish I could make amends to you."

Her lips stalled around her words. Her expression said she wanted to assure him, but that she didn't know how.

A fire sparked to life in his gut. All he could focus on was her mouth—her perfect, soft lips and the need to bend down and kiss her again. Even as he fought to restrain himself, he realized if he married her, he wouldn't have to withhold himself any longer.

"I shall do the right and honorable thing by you, Mercy," he said in a rush before he could find an excuse not to say it. "I shall make amends by marrying you."

At a knocking nearby, Joseph glanced around the deck again. He saw no evidence of anyone there. As far as he could tell, they were still alone.

"Be my wife, Mercy." He wanted to tug her into his arms and bury his face into the smooth span of her neck. But her eyes had widened, and her cheeks had changed from pink to pale in a single heartbeat.

Maybe he was going about this all wrong. Perhaps he ought to express himself better, tell her of his affection and how much he desired her. After all, Captain Hellyer had advised him not to put stock in class differences, hadn't he?

"We don't have to let your background and station stand in the way of our being together." He waited, expecting her eyes to alight with gratitude and happiness that he was willing to overlook their enormous differences.

Instead, lines creased her forehead.

"Please say something," he whispered.

"Aye. It's a really kind offer for a woman like me, to be sure." Her words sounded familiar. She'd said something akin to this when they were stuck together in steerage during the storm. And somehow, in both instances, the words didn't sit right but rattled noisily in Joseph's mind.

"We shall overcome any obstacles, you'll see," he assured, more for his own sake than for hers.

"I won't know nothing about being the kind of lady you need, Joseph."

"I shall teach you everything."

"What if I can't learn?"

"You will learn, trust me."

She didn't argue any further with him, but doubt emanated from her eyes.

The uncertainty knocked him off-balance. What was he doing proposing marriage to Mercy? Had he gone mad? Hadn't he told himself he wasn't ready for marriage, that he needed more time?

And what about Mercy? If he let her go with the other women into Victoria tomorrow, she'd find another man to be her husband. After all, that was what she'd come here for. From everything he'd heard, the men of Victoria were most eager to meet the women from the bride ship.

"I must admit," he said, "I own to jealousy at the thought of you going ashore tomorrow and letting another claim you."

"You needn't worry on that score."

"The fellows will take one look at you and fight over who's to have you." Though he tried to keep his voice light, darkness seeped into him at the very thought of another man claiming Mercy, touching her, kissing her.

She twisted her hands into her skirt and stared at the tips of her shoes sticking out from its very dirty hem. Finally, she looked up. "I'm not planning to get married, Joseph."

He watched the play of emotions on her face—guilt, uncertainty, as well as resignation. "I don't understand. Is that not why you came here? To find a husband?"

"Not at all. I didn't know this was a bride ship till I was aboard. My plan is to find a job, not a husband. I need to prepare for when Patience arrives."

"So you're not going ashore tomorrow looking for a husband?"

She shook her head solemnly. "I got my heart set against marrying."

He didn't know whether he should try to convince her otherwise or accept her decision.

"I never did see a happy marriage," she continued.

"That doesn't mean yours has to be the same."

"I'm not sure I'd know how to be different," she admitted. "Though I'm trying hard not to be Twiggy, seems I've got more of her inside me than I thought."

"No doubt we are all shaped by where we come from," he said. "But can we not chart a new course for ourselves? You have already begun to do so, have you not?"

She was quiet and contemplative, so that the ringing call of the gulls overhead reminded him they'd reached land and were no longer adrift at sea.

"I've not only got my heart set against marrying but against having babes. And I wouldn't never ask a man to give up having sons and heirs on account of me."

"You don't want to have any children?" After seeing how much love Mercy poured out upon others, especially the younger ones, her statement made no sense to him.

"Never," she said forcefully.

"But why?"

"Can't bring more babes into the world when there are already too many needing homes and help and love."

"Have you considered that perhaps the joys of marriage and having a family help people to endure the difficulties of life?"

"I don't rightly know."

"Surely God doesn't require that we deny ourselves pleasure until all problems are eradicated. Then none of us would ever find enjoyment in life, since this world will always have trouble."

"But if we can ease the trouble, shouldn't we do it?"

She sounded like Dr. Bates. Joseph didn't like to think of his friend back in London, struggling to keep the Shoreditch Dispensary open by himself, but the thought had continually nagged him nevertheless. At times like this, his heart felt heavy with the guilt of abandoning Bates when he so needed the help. He prayed his friend had found a way to manage without him, yet deep inside he feared Bates would eventually have no choice but to close up his practice at the dispensary.

He couldn't think of that now. Time was slipping away. He needed to return to the committee gathering before someone noticed he was gone and came looking for him.

"I am to assume, then, you've given me your answer regarding my proposal of marriage?"

She nodded.

"I cannot persuade you to change your mind?"

"No, Joseph."

He wasn't sure whether to feel relief or disappointment. "Can I at least persuade you to accept my apology?"

"It isn't necessary."

"You would ease my conscience if you kindly accepted it."

"Very well." Her tone contained a note of sadness.

Why was she sad? He studied her face, searching for clues. Was she distressed they wouldn't be together? At their inevitable parting? Or that he hadn't tried harder to win her hand?

He straightened his shoulders and lifted his head. He'd done more than most men would. And she clearly didn't love him if she could refuse him like she did. Not that he'd expected love. In truth, he wasn't sure what he'd expected.

"Good-bye, Mercy." His confusion warred with his desire to have her. "I wish you the very best here on Vancouver Island. I pray you find everything you've hoped for." The throbbing in his chest turned into a hard thudding. He needed to leave now before he did something he would later regret, such as pull her into his arms, kiss her, and plead with her to stay with him.

He forced himself to spin and walk away. He had to let her go. It was best for them both. Hopefully, his aching heart would learn the lesson soon enough.

twenty-four

Mercy leaned against her cabin door and tried to still her racing pulse. Her body screamed with the need to chase after Joseph and tell him she'd changed her mind, that she'd marry him, that she never wanted to leave him.

My stars. He'd proposed marriage. To *her*. And she'd turned him down.

She sank to her knees and buried her face in her hands. What had she done? All she'd had to do was say yes. One little word. And she could have stayed with Joseph and returned to that place where she was lost in his embrace, in his touch, and in his passion. That place where she could shut out her problems and pain. That place where, for just a little while, she could be happy.

"Surely God doesn't require that we deny ourselves pleasure until all problems are eradicated."

Joseph's words burst back into her thoughts. He was a wise man and never failed to challenge her. And that was just one thing of many she loved about him. But for all his qualities she admired and the friendship they'd developed during the voyage, was that enough reason to get married?

She shook her head. Even as he'd proposed, she saw the relief in his eyes when she turned him down. He was attracted to her right well enough and thought he was doing the noble thing by her after their kiss, but there wasn't a mite of thrill in him.

If she ever changed her mind and got married, she didn't want a man who was marrying her out of guilt and obligation. Nor did she want a man who was only putting up with her background and station.

Instead, she wanted someone who couldn't live without her and who loved her exactly for who she was. Aye, she'd want a man who thought being with her forever was just a bit exciting and not drudgery.

She'd never asked for much in life, had never expected more than her lot. Was she expecting too much now?

The question rose up to torment her. Everything Joseph had offered was like a fairy tale for a woman like her. Other women in much higher stations would covet the position she found herself in, to have his affection and his proposal of marriage. They wouldn't have hesitated to accept him, no matter his motivation for asking.

"No, you little wretch," she whispered. She'd made the right decision. Now she just had to convince herself of it.

A knock sounded on the door.

She sat up, her heart jumping into her throat. Had Joseph come back to plead with her? What if he declared his love? Could she turn him down a second time? Would she even want to?

The knock came again.

Pushing to her feet, she smoothed down her skirt. She hesitated before brushing stray strands of hair back, only then realizing her fingers were trembling. With a deep breath, she pulled open the door and at the same moment attempted a smile.

Mr. Scott stood before her, his shoulders rigid. "You have some explaining to do," he stated too quietly.

"I didn't think anyone on the welcoming committee would notice me gone. Honest."

"Your familiarity with Lord Colville must cease at once." His voice wobbled with an undercurrent of anger he was too pious to express.

The words silenced Mercy. Had Mr. Scott overheard her conversation with Joseph? If so, how much?

"'Course, sir," she replied, curtsying at the same time she lowered her gaze. Urgency propelled her into doing whatever she had to in order to protect herself, even if that meant groveling at Mr. Scott's feet. "There's nothing betwixt Lord Colville and me, sir. Nothing at all."

"It would appear you are in the habit of speaking falsehoods."

"No, sir—"

"Silence, you upstart!" His voice rose, but then he quickly stretched his neck before speaking calmly once more. "I heard every word of your conversation just now."

Mercy closed her mouth, her protest dying on her lips. Had he followed her or Joseph away from the gathering only to hide and listen to them?

He lifted his chin and seemed to be attempting to peer down his nose at her, except he only managed to reveal his nose hairs. "Not only have you been cavorting with the esteemed Lord Colville, but you have turned his pity upon you. You certainly do not think he cares about you other than how he might gratify his flesh?"

The bluntness of Mr. Scott's words slapped Mercy, leaving her mortified.

"No?" Mr. Scott said. "You are a greater fool than I thought if you believe for one moment a man of Lord Colville's station has any inclination toward you."

"I didn't know. Leastways I didn't think so."

"Believe me, girl, I know."

Girl. She thought back to the last time Mr. Scott called her this, when with Joseph, and how he hadn't liked it, how he'd taken her side.

She'd accepted her place in life. As a poor woman, she was the lowest of the low, a nobody. She'd never questioned her station or how others treated her . . . until Joseph.

Was Joseph right? Was Mr. Scott showing a lack of respect for her as a person? She and the poor girls were every bit as much human beings as the wealthy ladies on the ship. Why should he speak with them more kindly and with more dignity than he did to her and the others of her class?

Silence stretched out between them. Though she was tempted to peek at him and gauge his expression, she kept her head down.

"You cannot imagine the shame that would come to the Columbia Mission Society and to the illustrious sponsor of our trip, Miss Angela Georgina Burdett Coutts, if you carry forth with enticing Lord Colville into marriage."

Enticing? Mercy flinched. Was that what everyone believed she'd done to Joseph—entice him?

"Not only would such a union cause a scandal and disgrace for Lord Colville, it would disgrace the Mission Society, Miss Coutts, and all the other sponsors. They would become the laughingstock of London."

Mercy hung her head further. She surely didn't want to cause a scandal for Joseph or humiliate him.

"Oh my, oh my." Mr. Scott's voice began to rise again. "And you can guess where the blame for the scandal will fall most heavily, can you not?"

She shook her head.

"It will fall directly upon me." His tone was laced with genuine anxiety that bordered on panic. "I shall be ruined. Reverend Thomas Nettleship Staley, the newly consecrated Bishop of Honolulu, will suspend my license and perhaps ban me from service altogether. I shall be sent away and will lose all hope of patronage from any of England's fine and noble families."

Mercy didn't understand half of what Mr. Scott was saying. But it was clear enough that Joseph couldn't marry her, not even if she wanted it—which she didn't. He'd not only embarrass himself, but it would bring shame to everyone involved in the bride ships.

"What shall I do?" Mr. Scott began to pace the deck outside her door with his short, choppy steps. "What shall I do?"

"You needn't worry, sir." She wrapped her arms around her middle to ward off a chill that came from the inside out. "Nothing's to come betwixt Lord Colville and me."

Mr. Scott swung his hands back and forth vigorously, picking up his pace, walking five steps before turning and walking five more, then repeating.

Surely the reverend had heard her earlier when she'd told Joseph no, that she wouldn't marry him.

"How can he resist the temptation?" Mr. Scott murmured. "With such beguiling women enticing him at every turn and swaying his good judgment? He may very well continue the pursuit. Unless I am able to deter him . . ."

"I vow I won't sway him—"

"Lord Colville will most certainly thank me later for saving him from ruin and dishonor." Mr. Scott's voice grew louder with conviction as he continued his pacing. "Once we are away from the lair of the temptress, he will see how he was nearly seduced and ruined. In gratefulness to my service, he will no doubt wish to become my patron himself."

Abruptly, Mr. Scott halted. With a somber face and wide eyes, he lifted his chin and peered up at Mercy again. "I shall hold myself personally responsible for finding you an appropriate husband. In fact, doing so shall be my priority when we go ashore. I shall make sure you are married before I leave for Hawaii, and I shall perform the ceremony myself."

Mercy swallowed hard. "But . . . there's no need to trouble yourself, sir. Please, I'm right sure I'll be able to take care of that on my own."

"Since you explicitly told Lord Colville that you had no intention of finding a husband among the waiting men, then it would appear you do indeed need my assistance."

Her heart plummeted. "No, sir—"

"Not only would your marriage ensure that Lord Colville will remain unscathed and free from scandal, but you must also consider the kindness of the Columbia Mission Society. They graciously paid your expenses to travel here to Vancouver Island with the end goal of marriage and with the ideal of helping to populate and so colonize this heathen land with good Christian families."

Mercy tried to think of a rebuttal, but her mind was blank.

"The influence of wives," Mr. Scott continued in the monotone he used for delivering sermons, "cannot be understated in taming a man's wild nature and regenerating his lost soul. After all, Scripture clearly states that God created Eve because He determined it is not good for man to be alone. That is our mission and that is the prime reason for this voyage."

"But it won't make much difference if one woman chooses not to marry, will it?"

"The men here are expecting brides," Mr. Scott said firmly. "And that is exactly what we shall deliver to them."

"When I signed on, I didn't right know—"

"Then shall I send you back to our great motherland? Or perhaps you'd like to repay the Columbia Mission Society every pound they have donated, all with the intention of helping you have a better life. Would you throw their kindness back into their faces so cruelly?"

Mercy couldn't abide the thought of returning to England. She'd have no life save the workhouse. She needed to stay, needed to be here when Patience arrived on the *Robert Lowe*.

"I can see that my suggestion for a return voyage doesn't appeal to you."

"No, sir. I'm expecting my sister on the next ship. I cannot be a-going back."

"Ah, I see." Something lit in the man's eyes, something that told

Mercy she'd made a mistake by mentioning anything having to do with Patience. "Then you will indeed give me your fullest cooperation on the morrow as I go ashore and pick for you a husband."

The desperation inside Mercy tightened, nearly strangling her. "Please, Mr. Scott, I beg you, sir. I vow I'll not be speaking with Joseph—Lord Colville—ever again. I have no thought to marrying him. Not now. Not ever."

Mr. Scott started to retreat. "The news of your marriage to a local will surely come as a relief to Lord Colville, freeing him from any obligation he may feel toward you."

Joseph had told her he would be jealous of the other men claiming her affection. But would it come as a relief to know she was married, that he was no longer obligated to her but was free to live as he chose? Maybe it would.

Whatever the case, she couldn't let Mr. Scott trap her into marriage. Worse than the idea of marriage was the idea of marriage to a complete stranger.

She had to find a way out of her predicament and quickly. If only she had the slightest inkling how.

twenty-five

"James Bay ahead!" came a call from the quarterdeck.

Mercy clutched the railing of the Royal Navy gunboat HMS *Forward* alongside the rest of the women. The view of Victoria proper was just around the bend.

In moments they'd arrive at their new home, hopefully a place where they could finally eke out a new life that was better than what they'd left behind.

When they'd boarded the gunboat a short while ago, Lieutenant Robson had greeted them and informed them they had a three-mile trip from the *Tynemouth* at Esquimalt to the town of Victoria.

Thankfully, for mid-September the afternoon was mild, even sunny for the last part of their journey. They'd gathered at the railing to watch the passing scenery—the evergreens that seemed to go on forever in all directions with their boughs outstretched over the water as if to claim both land and sea.

Gentle waves lapped the rocky shore, the low tide revealing boulders thick with barnacles and stained shades of brown and red from seaweed. Across the strait, the mainland spread out for miles, small bays with sandy beaches, along with rugged inlets carved out of giant jutting stone.

Mercy hadn't expected the three miles to go so quickly. But it seemed only minutes had passed before the lieutenant called out that they were entering the inner harbor where they would drop anchor.

"Oh, gracious heavens," Miss Lawrence murmured from her spot several women down. "What have I gotten myself into?" She pumped her fan rapidly, her face pale, her auburn hair pulled back under a pretty hat.

In all the excitement before leaving the *Tynemouth*, one of the middle-class women had fainted while several others worked themselves into states of dizziness. And now Mercy could see that Miss Lawrence was about to faint as well.

Mercy released her grip on the rail and reached the delicate gentlewoman just as her knees crumpled. Gasps and exclamations broke out among the women that another of their own had succumbed to the excitement.

"There, there, dear heart." Mercy lowered Miss Lawrence gently to the deck. As she knelt, she wasn't surprised to see Joseph approaching.

After the earlier excitability, he'd announced to Mr. Scott that he planned to accompany the women ashore. When he'd boarded the *Forward* shortly after the women, Mercy attempted to stay as far away from him as possible and had avoided looking at him at all costs.

Mr. Scott's threat of the previous day to find her a husband had haunted her well into the night, growing more terrifying the closer she drew to the shore.

"Has she fainted?" Joseph asked, kneeling and finding Miss Lawrence's pulse.

"Aye, I'd say so." Mercy focused upon their patient and refused to look at Joseph, even though she desperately wanted to study his face for any lingering affection, to determine what he really felt for her.

Joseph checked Miss Lawrence's breathing and then dug

through the medical bag next to him. "Seems that many of the women are suffering from hysteria."

Mercy wasn't sure what hysteria was, so she only nodded.

"Are you not anxious as well?" His question was soft and meant for her ears alone.

She wanted to answer him truthfully, to tell him what Mr. Scott had threatened. But she suspected he'd only propose marriage again. He was noble like that. He'd marry a lowly woman like her without thinking of the cost to himself. And she couldn't let him do it.

"I'm ready to put my feet to the ground." She glanced sideways to where Mr. Scott stood at the railing with his wife and two daughters, and she prayed Joseph would finish up quickly and revive Miss Lawrence before Mr. Scott caught them speaking.

Joseph was still digging through his medical bag, albeit slowly, until he stopped altogether. He remained unmoving, his hand in the bag, until finally she looked up at him. His warm brown eyes were fixed upon her, waiting, desiring, asking.

A spot of heat settled in her abdomen, a spot that would easily spread if she dwelt upon how much she wanted to be in his arms, tucked against his chest, with his hands pressed against her back.

She forced her attention to Miss Lawrence but was sure the flush in her face had exposed her errant thoughts.

"I shall miss you, Mercy," he whispered.

"And I you," Mercy responded without looking up.

He waited another moment before resuming his search in the bag. This time he immediately found what he was looking for. He lifted out a tin flask, popped off the lid, and extracted a small clear bottle. "Hopefully a sniff of smelling salts will revive her sufficiently."

Mercy held Miss Lawrence's head as Joseph waved the vial in front of her nose. In an instant, the woman drew in a deep breath and her lashes fluttered up.

"Oh my . . ." Miss Lawrence said with a faint smile, first at

Mercy, then Joseph. "'Twould seem my poor nerves cannot handle such excitement."

"Then you must brace yourself," Joseph said. "You still have a great deal of excitement yet to come. Perhaps for now you should sit and rest in the shade."

Even as he spoke, the women at the railing began to make exclamations. In the distance came the sounds of cheering, whistling, shouting, and even clapping.

Joseph glanced up, as did Mercy, but they couldn't see past the swarm of women.

"Apparently the welcoming committee wasn't exaggerating yesterday about the men waiting to greet you." Joseph's voice was laced with derision as he helped Miss Lawrence to her feet and accompanied her down the deck away from the crowd, as gentlemanly and dignified as always.

Mercy returned to the railing. Joseph's words *I shall miss you* echoed through her mind and warmed her insides again.

"Strike me blind," Ann whispered as Mercy sidled next to the girl.

"You're not feeling faint now, are you?" Mercy took in Ann's exceptionally pale face and eyes the size of saucepans.

"What'll they do to us, Mercy?" Ann stared straight ahead.

"God save us," Flo said, shrinking against Mercy as though she could protect her.

Mercy peered at the shore and gasped out her own surprise at the sight of the crowds lining the waterfront. Now she understood the source of the cheering. She tried to swallow but couldn't make her throat work.

Beyond the numerous vessels moored in the bay were hundreds of men. They were swarming the shoreline, waving, laughing, grinning, and calling out greetings. Not even the *Forward*'s engines and the short blasts of her whistle could drown out the commotion.

"Are the men gonna grab us when we get off the boat and carry us off?" asked Minnie, her voice wobbly with alarm.

"No, of course not." Mercy tried to keep her tone light for the girls, even though a terrible dread began filling her. She pointed to the wharf. "Look. Policemen are there to guard us."

At least she hoped the police were there to guard them. From what she could see, there were four uniformed men among the horde. But was four enough to keep them safe? Or were they waiting like the others, intending to take a bride the instant the women stepped onto land?

Ann tucked her hand into the crook of Mercy's arm. "I ain't never seen goings-on like this."

Mercy wanted nothing more than to propel the *Forward* around, return to the *Tynemouth*, and climb back aboard. It didn't matter that she hadn't been on firm ground in over three months. It didn't matter she wanted a bath, needed to wash her hair, and longed to launder her clothing. The realization of the men awaiting them was enough to send even the stoutest souls back to England.

"At least they want us here." Kip dared to smile and wave back at the crowd.

Mercy understood the desire to be accepted and loved. All their lives they'd only ever been a burden, not just to their families but also to their country. Maybe Kip was right. Maybe here, in this new land, they'd finally be wanted.

The HMS *Forward* dropped anchor in the middle of James Bay, and shortly afterward a longboat pulled beside their vessel to begin ferrying the passengers ashore. The women resisted having to be the first to climb down the makeshift rope ladder into the waiting boat. Finally, given little choice, Mercy and the other poor women descended and huddled together on the benches.

"I shall accompany you." Mercy could hear Joseph talking to Mr. Scott on the deck above them. "You may need another escort."

"Thank you for your kind concern, Lord Colville," Mr. Scott replied. "You are most gracious to offer us your assistance. However, there is no need to trouble yourself as the committee has assured us the gathering will be orderly."

"You can see for yourself the men are quite rowdy," Joseph said bluntly. "God forbid that my services will be necessary. Nevertheless, I shall attend the women and be at the ready."

Mercy heard no more discussion after that. As the longboat dipped under the newcomers climbing inside, she sensed Joseph's presence not far behind her. Though she might never see him again after today, she wouldn't forget him or his kindness.

Within minutes, the men at the oars started rowing to shore. The cheering and whistling escalated. Some of the women were beginning to lose their fear and called back to the men, only to have Mr. Scott rebuke them to stay silent.

It was difficult to see Victoria beyond the crowds. From the little Mercy could glimpse, the town had an openness about it that was much different from the crowded alleys and streets of London. The area was cleared of trees, with homes and buildings lining wide dirt roads. Everything appeared to be new and freshly painted.

Once they reached the wharf, two men in blue uniforms came forward to assist the women from the boat. As Mercy's feet touched the wooden planks, she swayed for a moment, so used to the motion of the water that the solid steadiness of the land made her dizzy.

The other girls held on to each other, whether from fear or dizziness, Mercy couldn't tell, especially as the calls from the men rang out in increasing fervor. Ahead, at the end of the wharf, several of the older gentlemen from yesterday's welcoming committee were there to greet them once again.

Past them on the shore, ropes had been erected to form a pathway. More officers stood along the lane, apparently to hold the men back as they pushed forward for their first glimpses up close of the bride-ship women.

All Mercy needed was one look at the eagerness in their faces for fresh dread to soak into her. Men of all types, sizes, ages, and skin colors stared boldly back at her. Their excited grins and undisguised interest told her Mr. Scott had been correct. The men expected to secure brides.

It appeared as though the male population of Victoria far outnumbered the few matrons among the crowd. Even with the boatload of new women arriving, there wouldn't be enough women to go around. There would likely be many disappointed men who'd have to wait for the next bride ship to arrive—the one carrying Patience.

What would her sister think of all this? Would she be excited at the possibility of finding a husband, or would it fill her with dread too? Patience had never been opposed to marriage the same way that Mercy was. But she'd always been particular about men, telling Mercy she intended to marry someone who loved God just as she herself did. Maybe here in Victoria, Patience would finally discover a man like that.

Mercy focused on the wharf. As for her, she simply wanted to survive and find a way to escape.

"Duck your heads," she instructed her charges. Perhaps if they didn't make eye contact and kept their heads down, they'd draw less attention. She trembled to think of what would happen once they moved off the wharf. Would the men lunge after them, grabbing and fighting over their brides? Or would the women have to parade in front of the crowd first before arriving at some sort of platform to be displayed further?

"If you women will line up in twos" came the distinguished voice of Lieutenant Verney, one of the gentlemen who'd come aboard the *Tynemouth* yesterday, "Victoria's bluejackets will escort you to your accommodations."

Mercy took hope from the lieutenant's instructions. Perhaps the women wouldn't be distributed among the men right away after all.

"This is bedlam, Mr. Scott," Joseph said tersely from behind her. "We cannot subject the women to this humiliation. This is no better than a gauntlet."

"Rest easy, Lord Colville," Mr. Scott replied in his usual

patronizing tone. "While the men are certainly more exuberant than I'd expected, I am grateful we shall be able to locate suitable husbands for each woman so readily and expeditiously."

"The men need to be carefully screened," Joseph said. "I insist upon it and will speak to the Female Immigration Committee to ensure it."

At Joseph's declaration, Mercy breathed a prayer of thanksgiving for at least one friend among the masses. Maybe with Joseph's help she'd survive the day.

She didn't hear Mr. Scott's reply, as the women ahead of her began to walk down the wharf. Upon reaching land, one of the first women in line knelt to the ground, dug her hands into the sandy soil, then bent and kissed the earth.

Mercy wished she could feel the same joy at being on land after so long at sea. But with the prospect of facing the men, her insides were as topsy-turvy as if she were back on the ship during a storm.

At last, her feet connected with the sand and rocks and then, a few steps later, firmer ground. Her stomach began to churn. She'd never experienced the nausea of seasickness so many of the other women had. But here and now, on dry land, she felt the need to bend over and vomit.

Only Ann's trembling fingers in the crook of her arm kept her upright. The girls needed her to be strong, to set an example, to protect them.

The men loomed ahead, pressing and jostling against one another behind the ropes while the officers held out their arms to keep the onlookers from falling into the women.

"Lord have mercy," Ann whispered as they reached the crowd, the hooting and cheering almost deafening.

"Head down, my lamb," Mercy said, her eyes trained on the hard-packed earth, hoping Joseph wasn't far behind and that if the men tried anything, he'd rush to their defense.

The narrow path ahead past the shouting horde seemed endless, and no matter how hard she tried, she couldn't block out their cheers.

The women in front halted, forcing the line to a standstill. Mercy glanced ahead to see that a tall man from the crowd had hopped over the rope and now stood in front of one of the women. A hush fell, allowing her to make out the interloper's words.

"Miss, I'd be mighty pleased if you did me the honor of becoming my wife." The tall young man doffed his cap and rolled the brim in his hands. Even if his hair was overlong and his beard in need of a trim, his clothing appeared to be clean, his expression was earnest, and his eyes were tired but kind.

The stunned silence spread with murmurs of, "It's Pioneer, the Cariboo miner."

Mercy attempted to see which of the women had gained the proposal.

"Sophia Shaw," Ann whispered the answer.

Even as two constables wound their way toward the miner, Pioneer pulled something out of his pocket and shoved it into Sophia's hands. "If you take me up on my offer, here's two thousand pounds to use toward buying yourself wedding clothes."

At the generous offer, whistles and gasps filtered through the crowd. The constables stopped to watch Sophia, apparently as shocked as everyone else at the turn of events.

For a long moment, Sophia stared at Pioneer, then back at the wad of money in her hands. Mercy guessed Sophia had never held a single pound in her life, much less two thousand. She could only imagine the inner turmoil the young woman was going through. The man clearly wanted her if he was giving her so much money.

"These miners are a depraved lot," someone directly behind Mercy said in an angry tone. She didn't need to turn to know it was Joseph. "If any bloke tries that trick on you, I shall thrash him."

Mercy was relieved the offer had gone out to Sophia and not her. Mr. Scott probably would have pulled out his prayer book and started the wedding ceremony before Mercy could've turned the miner down.

All around, everyone was watching Sophia, waiting for her decision. Even Mr. Scott seemed to be too shocked by the proposal to offer any words of protest or caution. Or perhaps he was anxious to see all his charges married and didn't particularly care how it happened, so long as it did.

Pioneer's expression was taut, and he continued to roll the brim of his hat in his hands. "I promise I'll be the best husband you could ever dream of having."

Sophia again studied his face. Then she nodded. "Alright."

In an instant, the wariness evaporated from Pioneer's face, and hope moved in to replace it. "You'll marry me?"

"Aye, I'll marry you."

A roaring cheer rose from the men. When Pioneer held out his hand, Sophia gave him a tentative smile and placed her hand into his. With a wide grin and whoop of his own, Pioneer swept Sophia off her feet, climbed back over the rope, and strode away with her in his arms as the crowd parted and men slapped him on the back.

"This is madness," Joseph said. Mercy felt the brush of his fingers at the small of her back, as though he wanted to direct her away from the crowd. But they were both trapped here in the middle of hundreds of men. Even as the line of women ahead began moving again, there was no place for any of them to go except forward.

"Keep your face hidden, Mercy," Joseph said with quiet urgency from behind. "And don't make eye contact with anyone."

Mercy wished for Joseph's cloak again so she could throw it over her head and hide just as he'd instructed. But she'd already given it back to him after he'd insisted she keep it.

The men pressed in closer, emboldened after Pioneer's daring proposal. Finally, some of the women, frightened by the forthrightness, began to run. Mercy lengthened her stride, sure that at any moment someone would jump into her path and propose marriage. She couldn't let that happen.

When the blue-uniformed constables finally led them inside a large building still under construction, the women collapsed against one another in relief.

Mercy turned to thank Joseph and realized he was gone.

twenty-six

Outside the newly built legislative building, Joseph craned his neck for a glimpse of Mercy. The bluejackets had prevented him from entering earlier with the women. And now he was standing like a bumbling idiot with all the other men along the crowded fence that connected the building to several others, all of which were part of the government complex.

He'd already attempted to convince the constables to allow him inside by assuring them he was one of the party, the ship's surgeon, that he'd spent the past months with the women, and that he belonged with them. But the bluejackets had been instructed by the Female Immigration Committee not to allow any single men into the women's quarters, and no amount of cajoling or bribing on Joseph's part had worked to change their minds, not even when he informed them that he was Lord Colville, Baron of Wiltshire.

Of course, they'd profusely apologized but had maintained their strict stance. Joseph asked to see Lieutenant Verney or one of the other gentlemen on the welcoming committee. He was told that no one was readily available.

Finally, Joseph had wandered away, only to discover the women had been ushered into a side yard of the legislative building, where tubs of water were set up for them to wash their clothes. While it was a kind gesture from the ladies of the committee, little did they realize most of the poor women were wearing all they owned.

"I got my eyes fixed on that pretty gal right there," said one of the many men, pointing as he vied for a spot along the fence. Joseph followed the man's finger to the young women surrounding the tub closest to the back door of the building. He recognized the girls from Mercy's cabin and then spotted her standing with them as they dipped their arms into the water.

"The one with the fair hair?" said another man with a weathered face, who sat perched atop the fence. "That's the one I'm aiming to marry."

"Guess we'll see who gets to her first," remarked a fellow on the opposite side of Joseph.

He had no doubt they were speaking of Mercy. She was the fairest of the women present in the yard. And though some of the wealthy women might possess more elegant garments and hats, Mercy was still the prettiest. Not even her travel-worn clothing could detract from her beauty.

Every word the men spoke regarding Mercy sliced inside him like a scalpel blade. Still, he reassured himself by recalling his conversation with her, when she'd told him in no uncertain terms that she was opposed to getting married. These men could rave all they wanted about her, but she wouldn't give them a single second of her attention in return.

"Heard the reverend announce we could arrange a time to meet her," one of them went on. "Said her name was Mercy Wilkins. Got myself on the list straightaway."

"List?" Joseph asked, his heart rate spiking.

"Too late for you," laughed the man. "That list filled up faster than a tavern on payday."

Joseph didn't see the humor in the situation. The entire afternoon had been taxing. From the first moment he'd seen all the men on the shore, he should have realized he'd find the proceedings distasteful and barbaric.

The women shouldn't have had to walk through the crowds of leering and lusting men. About halfway to the legislative building he'd been tempted to hoist Mercy up into his arms and shout at everyone to stop their ogling.

Yes, he understood the men were isolated here in the colonies, that many of the miners who'd come down from the mountains had quite possibly gone for months without seeing a female. But that was no excuse for the vulgarity.

"That Pioneer," said another man down the fence. "Guess he's lucky with the gold and the girl."

"If I had two thousand pounds, I'd buy me a wife too—especially Mercy Wilkins. Instead I'll just have to win her over with my charm and good looks." The comment drew a slew of guffaws among the other men.

Joseph wanted to inform them that wealth wouldn't buy Mercy. After all, if his title and the aristocratic life hadn't attracted her, then two thousand pounds wouldn't either. If she didn't want to marry him, she certainly wouldn't want to marry any of these men. Would she?

He studied their eager, young faces. Most were of the laboring class, likely having emigrated from England, similar to the women they sought to wed. These were the kind of men Mercy was used to. Would she feel more comfortable with them than him? Would she eventually change her mind and marry one of them?

His body stiffened at the thought. Why was she arranging meetings anyway? After seeing the eligible men, had she already decided to put aside her reservations and get married?

"Why is there a list for Miss Wilkins?" Joseph asked again, trying for a measure of calmness he didn't feel. "What if she doesn't want to get married?"

"Oh, she does," chimed in a different fellow. "The reverend, who was her chaperone on the ship, informed us she'll pick a man and marry him by Sunday."

"What the devil?" Joseph shook his head. Impossible. Mercy

wouldn't do such a thing. Could it be they had her mixed up with someone else? "The one with the fair hair, at the tub near the door?" he asked.

"That's the one."

Her back was facing the men. He willed her to turn and see him, so he could beckon her. Even now he was tempted to shout her name and call her over. If only he could do so where he might have a moment to speak to her alone without half the town's male population watching them.

If Mercy had indeed changed her mind about getting married, if she really was picking a man and marrying by Sunday, then why had she turned down his proposal? She seemed to care for him. He assumed she'd enjoyed spending time with him as much as he had with her. Surely he hadn't imagined her passionate response to him the time he'd kissed her.

But what if he'd misread her signals? After all, he hadn't exactly courted or spent much time with women over the past few years. Perhaps his skills with the fairer sex were lacking. Maybe he'd only assumed she was attracted to him when instead she was relieved to be rid of him.

He shook his head. No. She'd been sincere earlier when she informed him that she'd miss him. And yet what if she would only miss him as a *friend*? Doubts piled upon doubts until he didn't know what to think.

"You fellows may as well go home and blubber," chortled a stocky man sitting on the fence. "One look at me and she'll take me right to her bed."

"Watch your tongue," Joseph rebuked sharply.

The man swiveled, glared at Joseph, then dropped to the ground. "You talking to me?"

"I'm talking to you and anyone else who decides to speak so obscenely about the women."

The man was short but swarthy. He quickly shed his coat, revealing thickly muscled arms. "Who woke up and made you king today?"

Joseph wasn't a man given to brawls, but he'd had to learn how to hold his own during his times at sea. After facing down mutineers, drunken sailors, and irate passengers, he wasn't afraid of an insolent miner.

"I wouldn't need to act like a king if you weren't behaving like a donkey." Joseph's comment brought several snickers. Part of him warned he should turn and walk away, that he was in no frame of mind to deal with this particular man. But another part of him churned with the strange need to fight.

"I heard you talking to that bluejacket and tellin' him you're a lord or baron or something and trying to push your way around." The man started rolling up his shirtsleeves. "If you think you can come here with all your highfalutin ways and start ordering us about, well, you got another thing comin'. We're not bowing and yes-sir-ing and as-you-pleasing no more to no one. Not here in this new land. Here we're free."

Before the man could swing the first punch, Joseph lunged for him, grabbed the front of his shirt, and lifted him off the ground. He leaned his face into the man's and glared. "If you treat the women with respect, I shan't need to push you around."

"Once I got me the woman, I can treat her any way I want," the man rasped, struggling to free himself from Joseph's grasp.

Joseph tightened his grip on the man's shirt so that it began to choke him. "She'll never be yours. Never."

The anger inside him built up like steam in a ship's boilers. The pressure hurt and needed release. But even as he brought his fist up, he shoved the miner, causing the man to stumble backward and fall to the ground, gasping for breath.

Without another word, Joseph spun and stalked away. Several of the others shouted after him, called him a coward for not finishing the fight. But Joseph kept on walking. He didn't know where he was headed, only that he had to get away.

Minutes later, he found himself back on the wharf, the one they'd used when first coming ashore. Now that the women had left and were at the legislative building, the waterfront was deserted, the longboat gone. Even the HMS *Forward* had moved on.

The pressure in Joseph's chest compelled him to keep going, to find someone to row him out to Esquimalt Lagoon near the naval base, where the *Tynemouth* was taking on fresh provisions and fuel in readiness for continuing the journey to the Hawaiian Islands. While the ship wasn't scheduled to depart until midweek, Joseph wanted to board and weigh anchor as soon as possible.

He clasped his hands behind his back and stared across the straits. His breathing was ragged, his muscles tight, and his chest still burned.

What was wrong with him? Hadn't he been looking forward to visiting Vancouver Island and exploring the area for the duration of the *Tynemouth*'s stay? And yet not once had he considered the landscape beyond a passing glance to the distant mountains. He hadn't even been able to take in the glorious sunset the previous eve when they'd entered the Strait of Juan de Fuca.

"Where is a ship when you need one?" he muttered, looking around at the small boats moored nearby. Surely there was a fisherman or some other local who might be willing to ferry him to the *Tynemouth*.

As far as he could see, only empty boats bobbed in the mostly calm waters. Apparently every able-bodied man in Victoria was either attempting to get another glimpse of the bride-ship women or celebrating their arrival at one of the town's many taverns.

He needed to leave and forget about Mercy. Then maybe the churning inside him would go away. Perhaps he'd find his sense of peace and adventure again.

But even as he attempted to rationalize his feelings, the gentle waves that rolled in and lightly rocked the wharf seemed to mock him. Had he sabotaged his proposal to Mercy yesterday so that she felt obligated to reject him? He certainly hadn't spoken eloquently or tenderly. Instead, he'd brought up their class difference and had likely made her feel inferior.

Even if Captain Hellyer believed him to be a man who didn't allow social status to influence him, clearly he still had much to learn about humility and treating others in a non-condescending manner.

With a groan, Joseph covered his face with both hands. He was a coward of the worst kind. Rather than staying and fighting for Mercy, for her reputation, for her safety, he'd started to run away again.

He turned back toward the fledgling town of Victoria. He'd find a way to meet with her again to discover the truth behind her plan to find a husband by Sunday. If she wanted marriage after all, then he'd have to convince her to choose him, this time asking for her hand with humility, as her equal. And if she still persisted with what she'd originally told him—that in fact she didn't want to get married—then he'd help her gain the freedom she longed for.

Either way, he wouldn't leave Victoria until he faced Mercy again and learned how she really felt.

twenty-seven

As Mercy hugged the girls from her cabin, an ache pressed against her chest, an ache she didn't want to dwell upon.

"I'll see you again, that I will," she said. "We'll be right close enough that we'll be neighbors."

They sniffled and brushed away tears even through their excited smiles.

"Come now, girls," said one of the matrons from Victoria's Female Immigration Committee who'd arrived at the legislative building a short while ago. "The representatives of your new homes are here. Please form a single line so that we may pair you with your new employers."

Mercy stepped away from the orphans and expelled a breath to ease the pain in her lungs and throat. Joseph's whispered words after Sarah's death rolled through her mind, a thick fog of an emotion she didn't care to name. *"If you push aside your pain, you can go on. But it's still there, buried deep."*

She'd never allowed herself to feel the heartache of the many children she'd lost over the years—not her baby siblings, not the neighbor children, not Sarah, and now not these precious girls. How could she endure it if she dwelled upon such things?

She'd survived this far by letting go of the pain and moving on with her life. And she'd have to do so again. Wasn't that what she was doing with Joseph? As hard as it was, she must push aside all thoughts of him. She had to do the same with the girls.

Mercy crossed to the other side of the large room, where some of the other poor women had congregated. After they'd finished washing up outside, the matrons from the committee ushered them back into the building and proceeded to divide them into three groups.

The first group consisted of the youngest girls. Mercy was relieved to discover that her sweet lambs were being placed directly into homes where they would live and work as domestics. The Female Immigration Committee had decided the orphans were too young for immediate marriage and should work until they were a bit older.

The girls hadn't protested. When they'd learned their wages were to be no less than twenty-five pounds a year, their delight had warmed Mercy's heart.

The committee then formed a second group, including a few widows and the wealthy middle-class women, who would be offered employment as teachers and governesses. From what Mercy could gather, some had positions already waiting for them. However, there weren't enough teacher or governess jobs available to match the demand, so some of these women were remaining behind to join the third group, the one Mercy had been put into.

"The rest of you shall be offered up as brides without delay," the committee woman had said. After walking through the horde a short while ago, as well as doing their washing with the men looking on, the committee member's remark had been met with a decided lack of enthusiasm.

If the other women felt anything like Mercy, then they were terrified by the overwhelming number of men and their wild exuberance about getting married. But as Mr. Scott had pointed out to her on the ship the previous day, the Columbia Mission Society had sponsored their trip, paid their fares, and made the arrangements for their care specifically to provide brides for the men in this new land. He'd made it quite clear that she was obligated to follow through with her part of the bargain, even if she hadn't known the purpose of the voyage at first. Either that or she'd have to return home to England or else pay the Society back for the cost of her trip.

Although she hadn't yet figured a way out of her predicament, she hadn't stopped thinking about her options. Perhaps her best course of action was to continue her pretense. She'd act like all the others and attempt some enthusiasm at the prospect of marriage.

And she'd pray hard Mr. Scott would give up his threat to make sure she was one of the first women matched to a man. Thankfully, he hadn't mentioned it again. Perhaps after Sophia Shaw's proposal, he'd put it out of his mind. Or perhaps now that he'd had the chance to see for himself exactly how many men were waiting for a wife, he'd stop worrying about her and Joseph. If she could avoid Mr. Scott until the *Tynemouth* left, he'd soon be gone and out of her life.

A giant of a woman with wide shoulders, thick arms, and a heavy girth entered the building through a back door. Mercy recognized her as one of the women of the Female Immigration Committee, particularly because of her hat with its colorful feathers, as though a flock of jungle birds had made a nest there. In addition to her outlandish hat, she was attired in a gown that was bright and flashy, certainly not as genteel or delicate-looking as the other committee members.

"Ladies," she said as she approached Mercy's group. "My name is Mrs. Moresby, and I'm here to escort you to your accommodations."

Mercy let the tension ease from her shoulders. From what she could tell, they weren't being married off tonight.

"We'll be walking a short distance to the Marine Barracks,"

Mrs. Moresby remarked, opening the door and holding it wide as the women filed past. Once they were all in the yard again, Mrs. Moresby moved to the front of the line.

"There are seven government buildings here in Victoria," Mrs. Moresby explained while waving at the brick structures that surrounded them. "All of them in close proximity of the main legislative building."

Mercy didn't listen to Mrs. Moresby's history of the order in which the buildings had been constructed. Instead, as they walked into view of the men who were still lined up along the fence, Mercy kept her head down and her attention on the dirt path.

Calls and whistles had accompanied the women all through their brief effort at washing three months of grime from their arms and faces. Mercy had done the best she could to remain quiet and avoid notice.

Now, as she made her way through the yard, she hoped no one would pay her any mind.

"Mercy Wilkins!" called one of the men. "Will you marry me?"

Upon hearing her name, Mercy stumbled and would have fallen if Miss Lawrence hadn't been next to her. The gentlewoman steadied her.

"I got five hundred pounds and a claim on the Fraser River!" the man shouted.

Mercy sidled closer to Miss Lawrence. How did this man know her name? Why was he singling her out?

"I'll make you a happy woman, I promise!"

Miss Lawrence quickened her pace, pulling Mercy along with her. "Don't respond," Miss Lawrence said. "Pretend as though you haven't heard him."

Thankfully, they reached the Marine Barracks within seconds, a spacious two-storied home that sat directly behind the legislative building. As they crowded inside the front room—the parlor, according to Mrs. Moresby—Miss Lawrence led Mercy to a cushioned chair and helped her sit down.

"Thank you for your help, miss," Mercy said, trying to still her rapidly beating heart.

"'Tis I who should be thanking you, Mercy." Miss Lawrence tugged up her high collar. "You've been more than kind to me this entire ordeal."

Mercy couldn't help but see the bite mark on Miss Lawrence's neck, the one she tried to carefully hide. The wound hadn't yet healed all the way. Maybe the mark would never go away. Miss Lawrence would likely have to live with her scars as glaring reminders of her past.

As though sensing Mercy's attention to her neck, Miss Lawrence fumbled for her reticule, unfastened the clasp, and pulled out a fan.

"You'll not be a-going with the other group to be a governess?" Mercy asked.

Miss Lawrence flipped open the fan and began pumping at her flushed face. "They're all very learned women. While I . . . I am more limited in my education."

Mercy doubted Miss Lawrence was as limited as she was. She'd never had *any* learning—not how to read or write or do sums. "No matter. I bet you'll find a fine gent soon enough. Those navy officers who came aboard yesterday seemed real interested, and it's no wonder with how pretty you are."

"You're sweet to say so. But it's you who will have your choice of suitors. Already they're lined up at the fence fighting over you."

Mercy waved her hand at the remark, wishing she could as easily wave away the men. "Stuff and nonsense."

"You're a beautiful woman, Mercy." Miss Lawrence spoke the words without a trace of envy, her eyes radiating sincerity. "It's easy to see why you've caught Lord Colville's eye."

Mercy glanced around, hoping none of the other women had heard her. She didn't want any gossip about her and Joseph getting back to Mr. Scott. Not now after the reverend's threats.

"'Tis no secret," Miss Lawrence said, softer this time.

"We're friends is all."

"Well, he's a kind and gracious man. And while the other ladies have attempted to garner his attention, we all know when the Baron of Wiltshire marries someday, he'll choose a woman of the aristocracy above any from our stations."

Mercy stared down at the rug that covered the polished wood floor. The words were similar to what Miss Lawrence had spoken on the ship when Mercy tended her. And they reminded her of Mr. Scott's worries from yesterday—the possibility of scandal if Joseph persisted in pursuing a lowly woman like Mercy to be his wife when he was destined for a much greater woman and partner.

Miss Lawrence reached out and gently patted Mercy's hand. "Now that we're here, you'll have your choice among all the young miners and laborers. In fact, you'll have the first pick of the best of them."

Mercy wanted to reassure Miss Lawrence that there wasn't anything to worry about, that she didn't have her sights upon Joseph at all. For even if she'd wanted to marry, she'd never consider stirring up trouble where Joseph was concerned.

Before Mercy could form a response, Mrs. Moresby clapped her hands to draw their attention. "Welcome, ladies," she said to the women squeezed into the parlor, which Mercy guessed to be about half their number from the bride ship. "You will stay here in the Marine Barracks until you're married or find employment. I'm sorry the accommodations are so basic. But as we didn't expect your ship to arrive for another month, this is the only suitable place that was available."

Mercy took stock of the room. The walls were whitewashed and clean of the coal smoke and dirty handprints Mercy had come to expect in her own family dwelling. The few pieces of furniture, like the chair, were simple but prettier than anything Mercy had ever seen. A fireplace against one wall was unlit, with a simple mantel surrounding it. The mirror above it was framed with gold and polished to perfection.

Though she was curious to see her reflection, she hung back, too intimidated to discover how she looked, especially after the months at sea.

"Commander Verney was kind enough to lend us his crew over the past few days since learning of your imminent arrival," Mrs. Moresby said. "The men painted, repaired, and scrubbed each and every room to make them as comfortable as possible for your stay."

Mercy guessed Mrs. Moresby had no notion of the condition of the slum hovels most of the poor women had come from, otherwise she might not have gone to so much trouble. She'd have realized that even dirty, this house was much nicer than any place they'd ever known.

"You'll have your own kitchen at the back of the house," Mrs. Moresby continued. "The Female Immigration Committee will provide the food, supplies, and utensils necessary for your welfare. However, you'll need to take responsibility—perhaps forming teams—for the preparation of the meals."

Beneath the brim of her flamboyant bird hat, the woman wore a remorseful expression as if she regretted they couldn't offer more. The truth was, Mercy had never had so much food readily available to her as she'd had on this trip. And she was grateful the committee would continue to provide for them and that they didn't need to fend for themselves in this strange place.

After Mrs. Moresby explained more about the accommodations, apologizing for the simplicity of the bedrooms and bunkbeds on the second floor and the cramped living space, she smiled at the women. "Hopefully, your stay here in the barracks will be short-lived and all of you will find loving husbands and new homes very soon."

Mercy glanced outside the large front window that overlooked the yard between the buildings. The evening sky was beginning to turn a violet blue with vibrant ribbons of purple and pink and orange threaded throughout in a stunning display of beauty, especially with the bay in the distance reaching toward the ocean.

From what Mercy could see, the men had finally dispersed from the fence that surrounded the government buildings, apparently having decided the women weren't coming back out.

She let her shoulders relax, and for the first time since coming ashore, she felt safe. Maybe there was hope after all. Hope that she could hide away in the barracks over the next few days and avoid contact with the men.

"Of course, you'll all have suitors who will want to come calling," Mrs. Moresby added, quickly breaking Mercy's fragile sense of peace. "The men will not be admitted inside the government complex without permission. But once you've obtained the proper consent, you may use this front parlor as a meeting room so long as you are chaperoned."

"How will we know who to invite," someone asked, "if we never have the chance to socialize and introduce ourselves?"

"Oh, you'll have plenty of chances to socialize," Mrs. Moresby assured. "Tomorrow we're having our annual regatta, and Commander Verney has graciously suggested you ladies spend the day on board the *Grappler*, so that you might participate in the festivities as guests of the navy. Afterward we'll have games and refreshments on the town green."

The news was met with whispers and smiles.

"Then on Sunday you'll join us for worship at Christ Church Cathedral, where you'll be given the opportunity to interact with many of our single male citizens."

Mercy decided she'd have to find excuses to avoid attending the events.

"In addition," Mrs. Moresby said, "your very own chaperone, Mr. Scott, has already been busy lining up appointments for several of you."

"Appointments?" echoed one of the women.

"Yes, for the men to meet you here in the parlor. As Mr. Scott is only here in Victoria for a limited time, he's such a generous man, agreeing to spend his evenings chaperoning the meetings."

Generous? Mercy tried not to shudder. Mrs. Moresby didn't need to mention the names of the women who would have appointments. Mercy could already guess she was one of them.

Mr. Scott was doing exactly as he vowed. He was determined to see her married before he left Victoria. She had to make sure he didn't succeed. But how?

twenty-eight

From her place on the blanket spread under an enormous oak tree, Mercy tried to keep out of sight amidst the other women and not call attention to herself.

The men lingered nearby along the edge of the cricket grounds on Beacon Hill, waiting for the opportunity to talk with them. Fortunately, the leaders of the Female Immigration Committee had cordoned off an area and were sitting close by under a large open tent with servants tending them.

After spending the morning aboard the HMS *Grappler* and watching the regatta, Mercy had hoped to find a way to return to the Marine Barracks. But again the committee had insisted all the women participate.

Mercy knew she should be grateful to these local gentlewomen. They meant well. On top of everything else they'd done, they even had two trunks of donated clothing delivered to the barracks early in the morning, after finally comprehending that many of the poor women had nothing but what they wore.

Having spent the past evening scrubbing her one outfit and hanging it to dry overnight, Mercy was as thrilled as everyone else at the fresh change of clothing. With her hair washed, her body scrubbed, and wearing the clean garments, Mercy felt almost like a new person.

She might have even enjoyed the activities of the warm autumn day if she didn't have the appointments looming ahead that eve. She glanced to the pavilion, where Mr. Scott sat with his family and the committee members, as well as the wealthier bride-ship women, Miss Lawrence among them.

Earlier, Mr. Scott had pulled her aside and informed her of the men who were scheduled to meet with her. He instructed her that she must pick one to marry by Sunday evening.

Of course, she'd wanted to refuse and tell him his plan was all rot, but his stern expression warned her that if she protested, he'd carry through on his threat to send her back to England. And if she returned to England, what would happen to Patience if she came on the next ship? Yet if she stayed, would she be trapped into marriage?

Her attention shifted to the men, many of whom were more interested in watching the women than the cricket game. Some of the women had been bold in flirting and making connections whenever possible, but Mercy only shuddered at the prospect of interacting with them.

A newcomer to the game caught her attention as he shook hands with his team members. He had a handsome profile and a muscular build with broad shoulders . . .

Her heartbeat lurched to a stop. *Joseph.*

He held himself with an air of confidence and strength that set him apart from the others. As he jogged out to his position, she couldn't help but admire him, just as every other eligible woman in Victoria was probably doing.

When she hadn't seen him that morning at the regatta, she'd begun to worry, even experiencing a surge of panic until she glimpsed Captain Hellyer and realized the *Tynemouth* hadn't left early, that Joseph was still in Victoria.

Even if she was forced to let Joseph go, she didn't want him to leave without saying good-bye. In fact, she couldn't bear the thought of his sailing away without speaking to him one last time—as a friend and nothing more.

Although she'd never watched a game of cricket before today, she didn't have a difficult time figuring out that Joseph was by far the best player on the grassy field. The handsomest too. She soon found herself on the edge of the blanket, unable to take her eyes off him.

Not for the first time, she was proud of him. Not just for being kindhearted, generous, and hardworking, but also for how skilled and athletic he was. He might be a gentleman, yet he wasn't above sweating and laboring and mingling with others of a lower rank.

Midway through the game, Joseph overthrew the ball to one of his teammates. It rolled toward the blanket and stopped almost directly in front of her.

She scooped it up and was about to throw it back when she realized Joseph was heading her way, his eyes upon her. There was something intense in his expression that made her stomach flutter and her breathing grow shallow. She knew she should toss him the ball, but she couldn't get her arm to obey.

When he finally reached her, she held out the ball.

"Miss Wilkins." He gave a gallant bow.

"Dr. Colville," she responded with a tilt of her head.

As he straightened, his eyes connected with hers. The rich brown depths churned with turmoil. He hesitated, and his brow creased as though he would speak his mind. A glance to the other women on the blanket as well as to the pavilion beyond revealed that all eyes were upon them.

All eyes including those of Mr. Scott.

A tremor of anxiety rippled through Mercy, and she shook her head, silently pleading with Joseph not to speak to her, not in front of everyone.

He took the ball from her without saying a word, giving her only a nod of thanks. Then he ran back to his teammates.

Mercy folded her hands in the layers of her new skirt and twisted the material. Silently she prayed the attention would quickly shift away from her and that everyone would soon forget Joseph had singled her out.

She hardly dared to budge for the rest of the game. Once it ended, she stood and moved into the sunshine as the committee and other important members of the community came out from the tent. She wished she could sneak away to the Marine Barracks, but the women from the Female Immigration Committee had warned them not to go about town unchaperoned, at least not until the excitement over their arrival had passed.

"Mercy Wilkins, isn't it?" came a voice next to her.

Mercy turned to find Mrs. Moresby. With her thick shoulders and torso, she had the build of a large man, but like yesterday her attire was feminine to the extreme. Her gown was trimmed with more lace and ruffles than Mercy had ever seen. Instead of feathers, today her wide hat was decorated with a bright array of ribbons.

"Aye, I'm Mercy Wilkins, ma'am." Mercy curtsied.

"No need to curtsy to me, Miss Wilkins."

Mercy straightened but kept her eyes fixed upon the woman's skirt—the layers upon layers of silky material.

"I hope you're enjoying your stay so far," Mrs. Moresby said.

"That I am. Right well, ma'am. Thank ye for making us feel welcome and for giving us so many nice things." Mercy patted her skirt to indicate her appreciation for the clothing.

"I'm glad to do it." Mrs. Moresby reached into her colorfully beaded reticule, retrieved a handkerchief, then pressed it against her forehead. "Do you mind moving into the shade, Miss Wilkins? Whenever I'm in the sun, I'm afraid I burn like bacon in a frypan."

"'Course, ma'am. Right away." Mercy walked with Mrs. Moresby into the shade, which took them a slight distance away from everyone else. She was struck again today as she was last evening that Mrs. Moresby was polite and considerate, more so than the others on the committee.

Mrs. Moresby stuffed her handkerchief back into her bag and then pulled out a fan. She unfolded it and began pumping the fan near her face, blowing the ribbons on her hat in every direction. Through the vigorous flapping, her gaze connected with Mercy's directly. "Lord Colville cares about you."

Mercy wanted to look away as she knew she should with someone who was her superior. But the woman's expression contained no judgment or even curiosity. She seemed matter-of-fact, as if she'd stated a simple truth like the sun was warm.

"That's the way Lord Colville is." Mercy was tempted to glance over to where he stood talking with his teammates. "He cares for people, that he does."

Mrs. Moresby's fan came to an abrupt halt, her hat ribbons falling flat. "No, Miss Wilkins. What I'm saying is that man is in *love* with you."

Mercy drew in a quick breath, and she checked to make sure no one had overheard Mrs. Moresby's bold claim.

Mrs. Moresby took up fanning herself again. "Don't worry, Miss Wilkins. No one is paying attention to our conversation, except for Lord Colville, who can't take his eyes off you."

"No, ma'am, I'm afraid you've got it all wrong," Mercy rushed to explain. "We're friends and that's all. I promise—"

"Mercy," she interrupted. "I may call you Mercy, may I not?"

"Aye, ma'am."

"And you'll call me Velva."

"Oh no, ma'am. It wouldn't be right. Not right at all. I couldn't."

"Nonsense. We're two equal women. Let's put away the formalities."

Mercy could only stare at Mrs. Moresby, who dwarfed her in size, especially with her overlarge hat and puffy garments, which only added to her height and girth. While the woman should have been intimidating, something in her eyes beckoned Mercy to trust her. In some ways, Mrs. Moresby reminded her of Joseph—his warmth and acceptance and his wish to put aside formalities.

What did Mrs. Moresby mean about Joseph not being able to take his eyes off her? And being in love with her? The woman had to be imagining things.

Mercy peeked sideways in Joseph's direction. He was still talking with the other men on his team. He wasn't paying her any attention.

"He's watching you, even though he's acting like he's not," Mrs. Moresby said. "You do know he purposefully threw that ball your way so he'd have an excuse to come over to you."

"No, ma'am. He didn't." Mercy started to panic. Where was this conversation headed? Had Mr. Scott told the matron about Joseph's shipboard proposal? What if Mr. Scott had asked Mrs. Moresby for help with finding Mercy a husband?

"You've no need to worry, ma'am," Mercy said. "I told Lord Colville no."

Mrs. Moresby's eyebrows rose. "No to what?"

"I'm not fit to marry a man like him," Mercy continued rapidly. "I'd embarrass him and cause him all kinds of problems, to be sure." Not to mention the shame she'd cause the Columbia Mission Society, as well as the trouble she'd bring to Mr. Scott.

Mrs. Moresby started to rapidly fan herself again. "My, my, my, it's no wonder Lord Colville is ready to tear to pieces any man who looks your way."

Mercy shook her head in denial, though a part of her wanted it to be true. Joseph hadn't been pleased with all the attention the men were giving the women yesterday after disembarking. Was he a little jealous?

The other women were beginning to stroll back to the Marine Barracks. Mrs. Moresby stuffed her fan back into her reticule, then tucked her hand into the crook of Mercy's arm. "Come. Walk with me, Mercy."

Even if Mercy could have pulled herself free from the woman's strong grip, she was too intimidated by Mrs. Moresby's forcefulness and frankness to do anything but try to keep up with the woman's long strides.

"When I arrived to Vancouver Island fifteen years ago, I came as a servant to Mrs. Archibald, wife to one of the commanders of Fort Victoria when it was still under the control of Hudson's Bay Company."

At Mrs. Moresby's admission, Mercy nearly tripped.

From beneath the array of flowing ribbons, the matron smiled at Mercy's reaction, as if she enjoyed shocking people with her story. "I never was a lady and still make no claim of being one."

"But you look and sound just like one."

Mrs. Moresby chuckled and patted Mercy's arm. "I married a very wealthy man, Mercy. Mr. Moresby made his fortune in the fur trade. He was, and still is, one of the richest men in Victoria."

Mercy allowed the woman to pull her along and attempted to digest the revelation.

"I understand you better than you think I do," Mrs. Moresby said with another pat. "Of course, Mr. Moresby isn't a nobleman like Lord Colville. Nevertheless, he's a very important man in the colony."

Mercy tried to picture Mrs. Moresby as a servant, but she couldn't imagine the woman without her colorful gowns and flamboyant hats. While they walked, Mrs. Moresby relayed the story of how she met her husband at a party the Archibalds hosted. They'd developed a friendship that eventually blossomed into love.

"So you see, Mercy," she said as they reached the door of the Marine Barracks, "we don't have to settle for a certain way of life just because that was what we were born into."

The very idea of socializing with women like Mrs. Moresby and the other members of the committee only frightened Mercy. She would have counted herself lucky to be a servant to such women, and never in a hundred years would she consider the possibility of becoming one of them.

"You've already started the journey to a new life by coming here," Mrs. Moresby continued. "It took a great deal of courage and strength to leave your family and country of birth behind."

The other women were passing them and entering the barracks, but Mercy wasn't in a hurry to part ways with Mrs. Moresby. Though the conversation was startling, Mercy wanted more. For a reason she couldn't explain, Mrs. Moresby's revelation and encouragement gave her hope.

"Just because you've arrived to Vancouver Island doesn't mean you have to stop your journey to a new life." Mrs. Moresby once again removed her handkerchief from her reticule and dabbed her forehead with it. "In fact, our whole lives are going to be filled with challenges, and our job is to keep growing and seeking after what God has next for us."

Mrs. Moresby's admonition sounded like something Patience would say.

"Don't get stuck, Mercy. Don't get stuck thinking you don't matter or you're not important enough. I know for people like us who come from lowly backgrounds, we all too often accept our place at the bottom and think that's where we belong. But that's just not true. God didn't create some people to be better than others. He created everyone to have equal value."

Mrs. Moresby's words were unlike anything Mercy had ever heard. She supposed here in the colony, away from the motherland, people were free to create a new life, to think differently, to break away from the customary ways of relating. Clearly, Mrs. Moresby had done so with her life.

And yet Mercy wasn't certain she could do the same or even if she wanted to. For so long, all she'd thought about was survival, for herself and for those she loved.

Mrs. Moresby patted her hand as though to encourage her to accept everything she'd just shared.

Mercy gave a brave nod, but inside she trembled. Mr. Scott's reminders for her to stay in her place were much more familiar, much easier to accept. But what if Mrs. Moresby was right? Was there more to her life than she'd believed possible?

Mercy stood behind the closed door of the kitchen. Mr. Scott had already called her several times, letting her know the men were lined up outside and ready to meet with her in the parlor. However, she couldn't get herself to move.

She'd considered tracking down Ann or one of the other girls from her cabin and asking them to hide her somewhere. She missed them all so terribly. After spending nearly every waking minute with the orphans over the past three months, she felt empty, almost purposeless today without them.

Her conversation with Mrs. Moresby following the cricket game kept coming back to her. What did God have next for her? Was it marriage to one of the men waiting to meet with her? Could she resign herself to taking a husband in order to stay in Victoria? Or did God have something else in mind?

What if it were possible for Mercy to find nursing work? She didn't have any official training, but she'd learned a lot from Joseph during the voyage. Surely she could be of some use at a hospital or maybe by assisting one of the local doctors.

She shook her head. Why would anyone let her help with nursing others? She was a nobody here.

"Mercy?" At the soft tread of footsteps entering through the back kitchen door, Mercy spun to find Miss Lawrence carrying in a pail of water. "What are you doing in here?"

Mercy had half a mind to ask Miss Lawrence the same thing. What was a gentlewoman like her doing in the kitchen? She'd come from a home and life where she had servants to run her kitchen and had likely never been in one in all her life.

"I thought you were meeting with your callers," Miss Lawrence said. "They're lined up outside the front door, down the stairs, and across the yard."

My stars . . . Mercy closed her eyes against the image and tried to tell herself they weren't all there to see her. A couple of the other poor women from the bride ship were also having visitors.

"'Tis very exciting," Miss Lawrence continued, stepping farther into the kitchen. "Didn't I tell you that you would have plenty of suitors?"

"I wish I didn't have any." The words were out before she could bite them back. Her eyes flew open to see Miss Lawrence studying her face, her head tilted and her brows arched.

"What I meant to say is that I wish I didn't have any *tonight*. It's so soon—"

"Mercy," Miss Lawrence interrupted, lowering the heavy pail to the floor. "It's perfectly normal to be frightened. I am as well."

"You are?"

"I am positively terrified."

Mercy sagged against the door and stared at Miss Lawrence. Always reserved and proper without revealing her emotions, the young woman's quiet admission was out of character.

As if recognizing the same, Miss Lawrence reached for the pail, turning away from Mercy's scrutiny.

Mercy wished she had the nerve to ask Miss Lawrence what she was afraid of, guessing that whatever had hurt her in England still haunted her.

Miss Lawrence crossed the room to the stove, where she made slow work of pouring the water first into one pot, then another.

"At least here we get to choose who we want to marry," she said after a moment, her back to Mercy.

Did that mean Miss Lawrence hadn't been able to choose for herself back home? That she'd been forced to be with a man she didn't want?

Before Mercy could figure out how to frame her question, Miss Lawrence spun around, a tight smile in place. "Take your time tonight. Get to know the men. I have no doubt you will find the husband of your dreams."

The husband of her dreams? There was only one man she'd ever dreamed about, and that was Joseph. But he could never be her husband. And they both knew it.

"Mercy Wilkins!" Mr. Scott called from the hallway, his tone edged with irritation. "You *must* come at once. Your first suitor is already waiting in the parlor."

Miss Lawrence nodded, her smile growing wider and more genuine. "Go. Before Mr. Scott comes in here and gives us both a sermon."

Mercy knew she ought to respond to the gentlewoman's attempt at a jest. But she couldn't muster the energy, even to smile, because she knew Mr. Scott would give her much more than a sermon if she didn't follow through with the interviews. He'd give her a one-way ticket back to England.

"I shall pray for you," Miss Lawrence added.

"Thank ye, miss."

Trying to keep her hands from shaking, Mercy opened the kitchen door. The clamor at the end of the hallway and in the open front door came to a halt. With at least a dozen pairs of eyes upon her, including Mr. Scott's, Mercy walked quickly to the parlor, entered, and crossed to the open chair opposite her first guest.

She sat down on the edge, folded her hands in her lap, and made herself acknowledge the stranger sitting across from her.

He was well groomed with a clean-shaven face and neatly combed hair. When he offered her an excited smile and began to speak, she could even acknowledge that he was somewhat good-looking and even slightly charming.

The trouble was that he wasn't Joseph. No one would ever be able to come close to Joseph. Not even if she met with every single man in the entire colony.

twenty-nine

Joseph flipped over in his hotel bed, the frame squeaking under his weight. The night was dark without moon or starlight or even streetlamps to provide the slightest glow. The darkness pressed in on him, suffocating him as much as the blankets that tangled around his body.

Although he'd fallen into a fitful sleep for a few hours, he'd awoken to the rapid beat of his heart and the urgency that had been building in his chest all day. And now he could do nothing but toss and turn, growing only more awake and more agitated with every passing second, especially as he reviewed his day.

A medical emergency had detained him from joining Lieutenant Verney aboard the HMS *Grappler* for the regatta. One of the local surgeon's assistants, Charlie Danbury, had called upon him to aid in a complicated surgery on a miner who'd been knocked over the head in a tavern brawl. A bottle of rum had been shattered against the man's skull, leaving a long sliver of glass embedded in his head.

Joseph wanted to help, for he knew the surgery would be more successful with the two of them working together and combining their medical knowledge and skills. And thankfully he and Charlie were able to remove the shard of glass without losing the patient.

As a result of the surgery, however, he'd not only missed the regatta but also part of the cricket game. By the time he arrived at the town green, the match was well under way and he hadn't been able to figure out how best to meet with Mercy in private. She was surrounded by the other women, and even when he'd overthrown the ball in her direction, all eyes turned upon them. Certainly not the place to have a conversation with her.

Afterward, he'd wanted to race after her, take her hand, and stroll next to her. But his teammates had him hedged in. By the time he realized Mercy had left, a chaperone was at her side and any hope of speaking with her privately had vanished.

Later, when evening came and Mercy had begun her appointments with the men, Joseph stood outside the Marine Barracks hoping and praying he'd be admitted, even though his name wasn't on the list to visit with the women who were accepting callers. He'd considered announcing his title and pushing his way through, yet the miner's statement from the previous day had humbled him. *"If you think you can come here with all your highfalutin ways and start ordering us about, well, you got another thing comin'."*

For all his talk of being fair and not letting social status stand in his way, he wasn't above taking advantage of his aristocratic position whenever it suited him. And while he'd been tempted to barge past the other men and shoulder his way inside the building, he held back.

With each passing moment, and with every new man who sat in the armchair across from Mercy, Joseph's stomach had clinched tighter with desperation. If only he'd been able to read her expression to know what she was thinking—to see for himself if this parade of men was what she wanted or not. Then he could be on his way and would never bother her again.

Unfortunately, Mercy was positioned in the parlor so that her back faced the window, leaving Joseph with nothing but his intuition to determine her state of mind. And his intuition warned him that something wasn't right, that he needed to see Mercy and find out the truth about what she really wanted for her future.

Even now, he still couldn't reconcile the fact that she was meeting with men and planning to choose a husband by this evening. Why?

As he had on the ship, he wondered if he was like Jonah in the belly of the fish? Certainly Jonah had been confused, frustrated, and a little hopeless. Nothing felt right anymore, not the journey to Vancouver Island, not his doctoring, not his relationship with Mercy, and not his plans to continue on to the Hawaiian Islands.

He sat up in the bed, untangled from his covers, and slid to the floor to his knees. "What do you want from me, God?" Bowing his head in his hands, the empty ache in his soul reminded him of the day Dr. Bates had come to him with the news that his family was dead. His old friend had laid a gentle hand on his shoulder, his eyes brimming with tears behind his spectacles.

A storm had raged to life inside Joseph, one that threatened to tear him apart. But instead of letting the storm take its natural course, instead of grieving his losses, he ran from his room and didn't stop until he'd reached the cricket field. Once there, he threw himself into a game and had played so hard that eventually he had to force himself to leave.

Ever since that day, Joseph hadn't stopped running. Though he didn't want to admit that Bates and Aunt Pen had been right, he could no longer deny he'd been running away from home so he could escape the painful memories that haunted him there.

Perhaps he was running away from Mercy too. Despite his excuses for not talking to her all day, maybe he was simply afraid of the finality of her rejection—of learning that she wasn't opposed to marriage, just marriage to him.

Even worse was the possibility that he'd easily accepted her rejection to his proposal on the *Tynemouth* because he was afraid. If he didn't allow himself to love Mercy, then he wouldn't have to worry about losing her the same way he'd lost his family.

Indeed, it would be easier to leave, forget the pain, and bury the hurts rather than to stand firm. It would be easier to cut

Mercy out of his thoughts rather than to dwell on what he was losing. And it would be easier to move on with his life, sail to the next destination, and find new sights with which to distract himself.

And yet could he ever really move on? He'd traveled all over the world and the pain of his family's death followed him everywhere. He suspected the same would happen if he ran from Mercy. The pain of losing her would follow him too.

"God," he prayed, "I'm sorry for running—especially from you."

Dragging in a deep breath, he did what he should have done the day Bates came to him with the news his family was gone. He silently lifted that burden up, raised it high, and placed it with his heavenly Father. He'd always miss his family, always feel the loss of their passing. But instead of running from the pain, he allowed himself to feel the grief and know that the One who walked next to him was holding him up.

He didn't know what God was calling him to do next, but he suspected part of His plan involved the partnership with Bates back in Shoreditch. His mind filled with the image of Mercy kneeling next to the lifeless girl, pressing a kiss to her forehead, and lifting her stricken eyes to meet his.

What about all the other people like her, those who needed assistance through their hardships and heartaches? He only had to imagine Mercy trying to fend for herself amidst the squalor for a burning to ignite in his chest, a burning to be there at the dispensary.

Perhaps Bates had already seen the potential for that passion in him when Joseph had yet been blind to it. Whatever the case, he resolved to stop running, face whatever came his way, and do whatever God asked of him.

And that included his relationship with Mercy. He had to stop making excuses, had to stop being afraid. He needed to speak with her again and soon.

Joseph sat rigidly against the hard pew of Christ Church Cathedral. The tall stained-glass windows, the high ceiling with its arched dome, and the imposing columns were all architecturally impressive for a church built so far from civilization. The enormous organ with its wall of pipes was equally extraordinary for a colonial mission.

However, he'd been unable to truly enjoy Victoria or Vancouver Island, especially not this morning with Mercy sitting only a few rows ahead of him with the other bride-ship women. Although every nerve in his body tensed with the need to go to her, he held himself in place by sheer willpower.

From the pulpit, Mr. Scott's monotone rang out over the silent audience. The bishop of Victoria had asked Mr. Scott, as a visiting reverend, to give the sermon today. The zealous man was taking the opportunity to admonish the brides to remember their religious duties, as well as their duties to their husbands and employers, so that they might prove to be a credit to their country and to God.

"And I beseech you, kind people of Victoria," Mr. Scott said, "to look well to the precious charges who have been placed in your keeping to the praise of His glorious name. I pray and hope that all the women here will soon be comfortable as English wives and mothers."

Joseph wanted to shake his head in protest. He didn't want Mercy to soon be comfortable as a wife and mother. It was selfish of him, he knew. She wasn't his. And yet the idea of another man pulling her close and kissing her about drove him mad every time he pictured it. His nerves tightened again so that when Mr. Scott asked the congregation to stand for the benediction, he shot up from the pew. With the final amen, everyone began filing out into the center and side aisles.

As Mercy turned to follow the other women, her sights snagged upon him. Like yesterday, he was struck by her loveliness. He'd never thought her anything but beautiful, even when they were both grimy from months at sea. Now, with her hair and skin glowing from a recent scrubbing, she had a fresh innocence about her like that of a spring blossom.

As if sensing his admiration, she glanced away shyly, her cheeks turning a pretty shade of pink before darting another look his way, a look that sent a sharp, almost painful need for her through his heart.

Joseph nodded toward the outer aisle, which was slightly more shadowed. It might not be private, yet it was a better place to speak with her than in the open.

He hurried from his pew without waiting to see if she was following and moved past the arches and pillars. At the sight of a darkened doorway of a side room, Joseph didn't hesitate. He stepped inside.

A moment later, Mercy entered. "Lord Colville," she whispered.

He reached for her and tugged her deeper into the shadows of what he guessed to be a prayer room or small chapel.

She offered no resistance, readily coming to him, smelling of sunshine and sea. He wanted nothing more than to pull her into his arms as the memory of their shared kiss burned within him.

"Mercy," he said, embarrassed that his voice came out so raspy, revealing his need of her.

Loosening his hold on her arms, he dropped his hands to his sides. He couldn't give in to his desires. He had to remain strong—if not for himself, then for her. She'd had so little in her life, and now that she was here in Victoria, she deserved to finally have the future she wanted. That was his purpose in this meeting, to discover what it was she wanted for herself. Wasn't it?

The dimness of the room hid her face. He could make out only her outline. "Lord Colville—"

"Joseph."

She didn't respond.

"Always Joseph and never anything else." He wasn't sure why it should matter how she addressed him since he was leaving in three days, except that he wanted her to know he didn't care one whit about their differences, that he'd been wrong to bring it up at all at their last parting. "Please," he whispered, wanting to reach out and caress her cheek until his name became a plea upon her lips.

"Joseph," she finally breathed.

He clutched his hands into fists to keep from touching her. He longed for her to say his name again, but he suspected she'd always hesitate in doing away with formalities until he convinced her their differences didn't matter. He had to believe it first and with his whole heart. Did he?

"I shouldn't be here with you," she said. "If Mr. Scott discovers I'm talking to you, he'll be cross, that he will."

Joseph appreciated the reverend for taking his duty as chaperone seriously and for doing his best to protect the women during the voyage. He could even respect the fact that Mr. Scott was still trying to protect them. After all, the eligible men of Victoria were hasty, overeager, and much too forward. But surely Mr. Scott had learned by now that he had nothing to fear from Joseph.

"Mr. Scott cannot protest my speaking with you for a moment."

She glanced over her shoulder so that the faint light coming from the doorway fell upon her, showing the strain in her muscles and her pinched brow. "He'll mind right well."

"Mercy . . ." He hesitated, unsure how to bring up the topic of her appointments with the men.

She swung her attention back to him, the shadows of the room once again concealing her features so he couldn't read her face.

"Tell me I've heard wrong. Tell me you're not choosing a husband for yourself by this eve."

Her silence sent a shiver of dread down his spine.

"Please tell me it isn't so," he insisted softly.

"You haven't heard wrong," she admitted just as softly.

"*Why?*" The desperate question spilled out before he could stop it. Without giving her time to answer, he pushed forward with the words that had been building inside him since he'd heard the news. "If you will marry, then why not wed me?"

She shook her head adamantly, which stirred his desperation all the more. "Please, Mercy." He hadn't proposed to her correctly the first time. And this time he had to do it right and wouldn't let his fears hold him back. He lowered himself on one knee and reached for her hand. "You have captured my heart, and I would be honored if you consented to be my wife."

"My stars, Joseph," she whispered, pressing a hand to her chest.

He hadn't drawn her into this alcove intending to propose marriage to her again, but now that he had, his entire body yearned for her to accept his offer. He wanted her more than he wanted anyone or anything ever before.

Did he indeed love her?

He hadn't believed it possible, hadn't known how love would feel. But now, faced with the possibility of losing her to someone else, his chest ached with something he could only describe as *love*.

Should he declare the intensity of his ardor? Would that sway her to accept his offer?

"Mercy, I didn't propose to you properly the first time." He took her hand more firmly in his. "I was a proud fool and see that clearly now—"

"No, Joseph." She cut him off, pulled her hand free of his grasp, and started to turn away.

"I love you." As soon as the words were out, the truth crashed into him with an intensity that left him weak and breathless. He loved everything about this beautiful woman. From the first time he'd met her until now, he'd known she was special, the kind of woman a man meets but once in a lifetime. If he let her go, he was certain he'd never meet anyone like her again, nor would he want to be with anyone else as much as he did with her.

Mercy couldn't move. Had Joseph really declared his love or had she only imagined it?

"I want to marry you because I love you," he said again, his voice ragged with emotion.

An ache formed deep inside Mercy, swelling with a storm of emotions—ecstasy, worry, desire, uncertainty, longing, reality. But most of all, fear.

He might think he loved her, but he'd remember soon enough just how different they were, just how incompatible. Not only were they from opposite worlds, but he was eventually going back to England. She couldn't leave Vancouver Island, not with Patience hopefully arriving on the next ship. And she couldn't ask Joseph to stay, not when his estate and life were back in England.

Besides, she had so little to give him. She had no money, no land, no title. She owned nothing but her clothing, and even that had been a donation. Mr. Scott was right. She'd utterly disgrace Joseph if she married him. She could see it now—all his friends laughing at him, at her. They'd want nothing to do with Joseph, and he'd lose the prestige and respect he deserved.

She couldn't let that happen, couldn't let him bring ruin upon himself because of her.

"Say something, Mercy," he pleaded.

"Joseph, I . . . I can't." The ache in her chest had expanded into her throat, making speaking difficult. If she told him the truth about why, he'd probably tell her none of her reasons mattered. But what if eventually he tired of the scandal and the shame that would come with their betrothal? What if later he realized he'd made a mistake?

"What is this really about, Mercy?" he asked, frustration in his voice. "Why will you consider marrying another man, a stranger, but not me?"

"I'm not considering anything of the sort!" she cried out, her own frustration getting the best of her. "Mr. Scott is *forcing* me into it."

"What the devil?"

"Mr. Scott has vowed to see I'm married before he sails away."

"I don't understand. Why is he so insistent upon it?"

Mercy hesitated. Should she tell Joseph that Mr. Scott had overheard his shipboard proposal and believed her unworthy? She suspected such news would only anger Joseph, leading him to confront Mr. Scott, who of course would deny it.

"Mr. Scott learned I'm not wanting to get married," she said at last. "He says that since the Columbia Mission Society paid for me to come here to be a bride, I must follow through with it. If not, I have to return to England or else pay back the cost of my fare."

"He has no business saying such a thing." Joseph's voice rose loud enough that anyone in the side aisle outside the alcove would be able to hear him and would surely come to investigate.

"He's right," Mercy continued, lowering her voice and hoping Joseph would do the same. "I'm in debt to the Columbia Mission Society. And I can't be a-going back to England, not when Patience will be expecting me here."

"I shall speak to Mr. Scott at once." He started to leave, but Mercy stopped him with a touch to his arm.

"No. He'll only make things worse." If that were possible.

Joseph nodded, then gave a sigh. "Tell me, did he orchestrate the appointments with the men?"

Mercy thought back to the previous evening, the parade of men coming in and out of the parlor. She'd hated every minute of it. Most of the meetings had been painfully awkward as each of the men attempted to prove why he was the better choice over the others. "'Twas Mr. Scott's idea, to be sure."

"And he wants you to choose a husband by tonight?"

"Aye. And if I don't pick someone tonight, he's planning to send me back to England straightaway." She thought over the blur of faces and names from last evening. She couldn't remember any of the men. How would she ever be able to choose?

"Mr. Scott may have zeal for accomplishing the goals of the

Columbia Mission Society," Joseph said with a growl, "but he's taken his duties too seriously. Much too seriously. And now he must be made to see the error of his ways."

"No, Joseph. Please . . ." If Joseph expressed his disapproval to Mr. Scott, there would be no telling what the man might do next. She couldn't chance it.

"I'm only sorry I did not step in and prevent him from ill-using you sooner." Once more Joseph started to leave.

Mercy clutched his arm to stop him. "You cannot talk to Mr. Scott about this. He'll punish me."

"I won't let him."

"He overheard us on the ship. He knows about your proposal to me, and he thinks I'm trying to trick you into marrying me." The embarrassing truth was out before she could stop it. "He knows that a union betwixt us will cause a scandal, and he's just wanting to protect you from ruination."

Joseph was silent for a long moment. Perhaps now he'd finally realize the foolishness of his proposal and see that he was better off without her.

"Promise me you won't talk to Mr. Scott," she said. "If you press him, he'll make me leave Vancouver Island."

"But if you have no desire to be married, I shall not allow him to coerce you into it."

She wished Joseph could find a way to save her from an unwanted marriage, but she feared his interference would have the opposite effect and make things worse. "Please, Joseph. I'm not doing this for me. I'm doing it for Patience."

Through the darkness of the room, his hand found hers. His fingers were warm and solid and strong. "Have no fear. I shall find a way to give you your freedom. It's the least I can do for you." He squeezed her hand and then slipped out of the alcove and was gone.

thirty

"Got ten acres of land overlooking the sea. Prettiest place on earth." The young man sat on the edge of the fancy chair, his hands trembling and his eyes twitching.

Mercy wished she could put him at ease, but she didn't know what to say and couldn't muster any enthusiasm. Her melancholy wasn't fair to her suitors. Her mood wasn't their fault, and they deserved better from her. But the truth was, the more she sat through the meetings, the more the life drained from her until she was all but emptied out.

In the end, what difference would it make whom she chose to marry? She'd never had much control over her life. Even if she'd come to a new place with the hope of having some say, she'd learned right well that wasn't likely to happen. The struggles of being poor and being a woman had followed her to her new home and seemed all too eager to stick with her. Would she be more satisfied if she simply accepted her lot in life?

As the man rose to leave, Mercy forced a smile and thanked him politely. Once he exited, Mr. Scott rapidly entered the room.

"He's the last one." The reverend eyed her with a solemn expression. "I shall wait as you take a few minutes to examine all the evidence presented to you and then make your choice of a husband."

She heard laughter coming from the room opposite the parlor, where two other poor women were meeting with suitors. If the laughter was any indication, they seemed to be enjoying the attention and flattery of the men.

"Well?" he asked.

Mr. Scott had given her but a few seconds to decide. She supposed that even if she had a few days, she still wouldn't be able to make a decision about which of the men to marry. She didn't want any of them. She didn't want any man . . . except Joseph.

In the hours since meeting with Joseph after the church service, she'd done little else but think about him, especially his declaration of love. But what did he see in her when he could have just about any woman he wanted?

She turned and found herself staring into a mirror. She'd steadfastly ignored her reflection thus far, not daring to look. Before she could truly focus, she shifted her gaze to the cushioned chair.

Was she afraid of what she'd see if she took a long look at herself?

"Don't get stuck thinking that you don't matter or that you're not important enough."

Mrs. Moresby's words had echoed through her mind since the walk home from the cricket game. Had Mercy gotten stuck thinking she wasn't important enough because she was poor and a woman? Had she too easily bowed her head, letting others dictate how she should live? Was she doing that even now with Mr. Scott?

Timidly, she glanced up and peeked at herself in the mirror. The person peering back at her was hanging her head and shoulders.

"For people like us who come from lowly backgrounds, we all too often accept our place at the bottom and think that's where we belong. But that's just not true."

Mrs. Moresby had been right. Mercy had always just accepted her place, had never questioned it. What made Mr. Scott know what was best for her life? Mercy straightened her shoulders and lifted her head, watching as the young woman in the mirror did likewise.

She'd left her home and everything familiar so she could forge a better life in a better place. But it was all too easy to keep walking the same old path, seeing herself as a nobody, viewing herself as nothing more than a servant, believing she didn't really matter.

If she wanted to move forward on her new journey, then she needed to accept what Mrs. Moresby had said, that God didn't create some people to be better than others, that He created everyone to have equal value.

Mercy stared at herself in the mirror without blinking. She lifted a hand and touched her cheek, her chin, then her nose and the dusting of freckles there. Her eyes were surrounded by long lashes. Her lips dipped into a heart shape. And the loose strands of her long hair softened her face.

Patience had told her she was beautiful like Twiggy. But Mercy hadn't wanted to be like Twiggy in any way, not even in her appearance. By avoiding mirrors, Mercy hoped she could make the similarity go away. And yet the face staring back at her now wasn't Twiggy's at all. Yes, there was some resemblance, like the eye and hair colors and maybe the shape of her nose and chin.

She blinked once. Then twice. Mostly she was different. Unique.

She'd tried so hard all her life not to be like Twiggy. But maybe she'd already been different all along and just hadn't realized it.

"I need your answer, Mercy," Mr. Scott said. "If you refuse to choose one of the men, then you will force me to do it for you."

Mercy stared at herself for another moment and then straightened her shoulders even higher. Taking a deep breath, before she lost her courage, she pivoted so that she was facing the reverend. Her stomach rebelled with a dizzying lurch.

"I'm not picking from any of the men, sir." Her voice quavered.

Mr. Scott took a step back, as if her defiant words had smacked him in the chest. He seemed to catch himself before narrowing his eyes. "I do not think I heard you correctly, girl. I demand that you choose one of the men, and then we shall have the business at hand concluded."

She had the overwhelming urge to lower her gaze and duck her head, to murmur her apology. But out of the corner of her eye she caught her reflection again. She was worthy of respect. She needn't cower in fear any longer.

With her chin held high, she looked Mr. Scott directly in the eyes. "I'll find a job here in Victoria, sir. And if someday I get a hankering to get married, I may do so. But for now, I'll make a way on my own right well, you'll see."

The words were the bravest she'd ever spoken to a person of authority. For a moment she half expected the reverend to cross the room, slap her face, and then force her to kneel and kiss his shoes.

Instead, Mr. Scott simply shook his head. "If you're aspiring to gentility, I assure you, you'll only be met with extreme regret."

She didn't know what *aspiring to gentility* meant but guessed it had something to do with Joseph.

"And I assure you that you'll also wish you'd done as I recommended, especially once you're back in England in debtors' prison. For not only will you owe the esteemed Columbia Mission Society the fees accumulated from the passage to Vancouver Island but also the fees for your return voyage."

"I'm staying, sir," Mercy insisted, glad her voice was steadier and stronger than her insides. "I'll save up my earnings and send them back to the mission just as soon as I can."

Mr. Scott's face became flushed, and his nostrils flared. "No, you will not—!"

A knock sounded against the doorframe, and they both startled at the sight of Joseph entering the room. Following close on his heels was Mrs. Moresby, bustling in amidst a flurry and swishing of her heavy skirts. She'd changed the hat and gown she'd worn to church earlier and was now attired in a vibrant blue velvet, glistening jewels, and a wide hat bedecked with matching velvet flowers and equally stunning jewels.

Every time Mercy saw Mrs. Moresby's opulent display of wealth, it was difficult to picture her as a much younger woman dressed in a simple skirt and apron, rushing about and doing the bidding of her master.

"Good evening, Miss Wilkins. Mr. Scott," Joseph said, taking off his hat and bowing slightly to them both. He was immaculately attired just as he had been at the church service that morning with his black dress coat, matching waistcoat, and pinstriped trousers. His dark brown eyes connected with hers for only an instant, but it was enough for her to glimpse the turmoil churning there.

From the heaviness of their breathing, Mercy guessed the two had hurried to arrive at the Marine Barracks just now. How much had they heard of her conversation with Mr. Scott?

"Lord Colville." Mr. Scott bowed low and held himself there as was his custom. She'd come to the conclusion that the length of the reverend's bow portrayed the depth of his respect. He clearly put a great deal of value upon titles, social standing, and wealth.

Perhaps other people weren't quite as blatant as Mr. Scott in their prejudices. No matter what she said or how she demanded his respect, he'd likely never be able to see her as anything other than a poor woman.

But she couldn't let people like Mr. Scott hold her back from respecting herself. If she learned to respect and hold herself in higher esteem, then perhaps one day others would too. Even if they didn't, she had to start somewhere.

Mrs. Moresby was watching Mr. Scott's bowed posture with ever-widening eyes. When she glanced at Mercy, her gaze was filled with both question and humor, so much so that Mercy had to look away to keep from smiling.

"I am deeply grateful you've chosen to grace us with the

pleasure of your company this evening." Mr. Scott finally pulled himself up so that he was as rigid as the prayer book he kept tucked in his coat pocket.

"May I present Mrs. Moresby?" Joseph motioned to the older woman.

"Mrs. Moresby." Mr. Scott nodded at her but kept his attention upon Joseph. "My lord—"

"I've heard a great deal about you, Mr. Scott," Mrs. Moresby said, her loud voice and large presence giving the reverend little choice but to acknowledge her again.

"I do hope Lord Colville has given me a fair report," Mr. Scott said gravely. "With all the time we spent together aboard the *Tynemouth*, may I be so bold as to say we've moved beyond mere formalities? It is my great hope that my wife and I and our lovely daughters may further our acquaintance with Lord Colville in the days to come. In fact, Lord Colville has already taken a liking to each of my daughters, so perhaps one day I shall have the privilege of an even more intimate acquaintance."

At the reverend's statement, Mrs. Moresby's mouth hung open. Her gaze once again swung to Mercy, her eyes dancing with mirth. This time Mercy couldn't hide her smile at the woman's reaction to Mr. Scott.

Mrs. Moresby snorted at the same time that Joseph spoke. "Mr. Scott, I may speak to you freely, may I not?"

"Indeed, my lord—"

"I am not, nor will I ever be, interested in your daughters beyond an acquaintance."

For once Mr. Scott clamped his lips together, clearly having no response.

"My sincerest apologies if I led you to believe otherwise." Joseph's brow creased. "They are indeed gracious young ladies, but my ardor and affection belong to another and always will."

Joseph didn't glance her way. Even so, Mercy's heartbeat picked up its pace at his admission. Even if he had confessed his love earlier, she still couldn't quite believe he'd be able to love—really love—a poor woman like her.

"Mr. Scott," Mrs. Moresby said, breaking the awkward silence that had settled in the parlor. "Actually, most of what I've heard about you has come from the bride-ship women. They've had much to say about you."

"I see." His voice was threaded with disappointment.

"I met with a number of the women individually this afternoon," Mrs. Moresby continued. "And not a one of them had anything positive to say about you. In short, they dislike you."

Mr. Scott blanched. "How dare you speak so harshly, madam? You have no right—"

"You'll have to forgive me for my bluntness, Mr. Scott. I'm afraid I don't have the same social graces as Lord Colville."

"Just as I have preached," Mr. Scott said. "That is precisely what happens when people aspire beyond themselves. They may imitate the manner and speech of those of a higher station, but they cannot hide their true nature indefinitely."

"I'm not hiding anything from anyone," Mrs. Moresby responded with a chuckle that shook her frame. "I am who I am. If you don't like me, then too bad."

Mercy watched with a mixture of awe and trepidation as the woman sparred with the reverend. She wasn't sure she'd ever have the same confidence Mrs. Moresby displayed, but she could certainly learn from her about self-respect.

Mr. Scott sputtered his response, but before he could formulate his thoughts, Mrs. Moresby spoke again. "After meeting with the women this afternoon and discovering the hard feelings, the Female Immigration Committee convened and just now decided to relieve you of your duties as chaperone."

"You may do no such thing." Splotchy red formed on Mr. Scott's face. "You have no authority to do so. I am a representative of the Columbia Mission Society, which is made up of illustrious and the most exemplary of sponsors. I report to them, not to a paltry handful of colonial upstarts."

"Mr. Scott," Joseph cut in, his tone calm but firm. "As we are departing from the colony soon, the oversight of the women's care must be transferred. You have done your duty, and now you must release it and look ahead to your next calling."

The reverend dipped his head in servitude to Joseph.

Mrs. Moresby apparently took that as her cue to continue. "The first thing the committee plans to make known is the policy regarding marriage of the bride-ship women. While it is our sincerest hope for all the women to eventually become wives and mothers, we don't think it's in anyone's best interests to rush the process. The marriages will be stronger and more enduring if the women have the necessary time to choose husbands wisely, rather than be pushed to decide by a deadline. Wouldn't you agree, Mr. Scott?"

At Mrs. Moresby's declaration, Mercy's attention jumped to Joseph, only to find him watching her. The sincerity of his expression told her everything—that he'd been the one to reach out to Mrs. Moresby today, to orchestrate the interviews with the other bride-ship women, and to coordinate the meeting of the committee. He'd done it all for her, to protect her and to fulfill his promise to help her be free, even though he wouldn't get anything out of it for himself.

Warmth bubbled up inside Mercy. She wanted to rush across the room, fling her arms about him, and embrace him. He was the kindest, sweetest, most considerate man she'd ever known.

Mr. Scott swallowed several times before managing to speak again. "No, madam, I do not agree. I'm afraid you have no inkling of what you're dealing with when it comes to these women. They are uneducated and unqualified to know what is in their best interests. They need the guidance of informed and well-meaning men like myself in order to step into their new roles as wives and mothers."

Mrs. Moresby shook her head, her wide hat swaying to and

fro like the ship in a storm. "After speaking with the women, I've concluded they are both smart and hardworking. Given time, they are more than capable of picking their own husbands. If some of them decide they aren't suited to married life, they will most certainly contribute to the welfare of the colony in other ways."

Mr. Scott wheeled to face Mercy, his expression growing even more severe. "This is *your* doing. You used your wiles and seductive nature to get your way."

"Mr. Scott," Joseph said sternly, his fists balled, his body rigid. "Say no more, sir, lest you inflict further shame upon yourself."

"I'll have you know," Mrs. Moresby interjected, "Miss Wilkins wasn't involved in any of the discussions today. She had no knowledge of the committee's meeting. But she, like all the others, should be free to make her own decisions regarding her future. And I trust that she will make the right decision."

Mrs. Moresby leveled a look at Mercy, one that censured her and implored her at the same time. What was Mrs. Moresby asking her to do?

"She has no notion of taking a husband!" Mr. Scott shouted. He quickly cleared his throat before speaking again in a much lower voice, "And certainly we can all agree that a woman's place is in the home. God created her to bear and raise children."

"Come now, Mr. Scott," Joseph said, "surely you cannot deny God has gifted women beyond childbearing capabilities. Miss Wilkins is a prime example. She has extraordinary nursing skills and 'twould be a shame if she could not serve God and others in that way."

"Whatever the case, she must be made to return to England," Mr. Scott said, "and repay the Columbia Mission Society for wasting their time and money on her."

Mercy was tempted to lower her head and allow the others to continue to speak on her behalf as if she were not present. But she glanced in the mirror and straightened her shoulders again.

She had to step forward and be confident and strong. If she didn't now, when would she?

Mrs. Moresby started to reply when Mercy spoke. "I told Mr. Scott I'd save my earnings to repay the Columbia Mission Society, and I vow I'll do it, that I will."

"That's an excellent idea," Mrs. Moresby said. "In fact, as we consider bringing more brides to the colony, we have contemplated how to fund the endeavor, as we cannot rely upon donations and charity indefinitely. Perhaps a system of repayment is the way to do it."

"Regardless of the ultimate decision," Joseph said, "you may put your troubled mind at ease, Mr. Scott. Upon my return to London, I shall personally make certain the Columbia Mission Society receives a sizable donation, part of which will most assuredly cover Miss Wilkins's passage here to Vancouver Island."

Mr. Scott bowed his head toward Joseph. "That is very generous of you, my lord. Very generous indeed."

Joseph nodded.

Mr. Scott took a tentative step toward him. "My lord, I hope you know I have only ever had your best interests at heart in this matter and that I desired to protect you and the Society from any hint of scandal."

Joseph narrowed his eyes upon the reverend.

Mr. Scott hurriedly added, "As young men are sometimes impetuous and lacking the foresight to know what is best for their futures, we who are older and wiser must step in on occasion and direct the situation. While such directives may seem unpleasant at the time, I have no doubt that in hindsight you will be much relieved and grateful for the intervention that is meant to protect your good name and reputation."

For a long moment, no one spoke. Mrs. Moresby's mouth hung open again, and Joseph's jaw flexed as he stared at Mr. Scott.

"As you say," Joseph finally said, his voice clipped, "there are times when young men do indeed fall prey to impetuousness and a lack of foresight. But this is not one such time, Mr. Scott. A wiser and older man I highly esteem recently told me not to let the barriers of class interfere with anything, not with work, life, or love. I shall hold to his advice as I believe it is the same advice my own father would have given me."

Mr. Scott's eyes had widened at Joseph's speech, and Mrs. Moresby had closed her mouth, the hint of a smile now playing on her lips.

Joseph put his hat back on. "As it appears our business here is concluded, I suggest we be on our way now. Shall we, Mr. Scott?" Joseph gestured toward the door, indicating that the reverend should precede him.

"Very well, Lord Colville." Mr. Scott fiddled with his collar and buttoned his coat before bowing again. "I bid you good day." When he exited the room, Mercy released a tight breath.

"I must be on my way as well." Mrs. Moresby bustled forward, but then stopped in the doorway and turned back to Mercy. "Again, I trust you'll make the right decision."

Mercy nodded. But as before, she didn't understand what decision Mrs. Moresby was referencing. Did she expect her to find a husband after all? Ultimately, did the kind matron believe as Mr. Scott did, that women needed to become wives and mothers? Or was she referring to Joseph?

When Mrs. Moresby was gone, Joseph hesitated by the door.

An invisible force seemed to pull at Mercy, urging her to close the span betwixt them and to throw her arms around him. Even as she fought against the force, the desire to go to him only increased. The desire to wipe her hand across his brow and smooth away the worried lines. The longing to ease the sadness in his eyes and bring a smile to his face. The wish to cling to him and never let go.

As his eyes connected with hers across the distance, her pulse slowed to a crawl. He'd told her he loved her and wanted to marry her. Would he do it again now?

A part of her wanted him to say the words once more. If he proposed again, she wasn't sure she'd be able to say no. He'd been there for her time after time during the voyage. He'd given of himself in countless ways. He'd never demanded anything in return, and he wasn't doing so now either.

Joseph Colville was an honorable and noble man. And her heart swelled with something she couldn't name.

"Thank ye," she said. The words were inadequate to express her gratitude for his help with her predicament and Mr. Scott. Even though she'd gathered the courage to take a stand against the reverend, ultimately it was Joseph's influence that had saved her and given her the freedom she sought.

His eyes held hers, giving her a glimpse of the turmoil that still raged in the depths of his soul. He opened his mouth as though he might say something. But then he pursed his lips, nodded, and tipped the brim of his hat. A second later, he pivoted and walked out of the room.

His firm footsteps thudded in the hallway, moving rapidly away. When the door closed behind him, the sound echoed with a finality that shook her to her very core.

thirty-one

Mercy clapped her hands to the music of the fiddler and watched the girls as they twirled. Ann, Minnie, Flo, and Kip had been allowed by their new employers to attend Sophia and Pioneer's wedding and the dance afterward. Most of the other bride-ship women were present too, along with half of Victoria.

The Swan Hall was full to overflowing. With the onset of the evening, the streetlights had been lit and people were dancing outside on the sidewalks and streets to the strains of music flowing from the open windows.

At the center of the hall, Sophia wore a lovely gown of ivory satin with a wide gathered waist, a neckline trimmed with lace ruffles, layers of full petticoats, and a wide crinoline hoop. If the rumors were true, Pioneer had instructed the local milliner that the bridal dress wasn't to cost less than four hundred pounds.

Pioneer, too, was attired in garments fit for royalty. His hair was neatly cut, his beard trimmed, and his face scrubbed to a shine. He hadn't stopped smiling the entire day, beaming down at his new bride as if he'd just gained the whole world.

Maybe he had. Maybe some marriages turned out well after all. At the very least, Sophia and Pioneer were looking for a bit of beauty amidst all the bleakness and finding joy in their union.

Mercy leaned against the elegantly papered wall and let her hands fall to her sides. She didn't mind her spot near the window and the heavy tapestry that half hid her. She'd already spent much of the day explaining to the hopeful men who approached her that she'd made her decision regarding a husband—that she wasn't choosing anyone at the moment and that she planned to take a job instead and live on her own.

Most of the men had taken her news with surprising grace. She supposed the wedding and the presence of all the women had made the rejection easier to take. They'd moved on to wooing and dancing with others, leaving Mercy content to mingle with the younger girls and listen to their tales about their new positions as domestics.

She was praying such an arrangement with a wealthy family would open up for herself. She'd be right happy being a domestic, a scullery maid, anything.

Miss Lawrence approached, fanning herself rapidly, her delicate face flushed, framed by her rich auburn hair. The beautiful gentlewoman had been surrounded by plenty of men, including the naval officer who'd been paying particular attention to her.

"Mercy," she hissed as she drew near, casting an anxious glance over her shoulder. "I need to hide."

"Hide?" Mercy scanned the crowd. "What's to hide from?"

Miss Lawrence was attired in a lovely gown of deep emerald that highlighted her pale skin and the stunning color of her hair. But even as she moved nearer, Mercy could see the tension in her thin body and the fear in her eyes.

"Please help me," she whispered, grasping Mercy with her silky gloved hands. "Please."

Mercy immediately stepped aside and drew the woman into the shadows of the tapestry so that the heavy curtains nearly concealed her.

"Is he looking this way?" Miss Lawrence asked.

"Who?"

"The man who just entered. The one with the bald head and red bow tie."

Mercy scanned the hall but found no one watching her or Miss Lawrence. There was indeed a short, balding man with a red bow tie, yet his attention was focused on one of the women of the welcoming committee.

"I see him—he's not paying you any heed."

Miss Lawrence poked her head out from behind the curtains. She watched the balding man for a moment before sagging back against the wall, the anxiety leaving her face, replaced by embarrassment. She extricated herself from the thick tapestry and took a wobbly step away from the wall.

Without explaining any further, Miss Lawrence began to skirt the room, hurrying toward the door, clearly wanting to exit the party. Why was Miss Lawrence so flustered?

"Come dance." Ann's voice interrupted Mercy's contemplation. The girl's face was pretty and full of life. Soon enough Ann and the other orphans would be attracting the men. But for now, Mercy was relieved that they could just be girls.

"I'm right happy to watch you dance," Mercy replied. "That's enough for me."

But was it enough? As happy as she was for her friends, and as happy as she was to be free from Mr. Scott's scheming, her heart had been heavy over the past couple of days. Maybe she'd be content once she had a job or was using her God-given gifts. Maybe she'd be content once Patience arrived.

Ann whirled back into the flow of the dancers, laughing with delight. Mercy couldn't help but think of the kind of life the girl might be living at this moment if she'd remained in London after being kicked out of the orphanage. She would've been homeless and probably ended up in a workhouse or brothel, where she would have wasted away.

This had been a voyage of discovery, courage, and freedom for all of them. Mercy was grateful and yet . . .

She sighed. As she leaned back into the tapestry again, the sight of Joseph in the wide doorway of the hall made her stomach spin like the dancers. Joseph paused in the center, a picture of elegance, distinction, and authority in his full dress coat, white vest, broad rolled collar, and silk hat.

Though their parting at the Marine Barracks on Sunday had felt final, she'd hoped for an opportunity to see him one last time and wish him farewell. However, she hadn't seen him at any of the festivities throughout the day and had begun to think he'd already boarded the *Tynemouth*.

The ship was scheduled to leave on the morrow. The girls had gleefully remarked that Mr. Scott and his family had gone out to the *Tynemouth* today. They were as happy as Mercy to be free of the man's strict control.

Mrs. Robb and her family were present at the wedding, but the dour matron had more easily given up her role as chaperone once the ship had arrived, and now she was busy settling in and starting her own new life.

Mercy wanted to start over, but somehow she couldn't make herself move forward quite yet. Maybe once she said good-bye to Joseph . . .

He peered around the room and seemed completely unaware of the attention he was drawing. Commander Verney approached him, as did several other important men who were members of the bride-ship welcoming committee. As Joseph greeted them and made conversation, his attention kept drifting.

Was he looking for someone? Perhaps her?

Mercy stepped out of the shadows of the tapestry and moved into the light spilling across the hall from the chandelier overhead. Did she dare cross to him? And speak to him one last time before he sailed out of her life forever?

He stood at the opposite side of the large room. Even if he glanced in her direction, he'd never spot her through the crowd. If she wanted to say anything, she'd have to go to him.

She took another step and was immediately bumped by a dancer. What if Joseph wasn't searching for her? What if he had no wish to see her again? After all, if he'd wanted to talk further, he could have sought her out over the past couple of days, especially now that Mr. Scott was no longer interfering.

She hesitated, letting another dancer collide with her, pushing her against the wall. She had no right to approach a man like Joseph. He was a titled nobleman, a wealthy lord, an important gentleman. Only the most significant of men dared mingle with him.

For several beats of the lively tune, she held back and watched him interact with his peers. He nodded at something one of them said and spoke politely in return.

Aye, he was a lord, but he'd also become her friend. And she couldn't let this opportunity pass her by. She had to say goodbye, and this was likely her last chance to do so. She might not be as significant as the men, but she couldn't forget she was just as valuable. She had worth. And she had to prove to herself she had every bit as much right to speak with Joseph as anyone else.

She thrust away from the wall, winding her way through the crowd until at last she was close enough that he would notice her if he turned.

His back was straight and his shoulders strong, his suit coat stretched taut at the seams. He continued to scan the dance hall even as he conversed with the gentlemen surrounding him.

What should she do? Sidle around until she stood in his line of vision and then wait for him to acknowledge her? She swallowed the old fears that whispered she wasn't good enough, that she'd never be his equal. She sucked in a breath and addressed him the way he'd asked of her. "Joseph?"

He froze and then spun to face her. "There you are." The relief in his voice and on his face reassured Mercy, even if the men on either side of Joseph raised questioning brows and peered down their noses at her.

"Will you please excuse me, gentlemen," Joseph said. "I must take some fresh air."

Without waiting for their responses, he took hold of her arm and steered her from the hall, past the crowds milling in the entrance, and out the front door.

The night air was laden with the scents of woodsmoke and pine. After almost a week in Victoria, Mercy was still amazed by the cleanliness of the buildings, streets, and the air. With the town only a few years old, most of the buildings were new and freshly painted, standing tall with pride. Of all the businesses, Victoria boasted mostly restaurants and saloons. There seemed to be a dozen on every street.

In spite of the vices, nothing could compare to the blackened, leaning, and terraced buildings that crowded London. The wide street before her contained a festiveness, a celebration of life that seemed to mock the desolation lurking in the narrow passageways of Nichol and other London slums.

She allowed Joseph to lead her past the revelers and past a gathering of Chinese men standing and talking outside a restaurant. She was fascinated by the various groups of people who populated Victoria. The Chinese and blacks had apparently come north from San Francisco to mine for gold. She'd expected to see more native people but had learned they'd been ordered to leave the town earlier in the year at the start of a smallpox epidemic.

Joseph stopped in front of what appeared to be a dry-goods store. The light from a nearby streetlamp glinted off the window display of tents, pots and pans, sleeping gear, mining tools, and other supplies for the miners working in the mountains across the bay on the mainland.

"Mercy," Joseph said, releasing her arm and taking a step away, "I'm taking passage out to the *Tynemouth* within the hour, and I didn't want to depart without bidding you farewell."

He was leaving in an hour? Her heart wrenched in protest.

"Forgive my intrusion," he said. "I know you are busy and likely have no wish to see me again—"

"That's not true," Mercy interrupted. "I wanted to find a way to say good-bye to you, but I didn't know how."

At her admission, some of the stiffness of Joseph's demeanor slipped away. "The *Tynemouth* weighs anchor tomorrow, and then we shall be on our way again, this time to the Hawaiian Islands."

During her days of being quarantined with Sarah, Joseph had read to her from his geography book, describing the Hawaiian Islands with great excitement. "I hope it's as beautiful as your book made it out to be."

He gave a little smile, not responding with the enthusiasm she expected.

"Will you get to visit the East Indies and China again?"

"Eventually, yes."

She waited for him to elaborate, to tell her something he was looking forward to seeing, but he remained sober and quiet.

"I'm sure you're thrilled about reuniting with your sister Patience," he finally remarked.

"Mrs. Moresby doesn't think the next ship will arrive for several more months. But she said our ship came sooner than expected, so it's possible the *Robert Lowe* will make it here earlier than scheduled too."

"Yes, let us pray for a swift and safe journey."

They fell silent again, the laughter and music from the Swan Hall filling the night air.

"Have you any prospects for employment yet?" He crossed his hands behind his back.

"No, but something's bound to open up right soon. It surely will." She tried to infuse her voice with confidence. She didn't want Joseph thinking she was worried or that he'd made a mistake in liberating her from the prospect of marriage.

"I shall speak to the gentlemen on the welcoming committee and inquire about positions in their households."

She shook her head in protest. "Everyone who needs help has already taken on the younger girls. If they hire me, maybe they'll have to let one of the girls go. And I don't want to chance that."

Joseph was quiet again.

"I'll be right fine. You'll see."

"I know you will. You're a strong and capable woman."

She would miss his confidence in her abilities. No one had ever believed in her quite the same way Joseph did, not even Patience.

Another long moment of silence spread between them. Mercy had a hundred things she wanted to say, but for some reason the words wouldn't come.

"If you ever have need of anything," Joseph said haltingly, "I hope you'll count me as your friend and contact me."

Although she was trying to move past her insecurities, she wasn't sure she'd ever be able to contact Joseph if she had a need. Even so, his offer was as kind as always.

"I am most sincere in my suggestion," he added, reaching for her hands and grasping them. His gloved fingers surrounded hers firmly.

"You're a good man, Joseph, and I thank ye for your friendship."

He shook his head as if in disagreement. "You've thanked me now and in the past for friendship, but 'tis I who should be thanking you. I'm a better person for having met and known you."

"You've taught me to be a better person too."

His grip tightened on her hands. "While I am still riddled with the arrogance of my station, perhaps these years of wandering have not all been in vain. After living aboard a ship and experiencing life in new places and among different kinds of people, God's beginning to humble me, though I still have much to learn."

"You are already the humblest man I've ever met." In fact, she didn't know of any other man who'd do all that Joseph had done. Perhaps Dr. Bates from the Shoreditch Dispensary. But there was still something about Joseph that was different, something that spoke of the greater things God would do through him someday.

"Please forgive me for ever insinuating I am better than you," he said softly.

"'Course I will, Joseph." She wanted to argue that he *was* better. But she couldn't now, not with so little time left.

The night air was balmy for the end of September, and a soft gust of wind brushed against Mercy's overheated cheeks. She shivered less from the breeze than from the realization Joseph was leaving and this was the last time she'd ever see him.

As if reading her mind, he expelled a sigh. "I regret I must be on my way. I need to return to my hotel to retrieve the last of my belongings before the boat takes me out to the *Tynemouth*."

"I understand." She tried to speak calmly but everything within her rose up in protest, making her want to scream at him not to leave. "Then I bid you farewell."

She squeezed his hands and started to let go. But he didn't release his grip. Instead, he clung to her as if he had no intention of releasing her. For just an instant, she pictured him sweeping her up in his arms, carrying her to the steamer, and sailing away with her.

As quickly as the image came, she forced it from her mind. She couldn't go anywhere. Not with the possibility of Patience arriving on the next bride ship. Even if she'd been free to leave, she wouldn't let him ruin his life and future. If the gentlemen at the dance had looked down upon her, how much more would his friends and family in England despise him because of her?

"Mercy, I—" he started, but then halted, closing his eyes and clamping his lips together. He held himself stiffly for a moment longer before pulling her closer.

She didn't resist but fell against him eagerly. His arms slid around her at the same time that she wrapped him into an embrace.

With the solid length of his body against hers, she was intensely aware of his thick arms about her, his broad chest, and his heartbeat thudding in tempo with hers. When he leaned in and buried his nose into her hair, warmth spread low in her abdomen, the same pool of desire that had formed when she'd kissed him on the ship.

If she lifted her face and gave him access, she suspected he'd kiss her. For as strong as he was, as much as he lived with integrity, their attraction was living and breathing and wouldn't easily be put to death, even as they went their separate ways. At least it wouldn't easily be put to death for her.

Instead, she pressed further into his chest and breathed in his clean musky scent. His hands at her lower back spread, as though he needed to hold more of her and couldn't quite get enough. He kissed the side of her head, his lips hard and possessive before he dropped his mouth to her ear, his breathing ragged and echoing into every limb of her body.

"Mercy," he whispered, longing stretching his voice taut. Was he asking her for a kiss?

She fought against the powerful, almost overwhelming sense of being pulled forward into him. She'd come out here to say good-bye, not to complicate the matter with passion and kisses and affection. As drawn as they were to each other, indulging in a farewell kiss would only make their parting more difficult.

"Good-bye, Joseph," she whispered, prying her arms away from him and taking a step back.

He visibly tensed as though he intended to draw her back into his embrace, but then he let his arms drop to his sides.

A tight ache formed in her throat along with the need to cry. She didn't want to lose him. He was her glimpse of beauty amidst the bleakness of life.

He closed his eyes. Was he fighting his own inner battle? She guessed he was and that she could help him best if she stayed strong. That way they could both move on separate from each other.

"I wish you well, Joseph."

His eyes flew open, almost frantic as he took her in. "I also wish you well."

The music coming from the dance hall wafted their way. Mercy didn't want to return to the festivities. Suddenly all she wanted to do was to run back to the Marine Barracks to her bedroom and throw herself upon her bunk where she'd be alone.

"I shall never forget you," Joseph whispered.

"Nor I you." Mercy let her eyes feast upon his face one last time before spinning and walking away. With each step, she waited for him to chase after her, grab her arm, swing her around, and tell her he couldn't live without her.

But an instant later, when she glanced over her shoulder to the front of the dry-goods store, Joseph was gone.

Joseph's lungs burned. His eyes stung. And his legs wobbled.

He wanted to fall to the ground and weep, to shout out his misery and frustration, to pound his head with his fists.

She'd walked away. And he'd let her . . .

Blindly he stumbled down the street, fighting the urge to turn around and sprint after her. This time he'd take her in his arms and wouldn't let her go. He'd kiss her until they both were breathless, and then he'd kiss her again.

But he knew he couldn't do that. Even though everything within him wanted Mercy, especially after holding her one last time, he needed to let her go. She wanted her freedom more than she wanted him. And he loved her too much to take that away from her when it had been so hard-earned.

After all, he'd asked her to marry him twice, told her he loved her, sought her out to say good-bye, and apologized for his arrogance in their relationship. If he hadn't persuaded her by now, what made him think he ever could? Besides, he didn't want to win her through coercion.

He should have stuck to his original plan not to say farewell.

He'd known deep down that doing so would tear him apart. But he'd gone to the dance anyway, and once he heard Mercy say his name in front of the other men, he became nearly crazed with the need to be alone with her—to discover if she'd changed her mind about him.

"Lord Colville" came a voice as though from a great distance. "I'd begun to think you left me behind."

Joseph halted and attempted to gain his bearings, but his head and his heart ached too much to see anything.

"Lord Colville," the same voice said again. "You don't look well. Why don't you sit down for a moment?"

Joseph blinked. In the light emanating from the entrance of the hotel stood a young man holding a haversack and a small surgeon's chest. Charlie Danbury, the assistant to the surgeon at the local hospital where Joseph had volunteered over the past few days.

They'd worked well together. When Charlie had said he was looking for passage back to England and asked if he could join him on the *Tynemouth* as an assistant, Joseph had welcomed it. Although he'd managed the voyage to Vancouver Island well enough on his own, an assistant would give Joseph more time to explore and take in the sights for the duration of the trip.

"I own to an eccentric feeling at present," Joseph replied. While feeling overwhelmed with melancholy, he couldn't admit his true state to Charlie. Somehow he had to withstand the sorrow and not allow it to break him. "Give me a moment, Charlie . . ." He drew a breath and attempted to push down his desperation and loss. "I must finish packing a few more items."

"Would you like me to help you, my lord?" Charlie asked, eager to please.

"I do appreciate your offer, but I shall attend to it and return shortly." He didn't wait for Charlie's reply but instead made his way to the hotel's second floor, stumbling and tripping as if he'd ingested an entire bottle of rum.

Finally entering his room, he closed the door and leaned back against it. In the darkness he released a long, low groan, giving way to his heartache and pain—chest-tearing, gut-wrenching pain. He needed to leave Victoria at once and get himself far away.

With trembling hands, he reached for the lantern on the writing table, lit it, and then began to stuff his remaining belongings into a satchel. He'd already sent his trunk to the wharf. These last few items were easy to pack: books, paper, an inkpot, pens, a half-finished letter to his aunt, and a few newspapers.

As he buckled the strap on the bag, he took stock of the room to make sure he'd gathered everything. The sooner he could board the *Tynemouth*, the sooner he could begin to forget about Mercy and move on with his life.

While pushing in the desk chair, his eye caught on something shiny beneath the table. He stooped to pick up the object. As his fingers closed around it, his heart lurched in his chest.

A simple gold band—Sarah's ring, the one she'd given to Mercy before she died, the ring Mercy had flung away in her effort to avoid the pain of the girl's passing. He'd meant to return it to Mercy, had thought about it on several occasions, bringing it ashore with him for that very purpose. Somehow the ring must have slipped from his pocket when he'd changed or packed his clothes.

He held it up to the lantern light. The faded gold chided him. He'd told Mercy to allow herself to grieve and feel the pain of Sarah's death, but now with his own loss, once again his first reaction was to run as far away from the pain as he could.

Slowly, he lowered himself to the edge of the bed. He stared at the spot on the floor where he'd knelt a few nights ago, when he'd cried out to God like Jonah and told God he'd stop running and do whatever He wanted of him.

How easy it was at the first sign of hardship to toss aside his resolve.

He twisted the ring, sliding his finger across the well-worn band. Things most definitely hadn't gone the way he'd wanted with Mercy. But he'd done what he needed to and had faced his fears. He couldn't forget that God was walking alongside him through the pain of the loss and rejection.

He didn't blame Mercy for not wanting to get married. He might not understand her need for freedom, but he wanted her to be happy and build a new life here—hopefully with Patience. Besides, it wouldn't be fair to ask her to leave the opportunity for a fresh start, only to go back to the despair and desolation she'd left behind.

Maybe he couldn't ask her to return to London. But nothing was stopping him anymore, was there? Nothing except himself.

Joseph sucked in a tight, aching breath and fought a stinging at the back of his eyes.

He knew what he needed to do. He needed to be faithful to the small part God was calling him to accomplish. And when he did that, God would give him just enough strength to complete the work. Wasn't that what Dr. Bates had told him the day he assisted at Shoreditch?

It had taken crossing an ocean and running halfway around the world for him to finally understand where he belonged. And that he could no longer wait. It was time to return home to do the work God had called him to.

Joseph unbuckled the leather strap on his bag, retrieved a pen, his inkpot, and two sheets of paper. He laid the pieces side by side on the writing table. He had two letters to write and not much time to write them.

thirty-two

Mercy squirmed in her chair, unable to focus on the tiny stitches in the hem she was sewing. After a sleepless night, her eyelids were heavy, her body was achy and restless, and her insides were upside down with turmoil.

She tried not to yawn again and draw frowns from the other women among the sewing circle.

"You're not making much progress this morning, Mercy," Mrs. Moresby said as she bent to examine Mercy's work, the long feathers on her hat tickling Mercy's neck.

"I'm right sorry, ma'am, that I am."

"You know I'm just doing my best to teach you skills that might help you find work." Mrs. Moresby straightened to her full height and pushed up the brim of her hat, the colorful feathers adding another foot to the woman's already-large stature.

"Aye, and I thank ye." Mercy brought the linen closer to her face and attempted to focus all her attention on her next stitch. She'd never been taught to sew proper-like and was mighty grateful Mrs. Moresby was instructing her and some of the other poor women how to sew, cook, and clean.

"It's as clear as daylight something's bothering you," Mrs. Moresby persisted as she stooped to examine another woman's work.

"Perhaps if you share what it is, you'll feel better and be able to concentrate on your work."

"Oh, no, ma'am. I couldn't share it." Mercy had spent the night trying not to think about her farewell to Joseph. She'd wrestled her thoughts of him away until both her stomach and head hurt with the effort. Even after the sleepless night of trying to push Joseph from her mind, her thoughts turned to him all too often, especially their last moment together in each other's arms.

He'd held her as though he still cherished and wanted her. But he hadn't spoken of his love again. Maybe he'd changed his mind about her. Maybe he hadn't found her worthy enough after all. The doubts crowded in and clamored for attention, and Mercy couldn't stop from paying them heed.

Mrs. Moresby moved on to the next woman while glancing over her wide shoulder at Mercy. "It couldn't possibly have to do with a certain young man leaving on the *Tynemouth*, could it?"

Mercy bent her face even closer to her stitching, wishing she could slip inside the material along with the thread and disappear. She could count on Mrs. Moresby for speaking her mind. If only the woman wasn't so outspoken this morn, not when Mercy's aching heart was still so tender.

"I say it's never too late to try to make things right," Mrs. Moresby offered.

Mercy didn't know how to respond, could feel the critical eyes of the other women upon her. Some shunned her, believing she'd tainted herself with Joseph during the voyage. Others resented that a rich man like Joseph had singled her out and treated her specially.

Of the women in the barracks, only Miss Lawrence had continued to treat her kindly. Even now, the beautiful gentlewoman brushed a hand across Mercy's shoulder. Miss Lawrence had volunteered to help Mrs. Moresby with the sewing class and was circling around giving instructions.

Mercy gave the woman a grateful nod.

Miss Lawrence smiled her encouragement, as if to let Mercy know she'd done the right thing in saying good-bye to Joseph and letting him go, no matter how hard it had been.

Tears stung Mercy's eyes, but she kept her attention on her needle and thread, even though she couldn't see them clearly anymore. She *had* done the right thing last night. Certainly she had.

Mrs. Moresby clucked, then shook her head and handed one of the women a seam ripper. "Your stitches are too big. Take them out and try again."

At a knock against the parlor door, Mercy looked up in time to see the constable who helped guard the complex. His eyes darted to one of the women, and they exchanged shy smiles.

"Yes?" Mrs. Moresby inquired.

All traces of the constable's smile quickly vanished, his expression turning severe. "A messenger came with a letter for Miss Wilkins, ma'am. Said to deliver it to her straightaway."

Mercy shot up from her chair, letting the shirt she'd been hemming fall to a heap on the floor. "I'm Miss Wilkins."

The constable retrieved something from his inner coat pocket and held it out to Mercy.

"Who is it from, Constable?" Mrs. Moresby demanded with a stern slant of her gaze.

"Don't rightly know, ma'am. But I was paid well to deliver it directly into the hands of Miss Wilkins herself."

If anyone could pay well, Joseph could.

Mercy's pulse sputtered faster. Mrs. Moresby was watching her, and she nodded as if coming to the same conclusion.

Was Joseph at the front door this very minute?

Anticipation began to break through the cracks of Mercy's heart. Had he come back for her after all?

She crossed to the constable, took the letter, and raced out of the room and down the hallway. As she stepped outside, her heart threatened to beat through her chest.

The morning sunshine was brilliant and sparkled off the bay, turning the calm waters into a glittering display of jewels, blinding her for an instant.

"Joseph?" she called, holding her breath, waiting for him to appear out of the shadows, to step up to the fence with a grin. But the area was empty of the usual men who lingered to get glimpses of the women.

Maybe she'd been wrong and the letter wasn't from Joseph. She broke open the envelope, slid out a piece of paper, and unfolded it to discover a gold band tucked inside. Sarah's ring.

She'd forgotten about the ring, had wanted to forget about it every bit as much as she wanted to forget about Sarah. Yet Joseph had kept it.

Why?

She scanned his letter. The long, sloping script flowed together to fill half a page. What did it say? She'd never cared much that she couldn't read, but at that moment she desperately wished she could read every word he'd penned to her.

Was this another good-bye? Had he come across the ring during his packing? Had he merely wanted to make sure she had it before he left? Or did the letter say more?

She searched the writing for the few words she'd learned to recognize. A moment later, she released a frustrated breath at the futility of her effort. She could no more read the letter than if it were a foreign language.

Part of her wanted to rush back inside and ask Mrs. Moresby for help. But another part resisted wasting another second of time. What if he hadn't left last night?

Mercy hurried to the fence and scanned the people loitering nearby and along the waterfront. No sign of Joseph anywhere.

"Was Lord Colville just here?" she called to a boy, who was leaning against the front of the legislative building.

"No, miss," the boy replied. He had hooked his fingers through his suspenders and was chewing on a long piece of grass.

She held up the envelope with her name printed on it. "Did you see who brought this letter to the constable?"

"Yep."

"Who?"

"Me."

Her heart began its pounding again. "Did you speak with Lord Colville this morning?"

"Yep."

Was Joseph still in Victoria then? Had he decided not to leave after all? The questions tumbled over one another in a dizzying swell. "What did he say? Where is he now?"

The boy pushed away from the brick building and twisted the stem of grass with his tongue, his face impassive, his eyes hard. "Lord Colville paid me to deliver the letter. That's all, miss."

Mercy had seen that look often enough to recognize the meaning. The boy wanted more money from her before he'd say more. She fisted her hands on her hips and gave him the stern glare she'd perfected with the unruly street urchins she'd encountered in London. "You know right well I don't have anything to give you. So you just go on and tell me all you know, d'ye hear me?"

"What's in it for me?" the boy persisted.

"Did Lord Colville leave on the *Tynemouth*?"

The boy stared at Mercy as though weighing how he might benefit from disclosing anything else. Finally he tossed the chewed-up weed to the ground. "Heard tell the ship's departure was delayed."

"For how long?"

He shrugged. "Do I look like I know everything?"

She expelled a breath and tried to control her mounting frustration. Fine. She'd seek out the information she needed another way. She rounded the gate and unlatched the wicket. With the constable still inside, likely engaged in making eyes with the women, there was no one to question where she was going or stop her from leaving the government complex.

She headed down the same dirt pathway she'd climbed last week when she'd come ashore. Only this time there were no ropes holding anyone back. And no hordes of men.

Gulls circled above, squawking out their displeasure at the billows of smoke rising from the twin stacks of a nearby steamship. The gangplank was still down, and two dockhands were rolling barrels up the ramp onto the main deck.

A handful of men tending boats along the wharf paused to watch her approach. As she stepped onto the planks, one doffed his hat. "Can I help you, miss?"

She paused and searched the faces of each man who lingered along the waterfront, but none belonged to the man she desperately wanted to see. "Do you know if the *Tynemouth* has weighed anchor yet?"

The man squinted out at the straits. "Don't see her sails. Guessing she's gone."

Mercy followed his gaze and prayed he was wrong, that she'd spot the mast and rigging, that Joseph would still be within reach.

Yet she saw nothing, not even the slightest hint of a ship.

"Last transport out to the *Tynemouth* left early this morning," the man added, as if the knowledge would make her feel better. Instead, it settled heavily upon her heart.

"Can we help you in any way?" He held his hat expectantly, his expression hopeful.

Mercy shook her head, her throat clogging. She swallowed hard and answered, "No matter. I thank ye anyway."

She walked away from the wharf, but instead of returning up the path to the government buildings, her feet took her along the shore, away from the men, away from the town. She wandered aimlessly, not caring where she went or where she ended up.

Finally, she reached the edge of a clearing and could go no farther, at least not without fighting her way through the overgrown woodland. She lowered herself onto a smooth boulder that faced the bay, the vast Pacific Ocean, and Joseph.

He was gone. And with him the hope that had been swelling within her since the letter arrived.

She stared at the vacant horizon, willing away the emptiness inside her. Emptiness had always been her companion. If she cleared her mind and ignored the loss, if she forced the memories away, then she wouldn't have to feel anything. She wouldn't have to worry about her sorrow overwhelming her.

The sea breeze nipped at her nose and cheeks with the chill of the autumn morning. She rested her hands in her lap, realizing she still held the letter and ring. Running her finger around the band, she traced the ring. Why had Joseph sent it to her when he knew she didn't want it, didn't want to remember Sarah. Was he trying to tell her something?

Maybe he'd written his explanation in his letter. She could only guess that perhaps he was encouraging her once again to grieve her losses instead of ignoring them.

Was Joseph right?

She slid the ring down her finger. Perhaps she'd buried her feelings for so long that she wouldn't allow herself to feel anything, not even love. Was this why she'd so easily thrown away her relationship with Joseph?

Aye, something was there betwixt them. She'd felt things with Joseph she'd never imagined possible. But had she ignored the feelings and walked away from him just as she had other people and situations when the emotions became too much to bear?

She held out her hand and studied the ring. Maybe she needed to allow the pain of Sarah's death as well as her many other sorrows to finally come to the surface.

"Oh, Sarah . . ." she whispered, forcing out the words she knew she had to say. "I'm sorry. So sorry. I wanted to save you, tried to save you, but I couldn't."

Her eyes and throat burned, and a frightened part of her wanted to stuff the burning back down, deep inside. And yet could she admit that holding in her emotions had failed to make her life any better?

"Patience," she continued, "I'm sorry I had to leave you behind, that there wasn't more I could do to help you."

Hot tears slid down her cheeks. She couldn't remember the last time she'd wept. But now that she'd started, she let the tears fall, let the pain come out—the pain of all the children she'd cared for but lost, the pain of never having Twiggy's love, the pain of being rejected by society, the pain of having to leave her family behind, the pain of struggling in an unfamiliar land, so far from home.

The pain of losing the man she loved.

Aye, she *loved* Joseph. She hadn't wanted to, but the truth was obvious now. She loved him deeply and passionately. And she'd gone and let him sail away without her.

She buried her face in her hands as wave after wave of silent sobs shook her body. The aching in her chest and throat was raw, and she didn't know if she could bear it. A part of her wanted to simply give up. But she forced herself to release her grief, even though it was excruciating, and prayed that the pain of it would eventually diminish.

"Oh, God," she whispered, "I've blamed you for so long, figured you didn't care. But I'm guessing you care even more about the lost ones than I do, that you're feeling the sorrow right well enough, but that you keep on loving."

Was that what she needed to do—let her sorrow increase her ability to love?

"Mercy?"

She sat up with a start. Gulping back her sobs, she swiped at her cheeks at the same time that she glanced over her shoulder.

It was Joseph. He stood only a few paces away with his chest rising and falling as though he'd been running. His hat was gone and his hair mussed. He looked in the direction of the harbor and the wharf before turning back to her. "You might not want to see me again, but I was aboard the steamer and noticed you by the wharf."

She slid off the boulder and wiped her cheeks once more. Joseph had seen her? And then followed her here? She turned to face him but couldn't speak past a new ache in her throat.

"I'll go back if you would rather be by yourself." As he studied her, his eyes widened with concern. "What happened? Why are you upset?"

She wanted to ask him why he was still here, why he wasn't on board the *Tynemouth*, only she couldn't formulate the words. Instead, more tears slipped down her cheeks.

He took a step closer to her, then stopped. "Please, Mercy, tell me what's wrong."

She held out his letter and the ring as if they explained everything.

"You read my note." His handsome face appeared haggard with dark circles under his eyes.

She shook her head. "I tried," she finally managed to say, "except I can't read but a few words here and there."

"I'm sorry. I should have realized . . ."

"It's alright." She knew she ought to feel embarrassed, even ashamed by her admission, but somehow it didn't matter.

"It doesn't say much." His attention dropped to the ring she now wore on her finger. "I just wanted you to have Sarah's ring. But I apologize if it upset you."

There was so much she wanted to tell him, about finally facing her past, about releasing all the pain, and yet she didn't know where to start and wasn't sure if she could get the words past the tightness in her throat.

"I didn't mean to disturb you," he continued, glancing back at the harbor again. "I should return to the steamer. The captain said he'd delay only a little while on my account."

She followed his gaze to the steamboat, still billowing black smoke. She wanted to tell him not to go, to stay with her, but she knew that wasn't fair. Maybe she'd changed, but their circumstances hadn't.

Even so, she'd nearly lost him, and now that he was here, standing so close, how could she let him go?

He shoved his fingers into his hair and looked as though he was about to speak. Then he dropped his hand and let his shoulders slump. "Good-bye, Mercy."

Good-bye? Again?

He spun and began to stride away.

Her heart chased after him, willing him to stop. She had to do something. She couldn't lose him. *Run after him. Don't let him get away!* Her mind screamed at her, even as tears began to slide down her cheeks once more.

"I love you." The words fell out, the only thing she could say, the only thing left.

His footsteps faltered and then he stopped. But he didn't turn around.

"I love you, Joseph," she said, louder this time. If they loved each other, surely they could find a way to overcome the obstacles that threatened to keep them apart.

Slowly he pivoted until he was facing her.

She tried to read his expression through her tears, but he was only a blur.

"I want to be with you," she continued. Now that she'd set her feelings free, she wanted to marry him and spend the rest of her life with him. But she knew he was too considerate to ask her again after he'd already done so twice, and after she'd rejected him both times.

It was her turn now.

She rubbed her sleeves against her tear-stained cheeks and started toward him. He didn't move but remained frozen in place. Except for his eyes, which were dark and fathomless, following her every move.

When she was standing in front of him, she reached for his hand and took a measure of courage when he didn't pull away. Without breaking her gaze from his, she lowered herself to one knee. "I want to be with you, Joseph. You and none else. I'd be right happy to marry you, if you'll still have me."

"I wanted to give you your freedom, Mercy," he whispered hoarsely. "I don't want you to be pressured into marrying anyone, not even me."

She brought his hand to her lips and pressed a kiss on the back of it. "You're not pressuring me at all, Joseph. This is what I want. You're what I want, and I'm just sorry it took me so long to figure it out."

His fingers tightened around hers, but otherwise he didn't seem to react to her declaration.

Her heart quavered at the prospect that he'd changed his mind about her. For just an instant, her old insecurities taunted her that he regretted his earlier proposals. "It's not too late, is it, Joseph?"

He tugged her up, giving her little choice but to stand. Once she faced him, she tried to quell her trembling but couldn't. Had she lost him this time for good? He lifted a hand to her cheek, hesitated, then gently combed back a loose strand of her hair.

"I'm finished running away from God," Joseph said quietly but with conviction, which told Mercy he'd found peace at last. "The captain of the *Callie Ellen* is waiting for me to board. I'll be going to San Francisco. From there I shall return to England directly, where I shall endeavor to take up my father's causes in Parliament, as well as work at the Shoreditch Dispensary with Dr. Bates." Joseph studied her face as if waiting for her reaction to his news.

"Then you're not a-going on the *Tynemouth* to the Hawaiian Islands or any of the other places you wanted to visit?"

"I've realized that was simply an excuse to avoid returning home. I wrote two letters last eve, one to you with the ring, telling you of my plans to return to London, and the second to Captain Hellyer of the *Tynemouth*, informing him that I wouldn't be sailing aboard his vessel. I sent an assistant in my stead."

She searched his eyes for any sign of disappointment or wavering or even regret, but his eyes were filled with confidence, with contentment.

"Before I left London, Dr. Bates asked me to take up the partnership with him at the dispensary. I tried to ignore the need, to run away from God's call, because I didn't want to stay in London and face the emptiness of my life there without my family. But I'm ready to go back now and help Bates. He needs me, and the community needs our medical practice."

It was her turn to reach up and touch his cheek. She did so tentatively at first, brushing her fingers along his jaw. It was bold, but she had to make him understand the depth of her love. "I'm right proud of you. You'll make a big difference there in the slums, that you will."

He nodded, swallowed hard, then took a deep breath. "I couldn't ask you to go back to London, Mercy. It wouldn't be fair, not after you've come this far to get away—"

She laid two fingers against his lips, cutting him off. "I'll go."

He started to speak again, but she pressed her fingers more firmly.

"I *want* to go," she said earnestly. "All I've ever wanted to do is help my people." Maybe her sorrows and hardships had all been part of the training for the greater things God had in store for her to do with Joseph. For so long she thought God had abandoned her. Was it possible He'd been there all along, even through the difficulties, making her stronger, working things out in His way so that eventually she'd be ready to go back?

"What about the scandal of our being together?" she asked. "I don't want to be causing you to lose your good name and reputation."

"It doesn't matter what others think," he stated. "Besides, I have a feeling we'll be too busy with the work God gives us to care about such things."

She hoped he was right. Even if they spent their time in the slums, she hoped she could lay claim to Mrs. Moresby's situation and learn to be the kind of lady Joseph might need from time to time. Whatever the case, she knew she couldn't let anything stop them from being together this time.

"Are you sure you don't have your heart set on having a new life here?" he asked.

"I want to work by your side, Joseph. Wherever that is, I want to be there helping you every day."

The velvety brown of his eyes caressed her. He shifted his lips against her fingers, moving down until the warm curve of his mouth connected with the soft flesh of her palm.

Without taking his gaze from hers, he pressed his mouth against her skin more fully as if making a claim upon her.

She sucked in a sharp breath. "Is this a *yes* to my marriage proposal?"

"No," he said, wrapping an arm around her waist and sliding her closer. "This is." His mouth found hers, covering and consuming her.

She let her fingers glide up his torso along the hard contours of his chest and shoulders and gave herself over to the pleasure of the kiss. This was where she wanted to be, the place she never wanted to leave. With him, in his arms, and by his side. Forever.

With a soft sigh, he broke the kiss and drew her against his body. The rapid rise and fall of his chest and the erratic thump of his heartbeat told her he was just as affected by their kiss as she was.

"Mercy?" he whispered.

"Hmmm."

"I love you and want to marry you today."

She pulled back to look into his beautiful eyes. She couldn't help but smile at the eagerness there. "Today? On board the steamer?"

"I've just decided I'm not leaving on that steamer."

"You're not?" She tugged away a little further, needing to put more distance between them so she could think clearly.

"I don't think God will mind if I wait here in Victoria a short while longer. Until Patience arrives and we make sure she's settled into her new life here."

At the tenderness in Joseph's eyes, she linked her arms around his neck and stood on her toes so that her mouth found his again. She leaned into him, letting her kiss tell him how much she desired and loved and needed him.

A clearing throat nearby interrupted them. Mercy jumped at the sound and would have moved away from Joseph had he not kept his arms securely locked around her waist.

"Lord Colville?" came a tentative voice. A uniformed steward stood a short distance away, his face red and his eyes averted.

"You may tell the captain I've been unavoidably detained," Joseph said, giving Mercy a sly grin. "If you would be so kind as to unload my trunk and other bags, I will more than make up for the inconvenience."

"Very well, my lord."

As soon as the steward started to walk away, Joseph pulled Mercy close again. "Now, where were we?" Thick desire melted the brown of his eyes into a warm liquid that threatened to drown her.

"We were speaking of our marriage plans," she replied.

As he bent to kiss her, she eagerly lifted her lips to his, relishing the feathery kiss that only made her impatient for more.

"Though I want to marry you today," he said, tilting his head back, "shall we wait until Patience is here? I should like a family member to see us wed."

Tears sprang to her eyes at the sweetness of his words. Still, she had to be honest with herself about Patience's arrival. She'd been clinging to the hope that Patience would survive the workhouse. But if she was truly going to start facing her heartaches, then she had to acknowledge the reality that Patience had been near to dying. If her sister was too ill for the passage aboard the *Tynemouth*, she'd likely be too ill for the *Robert Lowe* as well.

"I'm afraid Patience won't be making it here," Mercy said, her voice breaking at the thought of losing her sister.

Joseph didn't say anything but instead looked into her eyes as though attempting to peer into her soul.

"My sister was dying when I left her." Mercy spoke the words even as her heart broke to say them. "She made me leave so that I wouldn't see her die."

"And she made you leave so you could have a better life than she did."

"Aye." Mercy thought back to the last time she'd seen Patience at the workhouse and her words "*You know I'll always love you.*" Had Patience known it was good-bye forever?

"If she has half your strength, Mercy, then she'll pull through and get well."

"Do you think so?"

Joseph wrapped her into an embrace. "I don't know, but let's pray she survived." For a long moment, he just held her. After losing his family, he, more than anyone, could empathize with her. His arms tightened about her as if assuring her that he understood.

You'd be proud of me, Patience, she thought. Her throat burned and her eyes stung. *I'm here. I'm with the man I love. And I'll be okay.*

"Would it help if I sent Dr. Bates a telegram?" Joseph whispered against her ear. "I have already sent him one, letting him know I'm returning. But I shall send him another and have him inquire at the workhouse to discover what has become of Patience."

Mercy blinked back tears and met Joseph's gaze, filled with love and compassion. She couldn't find the words to respond to this man, who had captured her body and soul. So instead she offered him herself, giving her answer in the crashing of her lips against his—a sea-tossed kiss that tilted her world and threatened to sway her off her feet.

She sensed they were both losing themselves in the kiss when he wrenched away. Gasping for breath, she buried her face in his chest. His heartbeat thumped wildly against her cheek. Their passion was untamed and would be difficult to resist. The less waiting they had to endure, the better.

Even now, as his lips found the soft pulse at her neck, she dug her fingers into his coat and bit back a cry.

"My stars, Joseph." She forced herself to break free of his hold and tried to take a deep breath.

"Am I so irresistible?" He grinned but didn't make a move toward her, though his eyes said he wanted to sweep her up and kiss her until she was breathless again. "So irresistible that you rejected two of my proposals of marriage?"

She let her fingers glide along his cheek into his hair. "I'm right sorry for causing you more sorrow."

"I suppose God knew I needed to find the ring and make sure my priorities were in their proper place first."

She looked down at Sarah's ring on her finger. God had done the same with her.

"I'm finally ready to go back and face my past," he said. "And I would be honored to have you by my side for as long as we both shall live."

She guessed they both still had much to learn about dealing with the pain that life often brought. But together they'd find the joy amidst the heartache. "I don't want to be anywhere else but with you."

He bent in and let his lips touch hers again, the sweetness and softness stirring her hunger for him. His lips against hers had the ability to sweep her away, making her forget everything and everyone, so that only he existed.

This time she pulled away. "Oh, Joseph . . ." she whispered, her heart too full to find the words to express herself.

"I love you," he said. "Most abundantly."

"Aye." She smiled. "Your kisses are abundant to be sure."

He grinned in return. "I did once warn you that I am most reservedly saving my love for only one woman, the woman I plan to marry, and that I shall have an overflowing abundance of affection to bestow on her alone."

Overflowing abundance of affection. The eloquent words fanned warmth into her veins.

He let his gaze linger on each part of her face, her brow, cheeks, nose, mouth, neck. A smoldering passion and love shone from his eyes. "I vow to you a lifetime of my affection, Mercy. Forever and always."

Joy pulsed with each beat of her heart. God had indeed taken her on a voyage. Through it all, He'd done a mighty work inside her, changing her, teaching her to truly love, and making her ready for even greater things to come.

She couldn't ask for anything more.

thirty-three

"There you are, sweet lamb." Mercy rocked the infant, swaying back and forth on her feet. The tiny brown face was delicate and beautiful, even with newborn swelling and redness that would eventually fade. The babe's mother slept on a cot only a foot away, exhausted after a grueling labor and subsequent surgery. The woman seemed heedless of the cold, cramped, windowless shed that was filled with crates and boxes containing an assortment of medical supplies.

Though everyone else in Victoria's small hospital wanted to send the native woman away, regardless of her miner husband's pleas, Joseph had intervened. After assuring the staff that the woman wasn't infected with smallpox, Joseph had been allowed to bring her into a supply shed outside the hospital, where he tended to her all through the previous night, delivering a daughter at dawn.

The miner had wept his gratitude and had only just left after Mercy insisted he find himself a hotel room to get some much-needed sleep. For all the condemnation the miners received for intermarrying with natives, Mercy had no doubt this one loved his wife dearly. At the first sign of his wife going into labor, he'd traveled tirelessly for miles out of the mountains to bring her to a doctor. He'd gone without sleep for days in his attempt to save her life, along with that of his unborn child.

He didn't see the differences. He saw only the woman he loved.

She realized Joseph had grown into that kind of man too—the kind who'd learned to look past outward appearances and circumstances and value what was in the heart.

Mercy paused to touch the infant's hand, which had escaped from the tight swaddle. The tiny fingers were each so perfectly formed, with thin fingernails and dimpled knuckles.

Was it possible she could someday give Joseph a child of his own? Even though he'd expressed his willingness to adopt homeless children, perhaps she'd one day hold their child conceived in love.

Whatever the future brought, she was learning to trust that God was with her no matter where she was and no matter how difficult her situation. She had to remind herself of that oft, especially with fresh rumors regarding her and Joseph's relationship.

Once word of her engagement to Joseph had spread, the brideship women had despised her more than before. Mercy overheard their whispers and knew they believed she'd somehow coerced Joseph into a union. Most embarrassing were the rumors that Joseph felt obligated to marry her because she was expecting his child. She tried to ignore the glares and the cold silences, kept herself busy helping Joseph so that she wouldn't encounter the women, and trusted Joseph and Mrs. Moresby's assurances that the gossip would soon go away.

Thankfully, Miss Lawrence had been kind and asked her to live with her in an apartment. It was a temporary living arrangement, one that wouldn't last for either of them. But for now, Mercy was thankful for a reprieve from the condemnation of the other women, the type of censure she and Joseph were sure to face in London.

They were still waiting to hear back from Dr. Bates regarding Patience. Joseph had sent a telegram over a week ago. With the distance his telegram had to travel, Joseph hadn't expected a return message from Dr. Bates for some time. Even so, he certainly hoped to have heard from the doctor by now.

Mercy guessed Dr. Bates was having a difficult time discovering what had become of Patience. If Patience had left on the *Robert Lowe*, it was possible the workhouse didn't have record of it. Worse still was the possibility Patience had died and been buried in an unmarked grave. Without solid news, or even with bad news, it was no wonder Dr. Bates had delayed.

Mercy had told Joseph only yesterday that perhaps they ought to consider marrying without word of Patience. She longed to be with him all the time, never having to part ways again. Whenever they were together, the passion between them flared with growing intensity. And while she was grateful for Joseph's care in maintaining her integrity by visiting with her only in public places or with chaperones present, she longed to be with him, only him, and wouldn't be satisfied until she was.

The babe in her arms squeaked and began sucking her little fist. It wouldn't be long before Mercy would need to awaken the wee one's mother to nurse the babe.

A soft rap on the shed door was followed by the creak of it opening. Mercy expected to see the scraggly, bearded face of the miner and was surprised to see Joseph's handsome face instead.

His warm brown eyes found her, and something reserved within the depths of them sent her heart to spiraling.

He had news for her.

"You're back sooner than I expected," she whispered, needing to delay his message for as long as possible. "Just admit that, with each passing day, you want to be with me more."

"More than you can know," he whispered, his voice rumbling with a need that matched the glimmer in his eyes.

Heat shimmered across her skin and soaked down to her bones. This was how it was every time they were together. It was exquisite torture.

Joseph cast a glance at the native woman still sleeping on the cot before crossing two long strides to reach her. Before Mercy could protest that they weren't alone, he cupped both of her cheeks and leaned in to claim her mouth in a slow and delicate kiss, one that teased her with promises of what was to come.

At another squeak from the babe, Mercy forced herself back, breaking the kiss. "Joseph," she admonished, ducking her head as her cheeks flushed. She darted a glance at the mother, who remained motionless.

"Is one week enough time in which to plan the wedding?" he asked, clasping his hands behind his back, as if by doing so he could prevent himself from reaching for her again.

"One week?" Mercy's heart dropped. She knew what was coming and didn't want to talk about it. Frantically, she looked around the cramped shed, searching for anything else that might divert their attention. "But the *Robert Lowe* won't be here for weeks, if not months."

"Mercy," he whispered tenderly as if sensing her mounting panic. "Patience is not coming."

Swift tears filled her eyes. She'd guessed Patience had passed away, had tried to allow herself to grieve. But now . . .

Joseph removed a telegram from his coat pocket. It was dirty and beaten as though it had traveled through a battlefield to reach them. He pried open the envelope and pulled out a sheet filled with small black print.

She had the urge to run from the shed or at least plug her ears. As the infant's squeaks erupted into a sudden, piercing wail, she turned away from Joseph and the telegram. The mother's eyes flew open, and she struggled to sit.

Joseph was at the woman's side in an instant, easing her up even as Mercy placed the babe in her waiting arms. With the sutures in her abdomen, Mercy had no doubt the mother was in extreme discomfort. But other than the slightest wince, she didn't show it.

Mercy straightened and took a deep breath. She wouldn't ignore the hard news and the pain that came with it, as she would have done in the past. She had to make herself go through it.

"How did Dr. Bates find Patience?" She forced out the question even though it hurt to do so.

Joseph spoke quietly to the native woman, who understood a little bit of English. Then he rose and reached for Mercy's hand, drawing her outside the shed and closing the door behind them. The pump at the center of the yard was dripping water into the muddy puddle at its base, and the grass was starting to turn yellow, but the area was deserted, giving them a moment of privacy.

"How did Dr. Bates find my sister?" Mercy repeated. She held her arms tightly to her chest to ward off the cold breeze, forcing herself to stay put even though she wanted to escape.

"Dr. Bates didn't say how he found her," Joseph answered, "only that she's been living at the Shoreditch Dispensary since you left."

Mercy stared at Joseph, taking in every sincere line etched into his forehead. "She's living at the dispensary?"

"I'm sorry, Mercy," Joseph continued. "I know how much you wanted her to come on the *Robert Lowe*, but she's still too weak to travel. According to Dr. Bates, she probably won't ever be strong enough to make the voyage here."

Mercy couldn't move as she tried to figure out what Dr. Bates had done. He'd likely gone to the workhouse himself not long after she'd left his office. And he'd done more than help Patience. He'd rescued her out of the bowels of hell and single-handedly saved her life.

A tender, sweet lump in her throat swelled as sudden tears spilled over.

Joseph pulled her against his chest, wrapping his arms around her.

"She's alive, then?" Mercy whispered.

"Yes, she's alive."

Mercy buried her face against Joseph and wept. When she finally spent herself, she realized she was trembling—her arms, legs, and hands. Trembling from relief, from hearing that her sister had survived. Trembling because she was overcome with such gratitude for Dr. Bates, who cared enough to help one person at a time, one day at a time.

Joseph pressed a kiss to her temple.

"I can be ready for the wedding in a week," she said and offered Joseph a tremulous smile.

He used the pad of his thumb to brush away her tears. "I shall understand if you're not ready so soon—"

"I'm ready now, Joseph." Aye, she was ready to spend the rest of her life with the man she loved.

"Are you certain?"

This time her smile broke free. "I'm right certain." She'd never been more certain of anything in her life.

Author's Note

When I first heard of the concept of bride ships, I was utterly horrified and fascinated by the idea that women would willingly board ships, leave everything they'd ever known behind, and sail to a strange land, all for the purpose of marrying complete strangers. I couldn't help but ask myself what kind of woman would do such a thing and why?

In the 1860s, several bride ships left England's shores with the destination of Vancouver Island and British Columbia, which at that time were both separate colonies of England and not yet part of Canada. As I researched these ships and the women who took the voyages, I looked frantically for the answer to the question: What sort of desperation did these women face that would drive them to take part in one of the bride ships?

Indeed, most of the women were very desperate, particularly the poorest of the immigrants. In this first book in THE BRIDE SHIPS series, I hope I've given you a glimpse of the hopeless conditions that existed for the poor who lived in London's slums. Many of the women on the first bride ship, the *Tynemouth*, were from London's poorest areas and faced conditions very much like Mercy did. Without adequate food, lodging, and opportunity for employment, the future was bleak for many women, and often immigration wasn't something they could afford.

At the same time that well-meaning people attempted to take action to help London's poor, the colonies of Vancouver Island and British Columbia complained about a lack of women for the many men who lived and worked there. A missionary among the miners of British Columbia, Reverend Lundin Brown, wrote a letter to his sponsors in London, asking for Christian wives for the miners. As a result, the Columbia Mission Society soon began making arrangements for the transport of such women.

The *Tynemouth* was one of the bride ships to leave England for Vancouver Island and British Columbia. Most of the story of the voyage happened the way I've portrayed it. There were sixty women and two very strict chaperones, who cordoned off the women and didn't allow them to mingle with any of the other passengers or to go ashore for the entire voyage.

The *Tynemouth* really did experience a gale while in the English Channel, which caused most on board to become terribly seasick. The *Tynemouth* also met with a hurricane-like storm in the South Atlantic and was nearly sunk by the large waves and high winds. And the *Tynemouth* experienced several mutinies. The mutineers were subdued, and subsequently the male passengers volunteered to help with the ship's duties until more sailors could be taken on board.

After the time in the Falklands, the passengers experienced food poisoning from the wild fowl and so all the birds had to be thrown overboard. The ship went through a period of such calm that it began to run out of coal and had to burn furniture and other wood items in order to fuel the engines. One of the bride-ship women did in fact die during the passage. In real life she died before reaching the Falklands, but for the sake of the story's pacing, I took the liberty of moving the smallpox scare and the woman's death to a little later in the voyage.

I also portrayed the bride ship's arrival in Victoria according to the accounts that have been recorded. Hundreds of men really did come down to the harbor to greet the women as they stepped ashore. The women had to walk through a gauntlet of cheering men. And surprisingly, yes, the story of Sophia and Pioneer really did happen. Pioneer proposed to Sophia on the spot, offered her two thousand pounds, and she accepted. The women ran to the government building, where they had to do their washing in front of the ogling men.

Finally, the ship's surgeon really did leave the *Tynemouth* once he arrived to Vancouver Island, and he married one of the women from the ship who had possibly helped him nurse the sick while on board the *Tynemouth*, giving them occasion to get to know each other. The real ship's surgeon eventually returned to England with his wife and lived there.

While Joseph and Mercy are completely fictional, I did draw inspiration from the love story of the real couple. As with any fiction, I added elements and backstory that helped to explore the great chasm between the social classes of that time. While it wasn't my intention to portray Mercy as a weak woman, I did want to show how a poor woman of her era would have accepted her position at the bottom and wouldn't have questioned those in authority over her the way we might today.

As the physical voyage took place, I also took my characters on a voyage of self-discovery. The truth is, we are shaped by our pasts—both the good and the bad influence who we become. But the other truth is, our voyage isn't over. If we allow God to come in and guide our journey, He'll give us the courage we need to shift course when necessary, to battle the storms, and to move forward in His strength and with His purpose.

I pray that wherever you're at in your life, you'll invite Him in, give Him control, and rely upon Him to steer the course, doing your small part to make a difference with His help and guidance.

Jody Hedlund is the award-winning author of multiple novels, including the BEACONS OF HOPE and ORPHAN TRAIN series, as well as *Captured by Love* and *Rebellious Heart*. She holds a bachelor's degree from Taylor University and a master's degree from the University of Wisconsin, both in social work. Jody lives in Michigan with her husband and five children. Learn more at JodyHedlund.com.

Sign Up for Jody's Newsletter!

Keep up to date with Jody's news on book releases and events by signing up for her email list at jodyhedlund.com.

More from Jody Hedlund

When three orphaned sisters are left nearly destitute, they must journey from New York to the west where they strive through tragedy and loss for the hope of a better life—but they find that the promise of the orphan trains is not all that it seems. Along the way, they encounter the true meaning of family, friendship, and love...

ORPHAN TRAIN: *With You Always, Together Forever, Searching for You*